Queens

A collection (
the world's leading romance

Two powerful novels from
international bestselling author

SARA CRAVEN

PRAISE FOR SARA CRAVEN:

"Sara Craven's latest is filled with
drama and passion"
—*Romantic Times* on *The Token Wife*

"*The Forced Bride* by Sara Craven is a wonderful
love story between two characters who fall in love
in spite of their best intentions. Craven takes you
on a very satisfying emotional journey."
—*Romantic Times* on *The Forced Bride*

"Craven strikes the perfect balance of romance,
humour and drama in this fast-paced novel
that keeps the reader enthralled."
—*Romantic Times* on
The Count's Blackmail Bargain

100 Reasons to Celebrate

We invite you to join us in celebrating Mills & Boon's centenary. Gerald Mills and Charles Boon founded Mills & Boon Limited in 1908 and opened offices in London's Covent Garden. Since then, Mills & Boon has become a hallmark for romantic fiction, recognised around the world.

We're proud of our 100 years of publishing excellence, which wouldn't have been achieved without the loyalty and enthusiasm of our authors and readers.

Thank you!

Each month throughout the year there will be something new and exciting to mark the centenary, so watch for your favourite authors, captivating new stories, special limited edition collections…and more!

SARA CRAVEN

Marriage Vows

Containing

**The Marriage Truce
& The Token Wife**

*M&B™ and M&B™ with the Rose Device
are trademarks of the publisher.
Harlequin Mills & Boon Limited, Eton House,
18-24 Paradise Road,
Richmond, Surrey TW9 1SR*

Marriage Vows © by Harlequin Books S.A. 2008

The Marriage Truce and *The Token Wife* were
first published in Great Britain by Harlequin Mills & Boon
Limited in separate, single volumes.

The Marriage Truce © Sara Craven 2002
The Token Wife © Sara Craven 2003

ISBN: 978 0 263 86676 6

025-0508

*Printed and bound in Spain
by Litografía Rosés S.A., Barcelona*

The Marriage Truce

SARA CRAVEN

The
Queens of Romance
Collection

February 2008
Their Wedding Deal Helen Bianchin

March 2008
Engaged to be Married? Jessica Steele

April 2008
A Passionate Bargain Michelle Reid

May 2008
Marriage Vows Sara Craven

June 2008
Rogues and Rakes Paula Marshall

July 2008
Summer Delights Nora Roberts

August 2008
Summer Engagements Betty Neels

September 2008
Jet Set Wives Penny Jordan

October 2008
At His Mercy Linda Howard

November 2008
Baby Bonds Caroline Anderson

Sara Craven says

"Thank you to all my readers for sticking with me over the past thirty-three years. I've had a wonderful time, and I hope you've enjoyed it too."

Sara Craven was born in South Devon, and grew up surrounded by books, in a house by the sea. After leaving grammar school she worked as a local journalist, covering everything from flower shows to murders. She started writing for Mills & Boon® in 1975. Apart from writing, her passions include films, music, cooking and eating in good restaurants. She now lives in Somerset.

Sara Craven has appeared as a contestant on the Channel Four game show *Fifteen to One* and is also the latest (and last ever) winner of the 1997 *Mastermind of Great Britain* championship.

CHAPTER ONE

'ARE you telling me that Ross is here—staying in the village? That he's come back and you didn't warn me?' Jenna Lang's face was ashen, her eyes blazing. 'Oh, Aunt Grace—how could you?'

'Because we didn't know until a couple of days ago—not for certain.' Mrs Penloe's kindly face was crumpled with worry as she looked pleadingly back at her niece. 'I thought—I hoped—it was just a bit of village gossip, and Betty Fox had got it all wrong. After all, it wouldn't be the first time.'

She shook her head. 'It never occurred to me that Thirza could really be so insensitive...'

'Ross's besotted stepmother—in whose eyes he can do no wrong?' Jenna's voice was icy with bitterness. 'The woman who blamed me for the break-up of our marriage? Oh, I can believe it.'

'I suppose she's bound to be loyal,' Mrs Penloe said, trying to be fair. 'After all, he was only seven when she married his father—another one with too much charm for his own good,' she added grimly. 'And that's sure to create a bond. Although that's no excuse for what she's done...'

'What's Thirza doing back in Polcarrow, anyway?' Jenna demanded. 'I thought she was supposed to be spending the whole year in Australia.'

'Too hot and too many insects,' her aunt said distractedly. 'Or so she claims. Interfered with her inspiration. She came back about three weeks ago.'

5

'Brilliant timing.' Jenna laughed shortly and mirthlessly. 'She always knew how to pick her moments.'

'She claims she had no choice.' Mrs Penloe hesitated. 'Apparently Ross's been really ill—picked up some ghastly virus on his last trip. When he was discharged from hospital he needed somewhere to recuperate.' She sighed. 'Knowing Thirza, I don't suppose she gave Christy's wedding, or your role in it, even a second thought.'

'No,' Jenna said bitingly. 'I'm the one who'll have to seriously reconsider.'

'Oh, Jenna, my dear—you're not going to leave—go back to London?' Mrs Penloe asked anxiously. 'Because Christy would be devastated. And it's all my fault. I know I should have said something. I suppose I hoped it might all—go away.'

'Or that I might never find out?' Jenna asked ironically. 'Hardly likely when Thirza will probably bring him with her to the wedding.'

'Oh, Jenna—surely not even Thirza...'

Jenna shrugged. 'Why not? She's capable of anything. And I presume she's been invited?'

'Well, yes, but we never thought she'd come. We thought she'd still be in Australia.' Mrs Penloe ran a hand through her greying curly hair. 'Oh, what a mess. Why couldn't Christy have chosen a June wedding instead? Ross would be long gone by then. And the weather would have been better, too,' she added, momentarily diverted by the threatening sky with its ragged, hurrying clouds framed by the drawing room window. 'Not that it matters, of course, compared with the sheer *embarrassment* of Thirza's behaviour.

'Surely she could have found a good nursing home somewhere—and don't tell me that Ross can't afford it, for he earns a fortune and probably has the best health insurance money can buy. Or she could have looked after him in his own home—wherever that is now. Anything rather than this.'

'Maybe it isn't too late for that, even now,' Jenna said slowly. 'Do you think Uncle Henry would talk to her—persuade her?'

'Darling, that was the first thing I thought of. All he said was that Thirza might be his cousin but she was a law unto herself and always had been.' She drew a long breath. 'Also that he had enough on his plate with the bills for the wedding, and that as you and Ross had been divorced for two years it could be time for you both to move on.' She paused, giving her niece another pleading look. 'And I suppose, in a way, he does have a point.'

'I'm sure he's right,' Jenna said. 'But, unfortunately, it's a point I haven't reached yet. Because it wasn't just the divorce…' She stopped, biting her lip.

'I know, dearest, I know.' Mrs Penloe hunted for a handkerchief and blew her nose. 'So much sadness—and no one could expect you to forget…'

'Or forgive.' Jenna's voice was stony. She got to her feet, reaching for her brown suede jacket. 'I'm going for a walk, Aunt Grace. I need to think, and some fresh air might help.'

'Fresh air?' Mrs Penloe echoed. 'It's blowing a force eight gale out there.'

But her protest fell on deaf ears. Jenna was already heading out of the room, and a moment later Mrs Penloe heard the front door bang shut.

She sank back against the sofa cushions and indulged herself with a little weep. She had every sympathy with Jenna, but she was also the mother of a beloved daughter who was getting married in three days' time, and who might find herself walking up the aisle of the village church without her only cousin in attendance behind her.

Grace Penloe was not a violent woman, but she felt strongly that if she could have got her hands round Thirza Grantham's throat she would probably have strangled her.

Meanwhile, Jenna was striding through the garden, her face pale and set, her tearless eyes staring rigidly ahead.

Spring had come softly to Cornwall that year, and then, suddenly and maliciously, reverted to winter with driving showers of hail and sleet, and gales that sent the seas battering at the coastline.

The Penloes, who'd built Trevarne House on the headland that tapered into the Atlantic, had protected their grounds from the prevailing winds with high stone walls, but Jenna chose not to remain within their shelter.

Instead, after a brief battle with the heavy latch, she pushed open the tall iron gate at the end of the garden, and stepped out on to the short, stubby grass of Trevarne Head itself.

As she turned to pull the gate shut behind her the wind tore at her loose knot of chestnut hair and whipped it free, so that it streamed behind her like a bright, silken pennant.

For a moment she paused, trying to subdue it into a braid, then realised her fingers were shaking too much so gave up the unequal struggle and walked on, digging her hands into the pockets of her jacket, her head bent and shoulders hunched as she met the full force of the wind.

She had the headland to herself. The hurrying clouds and harsh wind had kept other people away, but for Jenna the weather suited the bleakness of her mood.

Long before she reached the small concrete observation platform which had been built into the turf she could feel the icy spray from the sea chilling her face, tingling against her skin, and paused, gasping for breath.

She would not, she decided, go any closer to the edge.

She was not prepared to risk the odd, erratic gust which might carry her over to the sharp rocks and boiling surf far below.

She might be upset. She was certainly angry. But she was sure as hell not suicidal.

She gripped the back of the bench seat, which was bolted to the platform, and looked at the dramatic panorama in front of her.

The sea was alive and furious, streaked in grass-green and indigo as it flung itself against the granite promontory. She could hear its boom and hiss as it raced up the inlet that divided Trevarne from the cliffs of Polcarrow itself, then fell back in frustration.

Lifting her head, she watched the sea birds that swooped and dived, and rode on the waves.

Tossed by fate, she thought ironically, as she was herself.

And she had not seen it coming, although she couldn't say she hadn't been warned.

'Are you sure you want to do this?' Natasha, her business partner, had asked, her slanting brows drawn together in a concerned frown. 'Isn't it asking for trouble?'

Jenna shrugged. 'Christy and I promised each other years ago that she'd be my bridesmaid and I'd be hers. She kept her side of the pledge. Now it's my turn, and I can't let her down.' She paused. 'Nor would I want to.'

Natasha gave her a wry look. 'Not even when it's the very same church that you were married in?' she queried. 'With all the memories that's bound to entail?'

Jenna bit her lip. 'It's a very old church,' she said quietly. 'And I'm sure a lot of happy marriages have been celebrated there, so it will have good vibes, too.'

'Well, it's your decision,' Natasha said. 'But I helped pick up the pieces the first time, remember, and I don't want to find you back at square one for the sake of a family wedding.'

Jenna lifted her hands. 'That's all in the past, I promise. Now all I care about is the present—and the future.'

Brave words, she told herself now, staring sightlessly at the grey horizon. And I might—just—have got away with them. If only Ross hadn't come back...

She couldn't believe the pain that had seized her—torn at her when she'd heard the news of his return. Or how easily her carefully constructed edifice of control and self-belief had crumpled.

She wasn't suffering from some reality bypass. She'd always known it was inevitable that she and her ex-husband would meet again one day. But she'd hoped desperately that the meeting would be far, far in the future, when she might finally have come to terms with his betrayal of her.

Yet it seemed it was to be here and now—in this remote Cornish peninsula which she had always regarded as her personal haven.

It was to Trevarne House that she'd come as a scared ten-year-old after her mother's death, to the care of her aunt and uncle, leaving her father free to assuage his own grief by abandoning the desk job he hated and roaming the world as a troubleshooter for the giant oil company he worked for.

And here, on her mother's soil, she'd put down faltering roots in the Penloes' kind, easy-going household, while she and Christy, both only children, had found in each other the sister they'd always wanted.

And when, a couple of years later, her father had been killed in a freak accident when his car tyre had burst on a tricky mountain road, she had been absorbed seamlessly into the family as another daughter of the house.

All the same, she'd thought long and hard before accepting Christy's invitation to the wedding, in spite of their childhood vow. Eventually she'd allowed herself to be swayed by the knowledge that Thirza Grantham, the only potential fly in the ointment, was on the other side of the world.

Where Ross himself was to be found had been anyone's guess. She went out of her way to ignore the scraps of information that filtered through concerning his whereabouts.

Impossible, of course, she'd discovered, to cut him out of her awareness completely. To forget, as she longed to do, that he'd ever existed. For that she'd need some kind of emotional lobotomy, she thought broodingly.

Besides, there was evidence of him everywhere. The photographs which he sent back to his agency from every trouble spot in the world were still winning him prizes and awards with monotonous regularity.

'It can't be a real war,' someone had once joked. 'Ross Grantham isn't there yet.'

No, his profile was far too public for her to be able to exercise any kind of selective amnesia where he was concerned, and somehow she had to live with that.

It was strange, she thought, that she hadn't run into him in London before now. On dozens of occasions she'd thought she'd glimpsed him on the street, or across busy restaurants, even among the interval crowds at the theatre, and had felt the swift wrench of panic deep in her guts, only to realise, belatedly, that she was running scared of some complete stranger.

But then wasn't that what Ross himself had always been? she asked herself with bitter irony. A charming stranger who had murmured words of love to her, slept with her, given her for a few ecstatic weeks the prospect of motherhood, then abandoned her to pursue a casual affair while she was still recovering from the pain and trauma of her loss.

She sank her teeth into her bottom lip until she tasted blood. That was forbidden territory to her now, and she would not go there.

She'd persuaded herself that, with Thirza away, Polcarrow would be safe enough. That Ross would not come visiting unless his stepmother was there—had, indeed, not been back since the divorce.

Only, unpredictable as ever, Thirza had returned...

And as a result her life had been sent spinning once more into confusion—and fear.

Although there was no reason for her to be scared of any confrontation, she told herself defiantly. She, after all, had been the innocent party in the collapse of their brief ill-starred marriage. It was Ross who'd been the guilty party—the deceiver—the betrayer.

He, she thought with sudden savagery, was the one who should be afraid to face her.

And maybe that was true. Perhaps he was equally disturbed to hear she was in the vicinity. Just as reluctant to undergo their eventual meeting.

Because, sooner or later, it was bound to happen. Polcarrow was too small a place for them to be able to avoid each other, even for a short time.

Although Aunt Grace had said he was ill. Too ill, perhaps, to leave Thirza's house?

Jenna shook her head, almost derisively. No, she thought. That couldn't happen. Impossible to imagine Ross as a sick man. To see that strong, lithe body suddenly vulnerable, aware of its own humanity. To hear him forced to acknowledge personal weakness when he didn't even know the meaning of the words.

When he had nothing but contempt for people who gave way to their emotions, no matter what the reason.

No question, either, of him tactfully pretending to be more ill than he was to dodge any possible confrontation.

Ross, she thought, her mouth twisting, had always erred on the side of brutal candour—as she had such bitter cause to know. No white lies or cover-ups. Just the truth, coldly told. Whatever the cost...

I should have known that, she told herself. Should have realised that, once the layers of charm, intelligence and sexual charisma were peeled away, I'd find ice at the core.

I suspected it years ago, when I first met him. How was it I could be more perceptive as a child than a woman?

Well, she knew the answer to that. As a child, her thinking hadn't been muddled by the treachery of love—the bewitchment of sexual desire. And yet...

She'd been just thirteen when Thirza had been widowed and returned to take up residence in the village. And it was only a few months later when her stepson Ross had paid her a first visit.

He'd been twenty-one then, and had already embarked on his high-flying and successful career as a photojournalist.

A tall, self-contained young man, black-haired and tanned, with eyes as dark as a moonless night. And as impenetrable.

Nor was he conventionally handsome. His straight nose was a fraction too long and his eyes too heavy-lidded for that. But the high cheekbones and the firm, sensuous mouth were exquisitely chiselled, and when he smiled Jenna, for one, felt her heart turn over.

'The looks of a fallen angel,' Aunt Grace had commented privately, her lips pursed. 'And trouble down to his handmade shoes.'

But Jenna and Christy hadn't considered him trouble-some at all. From the first moment they'd been open-mouthed at the sight of him, bowled over by the aura of easy confidence and sophistication that clung to him. Starry-eyed at this answer to all their burgeoning adolescent dreams, who was even—oh, joy—some kind of distant cousin by marriage. Unable to believe that for all this time they had been barely aware of his existence. But Thirza herself had been hardly more than a name to them either.

They'd been more than ready for breathless, unequivocal hero-worship—had Ross Grantham shown any sign of wanting their adoration.

But he hadn't. He greeted them with a cool civility bordering on indifference, and then appeared oblivious to their existence for the remainder of his stay.

Even after all this time, and in spite of everything that had happened since, Jenna could still wince at the memory of the lengths they'd gone to in their unavailing attempts to attract his attention.

Christy, who been reading Jane Austen's *Emma*, had bewailed the fact that all her shoes were slip-ons, and she couldn't stage an encounter by breaking a lace outside Thirza's cottage.

Jenna had had notions of persuading one of the amiable hacks they rode at the local stables to bolt with her when Ross was passing, so that he would be obliged to save her.

But before she'd been able to put this daring plan into action Ross had gone. He'd called briefly at Trevarne House to say goodbye, but the girls had been taken shopping in Truro by Mrs Penloe, so they'd missed him. And he had left no message for them either.

'Beast,' Christy had said hotly, her pretty face pink with indignation. 'Well, good riddance to him.'

Jenna had said nothing, aware only of a curious mixture

of emotion churning in the pit of her stomach. Her almost agonised disappointment at his sudden departure had warred with an odd relief that such an unsettling presence had been removed, and her life could resume its usual placid path.

Except that, in retrospect she could see it never really had. Ross had remained there, a shadow in the corner of her mind, never completely banished, even though it had been seven years before she saw him again, and when they finally met it had been miles away in London.

He'd been back to Cornwall, of course, during those years. He'd come regularly to visit Thirza—never alone, and rarely bringing the same girl twice, which had set local tongues wagging. But his visits had invariably taken place at times when Christy and Jenna had been away, first at school, then at college, pursuing their respective courses.

She suspected that this had probably been quite deliberate, because they'd made such pests of themselves the first time around, but Ross had always insisted it was just a coincidence.

And she'd believed him, just as she'd somehow convinced herself that someone who so clearly liked to play the field could change and become focussed and faithful.

Because he'd made her think that all that time he'd simply been waiting for the right woman to come into his life. And that she was that woman.

She'd let herself believe too that his wanderlust—the need to be where the action was—could be subdued, that he could be tied down to a desk job, running the agency in London, even though she had the example of her own father to warn her how unlikely this was.

Perhaps if he'd lived he would have uttered a word of caution about how hard it would be for a man who'd enjoyed Ross's kind of freedom to be suddenly fettered by domesticity.

Her aunt and uncle, when she'd told them the news, had the other concerns.

'Are you really sure he's the man for you, darling?' Mrs Penloe's brow creased. 'It's not just an extension of that silly crush you once had?'

'Oh, don't remind me.' Jenna shuddered, blushing a little. 'And this is entirely different. As soon as I saw him again—I knew. And it was just the same for Ross. As if we'd always been waiting for each other.'

Her aunt pursed her lips doubtfully, exchanging glances with her husband. They'd enjoyed a happy and tranquil marriage, based on affection, respect and shared interests, and in her heart Grace Penloe believed that was the right basis for a sound relationship.

'Well, it all sounds very romantic,' she said at last. 'But I have to tell you, Jenna dear, that Thirza's marriage to Gerard Grantham was volatile, to put it mildly, and no one should pretend otherwise.'

Jenna nodded. 'Ross told me about it—and that's why he's waited to settle down. Because he didn't want the same thing to happen to him. He needed to be sure.' Her voice quickened easily. 'And now we've found each other—and we are.'

Mrs Penloe looked as if she wanted to say more, but the blaze of happiness in her niece's clear hazel eyes seemed to forbid any such thing, so she sighed soundlessly and kept quiet.

Memo to self, Jenna thought, biting her lip as she remembered the exchange. Stop thinking I know best and occasionally listen to the people who love me, like Uncle Henry, Aunt Grace, and Christy. And Tasha, of course, who'd had reservations from the first about Jenna's new relationship.

Tasha maybe most of all, she thought. Because I owe her so much.

They'd met originally through work. Her art course completed, Jenna had found a job in a smart London gallery, where Natasha Crane was already working. She was several years older than Jenny, tall and slim and striking, with black hair drawn severely back from her face. At first Jenna had found her manner faintly chilling, and had been in awe of her new colleague, but eventually there'd been a thaw and they'd become friends. So much so, indeed, that, both unhappy with their flat-sharing arrangements, they'd moved into a place of their own together.

The gallery had been a successful one. The owner, Raymond Haville, had had a sure eye for talent, and a good commercial sense, but he'd been nearing retirement and basically indolent, preferring to leave the day-to-day running of the business to his assistants. In many ways this had been a baptism of fire for Jenna, but she'd soon found herself gaining confidence and enjoying the challenge.

'We make a good team,' she'd once said buoyantly to Natasha, who'd nodded thoughtfully.

'Something we should bear in mind for the future, perhaps,' she'd returned.

But shortly after that Ross had come back into Jenna's life, and it had seemed as if her future was certain—settled, and all else had been forgotten.

Until, of course, her new world had come crashing down in ruins around her, and then, suddenly, Tasha had been there for her, strong and supportive, and offering a different kind of hope.

Raymond Haville was finally giving up, she'd told her, and her elderly godfather had also died, leaving her his antiques business, which had seen better days but was based in excellent premises.

'So why don't we go for it?' she'd urged. 'Pool our resources and open our own gallery. Raymond will let us use his contacts, and we know more than he does about the admin side.'

At first Jenna had been reluctant, unsure whether she was ready to cope with such hectic demands on her time and energy, but Tasha had been firm.

'I think it's exactly what you need,' she'd said. 'Something to take your mind off—everything else. I know you still need to grieve, honey,' she'd added, more gently. 'But you won't have time to brood. So, let's give our team a chance.'

So, almost before she knew it, Jenna had found herself a partner in a modest gallery, selling paintings, pottery and small sculptures. And discovering success.

Ross had moved out of the house they'd shared, and disclaimed any financial interest in it, so Jenna had sold up. Impossible to remain there alone, haunted by her delusions of happiness. She'd bought a smaller place, investing the surplus funds in the business and giving herself an equal stake with Natasha.

So now, two years on, she had a home and a career, for both of which she was inordinately grateful. Professionally, her life was fulfilling. Socially too she kept busy. She went to the theatre and the cinema, with Natasha and other friends. And as her circle of acquaintance had widened she'd begun to attend dinner parties. She smiled and chatted to the pleasant men who'd been invited to partner her, and, watched with wistful anxiety by her hostesses, politely evaded the inevitable follow-up invitations.

There would come a time when her personal life would

need fulfilment again; she was sure of it. But that time was not yet. At present, celibacy seemed much the safer option.

And right now she had another choice to make. Should she stay, or should she run? Her primary instinct told her to get out, and fast. She had suffered enough already at Ross's hands.

But reason advised caution. Maybe this meeting, so long dreaded, was the very catalyst she needed in order to close the lid on the past once and for all. Achieve some kind of closure on a relationship that should never have existed in the first place.

And there were other factors to take into account—Christy's disappointment at losing her matron of honour not being the least. It would be selfish and unkind to upset arrangements that had been months in the planning. And it was improbable that anyone else could possibly wear the slender sheath of primrose silk that she planned to wear as she followed Christy up the aisle.

Besides—and this was important too—Ross would doubtless be expecting her to vanish back to London—to take the coward's way out, she thought, her mouth twisting. And why should she oblige him by being so predictable?

Far better to let him see how little she cared about the past by standing her ground and toughing it out.

After all, it was only three days to the wedding, and then she could quite legitimately return to London—although she knew her aunt and uncle had been hoping she might stay on for a few days.

I, she thought, can survive three days.

'Jenna.'

Over the boom of the surf, and the mourning of the wind, she heard her name spoken.

For a moment she was very still, telling herself with a kind of desperation that it couldn't be true. That it was just a figment of her imagination, conjured up because she had allowed herself to think about Ross—to indulge memories that were best ignored.

'Jenna.'

She heard it again, and knew there could be no mistake—and no respite either. The moment she had feared all these months was upon her at last.

Because no one else had ever said her name with quite that same intonation, the first syllable softened and deliberately emphasised.

There was a time when that sound alone had had the power to melt her bones, as if she felt the touch of his hand, the brush of his lips on her naked skin.

Now it seemed as if a stone had lodged, hard and cold, in the pit of her stomach. Her hands tightened briefly, convulsively, on the back of the bench, and the roar of the sea was no louder than the thunder of her own pulses as slowly she turned to face him.

He was, she discovered, startled, only a few yards away from her. How could she not have known—not been aware of his approach? Her emotional antennae must have been dulled by all those false alarms in the past.

Striving for composure, she balled her hands into fists and thrust them deep into the pockets of her jacket. If they were going to start shaking it was no one's business but her own, she thought, and she made herself meet his gaze.

Although it was not easy to do so. His eyes went over her, slowly, searchingly, the straight black brows drawing together in a slight frown.

She knew exactly what he was seeing. The brown suede covered a tawny jersey. A silk scarf was knotted at her throat, and her long legs were booted to the knee under a brief skirt in pale tweed.

A successful, even affluent look—casual, but confident.

And she needed every scrap of confidence that was at her disposal.

He, she saw, was wearing black. Close-fitting pants that stressed the length of his legs, a roll-neck sweater and a leather jacket.

Belated mourning? she wondered bitterly, as the block of stone inside her twisted slowly. Agonisingly.

He said abruptly, 'You're thinner.'

It was so totally typical of him, Jenna thought, almost stung to unexpected laughter. None of the niceties or formalities of polite conversation for Ross. No cautious breaking of the ice between two people who had parted badly and never met since.

Well, if that was how he wanted to play it...

She shrugged. 'Then I'm in fashion.' She kept her tone cool to the point of indifference.

He smiled, that familiar, ironic twist of the mouth. 'Since when did you care about that?'

'Perhaps I've changed,' she said. 'People do.'

He shook his head slowly, his eyes never leaving hers. 'You haven't changed so much,' he said. 'Or how would I have known where to find you?' He gestured towards the sea. 'This was always your favourite place.'

'You came—looking for me?' She could not suppress the note of incredulity, but managed a tiny laugh to cover it. 'And I thought it was just a ghastly coincidence.'

'I thought perhaps we should—talk a little.'

'I really don't think we have anything left to talk about,' Jenna told him crisply. 'Our lawyers said all that was necessary quite some time ago.'

'However, they're not here,' he said softly. 'But we are. And that's the problem.'

'Is there a problem? I didn't realise...'

He sighed. 'Jenna—do you want to play games or talk

sense?' He paused questioningly, and when she did not reply went on, 'Can we at least agree that this isn't a situation either of us would have chosen?'

'Your stepmother clearly thinks differently.'

'Thirza is a genuinely kind woman,' he said. 'But sometimes her kindness leads her in strange directions.' He shrugged. 'What can I say?' He was silent again for a moment. 'Please believe that she didn't see fit to mention to me that Christy was to be married at this time—or that you would be attending the wedding. Otherwise I would not be here.'

'Well,' Jenna said, trying for crisp lightness, 'no one told me about you either. You'd almost think they were playing a late April Fool on us.'

'And I think, unless we are careful, we could both end up looking like fools,' Ross returned tersely. 'So, if you're thinking of doing a runner back to London, I advise you to forget it.'

Jenna gasped. 'May I remind you that you no longer have the right to dictate my actions?'

He said gently, 'And may I remind you that it was never a right I chose to enforce, anyway?'

She bit her lip. 'You realise the local gossips will have a field-day if we both stay.'

'They will have even more to enjoy if we leave.'

'Why?'

'Because they will think it means that we still matter to each other—when we know that's not the case.'

'On that,' she said, her tone gritty, 'we can agree, at least.'

'Good,' he said. 'We're making progress.' He paused. 'Unfortunately, it will be equally harmful if we each pretend the other does not exist—and for the same reason.'

'Ye-es,' she acknowledged, slowly and reluctantly. 'I suppose so.'

'Then I suggest that for the duration of the wedding celebrations we maintain a pretence of civility with each other.' He spoke briskly. 'Not for my sake, of course, or even yours, but for Christy.' He paused. 'I don't want her big day to be marred by the spectacle of us making ourselves ridiculous—or an object of speculation for the whole community, either,' he added grimly. 'I'm sure that's a point of view you can share.'

'How reasonable you make it sound,' Jenna said with a snap.

'Fine,' he threw back at her. 'Then go back to London. Let them think that you still care too much to be near me, even in public.'

'Now you really are being ridiculous,' she said coldly. 'As a matter of fact, I'd already made up my mind to stay. But I admit I hoped you'd have the decency to keep out of the way.'

'Decency was never one of my virtues.' His drawl taunted her. 'And I gather Thirza has already told the Penloes that I will be escorting her to the wedding. So I think we're going to have to—grin and bear it.'

'By taking refuge in clichés?'

'By doing whatever it takes.' He paused again, and she was uneasily aware of that intent, assessing stare. 'So, shall we each take a deep breath and declare a temporary truce— for the duration of the wedding?'

Jenna bit her lip. 'It seems there is no alternative.'

'Then shall we shake hands on it?' He walked towards her, closing the space between them, and she couldn't retreat because the damned bench was in the way. Could do nothing about the fact that he was now standing right beside her.

He held out his hand, his dark eyes mesmeric, compelling. Then a mischievous gust of wind suddenly lifted her loosened hair and blew it across his face.

Ross gasped and took a step backwards, his hands tearing almost feverishly at the errant strands to free himself.

For a crazy moment she wondered if he was remembering, as she was, the way he'd used to play with her hair when they were in bed together after lovemaking, twining it round his fingers and drawing it across his lips and throat.

And how she would bury her face in his shoulder, luxuriously inhaling the scent of his skin...

Sudden pain wrenched at her uncontrollably. Blood was roaring in her ears. Hands shaking, she raked her hair back from her face and held it captive at the nape of her neck.

She said hoarsely, looking past him, 'I—I think the weather's getting worse. I—I'll see you around—I expect...'

She walked away from him, forcing herself not to hurry, across the short, damp grass.

And if he said her name again as she went the wind carried it away and it was lost for ever. And she could only be thankful for that.

Once safely inside the garden she began to run, stumbling a little as her feet crunched the gravel.

She fell breathlessly through the front door and met Christy, back from her shopping trip to Truro, coming downstairs.

'Darling,' Christy's blue eyes searched her face. 'Are you all right? Ma was worried about you...'

'I'm fine,' Jenna said, eyes fiercely bright, cheeks hectically flushed. 'And, for good or ill, I'm staying. But on one condition—and it's not negotiable.'

'Oh, Jen.' Christy hugged her. 'Anything—you know that.'

Jenna took a deep, steadying breath. 'I'm going into Polcarrow tomorrow—and I'm having my hair cut.' She paused. 'All of it.'

CHAPTER TWO

THE wind dropped during the early hours of the morning. Jenna could have timed it to the minute, if she'd felt inclined, as she'd done little else since she got to bed but lie staring into the darkness and listening to the grandfather clock in the hall below sonorously marking the passage of the night.

If I don't get some sleep soon I'm going to look and feel like hell in the morning, she told herself, turning on to her stomach and giving her inoffensive pillows a vicious pummelling.

Even so, there was no way she would look as bad as Ross had done yesterday, she realised with a pang of reluctant concern. Any doubts she might have had about the seriousness of his recent illness had shattered after the first glance. Because he'd looked as if the virus he'd picked up abroad had taken him to death's door and back again.

He had told her she was thinner, but he too had lost an untold amount of weight, and his dark face had been haggard, and sallow, with deep shadows under his eyes. He'd looked older, too, and quieter. And oddly weary. For a moment she had found herself confronted by a stranger.

She could understand now why Thirza had been so worried about him, even if she did not relish the solution that worry had produced.

She sighed, burying her face in the pillow. For a while she'd been seriously tempted to keep quiet about their encounter on the cliff, but she'd soon realised that would be impractical. Besides, the way that she and Ross planned to deal with each other would have a direct bearing on the next few days, and affect her family, so they probably had a right to know.

She'd broken the news of their truce over dinner, keeping her voice light and matter-of-fact.

'The last thing either of us wants is to make the situation more awkward than it already is.' She had tried to smile. 'So, we plan to be—civil.'

There was a silence, then Aunt Grace said, 'Oh, my dear child, how desperately sad.' She directed a fulminating stare at her husband, who was placidly eating his portion of chicken casserole. 'Henry—how long have you known that Ross would be bringing Thirza to the wedding—and why on earth did you agree?'

'She rang to inform me just this morning.' Mr Penloe smiled at his wife. 'And she didn't ask my permission,' he added drily.

'Typical,' Grace Penloe said hotly. 'Absolutely *typical*. If she'd had the least consideration for us all she'd have stayed away herself.'

Jenna laid a placatory hand over her aunt's. 'Darling, it's all right—really. I admit I was upset when I first heard Ross was here, but that was—just me being silly.' She gave a resolute smile. 'It could be all for the best,' she added, with a sideways glance at her uncle. 'After all, we had to meet again some time.'

'Probably,' said Mrs Penloe. 'But, for preference, not under the Polcarrow microscope. Oh, Betty Fox will make a meal of this,' she added, stabbing at a mushroom as if it were the lady in question.

'Betty Fox will have enough to do, criticising what we're all wearing and finding fault with the decorations in the church hall and the caterers,' Christy said, pulling a face.

'Even she can't make much capital out of a divorced couple being polite to each other.'

'That's what you think,' her mother said tartly. 'Oh, damn Thirza.' She paused ominously. 'And, Jenna, what's this Christy tells me about you making an appointment at the hairdresser tomorrow to have your hair cut?'

Jenna shrugged. 'New attitude—new image. I've had long hair all my life. It's time for a change.'

Mrs Penloe gave the smooth chestnut coil at the nape of her niece's neck an anguished look. 'Oh, Jenna, don't do it. At least, not now. Wait until the wedding is over, please.'

Jenna stared at her. 'Aunt Grace, I'll be wearing a spray of freesias in my hair. The style won't make any difference.'

'I wasn't thinking of the headdress.' Mrs Penloe shook her head. 'Oh, dear.'

'You'd think,' Jenna said later, as she gave the condemned hair its final nightly brushing, 'that I was having my head cut off instead.'

Christy, who was sprawled across the bed, turning over the pages of *House and Garden*, frowned. 'Ma did over-react slightly,' she agreed. 'I can't say I'm entranced with the idea myself, but it's your hair, and your decision.'

She pulled a face. 'Perhaps the wedding is starting to get to her at last. She's been amazingly calm and organised so far, until dear Thirza dropped her bombshell, that is. I've told Pops that when it's all over he should take Ma away for a holiday.'

A sharp gust rattled the window, and the girls exchanged wry glances.

'Preferably somewhere warm and peaceful,' Jenna said drily, putting down her brush.

'Thank heavens we decided to have the reception in the church hall, instead of...' Christy paused awkwardly.

Jenna sent her a composed smile. 'Instead of a marquee on the lawn as I did?' she queried. 'It's all right. You can mention it without me having hysterics.' She pulled a face. 'I suspect I'll need to grow another skin over the next few days, anyway.'

Christy shut the magazine and sat up. 'Jen—I'm so awfully sorry you should be put through this.' She paused. 'The village rumour mill had Ross totally bedridden and being fed intravenously, of course, so you'd hardly expect him to pop up on Trevarne Head, being civilised.' She gave Jenna an anxious look. 'Seeing him again—was it as bad as you feared?'

'Heavens, no,' Jenna said lightly. *Worse—much worse.*

'Well, that's a relief.' Christy shook her head. 'Not that it lets Thirza off the hook. As a contributor to consideration and family unity, she makes a terrific fabric designer.'

'Well, she's certainly that, all right,' Jenna agreed. 'In fact, I've often thought I'd like to stage an exhibition of her work at the gallery.'

'You could always suggest it.'

Jenna shook her head. 'She'd refuse. I was never her favourite person, even before the divorce.'

'I could never figure that,' Christy said thoughtfully. 'After what she went through with her own husband, I'd have said her sympathies would have been with you.' She paused ruefully. 'Ouch, my big mouth again. Jen, I'm so sorry...'

'Don't be,' Jenna said briskly as she applied her moisturiser. 'Now, tell me about the best man instead. He's supposed to be my perk, isn't he?'

'Oh, Tim's adorable.' Christy cheered noticeably. 'He works in the City, too, and he and Adrian have been friends since university. They're arriving in time for lunch tomorrow.' She lowered her voice confidentially. 'And I happen to know Tim's not seeing anyone just now.'

'Christy,' Jenna said gently, 'be content with your lovely Adrian, and don't try matchmaking for other people. I was thinking of having a dance with Tim—nothing more.'

'Why not have two or three dances?' Christy suggested, unperturbed. She gave a sly smile. 'He'll make excellent camouflage, if nothing else.'

'I'll think about it.' Jenna rose from the dressing table. 'Now, push off, bride, and get some beauty sleep.'

'There are still three days to go,' Christy protested as Jenna ushered her inexorably to the door.

'True, but you need all the help you can get,' she said wickedly, and closed the door, laughing, on her cousin's outrage.

Now I'm the one who needs help, she thought drily, as she turned over in bed yet again, trying to relax and failing. This insomnia is probably Christy's curse on me.

But in her heart she knew that it was not that simple. That her restlessness and unease were really due to Ross's reappearance in her life and nothing else.

Which was quite ridiculous, she told herself forcefully. Because he wouldn't be losing a moment's sleep over her, in Thirza's slate-roofed cottage on the outskirts of the village.

Once again so near, she thought, yet so far away. Which seemed to sum up the entirety of their brief marriage.

Once before, on the night before their wedding, when she hadn't been able to sleep because she was too keyed up with joy and excitement, she'd tried to work out exactly what the distance was that separated them from each other, mentally retracing her steps down the drive from Trevarne House to the lane, narrow between its high summer hedges, and down its winding length to the steep sprawl of

Polcarrow, counting her paces as she went. Imagining him opening the door of the cottage to smile at her. Holding out his arms to enfold her...

Suddenly Jenna found herself sitting up, gasping for breath. She was shaking all over and her nightdress was clinging to her sweat-dampened body. She fumbled for the switch of the bedside lamp, then poured herself some water from the carafe on the night table, gulping its coolness past the constriction in her throat.

'Oh, you idiot,' she whispered to herself. 'You pathetic fool.'

The phrase 'don't even go there' had never seemed more appropriate, yet she almost had. She'd created a trap for herself and nearly fallen into it. Because she couldn't afford these memories. They brought too much pain with them.

The ending of her marriage had been a war zone, and she still bore the wounds. And this truce that she'd agreed on with Ross was meaningless, because it would never lead to a lasting peace.

That was impossible, she thought. Too much had happened.

Most of it she'd managed to block out over the past months by working hard and making sure her leisure hours were full, leaving little time for introspection. But now there was a crack in the dam, and she was terrified of what might follow.

She switched off the lamp and lay down again, aware that her stomach was churning and a mass of confused thoughts were jostling for precedence in her tired mind. And, with them, memories as sharp as knives.

Memories that she needed to deal with and forget. As Ross himself, no doubt, had done long ago.

And that, she realised unhappily, was no comfort at all.

*   *   *

'Are you sure about this?' said Stella, picking up a length of Jenna's hair and brandishing it.

She was short, wiry and feisty, with hair that—this week—was the colour of pewter. She was an 'incomer' too—someone who'd come to Cornwall on holiday and fallen in love with it, then decided to throw up her job in a top London hairdressing salon and make a new life for herself in Polcarrow.

She'd lost no time in opening her own premises in the village's steep main street, and her skills had attracted clients from all over the Duchy.

On Saturday she would be bringing two assistants and a friend who was a beautician and manicurist to Trevarne House to attend to the needs of the bride and her family.

In the meantime she'd agreed to squeeze in an appointment for Jenna. But she clearly wasn't happy about it.

'What happens if I start and you change your mind?' she demanded pugnaciously, hands on hips. 'I can't stick it back on, you know.' Her tone changed, became wheedling. 'Why don't I just give it a good trim instead?'

'I'm quite serious.' Jenna said flatly. 'I want it short.' She opened the style book and pointed. 'Like that.'

'Hell's bells,' said Stella, blinking. 'All right, then, love. But it's your funeral.'

Three quarters of an hour later, Jenna found herself regarding a stranger in the mirror. Her chestnut mane had been reduced to little more than a sleek cap, skilfully layered, which emphasised the shape of her head and lay in feathered fronds across her forehead and over her ears.

'Actually, it works,' Stella conceded unwillingly. 'It shows off your cheekbones and that. And on Saturday I can fix your flowers—like this.' She demonstrated.

Jenna smiled at her. 'Stella—you're a genius.'

'Yeah,' said Stella, who did not count mock-modesty as

a virtue. 'But I still say it's a shame. All that lovely hair.'
She paused. 'Want a bit to keep? Reminder of past glories,
eh?'

'No,' Jenna said quietly. 'I don't think so, thanks.'

Her head felt incredibly light as she emerged into the
street, and the sun had come out too—doubtless in honour
of her new image.

She had parked her car down by the harbour, and progress back to it was slow. Every few yards, it seemed, people were stopping her to welcome her back, to tell her she
looked wonderful, and say that it looked as if the weather
might clear up after all for the wedding.

And she smiled back, and thanked them and agreed, saying she would see them on Saturday.

Amid the general euphoria of welcome it took a moment
to register that she was being watched with less than
warmth from across the street. She glanced up and saw that
Ross was standing on the narrow pavement, outside Betty
Fox's general stores. He was still to the point of tension,
staring at her, his brows drawn together in thunderous incredulity.

Jenna's instinct was to make a dash for the car, but instead she made herself smile weakly and lift her hand in a
half-greeting.

He moved then, crossing the street, weaving his way between two vans and a bicycle with the long, lithe stride that
was so hauntingly familiar.

What a difference a few hours could make, Jenna thought
in astonishment as he reached her. Yesterday on the cliff
he had looked tired, almost defeated. Today he was clearly
incandescent, and her heart began to thud in alarm.

His hand closed, not gently, on her arm. 'In the name of
God,' he grated, 'what have you done to yourself?'

'I've had my hair cut.' She tried unavailingly to free herself from his grasp. 'It's not a crime.'

'That,' Ross said crushingly, 'is a matter of opinion.'

'And, anyway,' Jenna went on, her own anger sparking into life, 'it's none of your damned business what I do.'

'So, if I see an act of vandalism being committed—a work of art being defaced—I'm to say or do nothing? Or should I stand back and applaud?'

'Don't be ridiculous,' she snapped. 'It's not the same thing at all, and you know it.'

'No,' he said. 'It's far worse. It's a travesty—a sacrilege.' His eyes held hers. The noise around them—the hum of voices, the stutter of traffic, and the crying of gulls from the harbour—seemed to fade, enclosing them in a strange and potent silence.

Then, over his shoulder, Jenna saw Betty Fox emerge from her shop, ostensibly to rearrange the newspapers in the outside rack, her glance darting avidly towards them, and the spell was sharply broken.

She said tautly, 'I thought we had a truce. Yet here we are brawling in public, for all the world to see. Now, will you kindly let go of me?'

'No,' he said. 'Not yet.'

He set off down the street, still holding her arm, taking Jenna with him whether she wanted to go or not, turning the corner on to the harbour.

'What the hell do you think you're doing.' She was flushed, breathless with indignation at being whirled along in this undignified manner.

He had always done this, she thought. Starting with that night in London when they'd met again. Recognised each other in a totally new way…

'Come.' He'd taken her arm then, hurrying her from the

room—from the building and into the street. Striding so
fast that she'd had to run to keep up with him.

'Where are we going?' She'd been overwhelmed by all
she felt for him—scared, joyous and hungry all at the same
time.

And he'd stopped suddenly, and turned to her, his hands
framing her face with heart-stopping tenderness. 'Does it
matter?'

Now, even though there was nothing remotely lover-like
in his touch, she was shocked to find it could still shake
her to the core. Or was that the memory it evoked?

'Making amends, darling,' he flung back at her. 'Being
amazingly civilised.'

He pushed open the door of the Quayside Café and
marched her in. For a startled moment the buzz of conversation at the occupied tables faltered, then resumed at a
slightly higher pitch as Ross ushered Jenna to a table beside
the window and ordered two coffees from the flustered pro-
prietress.

'Would you like something to eat?' he asked Jenna,
glancing towards the counter laden with cakes, biscuits and
scones.

'Thank you, no,' she returned glacially.

His face relaxed into a sudden grin. 'Because it would
choke you?'

It did not help her temper to know she'd actually been
tempted, just for a moment, to smile back. 'This is all a
big joke to you, isn't it?' she said in a furious undertone.

His brows lifted. 'Far from it, sweetheart,' he drawled.
'A tragedy, perhaps.' He paused. 'Now, perhaps we should
find some bland neutral topic to keep us from each other's
throats until the coffee comes.'

'You think of something,' she said curtly. 'I'm not into
small talk.'

'Fine.' He thought for a moment. 'Are you planning to go on holiday this year?'

'I haven't decided yet.' She looked down at the checked tablecloth. 'I might go for a last-minute booking on some Greek island.'

'Alone?'

She shrugged. 'I can hardly go with Natasha. One of us has to be there to run the gallery.'

'Yes, of course,' he said softly. 'Thirza told me that you were now in business together.'

There was a note in his voice that reminded her that Natasha's low opinion of him had been entirely reciprocated.

She lifted her chin. 'How kind of your stepmother to take such an interest in my affairs.'

'A slight exaggeration.' The dark eyes glinted. 'She merely mentioned it in passing.'

'I see.' She hesitated. 'What about you? Are you—planning any kind of vacation?'

He smiled faintly. 'For me, as ever, a holiday is simply to stop travelling.'

But you did stop—when you married me. You said you'd finished with that kind of life. The thought forced itself upon her before she could prevent it.

'But I suppose I'll go back to the house in Brittany,' he went on. 'Apparently the last lot of tenants weren't the most careful in the world, and it needs some work.'

'You've been renting out Les Roches?' *The place where we spent our honeymoon?* 'I—I didn't know.'

Ross shrugged. 'Houses shouldn't be left empty, or the heart goes out of them.'

Jenna examined a fleck on her thumbnail. 'You've never considered selling it?'

'No.' The response was crisp and instant. 'It's always

been a family home.' He leaned back in his chair. 'And one day I intend to have a family there.'

She had not seen that coming, and she felt as if she'd been punched in the solar plexus. There was an odd roaring in her ears, and when she parted her lips to say something—anything—no sound would come.

The arrival of the coffee saved her. By the time the cups had been placed on the table, and cream and sugar brought, she was able to speak again. To cover, she hoped, the momentary hiatus.

'My God.' She even managed a little laugh. 'Is the rolling stone coming to rest at last?'

'It would seem so.' His mouth twisted. 'As they all do—eventually.'

'I thought you might prove to be the exception.' She could only hope the lightness in her tone was convincing. 'What's caused the change of heart?'

'I became ill.' His gaze met hers. 'And, as you know, I'm not used to that. It made me think. Perhaps—adjust my priorities.' He was silent for a moment, then he said, 'Also, there is—someone in my life. Someone important.' He shrugged. 'What can I say?'

'There's nothing that needs to be said.' Stunned as she was, somehow she found the words. Made her lips utter them without faltering. 'After all, we're both—free agents. When—when's the happy day?'

'Nothing's been decided yet. It is still a little too soon for her. She's been married before as well, and there are adjustments to be made.'

'Well,' she said, smiling resolutely, 'naturally you'll want to be sure—this time.'

'Yes,' he said. 'I will.' His brows lifted. 'You're—very understanding.'

She murmured something and looked down at the table.

The compliment was undeserved, and she knew it. She understood nothing. Under her façade of composure she was seething with questions that she would not—could not ask him.

Do I know her? being the foremost. To be followed by, *Is it Lisa Weston? And, if not, why not? What happened to the woman for whom you ended our marriage?* And, *Did you tire of her, too, in the end?* The words were tumbling over themselves in her mind, demanding answers.

But these were places she dared not go. Because once the questions started she might not be able to stop them.

And the inner ice she relied on might crack, and all the pain—all the loss—might come pouring out at last. Betraying her utterly.

Revealing to him, once and for all, how deeply he had wounded her.

And revealing, most damagingly of all, that she still bled—still grieved in spite of the two years' total separation between them.

And if he ever suspected the healing process in her had not begun, he might ask himself why. And she could not risk that particular humiliation, she thought breathlessly, or any other.

Aware that the silence between them was lengthening, she looked up and smiled brightly at him across the table.

His own glance was hooded, meditative. 'And what about you, Jenna? Is there someone for you?'

'No one that special.' She lifted a nonchalant shoulder. 'But I'm enjoying playing the field. I never really did that before.'

'No,' he said. He drank some coffee, grimaced and put down his cup. 'This place serves the worst coffee in the world.'

'You've said that every time we've been here.' The

words were out before she could stop them. They were loaded with shared memory. And just when she needed to make him think the past was a closed book, she thought, biting her lip.

'That could be because it's always true.' He glanced at his watch. 'Maybe it's time to bring our demonstration of ex-marital harmony to an end.'

'Yes—yes, of course.' She made a business of picking up her bag, watching from under her lashes as he walked to the counter to pay the bill, smiling at plump Mrs Trewin and saying something that made her bridle girlishly.

But that was Ross, she told herself stonily. He could use charm like a weapon, and it was something to which his new lady would have to accustom herself.

However, she couldn't get over the astonishing change just a few hours had wrought in him.

He looked, she thought wonderingly, as if he'd woken, refreshed, from a deep sleep. He was still too thin, of course, but the lines of his face looked sharper, more dynamic this morning, and the old glint was back in his eyes—sexy, humorous, and as devastating as ever.

Perhaps he was looking for closure, too, wanting to go into his new relationship without baggage from the past to slow him down.

And that, of course, was what she should be seeking, too. Had always told herself that she was striving to attain.

Christy's wedding was supposed to be a step on the path to her own regeneration. She had known ever since she received the invitation that she would have to be strong to cope with all the implications and resonances of the occasion. But that had been before the bombshell of Ross's presence had been exploded, and all that had happened since.

Culminating in the revelations of the past half-hour.

And now, she knew, she was going to need every single weapon in her armoury of self-protection to get her unscathed through the next few days, let alone the eternity to come. And she was frightened.

She walked ahead of him out on to the cobbles, and stood for a moment, shading her eyes, looking at the familiar mix of fishing boats and sailing craft in the harbour, thankful to have something else to focus on.

Ross came to stand beside her. 'You must miss this place—the sea—very much. Do you think you will ever come back?'

'It was a wonderful place to spend my childhood.' She kept her voice steady. 'But I'm grown-up now, and my life is—elsewhere.'

'London?' His mouth twisted. 'Even when we lived there together I was never convinced it was the right place for you.'

'Perhaps it wasn't the environment,' she said tautly, 'but other factors that were wrong. Anyway, I'd prefer not to discuss it.' She squared her shoulders. 'My car's over there. Do you want a lift back to Thirza's?'

He said slowly. 'That would be kind. But are you sure you wish to do this?'

She didn't look at him. 'We may as well keep the charade going to the bitter end.'

There was still a breeze, but it was turning into a perfect spring day. The clouds were high and broken, and the sun was hot and bright on Jenna's newly shorn head as they walked along the quayside. She slipped off the quilted gilet she was wearing and pushed up the sleeves of her thin wool sweater.

He said suddenly, his voice faintly hoarse, 'Dear God— did I do that?'

Glancing down, Jenna saw the red marks, clearly visible on her bare arm, where his fingers had gripped her.

She said, 'It's—not important. And the dress I'm wearing for the wedding has long sleeves. Besides,' she added, coolly and pointedly. 'I always did bruise easily.'

His swift smile was humourless. 'Ah, yes. Of course. How could I forget? Whereas I, on the other hand, remained unmarked and untouched by everything—always. As if I have chain mail instead of skin. Is that what you're saying?'

She bit her lip. 'Not exactly. I—I couldn't expect you to care about—some things in the same way as I did.'

'Presumably because I am an insensitive boor of a man, who understands nothing of a woman's innermost feelings.' His tone was suddenly icy. 'You have a short memory, Jenna. In those first few months of our marriage I came to know all your most intimate secrets—including some you'd never been aware of yourself until then.'

Her suddenly flushed cheeks owed nothing to the heat of the day.

She said in a suffocated voice, 'You have no right to talk to me like this. No right at all.'

'I need no reminder,' Ross said softly, 'of all the rights in you that I was fool enough to surrender.'

His words seemed to hang in the air between them, challenging, even threatening. Reviving old memories—old hungers. Shocking her with their potency.

He was watching her, the dark eyes glittering as they travelled over her in unashamed exploration. The cream round-necked sweater and close-fitting blue denim jeans she wore were no barrier to the intensity of his scrutiny, she realised as she stared back at him, eyes dilating, lips parted. Aware of a small, unwelcome stir of excitement deep within her.

Because he knew—none better—how she looked naked, after all the times he'd removed her clothes, his hands sometimes tender, often fiercely urgent. His lips caressing the warm skin he'd uncovered.

She was horrified to feel her nipples hardening involuntarily under the sudden force of the recollection.

This was what she'd always feared, she thought, swallowing. This was why she'd refused to allow any personal contact between them during the divorce, even in the safety of the lawyers' offices. Or afterwards.

Because she knew she could not guarantee to control her physical responses to him.

However much she might have trained her mind to reject him, her body still shivered with remembered desire in his presence.

Suddenly she felt heat blaze from him like a dark sun.

And realised with swift, scared certainty that all she needed to do was reach out her hand...

Her throat tightened. She thought, 'I can't do this.' And only realised she had spoken aloud when she saw his face change. The firm mouth harden.

Saw him take a step backwards, deliberately distancing himself from her.

He said quietly, 'Unfortunately, you don't have a choice, Jenna. And neither do I.' He paused. 'However, it might be better for me to walk back to Thirza's. I'll see you later.'

He turned and strode off down the quay.

For a moment Jenna stood where she was, watching him go, then, slowly and shakily, she made her way across the cobbles to her car.

She unlocked it and got in, stowing her bag on the passenger seat. Even fitting the key in the ignition. But she made no attempt to start the engine.

Her heart was thumping rapidly and noisily, and she felt

slightly sick. Certainly she didn't trust herself to drive. Not unless she wanted to find herself, and the car, on the bottom of the harbour.

She thought, I have to pull myself together.

But that, of course, was easier said than done.

She drew a deep breath and made herself review the situation. It had been lousy luck running into Ross two days in a row, but she'd make sure it didn't happen again.

She was bound to see him at the wedding, of course, but there would be plenty of other people around, and he would be easier to dodge in a crowd. And there would be the unknown Tim to act as safeguard, anyway.

Apart from the wedding rehearsal tomorrow, there was no need for her to leave Trevarne House at all, and she would make sure that her every waking moment was full— even if all she could find to do was soothing Aunt Grace.

She folded her arms on the steering wheel and leaned her forehead against them, feeling the prickle of tears against her closed eyelids.

But who, she thought, with sudden desolation, is going to soothe me?

And for that she could find no satisfactory answer at all.

CHAPTER THREE

THE car was a cocoon. A refuge closing her away from everything except her thoughts. Those she could not escape, or even evade. Not any more.

Her mind was in chaos, yet somehow she found she was being dragged inexorably back in time to that night over three years ago when she, a child no longer, had met Ross again.

There'd been a private view at the Haville Gallery for a talented young painter having his first exhibition. The evening had gone well, and a number of pictures had displayed the red dot of success. People had begun to drift away when, suddenly alerted by an odd tingle in her senses that she was being watched, Jenna had turned and seen Ross standing a few yards away, his eyes narrowed in a kind of stunned disbelief as he looked at her.

They might have been alone. None of the chattering groups around them had seemed to exist any longer.

All the breath seemed to leave her body in one deep, startled gasp as her gaze had locked with his. Read what he was thinking as if he had shouted it aloud. The total astonishing certainty of the moment had taken her a willing, helpless prisoner. Joined them both in a new and devastating recognition.

It had been as if some lifelong search was suddenly over, and the hidden treasure—the Holy Grail—was there waiting for her.

Her stomach had churned—her pulses had gone crazy.

A delicious heat had spread through her veins, and her senses had gone spinning into a kind of delirium.

And then she'd seen him smile and start towards her, and she had moved, too, going to meet him halfway. More than halfway. People had spoken to her, but she hadn't heard what they said. She'd been oblivious, every fibre of her being focussed on this man now re-entering her life with such unbelievable impact. She'd realised that she was accepting without question that here was the only man in the world whom she would ever want.

And that it was how, in some strange unfathomable way, she had always known it would be.

When she'd reached him, her voice had been a little husky croak. 'What are you doing here?'

'I was invited. Someone I met at a party.' She watched him draw an uneven breath. 'I—I almost didn't come...'

And they both laughed in derisive rejection of the very idea. Because they knew that since time began it had been inevitable that they would meet again at this place—at this moment. That this was what they had both been created for, and that there was nothing that could have kept them apart.

She said, her voice smiling, 'You recognised me—in this crowd?'

He said slowly, 'I'd have known you anywhere.' He paused. 'But why are you here?'

'It's where I work.'

'Of course.' He shook his head. 'Thirza told me that you'd done an art course.'

'I'm surprised she remembered.'

He said quietly, 'But I asked about you, Jenna. I always—always asked about you.'

And as she met his eyes, and saw the flare of passion, the unhidden hunger, she felt her skin warm passionately and involuntarily, and her throat tighten in a sweet excitement she had never known before.

She said, in a whisper, 'I—I don't understand. What is happening?'

'We are.' His voice was almost harsh. 'We're happening to each other. At long last.' His hand touched her cheek, stroked its curve, and she turned her head in a swift, involuntary reaction, finding his caressing fingers with her lips.

'Jenna.' He spoke in a tortured whisper. 'Dear God, Jenna...'

For a moment he was silent, mastering his breathing. Then, 'Come.' He took her arm, hurrying her from the room—from the building and into the street. Striding so fast that she had to run to keep up with him.

'I can't just leave...' But her protest carried no real conviction.

'You just did.'

'Where are we going?' She was overwhelmed by all she felt for him—scared, joyous and hungry all at the same time.

And he stopped suddenly and turned to her, his hands framing her face with heart-stopping tenderness. 'Does it matter?'

And she replied simply and seriously, 'No.'

They went to his flat in a warehouse development overlooking the Thames. As he sat beside her in the shadowed intimacy of the taxi Ross took her hand and held it. There was no real pressure in the clasp of his fingers, but his touch seemed to penetrate to her bones, and she began to tremble inside.

Yet as they rode in the lift to the upper floor Jenna found her first euphoria evaporating, leaving her feeling shy and vulnerable. She cast a swift, sideways glance at Ross, but there was nothing to be read from his expression. Suddenly he seemed to be the cool, enigmatic stranger of her teens again, and she was assailed by a pang of real doubt.

What am I doing? she thought. Why am I here?

Well, she knew the answer to that, of course. She might be inexperienced, but she wasn't naïve. And she had gone with him of her own free will, so she could hardly protest if he expected her to keep the promise that her capitulation implied, she thought, swallowing.

But her first glimpse inside the flat itself drove everything else from her mind. Eyes widening, she stared round at the high vaulted ceilings and enormous windows which provided untrammelled views of the river from the main living area. The wooden floors gleamed with the patina of gold, and the pale walls provided a neutral background for furnishings and drapes in warm earth colours.

'I bought the shell,' Ross told her, as he began to make coffee in the streamlined galley kitchen. 'Then I got a mate of mine who's an architect to design the interior, because I needed space for an office and a dark room.'

'He's made a wonderful job of it.' Jenna's eyes shone as she looked around her. 'It's amazing.'

He grinned at her. 'And that's even before you get the guided tour.' He paused. 'Have you had anything to eat this evening—apart from those little bits of nothing on toast?'

'I'm glad Mr Haville can't hear you,' Jenna told him with severity. 'Those were canapés from very expensive caterers.'

'Which could explain the fashionable minimalistic effect. And also why I'm starving.' Ross briskly abandoned coffee-making and produced a pack of dried pasta from a cupboard instead, rummaging in the fridge for eggs, pancetta and a carton of cream. 'Spaghetti carbonara?'

'Yes, please.' Jenna nodded vigorously. 'Can I help?'

'There's some rocket and stuff in the salad drawer. You could make a dressing for that.' He pointed. 'You'll find what you need in that cupboard.'

They worked for a few minutes in a silence that managed, incredibly, to be relaxed and companionable. As if, Jenna thought wonderingly, they'd been doing it all their lives...

And she was frankly relieved to find that he had no intention of dragging her into bed immediately. Because, however much her body might be clamouring for him, her first physical surrender was going to be a tremendous mental and emotional hurdle for her.

But I'll deal with that when I have to, she told herself.

As she tossed the salad leaves in a bowl, she said, 'I still can't believe this is happening.'

'You're on some strange diet that forbids evening meals?'

'I mean that we're here—like this.' She shook her head in bewilderment. 'Yet really we're practically strangers.'

'You and I have always known each other.' Ross rinsed his hands and dried them on a towel. 'And I don't mean the fact that we're probably fourth or fifth cousins by marriage. There was an awareness there from the first.' He paused. 'I think you sensed it, too.'

She blushed a little. 'Even when I was being a brat?'

His face was solemn, but his eyes were dancing. 'Particularly then.'

'But—you always ignored me.'

'Have a heart, my love.' His tone was gentle. 'You were still a child. I had to keep my distance for all kinds of reasons. You must know that. Your uncle Henry certainly did,' he added drily. 'He was very kind about it. Told me I had nothing to be ashamed of. Congratulated me on identifying a potential problem and dealing with it before it became serious. Said that young girls had no idea of their own power, but enjoyed testing it anyway. That I'd been very patient and must continue to be so.'

She said in a stifled voice, 'You talked about me—like that? As if I was some junior tease? Oh, God...'

He shook his head. 'No, darling. Because we both loved you. Besides, he was quite right. I'd been shaken at the depth of my own feelings. And I couldn't explain to him that it wasn't just a physical thing. That what drew you to me was that sense of inner calm you already possessed. Christy was the open, flirty one. But you had a quality of stillness that was like a magnet to my type of vagabond. So the only answer was to go away, and stay away until you were older.'

She bent her head. 'Ross, I grew up a long time ago. But, even so, you—stayed away.'

'Yes,' he said slowly. 'Because over the years it all began to seem like an illusion. One of those private dreams that you keep locked away, because you know it can never be fulfilled.'

He paused. 'It occurred to me too that it could all be completely one-sided. That the strange feeling of attunement—of coming home—that I'd sensed had just been a figment of my imagination.'

She said huskily, 'You knew better than that.'

'Perhaps—but life moves on, and I could have missed my moment. You might easily have met someone else.' He shook his head. 'Each time I saw Thirza I was half expecting her to tell me that you were engaged or married.'

'No,' she said. 'There's never been anyone—anyone serious, that is.'

And her heart cried, *Because I was waiting for you—*

only I didn't realise it. I only knew when I saw you again tonight.

He was silent for a moment, the dark eyes quizzical as he studied her.

Then he said quietly, 'I see.' And continued with his preparations for supper.

And she knew that it was true. That he recognised her longing, and her fear, and understood them both. And tonight would be a new beginning.

There was warm ciabatta bread with the food, and a dry, crisp white wine which cut across the melting richness of the pasta. And afterwards there was cheese, and a platter of fresh fruit.

In spite of the nervous flutters in the pit of her stomach, Jenna managed to eat a perfectly reasonable meal. It was partly a matter of pride. She needed to prove to herself as well as Ross that she possessed at least a modicum of sophistication, even though she might be embarking on uncharted waters.

The conversation helped reduce tension, too. They chatted easily, filling in the gaps in the years they'd been apart.

However, she was bewildered by the fact that he made no attempt to touch her at all. Indeed, in the kitchen, during the final preparations for the meal, he seemed to have gone out of his way to avoid physical contact.

Perhaps his realisation that she was still a virgin was an unwelcome one, Jenna thought unhappily. Maybe he needed someone who could meet him at his own level of experience.

Even when dinner was over, and they took their coffee and brandies with tacit consent to one of the enormous sofas, they occupied opposite corners, several feet apart.

Surely, Jenna thought, biting her lip, he couldn't be waiting for her to make the first move.

Whatever the reason, Ross seemed quite happy to go on chatting, exchanging reminiscences, and Jenna found herself catching her breath as he described, almost laconically, some of the adventures and dangers his chosen career had involved.

'I feel as if I've been living on a different planet,' she said ruefully, curled up tautly amongst the deep cushions, her feet tucked under her. She ticked off on her fingers. 'Home, school, college, job. A very sedate progression. Not much excitement there.'

'Is that what you want—excitement?' There was a smile in his voice. He was leaning back, totally at ease and sexy with it, tie loosened and the top buttons of his shirt undone, its cuffs turned back over tanned forearms.

'I don't know.' She swallowed past a sudden tightness in her throat as she realised the mood of the evening had shifted. 'I never thought about it before.'

'And now?'

'I'm still—not sure.' She shook her head, punching a clenched fist into the arm of the sofa. 'Oh, how feeble does that sound?'

He said quietly, 'Darling, there's no need for you to beat yourself up over this, I promise you.' He paused. 'Or to be scared, either.'

'I—I'm not...'

'No?' His eyes were quizzical. 'You're so brittle that if I laid a hand on you, you'd probably shatter into a million pieces.'

She lifted her chin, meeting his gaze. 'Maybe I'm tougher than I look. And I have been touched before,' she added for good measure.

'Really?' The dark eyes studied her, lingering with sensuous candour on the curve of her breasts, then travelled slowly down to the slender outline of her thighs under the cling of her simple black dress. 'Would you care to specify how—and where?'

She said, 'You're laughing at me...'

'I promise I was never more serious.' There was a sudden harshness in his voice. 'Make no mistake, I want you very badly, Jenna. I need you to stay with me tonight, but I won't force you into something you're not ready for.'

He took a deep breath. 'If it's all too soon, and too sudden for you, then you only have to say so. It's not a problem. I have the number of a reliable cab company to take you home.'

She said with difficulty, 'And then?'

He shrugged wryly. 'Then I practise superhuman patience—and wait.'

'But for how long?'

His mouth tightened. 'You want your pound of flesh, don't you? Very well. The answer is for as long as it takes—but no further than our wedding night,' he added drily. 'Because then I might have to insist.'

She stared at him. 'You—want to—marry me?'

He moved then. Closer, but still not crowding her. Reached out a hand and took a long strand of hair, winding it round his fingers.

He said quietly, staring down at its glossy sheen, 'You surely can't think that, having found you, I'm ever going to let you go again?'

Her heart was pounding like a beaten drum.

'Isn't it usual to make some kind of formal proposal?'

His grin was rueful. 'I planned to—in the morning.'

'Oh,' she said slowly. Then 'May I use your phone?'

'Of course.' He released her immediately. 'You'll find the card for a minicab tucked inside the directory.'

Jenna shook her head. 'I'm calling my flatmate—to tell

her I won't be back tonight.' She smiled rather waveringly. 'You see, I really don't do this, and she may—worry.'

'Darling.' He slipped off the sofa and knelt in front of her. His voice was very gentle. 'Are you sure about this?'

'Yes,' she said. 'I am now. I'm quite certain that if I'm going to spend the rest of my life with you I'd like it to begin tonight.'

Ross bent his head and rested his cheek for a long moment against her stockinged knee. He said softly, 'Then so it shall.'

She got the answering machine when she called the flat. Perhaps Natasha was already in bed, she thought, glancing at her watch. Or, worse, still at the gallery, helping to clear up after the private view.

But no amount of guilt could hide the note of lilting joy in her voice. 'Hi. This is to let you know that I'm fine—and I'll see you in the morning.'

Then she replaced the handset and, smiling, her heart in her eyes, walked sweetly and simply into Ross's waiting arms.

God, but he'd made it so easy for her, Jenna thought wearily, remembering. But then he'd hardly had to try.

It had been the kind of seduction that dreams were made of. A long, sweet ascent to pleasure which had made the blood sing in her veins.

From the moment his mouth had touched hers, parting her lips in unquestioned mastery, she'd been lost, drowning in sensations she'd never guessed could exist.

She'd yielded herself totally to his kisses, returning them with eager abandonment, her whole body shivering with delight as he'd lifted her into his arms and carried her to his bed.

Any last traces of shyness, any lingering doubt had been

superseded entirely by a burning, overwhelming hunger which had demanded a surcease that only he could give.

She had not even questioned the practised fingers that slid off her clothes, uncovering her body in the lamplight for the arousing beguilement of his hands and lips. Nor wondered, as she'd come to do later, how many other women had moaned their longing under his smiling mouth, or arched in trembling greed for his caress.

Then, she had been blind and deaf to everything but the need to take, and be taken.

His hands had been warm as they'd explored the satin of her skin, paying a leisurely homage to every slender curve, every plane and angle of her body.

Through half-closed eyes she'd been aware that he was watching her, his own gaze intent on the play of colour under her pale skin, the drawn breath that had become a sob, the restless movement of her head on the pillow—all the small sighing answers of her body to his caresses.

She had given herself up to him with total ardour, whimpering her pleasure into his shoulder as he'd stroked and kissed her breasts, teasing her eager nipples with his tongue so that they stood proudly erect.

Her fingers had been shaking and clumsy as she'd helped to strip off his own clothing, gasping soundlessly as she'd experienced for the first time the heated power of him, naked against her nakedness.

As she'd felt the strong, clever fingers part her thighs, and discover, slowly and exquisitely, the scalding quivering centre of her being. As he'd found the tiny hidden bud and coaxed it to vibrant life, so that everything was forgotten but the agonising, essential play of his hands.

As he had drawn her slowly through the fever and torment of desire to the ultimate pinnacle and held her there for endless moments, before sending her shuddering into the stark glory of her first climax.

The ripples of delight had still been coursing through her when he'd entered her in one swift, fluid movement.

Jenna had cried out, not in pain, but in surprise and a kind of awe, her eyes dilating as they'd looked into his.

He had said her name, softly, huskily, and begun to move, gently at first, then with increasing power. And she had responded from sheer instinct, echoing the driving rhythm of his possession, her hands clasping his sweat-dampened shoulders, her slim legs locked round his lean hips, her breathing shallow, almost startled.

And she had felt, deep within her, the same primitive, devastating pressure that she'd just experienced building again. And thought, almost with fear, No—that cannot be...

Ross must have sensed her bewilderment, her momentary hesitation. His voice had reached her almost harshly, 'Darling—don't hold back. Let it happen.'

And she gasped, her head falling back on the pillow, as sheer sensation overtook her, tearing her apart in one aching convulsion after another until she thought she might die. And somewhere in the swirling golden light that consumed her she heard Ross's groan of ecstasy as he reached his own release.

A long time later, he said, 'Now you'll have to marry me.'

She lay back, smiling, in his arms, her head pillowed on his chest. 'Shouldn't that be my line?'

He dropped a kiss on her tangled hair. 'Perhaps I'm afraid you won't say it. That you'll decide you prefer just a one-night stand.'

'No,' she said, stretching luxuriously. 'That wouldn't suit me at all. And if this is domesticity, I'm all for it.'

His voice quivered into laughter. 'I'll try to give satisfaction, ma'am.'

She turned to look up at him, lifting a hand to touch his cheek. She said in a low voice, 'Ross—I never dreamed...'

He captured her hand, carrying it to his lips. 'Nor I, my love. Nor I.'

'But that can't be altogether true.' Even in her state of blissful euphoria the voice of reason intervened. 'You must have had so many women...'

'Well, that's true,' Ross said cordially. 'It's amazing I find time to eat, let alone earn my living. In fact, there's probably a queue outside now, waiting for you to leave.'

'Oh.' Jenna attempted to exact retribution, only to find herself being kissed into breathlessness. When she emerged, she said with dignity, 'I meant that you actually knew what to expect.'

He said gently, 'But not with you, Jenna. I was told once that sex moves to another dimension with someone you love, and I found out tonight that it's true.' He kissed her again. 'My warm, perfect girl,' he murmured with deep content.

Later still he said, 'Do you think you could live here, or would you rather look for somewhere that's new to both of us?'

'No,' she said. 'I think I could be very happy here.' She paused. 'Of course, we might have to move once we start a family.'

'Hey.' Ross sounded slightly startled. 'There's no real hurry for that, surely? Let's have some marriage first.'

'But you do want children?'

There was a slight pause, then he said, 'Yes—eventually.'

'Then that's all right.' Jenna sighed happily. 'There's still so much we don't know about each other. It's going to be wonderful finding out.'

'There could be some nasty shocks along the way, too,' Ross suggested drily.

But Jenna only laughed. 'Not a chance,' she told him airily. 'Not a chance.'

'So,' Ross said, 'as a first step on this voyage of discovery, when are you going to move in here? Do you have much stuff to shift from your present flat?'

Jenna raised her head and stared at him. 'You mean you want me to live here—before we're married?'

His brows drew together. 'That was the plan, yes. Do you have a problem with it?'

'No, but my flatmate certainly would.' Jenna's tone was rueful. 'For one thing, she relies on me for half the rent. I couldn't possibly just abandon her. I'd need to stay until she finds someone else to take my place.'

She paused. 'Besides, I've always despised women who dump their girlfriends as soon as they fall in love. And Natasha's been good to me, ever since we started working together at the gallery.'

There was an odd silence, and Jenna realised that the arm that held her had become tense. That he was staring ahead of him, his jaw set.

He said, 'I didn't realise you shared a flat.'

'Well, yes. Most people do, if they want to live somewhere half decent.'

He shrugged. 'Perhaps. I never have.' His tone was almost abrupt.

Jenna sat up. 'Ross—you really mind about this, don't you?'

He didn't reply at once. At last he said quietly, 'Is that really so strange? I—want you with me.'

'And that's what I want, too.' She looked at him appealingly. 'But you must see that I can't let Natasha down. It wouldn't be right, especially when we work together as well.'

'No,' he said. 'I suppose not. And I should admire your loyalty.'

She said slowly, 'You—you can't be jealous, surely…?'

'Can't I?' His mouth twisted. 'Maybe this is the first of those nasty shocks I mentioned.'

'I am surprised.' She smiled at him. 'Perhaps I should be flattered.'

His own grin was wry. 'I can't even use the excuse that I'm an only child and not used to sharing, because you're one, too.'

'Oh, my willingness to share has its limits.' She bent and kissed him. 'For instance, I claim exclusive rights in you,' she added softly. 'And that's not negotiable.'

'I can't wait to sign the contract.' He drew her down to him again, with sensuous purpose. 'Even if you don't move in,' he said softly, as his lips tantalised the aching peaks of her breasts, 'I hope that you'll be able to spare me the occasional night? Or several?'

'Yes,' Jenna said. 'Oh, yes.' And then she said nothing more at all for a long time.

They'd been so happy—so totally absorbed in each other, Jenna thought, her mind wincing helplessly as she remembered.

She'd been floating on a cloud by the time she'd got back to her own flat early the following morning. Unable to think of anything but how to get through the day as quickly as possible, so that she could be with Ross again that night.

She'd let herself in quietly, almost guiltily, she recalled, and crept into her room to grab a handful of clean underwear and one of the neat shirts and skirts she wore for work.

She had showered, and washed her hair, and had been sitting in bra and briefs at her dressing table, busy with the hairdryer when she suddenly realised that Natasha had appeared in the doorway behind her.

She had turned, smiling carefully. 'Oh, hi.'

'Where did you get to last night?' Natasha's eyes were fixed on her. 'You suddenly—vanished.'

'Yes.' Jenna could feel herself blushing, and cursed under her breath.

So much for playing it cool. 'I suppose I did, and I'm sorry.' She paused. 'You did get my message?'

Natasha shrugged. 'It didn't actually say much.'

'No.' Jenna bit her lip. 'You see—I accidentally bumped into an old friend—someone I haven't seen for a very long time.'

'At the viewing?' Natasha's tone was suddenly sharp.

'Why—yes.' Jenna bit her lip. 'And, naturally, we had a lot of catching up to do,' she added rather lamely.

'Did you, indeed?' Natasha said softly, her smile glinting. 'Well, it looks from here as if it was a very successful reunion. A night to remember, in fact.'

Jenna was already deeply conscious that her face was a total betrayal, her eyes shadowed and weary with sex, her skin luminous, her mouth lushly swollen. But she had nothing to regret or be ashamed of, she told herself defiantly. It wasn't as if she'd taken a vow of celibacy. And Ross was her love as well as her lover.

Her flush deepened. 'I really didn't mean to leave you in the lurch at the gallery.'

'Only you were carried away by your feelings.' Natasha paused. 'There's no need to worry. I don't think Mr Haville even noticed.'

'It went well, didn't it—the private view?' Jenna turned eagerly to an impersonal subject. She didn't want to talk about Ross, she realised. He was her sweet secret, too new and precious to be shared, even with Natasha.

Who was shrugging. 'I guess so. We certainly sold a lot of pictures.'

'Well,' Jenna said, switching off the dryer, 'that was the whole purpose of the exercise.'

'Yes,' Natasha said slowly. 'Of course it was.' Her hands tightened the belt of her robe. 'Work beckons, so I'd better get dressed.'

At the door, she paused. 'I don't mean to carp,' she said, 'or pry. But isn't all this rather out of character for you?'

Jenna bit her lip. 'I certainly didn't plan it, if that's what you mean,' she replied stiltedly. 'In fact, I had no idea Ross was going to be there, but...'

'But your eyes met across a crowded room and that was that?' There was a faint note of derision in Natasha's even voice.

'Yes.' Jenna shook her head. 'Tasha—it was incredible.' She paused, then plunged recklessly. 'He's asked me to marry him.'

There was a silence, then Natasha said softly, 'Marriage? To someone you haven't seen for years on your own admission? Are you quite mad?'

'No,' Jenna defended, then shook her head ruefully. 'Well, maybe. I don't even know any more. But I'm quite sure that I'm in love. And I've never been so happy.'

'And all this on the strength of one night.' Natasha laughed harshly. 'This Ross must be quite a stud.'

Jenna winced away from the crudity. 'It wasn't like that.' Her voice was almost stern. 'It was beautiful—and right. As if we were the other halves of each other. And that's how Ross feels, too.'

'Oh, spare me the details, please.' Her flatmate spoke with unwonted sharpness. 'The fact is, Jenna, that you got laid—at last. And I'm glad it was good for you. But it's hardly enough to build a future on. You'd do better to play the field—see what's out there.'

Like you do? thought Jenna. A series of encounters leading nowhere while you pretend not to care?

Aloud, she said gently, 'Tasha—that's not what I want.' She shook her head. 'Perhaps I'm a one-man woman.'

'If there is such a thing.' Natasha shrugged. 'I only hope,' she added, 'that you know what you're doing.'

'Yes.' Jenna lifted her chin. 'Of course.'

Again she was accorded that flat, glittering smile. 'Well,' Natasha said softly, 'we shall see.' And went out.

But I love him, Jenna wanted to call after her. And he loves me. And he's all that I shall ever want.

All the same, some of the shine had gone out of the morning, and she put down her brush, staring at herself in the mirror. Seeing the face of a woman she barely recognised.

She thought, with an odd sense of desolation, I need Ross—here and now—to hold me. To tell me that everything's going to be all right. Oh, I need that so badly.

But she was alone.

In retrospect, Jenna could see that had been an omen, foreshadowing a tragic chain of events that had already been set in motion.

And even if she'd realised unhappiness and betrayal awaited her, would she have had the strength to break Ross's spell and walk away?

After all, everyone had tried to talk her out of her hasty marriage—had begged her to wait—give herself a breathing space. But she'd refused to listen.

Ross had warned her himself, of course, that their life

would not be plain sailing. Demonstrated that he might have a darker, more complex side. Why hadn't she believed him either—and thought again?

Because I was in love, she thought tiredly. And I thought—I believed with all my heart—that it would be enough. That it would get us through anything life might throw at us.

Which makes me all kinds of a fool. But I'm older now, and wiser—and I'm never, ever going to make that same mistake again. And that's a promise.

CHAPTER FOUR

THE sudden rap on the side of the car brought her, startled, back to the present and stark reality. She tensed, her heart thumping, turning frightened eyes towards the window, only to see Polcarrow's one and only traffic warden mouthing at her that her parking time was up.

My God, she thought, torn between shock and relief. I've been sitting here for twenty minutes. I must be crazy.

She gave the warden a jerky nod, and started the engine. Deliberately, she chose the back road out of the village rather than the direct route which would take her past Thirza's cottage.

It might be the coward's way out, but she could not risk another confrontation with Ross. Not yet, anyway. She was feeling too raw—too vulnerable after her unwise visit to the past.

Even a fleeting glimpse of him might prove more than she could bear at the moment. Because, in spite of everything he'd done, it seemed he still had the same devastating effect on her that he'd always done.

Oh, God, she thought, her hands tightening on the wheel. That's so unfair. I don't deserve it.

It was like a micro-version of the chaos theory, she decided bitterly. But instead of a butterfly flapping its wings in the jungle a virus had stirred. And it was only her life that had been thrown into turmoil as a result.

When she reached the crossroads at the top of a hill she paused, then reluctantly took the fork which led back to Trevarne House, when every instinct was encouraging her to drive in the opposite direction altogether. To put as many miles between herself and Polcarrow as it was possible to achieve in one day.

Because what was she going to say when Aunt Grace asked, as she surely would, if she'd met anyone in the village?

There was no point in fibbing, or pretence. News of her confrontation with Ross would soon filter back anyway, she thought, grimacing. Because that was how village life worked, which was why she couldn't wait to get back to the city, and its comparative anonymity.

If she had indeed encountered Ross in London it would have been no one's business but her own, and she could have handled it better there. Couldn't she? Or was she just fooling herself? Wouldn't it have provoked exactly the same wretched, inescapable memories?

And just how long would it be before she would finally be able to forget—to put behind her for ever their short-lived passionate marriage and the nightmare of disillusion which had followed it?

After all, she had just proved to herself beyond all doubt that every detail of their relationship was still only too fresh in her mind, she thought, biting her lip savagely.

Well, she would get through the wedding as best she could, and wearing a smile, too, even if she had to nail it there. And then she would go away somewhere and begin the entire healing process all over again.

Somehow she would find the means to come to terms with the situation once and for all, and this time she would succeed. Because there was no other choice open to her. Except despair, and that she would not allow. She'd been down that road before, and she would not—could not tread there again.

Especially when Ross had made it clear that he'd put

their relationship behind him and that his new life was already in place.

She tried to cheer herself with the reflection that any lunchtime inquisition was bound to be inhibited by the presence of Adrian, and, of course, the unknown Tim. Her potential saviour. Or at least another focus for her attention for a few necessary hours.

Someone to chat and laugh and dance with at the wedding. Someone with whom she could pretend to be carefree, and even available.

And, hopefully, the demands of hospitality would also divert her aunt's attention from the vexed question of her shorn hair, she thought, touching the silky strands with a protective hand.

Also, with the arrival of the groom and best man, the wedding would take over to the exclusion of everything else. The countdown would begin, giving her, she prayed, no time to brood.

The last few days before her own marriage had merged into a kind of blur through which she'd floated in a blissful dream, thinking of nothing but the moment when she would belong to Ross at last and for ever.

She had never felt so cherished or desired in her life. No bridal nerves or last-minute doubts had troubled her either, in spite of the openly expressed anxieties of family and friends, who had begged both of them to extend the length of their engagement.

'But why should we wait?' she'd appealed to Uncle Henry. 'I thought you at least would understand. I thought you liked Ross.'

'I do, my dear.' He was silent for a moment. Frowning a little. 'But I'm not sure you have the same objectives in this marriage. At least not yet. Your aim is making a home, having a family with the man you love.'

'Is that so wrong?' she asked, hurt.

'No,' he said. 'But Ross, I think, only wants you. And that's not the same thing at all.'

To Jenna's additional distress, Natasha was not even going to be there, but was spending the weekend in Vienna. She had apologised, claiming it had been booked for ages, but Jenna wasn't convinced. The older girl had never openly expressed her disapproval, apart from that first morning, but it was always there, like a shadow, just the same.

Each time Jenna spent the night with Ross, she was aware, the following day, of Natasha's narrowed gaze assessing her almost tangible glow of fulfilment. And this had created an awkwardness that, for the first time in their relationship, simmered on the edge of resentment.

But that might be because her flatmate's own love life didn't seem to be going too swimmingly, Jenna reminded herself. She had overheard her talking on the phone one day at the gallery, her voice low and intense.

'How dare you treat me like this? I won't just be brushed aside from your life,' she'd been saying.

Jenna, embarrassed, had made herself scarce. As she'd brewed some coffee in the tiny kitchen, she had found herself wondering if Tasha had become involved with yet another married man.

Hasn't she learned by now that there's no future in such relationships? She'd thought, with an inward sigh. Just heartache?

She had never been able to understand why Natasha had no one permanent in her life. She was beautiful and intelligent, but though she always had plenty of dates none of them seemed to develop into a steady relationship.

Jenna, puzzled, had asked her once what she was looking for in a man, and the older girl had shrugged.

'When I find it,' she'd countered. 'I'll let you know.'

Leaving Jenna none the wiser.

She'd been genuinely anxious at the beginning for Ross and Natasha to meet, and had counted on them liking each other—for her sake, if no other. She'd told herself this would be bound to ease the situation.

But it had never happened. Their first encounter had been conducted in an atmosphere of hostility that had been almost tangible. Like two dogs circling each other, preparing for a fight, Jenna had recognised with astonishment. And things had never improved between them. At best, they treated each other with wary civility. At worst, it was like walking headlong into a wall of ice.

She'd had a desperate try at lightening things up by giving a dinner party, and Ross had brought along Seb Lithgow, a journalist friend, to make up the foursome. But it had still turned into another evening of forced conversation and awkward silences, even though Seb, who was tall, with dark blond hair and charm enough for several, had done his best.

An embarrassed Jenna had been aware that Natasha had barely exchanged two sentences with him.

'No more evenings like that, please,' Ross had said when they were alone.

'I know—it was awful.' She'd hugged him close, her face rueful. 'But she's in a funny mood these days. The hunt for my replacement isn't going too well, apparently.'

She'd expected some barbed rejoinder, but he'd said nothing. However, when she had glanced up at him she'd seen that his eyes were hooded and his mouth tight-lipped to the point of grimness.

In hindsight, Jenna could understand why the friction between them had existed.

Natasha must have seen right through him from day one,

she told herself. And she knew, somehow, that he would break *my* heart. So she was just acting out of concern.

But when it happened, she never once said *I told you so*, and I'm so grateful to her for that.

She turned into the drive and parked on the gravelled sweep in front of the house, beside Adrian's Porsche.

There was a buzz of conversation coming from the drawing room, so she took a deep breath, nerving herself to push open the door and walk in as if nothing had happened.

Adrian was the first to spot her, and he strode over, grinning broadly, lifting her off her feet and kissing her soundly.

'What a transformation,' he commented as he put her down. 'Very chic, sweetheart. What's brought this on?'

Jenna touched her hair with a self-conscious hand. 'I felt a change was long overdue, that's all.'

'Well, it's absolutely terrific,' Christy said as she joined them, handing Jenna a glass of sherry. 'And it makes you look even younger, if that's possible.'

Jenna turned to Mrs Penloe. 'You see, Aunt Grace. Short hair suits me.'

'If you say so, dear,' said her aunt. 'I'm sure you had your reasons for having it cut—and of course it will always grow back again.'

Jenna exchanged a resigned look with Christy, then glanced round the drawing room. 'So, Adrian, where's this best friend of yours that I've yet to meet?'

'You'll have to wait until tomorrow for that,' Adrian said cheerfully. 'He wasn't feeling particularly great yesterday, so he decided to give it another twenty-four hours.'

'It must have been a hell of a stag night,' Jenna teased.

Adrian shook his head wryly. 'Not at all. A crowd of us went out for quite a sedate dinner, and I really didn't think Tim had drunk that much. Unless he started again once we got home,' he added with a frown. 'But he's sworn that he'll catch the early train and be here in time for the rehearsal tomorrow afternoon, hungover or not.' He grinned at Jenna. 'I've given you the big build-up, honey, so he's dying to meet you.'

Jenna forced a cheerful smile in response. 'Sounds promising.'

Just as she'd hoped, the wedding was the sole topic of conversation over lunch, and when the meal was over Adrian had a stack of wedding presents to bring in from the car, to be opened and admired, and put with all the others in the morning room.

'You've had some lovely things,' said Mrs Penloe. 'And so many of them, too,' she added worriedly. 'The two of you should sit down quietly this afternoon and make a list of them, with their donors, in case any of the cards get mislaid later on in the excitement.'

Jenna took one look at Adrian's face and bit back a smile. 'Why don't I do that?' she suggested. 'While you take Christy for a drive. Enjoy the calm before the storm.'

He grinned at her. 'You're an angel.'

Watching Aunt Grace bustling around with a sheaf of papers in her hand, her glasses on top of her head, muttering worriedly, Jenna realised with affection that she was in her element.

Of course, she'd seen her in action before, she reminded herself as she went into the morning room and started the list.

Once her aunt had seen that Ross and Jenna were not going to be deterred from their hasty marriage she'd moved into another gear.

Jenna had been perfectly ready to have a simple London ceremony in front of a registrar, but Aunt Grace had put her foot down with a firmness that brooked no further argument.

Jenna, she had said, would be married from the parish church in her own home village.

From then on her niece had watched in awe as Mrs Penloe had bullied the local bakery into making a cake, contacted a florist, discovered a catering company who had an unexpected gap on their calendar, and briskly despatched Jenna and Christy to an upmarket dress-hire boutique.

There had been no time for a full-blown reception, with a dance in the evening. As the wedding was to be sandwiched between photographic assignments to which he had already committed, Ross was taking his bride to Brittany for their brief honeymoon, and they'd need to catch an afternoon ferry.

They had stood together, the day before, watching the small round marquee, with its blue and white stripes, being erected briskly on the lawn.

'Heaven knows where Aunt Grace found it, but isn't it sweet?' Jenna leaned back into Ross's embrace. 'It looks like one of those little tents they used to have at medieval jousts.'

There was a smile in his voice. 'You're not expecting me to arrive at the church on horseback, carrying a lance, I hope?'

'Not unless you want to upset all Aunt Grace's arrangements and see her turn into a dragon.' She paused. 'If we'd lived in those days, would you have fought for me?'

His lips touched her hair. 'Against all the world.'

And I believed him, Jenna thought flatly. I thought we'd belong together for ever. I had all the confidence in the world.

Thirza had called to see her that evening, she remembered, wearing a striking silk dress in one of her own exotic prints and bringing with her a flat leather case.

'I don't know whether you subscribe to the old superstitions,' she said, 'but I've brought you something old.'

Jenna gasped when she opened the case and saw the string of gleaming pearls lying on a black velvet bed.

'But they're beautiful. How can you bear to part with them?'

Thirza shrugged. 'They're not my style. Besides, they belonged to Ross's mother originally, and I decided long ago to keep them for his wife.'

Jenna touched them almost reverently. 'I truly don't know what to say. How to thank you.'

Thirza shrugged. 'Just make him happy,' she said abruptly. 'If you can.'

Jenna gasped. 'Of course I shall.'

'I'm sure you think so,' the older woman returned more gently. 'But there are a lot of adjustments to be made on both sides, and it's not going to be easy.' She paused. 'He tells me he's decided to give up overseas assignments and run the London desk at the agency. That's quite a sacrifice.'

Jenna lifted her chin. 'It was his own idea. I didn't ask him to do it.'

'No, but you didn't tell him not to, either,' Thirza said crisply. She shook her head. 'Jenna, I know your father went away and didn't come back, and for that I'm truly sorry. But you can't compensate by keeping Ross tied at home. It doesn't work like that. And he's not a substitute either.'

Jenna bit her lip. She said stiffly, 'That—never even occurred to me.'

'I'm glad to hear it. But please think about what I've said,' Thirza urged. 'It's not too late for him to change his mind.'

'It's Ross's own decision,' Jenna defended.

Thirza sighed. 'As you wish. But you'd do better to let Ross have his freedom now, while he's still flying high. I promise you it won't be a problem in the long term. He'll be even keener to settle down if you don't clip his wings now.'

'Why don't you say all this to him?'

'I already did.' Thirza gave a tight-lipped smile. 'And now, having put your back up permanently for the best possible motives, I'd better go before you throw me out. Enjoy your day tomorrow. I'm sure you'll make an exquisite bride.'

And she went, leaving Jenna staring after her.

Perhaps she was right, Jenna thought now, trying to decipher the name scrawled on a card accompanying a Lalique figure. Maybe I did try and tie him down to domesticity too soon. But if I'd turned him loose, in all probability he would simply have been unfaithful that much sooner.

Presumably, Thirza herself had been prepared to put up with that kind of treatment from his father.

Perhaps those were the adjustments she told me I'd need to make. Only I wouldn't. I couldn't.

Not when I was already at my lowest ebb anyway, after losing the baby.

The child Ross didn't even want.

I should have remembered pearls are for tears and left them in their case.

Her throat tightened uncontrollably and she hunted in her pocket for a tissue and blew her nose.

I was crazy to come here, she thought wretchedly. Mad to put myself through this all over again.

And I'm going to be counting the hours until I can turn my back on this place and its memories, and rejoin the real world.

They weren't dining at home that night. They were joining Adrian at the Fisherman's Arms in Polcarrow, where he and Tim would be staying until the wedding.

Jenna had a relaxing soak in the tub, then applied her favourite scented body lotion. She kept her make-up light, then put on one of her favourite dresses—a plain slip style in a silky apple green fabric, with narrow straps and a skirt cleverly cut on the bias. Her sandals were green, too, and she flung a silvery pashmina round her shoulders.

'Very elfin,' Christy said approvingly when she saw her. 'What a pity Tim isn't around to be led astray.'

'Oh, I'm fresh out of fairy dust,' Jenna said lightly. 'Did you have a pleasant afternoon?'

Christy blushed revealingly, indicating that the drive out had probably only taken them as far as Adrian's room at the hotel. 'You could say that.' She paused. 'I hope Ma didn't get too heavy about everything.'

'She found a number of little jobs for me,' Jenna admitted. 'But at least they stopped me from being bored.' *Or thinking…*

The hotel was a popular venue for diners, specialising as it did in fresh fish and seafood, and most of the tables in the low-ceilinged room were already occupied when the party from Trevarne House arrived, to be given prime position in the big bow window which overlooked the harbour.

And Adrian had arranged for champagne on ice to be waiting for them at their table.

'How splendid,' Mrs Penloe said happily as she sat down. 'You're spoiling us, my dear.'

'It's a time for celebration,' Adrian returned as the wine

waiter removed the cork and filled their glasses. 'We're all together—and for the best of reasons. So let's drink to that.'

'Not quite all of us,' Christy objected. 'Tim's not here, remember.'

'All right,' her fiancé said, unperturbed. 'We'll drink to "absent friends" instead.' And he raised his glass.

The words sent an odd shiver crawling down Jenna's spine. A goose, she thought, walking over her grave...

'Oh, no, not that.' Her voice was raised and slightly brittle. She flushed as they all looked at her in surprise. 'I mean—we can do that later. But first I'd much rather drink to you and Christy,' she went on, stumbling a little. 'To—to your happiness.'

'Then we shall,' her uncle said quietly. 'To Christy and Adrian. May love be long and life be kind.'

As he spoke he glanced at his wife and smiled, and she put her hand gently on his sleeve.

He was describing his own marriage, Jenna thought, a lump in her throat as she watched them. An affection that had remained undimmed down the years.

And yet, on the face of it, they weren't the most obvious of soulmates. He quiet, humorous and laid back, happy to be semi-retired from his successful architectural practice and pursuing his passion for Cornish history. Aunt Grace more volatile and sociable, always busy, too, revelling in her involvement in local affairs and organisations.

But it worked, Jenna acknowledged with a small inward sigh. Oh, God, how it worked. And made the failure of her own marriage more poignant by comparison.

But she was not here to be the skeleton at the feast, she reminded herself forcefully, but to enjoy the food and company. And she would do exactly that, or die in the attempt.

And champagne was always a good start, she told herself, relishing its dry chill against the tightness of her throat as she accepted the menu she was being handed with murmured thanks.

She'd decided on griddled scallops and king prawns with rice for her main course, and was hesitating between gazpacho and red pepper mousse as a starter when she was aware of a stir in the restaurant and glanced up casually.

She stiffened, her hands tightening their grip on the leather-bound menu until the knuckles turned white, as she watched with utter disbelief Thirza threading her way through the restaurant, with Ross one pace behind her.

One swift glance around her revealed her aunt and uncle exchanging appalled glances and Christy sitting frozen, her bottom lip caught in her teeth, while Adrian muttered something under his breath.

There was only one unoccupied table, she realised swiftly, and that, thankfully, was in the opposite corner of the room—about as far away as it was possible to get.

She paused, her heart thudding in sudden panic, as Thirza suddenly changed track and came towards the window table and its transfixed occupants. She looked magnificent, in an ankle-length indigo dress topped by a loose floating jacket, blocked in jewel colours like a stained glass window, as she loomed over them all. Ross waited a few feet away, his face saturnine, his hooded eyes unreadable.

'Henry—Grace—what a marvellous surprise.' Her voice carried through the room. 'A cosy little family party. How are you, Christy? Adrian, you're looking well.' A pause. 'Good evening Jenna.'

There was an awkward chorus of responses.

'Thirza, my dear.' Henry Penloe had risen politely. 'How good to see you. I didn't know this was one of your haunts.'

'It isn't, but I felt poor Ross needed a break from my cooking.' She was laughing, gesturing expansively. 'After all, he's supposed to be convalescing, and I don't want to make him ill again.'

Another pause, and Jenna felt suddenly as if she was on the edge of a precipice.

Then, 'I see,' Thirza said, smiling, 'that the table is laid for six. Are you expecting another guest?'

'We were,' Mr Penloe returned. 'A friend of Adrian's. But unfortunately he's been delayed until tomorrow.'

'Then why don't we get Carlo to lay an additional place and join you? After all, we're family, too, don't forget.'

There couldn't be a soul in the room unaware that some kind of drama was being played out, Jenna thought bitterly. And Thirza had stage-managed it beautifully, making it impossible for the Penloes to refuse. But why? *Why?*

Christy rose to the occasion. 'Of course,' she said brightly. 'If we all move round a little there'll be plenty of room.' And in that way Jenna would be safely flanked by her uncle on one side and Adrian on the other, was her unspoken message.

Chairs were shifted, the head waiter summoned, cutlery and glassware brought, and the thing was accomplished. And Jenna found herself vulnerable in a different way, facing Ross across the table.

But apart from a cool smile, and a murmured acknowledgement of her presence when he first sat down, he paid her no direct attention at all, chatting instead, with apparent ease, to Christy and Mrs Penloe.

And then there were food orders to be taken, and wines to be chosen, which did away with any potential awkward silences. Although Thirza would not have allowed those anyway. From the first she set out to be the life and soul of the party, chatting and laughing about her curtailed trip to Australia.

Under cover of a sprightly description of Alice Springs, Adrian said quietly, 'I'm sorry about this, Jenna.'

'It's not your fault. My uncle calls Thirza a law unto herself. A force of nature.'

'I'm sure he's right. However, I wasn't referring to her but to your ex-husband.'

'Well, don't worry about him.' Jenna smiled tautly. 'Didn't Christy tell you that an armistice has been declared for the duration of the wedding?'

'She mentioned something, yes, but it sounded iffy to me.'

'Oh, it's perfectly genuine, I assure you.' She managed a shrug. 'Besides, Ross being around really doesn't bother me any more. I'm through with all that now.'

'Really?' Adrian's smile was kind but sceptical. 'Anything you say, sweetheart.'

She was glad to turn to Uncle Henry, who engaged her in a gentle flow of chat about a book he was considering writing on some of the Duchy's great houses and their architecture. That, and the arrival of the food, should have been enough to distract her, but in reality nothing seemed able to dispel her tingling, uneasy awareness of the man sitting on the opposite side of the table.

Across the central cluster of candles and flowers she could feel him watching her. Could sense unerringly that his eyes were studying her face—then moving down to the first swell of her breasts above the low neckline of her dress, just as they'd done so many times before. And now, as then, she felt her skin warming helplessly under his scrutiny.

What the hell did he think he was doing? she raged inwardly. Or was it just an automatic reflex when he was confronted by a woman—any woman?

Whatever the reason, he was not, she thought bitterly, playing fair. But, then, what was new about that?

Her best—her only response was to appear oblivious to his regard, but this was easier to decide than perform, because that familiar trembling ache was stirring into life again deep inside her. A response that, to her shame, he had always been able to evoke, even when their relationship had been falling apart.

The food was delicious, but Jenna had to force herself to eat and echo the appreciative noises from her neighbours. Ross, a lightning glance told her, had no such problem, but appeared to be enjoying every mouthful of his sea bass.

When the dessert menus appeared she was able to say with perfect truth that she couldn't manage another thing. On the other hand Ross, she noted crossly, asked for the cheeseboard.

'It's so good to see him eating at last,' Thirza proclaimed. 'He needs to build his strength up after that awful illness,' she added, looking round fiercely as if daring them to contradict her.

'How long do you plan to stay in Cornwall, Ross?' Mr Penloe asked quietly.

'I'm seeing the consultant next week,' Ross returned. 'Once he gives me the all-clear I can start finalising my plans.'

'You must be keen to get back to work,' Christy commented.

His smile was cool. 'Of course, but that's only part of it.' He paused. 'I'm hoping to be married again quite soon.'

There was a shocked, deafening silence. Under cover of the tablecloth Jenna's hands were clenched together so tightly that she could have cried out from the pain. So, she thought, that was that. And she couldn't say she hadn't been warned.

She realised that everyone was studiously not looking at her—apart from Ross, who was leaning back in his chair, an unsmiling challenge in his dark eyes.

A challenge that she had to meet—and fast. She lifted her chin. 'Congratulations.' Her tone was light, almost amused. 'Your plans weren't quite so finite when you mentioned them this morning. That's—quite a step forward.'

'The world's an uncertain place,' he said. 'Life can be short and brutal. So—I talked things over with her, and a decision was made.'

'That's really good news.' The words scraped her throat like sharp knives. She lifted her glass. 'Here's to better luck—the second time around.'

She paused. 'For both of us.'

'Why, Jen...' Christy's face was bewildered. 'Have you met someone, too? How marvellous. You never mentioned it.'

Jenna shrugged. 'Oh, it's early days. And, anyway, I'm enjoying the single life.' She met Ross's gaze. 'I have no plans to remarry. I think it's an unnecessary complication.'

She was lying—continually and desperately. Trying to shield herself from the devastating and unwelcome truth that had just exploded in her mind.

The realisation that, in spite of everything that had happened between them—all the harrowing sadness and betrayal in their relationship—she was indeed a one-man woman, and always would be.

And, heaven help her, Ross was the one and only man she would ever want.

A man, she acknowledged, that she had just lost for ever.

And somehow, however agonising it might be, she was going to have to find some way to go on living without him.

CHAPTER FIVE

JENNA never knew how she got through the rest of the meal. From some depth of her being she managed to dredge up the ability to stay outwardly composed, and even radiate charm and interest in what was going on around her.

She chatted and laughed, and even accepted admiring tastes of other people's desserts, when all she really wanted to do was crawl into some dark and deserted space and howl her shock and wretchedness to the moon.

How could she possibly still care for someone who had behaved so badly and so callously? she asked herself with wincing incredulity. How could anyone be such a pathetic fool?

She told herself with increasing desperation that it must be a delusion. Had to be. That seeing Ross again so un-expectedly—being thrown together with him like this—had knocked her sideways. Made her a little crazy.

That could be the only feasible explanation for the chaos of her thoughts.

And, yes, she still wanted him physically. That was something she could no longer deny.

His lovemaking had created this burning hunger in her, and for many long months it had gone unsatisfied, leaving her sexually bereft. Now, as she had discovered to her cost, simply being near him was enough to light the fire all over again. And her suffering was exquisite. Unbearable.

She'd looked at him this evening, sitting across the table from her in all the formality of a dark suit and silk tie, and had a vision of him leaning over her naked, his eyes drowsy with passion, his mouth warm as it sought hers in the long, sweet prelude to possession.

In those first months of loving, his body had become as familiar to her as her own, and her hands had memorised him with rapturous joy, lingering over the strength of bone and play of muscle, making him groan softly with desire in turn.

And now some other unknown girl would arch in pleasure beneath him and cry out wordlessly at the culmination, and the knowledge of that was tearing her apart. Someone else would have his baby and he would probably never remember, in his new-found delight, that there had once been the prospect of another child. Short-lived. With her.

And, for her, an ever-present pain.

Her nails scored the palms of her hand beneath the shelter of the cloth. She thought, I need to get out of here. I want to be on my own. But there was little chance of that. When they arrived back at Trevarne House both Christy and Aunt Grace would be eager to discuss the evening, and Ross's startling revelation.

And somehow she would have to pretend that it didn't matter. That, for her, it was a positive step, drawing a final and much needed line under her brief marriage. But how long would she be able to sustain this charade of indifference when, emotionally, she was coming apart at the seams?

Also, she supposed dully, she would have to admit to the Penloes that there was no one in her own life, after all. That what she'd implied was simply a face-saving exercise. They would understand, of course, because they loved her, and were loyal. But then they would expect her to move on, too. To follow Ross's example and establish a new relationship. To seize a second chance at happiness.

And only she knew how impossible that was.

She was thankful to see her uncle signalling for the bill, but less happy when Ross intercepted it on its arrival at the table, tossing his credit card on to the salver.

'No, I insist.' His smile was faintly tight-lipped as Mr Penloe and Adrian protested. 'After all, we were the intruders on a private family occasion. This is by way of amends.'

Emphasising that, no matter what Thirza might say, he no longer considered himself part of the family since the divorce, Jenna thought with a pang.

She trailed in the rear as they left the restaurant, and waited unobtrusively while goodnights were being said—Aunt Grace constrained and faintly on her dignity, she noted with reluctant amusement. But any hopes of a speedy exit were unfulfilled when Adrian was called away to the telephone by the receptionist.

And, to her dismay, she saw Ross coming towards her.

'I wanted to thank you,' he said abruptly. 'Your comments just now were—generous.' He paused. 'Maybe the truce could last beyond the wedding. What do you think?'

'I don't really see the necessity.' Jenna met his gaze coolly. 'I think a clean break divorce should be exactly that. And nothing's changed.'

'"Shake hands for ever. Cancel all our vows,"' Ross quoted softly. 'Is that how you see it?'

'No,' she said. 'That's how it really is. Subtle difference.'

'Some divorced couples manage to remain friendly,' he said meditatively. 'And no one can have too many friends, Jenna.'

She shook her head, looking past him, noting almost absently that Adrian had emerged from the phone booth looking strangely agitated.

'We were never friends, Ross,' she said. 'Perhaps that was part of the trouble.'

'Ah,' he said softly. 'The trouble. What a multitude of sins that could be said to cover.'

He paused. 'You know, Jenna, I'd really like to get together with you one day soon and have a look at everything that happened between us. The retrospective viewpoint can sometimes be valuable—don't you think?'

'No,' she said tautly, 'I don't. History was never one of my favourite subjects.'

He smiled faintly. 'And that's what we are?'

'Of course,' she said. 'And it's time to move on. Look forward, not back, and get on with our lives.' Keep saying it—repeating it, she thought, and maybe one day it will come to mean something.

'Difficult,' he said. 'When there's so much unfinished business to resolve.'

'Consider it done,' she said. 'I had a miscarriage. You had an affair.' She managed a shrug. 'End of story.'

He said slowly, 'I said just now you were generous, but apparently that's a quality you reserve for public occasions.'

'And there aren't many more of those to go.' She lifted her chin. 'Once Christy and Adrian are married we won't be meeting again.'

'That's if there is a wedding,' Ross remarked, his brows drawing together. 'There seems to be some kind of fuss going on over there, and your cousin is in tears.'

'Oh, God, so she is.' Trying not to be thankful that she was off the hook, Jenna flew to Christy's side. 'Darling— what is it?'

'It's Tim,' Adrian replied tersely, his arm protectively round his weeping fiancée. 'That was his mother on the phone. It seems he wasn't hungover at all. It was chicken pox, and he can't make the wedding.' He attempted a rueful grin. 'So, as of this moment, I don't have a best man.'

'Oh, my dear,' said Mrs Penloe. 'Surely one of your other friends…?'

Adrian shrugged unhappily. 'Maybe, but it's a hell of a thing to dump on someone at the last minute. There's the speech, for one thing. I can ring around in the morning, but quite a few of them will be already on their way down.' He shook his head. 'Thank God I brought the rings with me.' He delved into a pocket and produced a handkerchief, and began to dry Christy's eyes. 'Don't cry any more, darling. We'll sort something out, I promise.'

'Ross can do it,' said Thirza.

There was an astonished silence.

Jenna felt a sudden roaring in her ears. The word *No* was pounding so violently at her consciousness that she thought she might have shouted it aloud.

But Aunt Grace was the first to speak. 'I hardly think so, Thirza dear,' she said with unwonted frostiness. 'As you pointed out at dinner, Ross is still recovering from a serious illness, and would hardly wish to take on so much responsibility so soon.'

Ross looked across at Jenna, his mouth twisting sardonically—as if in acknowledgement of the inner disquiet that only he could see.

'Damn you,' she whispered under her breath. 'Damn you to hell.'

He said coolly, 'I hardly think it will bring on a relapse, Mrs Penloe, but thanks for your concern.' He paused. 'As it happens, I'd be happy to do it, if Adrian agrees.'

'Well, of course he agrees,' Thirza said impatiently. 'It's the obvious—the only solution.'

'A morning suit.' Aunt Grace was battling bravely on. 'What are we going to do about that? Unless by some

amazing coincidence he happens to have one with him,'
she added with a touch of edge.

'I don't possess that amount of foresight,' Ross said
drily. 'But I can hire one. It's not a problem.'

'As a matter of fact,' Adrian said slowly, 'I brought
Tim's suit down with me, and I think you're pretty much
the same size.' He paused. 'You could always try it and
see.'

A flushed Christy parted her lips to speak, caught Jenna's
eye, and subsided.

'That's fine with me.' Ross's gaze swept the stunned
semi-circle in front of him. 'Unless anyone has any further
objections.'

Jenna cut in smoothly, before Aunt Grace could launch
herself again. She was trapped, and she knew it, and so did
he. All that remained was damage limitation. The mainte-
nance of the pretence she'd been forced into.

'On the contrary, it seems the ideal arrangement,' she
said. She even made herself smile. 'It's really good of you,
Ross, to fill the breach like this.'

He said softly, 'It will be my pleasure, believe me.' He
turned to Adrian. 'Should we have a look at that suit now?
Just in case I need to make an early start with the hire
companies?'

'Er—yes. Absolutely.' Adrian gave Christy a swift kiss
and an anxious look. 'I'll see you in the morning, darling.'
And he and Ross disappeared towards the stairs.

Uncle Henry muttered something about fetching the car,
and Mrs Penloe and Christy followed him to the door.

Leaving Jenna momentarily alone with Thirza. Their
glances met—clashed—leaving Jenna in no doubt that here
was someone else she hadn't fooled by her acquiescence.

She drew a deep breath. 'What exactly do you think
you've been doing tonight?' she demanded shakily.

'Righting a few wrongs.' Thirza's tone was steely. 'I've had enough of seeing my stepson treated as a pariah while the world tiptoes round you, the poor little victim.'

Jenna sank her teeth into her lower lip. 'I wasn't the one who ended the marriage,' she said. 'I didn't have the affair.'

'I don't condone what Ross did.' Thirza's mouth tightened. 'But the marriage was in trouble long before he went astray. Think about that, princess, next time you feel like shining up your sense of grievance.'

Jenna said thickly, 'You've always taken his side.'

The older woman shrugged. 'Someone had to,' she retorted brusquely. 'Why wasn't it you, Jenna?'

And she turned away and walked into the bar, leaving Jenna, white-faced and speechless, staring after her.

Jenna sat on the window seat in her bedroom, leaning her aching forehead against the chill of the glass and staring unseeingly into the darkness. She wanted to sleep. She needed to sleep. But she knew it wasn't going to happen. Not while her mind was teeming relentlessly like this.

How dared Thirza? she thought numbly. How dared she say those things? Imply that I was the one at fault?

The older woman's words had touched all kinds of nerves, and left her feeling sore and on edge. But it had been the earlier encounter with Ross which had done the most damage, she realised wretchedly.

She had been silent during the car ride home, but Aunt Grace had more than made up for it, inveighing bitterly against what she called 'that shameless intrusion'.

'And now Ross is going to be best man,' she'd added bitterly. 'What can Adrian be thinking of?'

'Of the difficulty of finding someone else at such short notice,' said Christy bleakly. 'Even I can see that. And if Jenna says she doesn't mind, why should we?' She shook her head. 'Oh, I could strangle Tim. How on earth does a grown man get chicken pox?'

The million-pound question, Jenna thought, biting her lip. The shield she'd hoped for was gone. Now all she had to rely on was her own resources.

And the fact that they were now playing opposite each other in leading roles at the wedding was bound to attract the sort of attention she'd desperately hoped to avoid.

'Oh, God,' she groaned under her breath. 'What am I going to do?'

Back at the house, she silently shared coffee and recriminations with the others for a while, then concocted a series of elaborate yawns, announced she was dead on her feet, and went thankfully upstairs.

On the landing, she encountered Uncle Henry. She was about to slip past with a murmured 'Goodnight' when he detained her with a gentle hand on her arm.

'Jenna, my dear.' His voice was kind. 'I can probably put a stop to this situation, if that's what you wish.'

'But I don't,' she said, too quickly. She gave him a resolute smile. 'It's going to prove to everyone, once and for all, that Ross and I have agreed to put our—difficulties behind us.'

'And become just good friends?' Her uncle's expression was quizzical.

Jenna hesitated. 'Well, not that, perhaps. But maybe we can turn our differences into indifference. That would be a positive step.'

'And is that what Ross wants, too?'

Jenna bit her lip. 'I have no idea—what Ross wants.'

Mr Penloe gave a quick sigh. 'No,' he said. 'Probably not. But it's something you might choose to consider— even now, at this late stage.' He patted her on the shoulder and went on his way.

Jenna was frowning as she went into her room and closed the door behind her. Was Uncle Henry also hinting that she hadn't been completely an innocent party in the breakdown of her marriage? Surely not, she thought in bewilderment. She'd always known she could count on his sympathy and support ever since she'd first come to live at Trevarne House. All these years, he'd been her rock.

Now, once again, she felt as if the ground was shivering under her feet.

She undressed, putting on her nightgown and her robe, but she made no attempt to get into bed, although she switched off the light to give the deliberate impression that she was already asleep and deter late-night visitors. Much as she loved Christy and Aunt Grace, she acknowledged ruefully, she didn't want to talk any more about what had happened, or how it would affect the wedding.

It was still too raw in her mind. Besides, she could only think about what it was likely to do to herself. She couldn't summon up enough generosity of spirit to take the broader view.

In fact, she couldn't find much spirit at all, she thought wearily. Over the past couple of days she seemed to have taken one blow after another.

And the worst of them all was tonight's recognition of her own terrible weakness.

Since the breakdown of their marriage, out of the morass of heartbreak and bitterness, had come the conviction that she hated Ross, and always would. Over the months it had become her armour and salvation. Yet, when put to the test, it had proved no protection at all.

Now I only hate myself for still wanting him, she thought, wrapping her arms convulsively round her shivering body. And I despise myself, too. Especially as I know beyond doubt that this need is totally one-sided.

But then it probably always had been...

She'd told herself from the very first that to forgive Ross was out of the question and to forget was equally impossible. Yet the sobering fact was she'd been called on for neither option.

When she'd confronted him, accusing him of having slept with Lisa Weston, she'd expected him to deny it. Had prayed that he'd offer proof of his innocence.

Instead he'd acknowledged his transgression, coolly and frankly, expressing regret but offering no excuse or even explanation for his conduct. Leaving her stricken to the heart.

Presumably, Jenna thought wearily, he'd been convinced that he wouldn't be found out, and that he could continue to live his bachelor life within the framework of marriage.

And when, shocked and humiliated, she'd ordered him, weeping, out of the house and her life, he'd turned and left without a single word of protest.

She'd told herself that he would return in a few days, asking for another chance, and that no matter how much he begged and pleaded she would not take him back. That justice demanded he should be made to suffer as she was doing.

Only he'd never come back, and the certainty that it was not an isolated fall from grace—that he was now permanently with his mistress—had pushed the knife deeper and twisted it. Forcing her to face the reality that she'd been fooling herself. That her marriage was over, almost as soon as it had begun. That all those dire warnings had been perfectly justified.

I truly thought we were happy, she told herself desolately. At least until we lost the baby.

Not that we agreed on everything, of course, but, then,

who does? I thought it was all part of learning to live together. So when did it all start to unravel in earnest?

If she was honest, she had to admit that Ross had been something of an enigma from the first. There were whole layers of his life that he had chosen not to disclose, or not immediately, anyway.

He had been still very young when his mother died, but from comments he had made she'd gathered that his parents' relationship had been a stormy one, and he'd been fully aware of this.

And when, barely two years later, he'd found himself with Thirza as his stepmother, it had proved no different.

Jenna had learned that Ross's father had been a serial womaniser, who'd also liked to gamble, and that as a result, Ross's maternal grandparents had quarrelled with their daughter Marina at the time of her marriage and continued to stay aloof after her death.

It was through them, however, that he'd acquired Les Roches, the old stone house on the Brittany coast where Jenna had spent her brief, idyllic honeymoon.

'My great-grandfather was a fisherman,' he'd told her. 'And Grand-mère Marianne was his only child. She met my grandfather during the war, when he was with the SOE and she was helping the Resistance.'

Jenna's eyes widened. 'How very romantic.'

'I doubt that,' Ross said wryly. 'Dirty, dangerous and bloody terrifying, I'd have said. But when the war was over he came back for her. And when she inherited the house they used it as a holiday retreat.'

'And then they left it to you—their only grandson?'

Ross shrugged. 'Under French law they had little choice,' he returned drily.

'But you were reconciled with them after your father died?'

'To a limited extent, but we were never really close. Too much had happened in the past. And they didn't really want anyone else. They were lovers all their lives, totally sufficient for each other.'

'Oh,' she said. Then, 'That's really—rather wonderful, isn't it?'

'Is it?' His mouth twisted.

'Yes,' she said. 'Of course. And that's exactly how we'll be, too.'

'You really think lightning can strike twice—in the same family?'

'I'm sure it can.' She spoke defiantly.

'If you say so.' He kissed her troubled mouth. 'Poor Jenna. You want the world to be neat and tidy, with no dark corners or skeletons in cupboards. And it isn't like that. It can't be.'

She sighed. 'You're laughing at me.' She paused. 'Are you talking about yourself? Do you have a skeleton in your cupboard, Ross?'

'Dozens of them.' He pulled her closer, his mouth teasing on hers, then suddenly hungry. 'So beware what doors you open, my love.'

And I, Jenna thought, wincing, was fool enough to believe he was joking.

Their marriage service had been simple but beautiful, using the words of the old prayer book. As she made her vows Jenna had felt a rush of emotion that seemed to lift her to a higher sphere.

She was going to make him happy, she had resolved passionately. Happier than he had ever dreamed. And people would look at their marriage and sigh with envy.

It had been dark when they'd arrived at Les Roches, and Jenna had been too tired after the excitement of the day, and a Channel crossing that had been less than tranquil, to pay much attention to her surroundings.

She'd been dimly aware of flagged stone floors, pale walls and low ceilings as Ross had guided her up the steep staircase. The bedroom was raftered, with fur rugs on the wooden floor and the window open to the sound of the sea. The bed was enormous, with carved head and foot boards, and the crisp linen was scented with lavender.

'It's very old,' Ross told her softly. 'A proper *lit matrimoniale*. My ancestors, as you see, took their marital duties very seriously.'

'And do you plan to follow their example?' she whispered back.

'Certainly,' he said. 'But not tonight.'

'Why not?' She did not hide her disappointment.

'Because it's been a long day,' he said simply. 'And I want to lie, holding you in my arms as you sleep. Enjoying being your husband at last. We have all the time in the world to make love, my beautiful wife, but tonight I want to cherish you, just as I promised a few hours ago.'

He undressed her slowly, his hands gentle. Slipped over her head the folds of the cobweb nightgown she'd never thought she'd wear and lifted her into the waiting bed. Swiftly he shed his own clothes and joined her, drawing her into his arms, against the lean warmth of his body.

Fighting her drowsiness, she said, 'But we have champagne...'

'We'll drink it later.' His lips caressed her hair, her closing eyelids. 'After all, my love, we have the rest of our lives. Now, sleep.'

And sleep she did. Deeply and dreamlessly, with her head pillowed on his chest.

When eventually she awoke, stretching languidly, the sun was pouring through the shutters and Ross was nowhere to be seen. She pushed back the duvet and slid out of bed. She padded to the door and called his name, but there was no answer.

Puzzled, she went to the window and opened the shutters, and it was then, as she turned back towards the bed, that she noticed the slip of paper pinned to the adjoining pillow and its laconic message— 'Gone shopping.'

Jenna showered swiftly in the large, old-fashioned bathroom, then pulled on a pair of white shorts and a pale pink cotton shirt which she tied under her midriff, slipping her feet into simple canvas shoes before descending the stairs.

The front door stood wide open, demonstrating that casual crime was not a consideration, and she went out into the sunshine and stood looking round her, lips parting in a gasp of delight.

Sheltered by a tall cliff, and standing on a broad jetty, with the sea glittering and dancing only a few yards away, Les Roches was a long, low house built in grey stone, which gave the impression that it had been hewn out of the living rock that guarded it. The shutters were a faded blue, and wooden tubs filled with summer blooms flanked the doorway.

Opposite, a flight of ancient stone steps, green with weed, led down to a crescent of beach.

Jenna drew a blissful breath, absorbing the salty tang in the air, listening to the cry of the gulls as they wheeled and swooped.

There were no other houses to be seen anywhere, and the steep access road, she realised, was little better than a track.

This, she thought, was seclusion of a very high order.

She heard the sound of an engine, and turned to see Ross's car descending towards her. She saw his smile through the windscreen and lifted her hand to wave in response, feeling suddenly and ridiculously shy.

He parked by the wall of the house and collected a series of bulging carriers from the boot, which he took into the house. It necessitated two trips.

When he finally emerged he came over to her, pulling her into his arms for a long, very thorough kiss.

'Good morning,' he murmured. 'Welcome to married life. I hope you appreciate how well-trained I am.'

'I'm seriously impressed.' She linked her arms round his neck. 'Are you stocking up for a siege?'

'Something like that.' His grin was slow and sexy. 'Let's say I don't see us travelling far from the house for a while.'

'And I thought you had a full sightseeing programme planned.' Jenna pretended to pout.

'Oh, I have.' He kissed her again. 'Starting almost at once.' He paused. 'Tell me, my sweet, are you wearing anything at all under this fetching outfit?'

'That,' she said, 'is a leading question.' She turned to look at the sea. 'This is a wonderful place.'

'I'm glad you approve. I wondered if you might find it too similar to Cornwall. If you'd have preferred a city break to another seascape.'

'Never.'

He slid his arms round her waist, his hands lifting to cup her breasts through the thin shirt, his thumbs teasing her nipples.

He said with a note of laughter in his voice, 'Did you sleep well.'

'Beautifully.' Jenna arched like a purring cat under his caress.

'And you're not tired any more?'

'Not even a little bit.' Her lips curved mischievously.

'I disagree.' He bit her earlobe very gently. 'I feel very

strongly that you should go back to bed at once and stay there, while I provide tender loving care.'

'And will that make me feel better?' she asked demurely.

'I guarantee it.' His fingers slid inside the waistband of her shorts, stroking the warm flat plane of her stomach, then moving lower.

'And will I ever be cured?' Her voice was beginning to sound breathless.

'Never,' he said. 'Because I intend the treatment to last a lifetime.'

And he picked her up in his arms and carried her into the house, and up the stairs to where their marriage bed waited.

It was a day from Paradise. Jenna had thought that Ross had already shown her all that sexual pleasure could afford, but during the long, sweet hours that followed they seemed to ascend together to new, undreamed of heights. Any lingering inhibitions she might still have possessed vanished for ever as Ross's hands and lips coaxed her to a rapture so piercing she thought she might die.

And she gave as much back to him in turn, freely and glowingly, matching his overwhelming generosity.

And when, at last, she slept once more in his arms, spent and drained from passion, she was drowsily aware of his voice whispering that he loved her.

Much later, hunger drove them, laughing, down to the kitchen for bread, pâté and cheese, and the long-neglected champagne.

Later still, they took a bath together in the deep, elderly tub. Lying back in his arms, Jenna said dreamily, 'I could stay here for ever.'

'I don't advise it.' Ross scooped up some scented foam

and decorated the peaks of her breasts with judicious care. 'We'd get all white and wrinkly.'

She sighed. 'You're such a fool. I meant stay in this house. Live here.' She looked round at him. 'Why don't we?'

'Because we have careers—a life elsewhere.' He kissed the side of her neck, making the pulse quicken. 'This is an interlude, darling, and for now that's all it can be. After a while, the big world would beckon us back.'

She pulled a face. 'I suppose...'

'Hey.' Ross nibbled her damp shoulder. 'This is our honeymoon. You're supposed to be happy.'

'I'm delirious.' She snuggled closer to him. 'For one thing, I've just realised I'll never have to creep guiltily back to the flat ever again, running the gauntlet of Natasha's disapproval. I might even get to eat breakfast.'

There was a sudden tension in the arm that encircled her. 'Natasha gave you problems? You didn't tell me.'

'Well, nothing was ever said,' she admitted. 'At least, not out loud. But there was sometimes a bit of an atmosphere.' She sighed again. 'I wish she could find someone and be happy, too. Because she's so beautiful. Don't you think so?'

Ross turned her in his arms and kissed her mouth. He said quietly, 'I think you're beautiful, and that's all that matters.'

Eventually, they put on some clothes and went downstairs. Ross put the chicken he had bought in the stove to cook, while Jenna prepared the vegetables to accompany it.

While their evening meal was cooking they went for a stroll along the beach at the edge of the sea, where a glorious sunset promised more golden days to come.

As they walked back Jenna glanced over her shoulder

and saw the imprint of their footsteps side by side in the damp sand.

It seemed like a good omen—a symbol of the journey they'd embarked on together, she decided, then laughed at herself inwardly for the sheer romanticism of the thought.

But when she reached the steps Jenna looked back and saw that the encroaching tide had covered the marks of their feet, erasing them as if they had never existed.

Transient, she thought. Not eternal.

And found, suddenly, she was shivering.

CHAPTER SIX

JENNA rose from the window seat and began to pace up and down the room.

They had indeed been golden days, she told herself. And she was thankful she hadn't known how few of them there were to be, or her heart would have broken right then and there.

Anyway, she should not be remembering how good things had once been between them. She should be reminding herself of how it had all collapsed in ruins. Rebuilding her defences.

But the temptation to relive that happy time in Brittany was overwhelming. The weather had been kind throughout their stay, and they'd swum in the sea and sunbathed on the beach, explored the surrounding countryside on foot and in the car. They both loved seafood, and Ross had introduced her to the joys of the great platters of *fruits de mer* that were a local speciality. Sometimes they'd cooked at home, but more often they'd visited one of the numerous small restaurants in the vicinity.

But most of the time they had been happy just being at Les Roches together in the private world they had created together.

In fact, learning to live with Ross had never been a problem, she reflected. There'd been differences in temperament, of course. He was scrupulously tidy, and she wasn't. If annoyed, he tended to retreat into silence, while she fired from the hip.

But she had soon settled into the shared intimacies of

marriage, realising that these had as much to do with the joint occupation of space as they had with sex.

She had soon grown accustomed to Ross shaving at the bathroom mirror while she was in the bath, and sprawling across the bed, chatting to her as she dressed and put on her make-up. And when she did her hair he would often take the brush from her hand, smoothing the long chestnut strands with almost reverent care, then spoiling the effect altogether by burying his face in the silken, scented mass.

But if she'd thought the honeymoon had taught her everything she needed to know about her new husband, she had soon discovered she was mistaken. That there were areas of his life into which she was not invited.

A couple of times she had overheard him on the telephone, his voice brisk and incisive as he dealt with business matters that clearly had no connection with photography, or the agency. And it had occurred to her that they never really talked about finance, or how he managed to fund that glamorous riverside apartment quite apart from this house.

But when she'd asked, half joking, half in earnest, how many jobs he had, he'd smiled and shrugged.

'Checking that I can afford to support a wife, darling?' he'd countered, which had been no answer at all.

They hadn't been left alone for the duration. After a few tactful days, there'd been visits from neighbouring families, all eager to meet Ross's new wife. All keen to assure her how welcome she was in their community.

And now they would be asked to welcome someone else, she thought, biting her lip.

Another girl would soon walk along the beach hand in hand with Ross, and sleep with him in the comfort of that enormous bed, soothed by the whisper of the sea. A thought that sliced into her heart.

Jenna took off her robe and tossed it across a chair. It

was time to stop tormenting herself and get some sleep, she told herself with resolution.

Tomorrow promised to be a day from hell, and she needed to be rested in mind and body in order to cope with its demands.

Of which Ross was only one, she reminded herself.

She lay very still, eyes closed, seeking to empty her mind of disturbing images as she went through the relaxation exercises that someone had once recommended to her for insomnia.

And eventually she found herself drifting slowly down into slumber. But there were dreams waiting for her.

Dreams where she walked alone along an endless beach and her bare feet left no trace of her presence. No trace at all.

When she went downstairs the next morning, she found only Aunt Grace presiding at the breakfast table, lips pursed like the Prophet of Doom.

'Christy's gone into Truro to pick up her wedding dress,' she said. 'And Adrian telephoned.' Ominous pause. 'It seems that the suit fits Ross perfectly.'

The condemned woman ate a hearty breakfast, Jenna thought, accepting the cup of coffee poured for her and reaching for the toast rack.

'Well, that's good news,' she said lightly. 'It saves a lot of trouble for everyone.'

'Good news?' Mrs Penloe stared at her, then shook her head. 'I declare, Jenna, there are times when I cannot understand you.'

And long may that continue, thought Jenna. Or at least for the next thirty-six hours.

Aloud, she said calmly, 'The rehearsal's at four o clock,

isn't it? Would you like me to go down to the village hall, presently, and supervise the setting up?'

'Oh, my dear, would you? Mr Sandown means well, but he will insist on using the old trestle tables, and they're really not reliable any more. One of them actually collapsed at the Garden Club coffee morning—the mess was unbelievable. And the caterers have sent a last-minute list of kitchen requirements like the United Nations charter,' she added bitterly. 'So no doubt he'll be grumbling about that, too.'

'Don't worry about a thing, darling.' Jenna helped herself to marmalade. 'I've always been able to handle Mr Sandown. He's a pussy cat. I'll make sure Christy's buffet is on safe legs.'

'Mrs Withers has laundered all the tablecloths, so you'll need to collect them from her,' her aunt mused. 'And then there are the evergreen garlands from the garden centre…'

'I'll do all of it,' Jenna said cheerfully. *Anything—anything to keep my eye on the ball and stop me from thinking.* 'Just make me a list.' She paused. 'Do you want me to hang the garlands as well?'

'Your uncle and Adrian are going to do that,' Mrs Penloe said firmly. 'I don't want you falling off any ladders.'

'The bride's father and the groom being dispensable, of course.' Jenna gave her an affectionate grin, then finished her toast and coffee. 'I'd better get cracking.'

'Thank heaven Christy's an only child,' said her fond mother, rising from the table. 'I don't think I could bear to go through all this again.'

In spite of her best efforts, Jenna was late arriving at the village hall. She had gone to the garden centre first, where, she'd discovered, the garlands with their dark green glossy leaves studded with tiny white and yellow jasmine-like flowers were still being packed in long boxes. And while she'd been waiting for this task to be completed, and the boxes to be placed in the boot of the car, it seemed that everyone who worked there had sought her out for a few words. As she'd known them all for most of her life, she hadn't been able to simply rush away.

But the real delay had come when she'd arrived at Mrs Withers's terraced cottage to collect the table linen. As she'd reached for the gleaming brass knocker the door had been snatched open, and Mrs Withers, minute in a blue-flowered overall, had surveyed her from head to foot, her small dark eyes snapping with mingled pleasure and curiosity.

'Dear life,' had been her greeting. 'So you're back where you belong, and not before time, too.'

An imperious gesture summoned the reluctant Jenna into the cottage and into a spotless living room, bright with polish, where a small fire burned contentedly in the hearth. Before she could protest, she found herself being plied with over-milky tea and home-made biscuits.

'Skin and bone, that's what you are, my little bird,' Mrs Withers commented critically, observing Jenna's ribbed sweater and slim denim-clad hips. 'Comes from fretting, I dare say.'

'Nothing of the sort.' Jenna kept her tone light and upbeat. 'Actually, I'm the ideal weight for my height,' she added, ignoring her hostess's derisive snort. 'And I have a full and busy life in London.'

'London,' Mrs Withers said loftily. 'I went there once. Couldn't abide un.' She added a heaped spoonful of sugar to her cup and stirred it vigorously. 'So you're bridesmaid-ing Christy Penloe tomorrow. Seems only yesterday you were a bride yourself, with your Ross.'

'Pure coincidence.' Jenna kept her bright smile nailed in

place. 'And he's not "my Ross" any longer. We're divorced, as I'm sure you know.'

'Then more's the pity. A handsome couple you made, and no mistake.' She paused insinuatingly. 'And now he's back here, too. Funny, that.'

'Pure coincidence.' Jenna said again briskly, draining the last of her tea with a repressed shudder. 'And I'm sure you know the old saying "handsome is as handsome does."'

'I know it.' Mrs Withers nodded fiercely. 'And I also know that a woman without a man is a poor sort of thing. It's been four years and more since I buried Withers, and not a day of it that I haven't missed him cruel.'

It occurred to Jenna that burly Mr Withers with his booming laugh and kind eyes had probably never had an unfaithful thought in the whole of his marriage.

She wanted to cry out, But you don't understand... And bit her lip when she saw the older woman's eyes were sparkling with something other than curiosity.

She said gently, and with real sincerity, 'Well, we can't all be as fortunate as you were, Mrs Withers.' She rose to her feet. 'Now, if I could just have the tablecloths, please? I really do need to get on.'

She laid the plastic bags of snowy linen carefully on the rear seat of the car, and drove off with a final wave.

Once out of sight of the cottage, however, she felt her shoulders drooping slightly. This was the disadvantage of coming back to a place where your life was an open book and thus available for comment, she thought ruefully.

Mr Sandown was the only person waiting for her at the hall, and now he helped her unload the car, complaining in an undertone about his bad back.

'I thought Adrian would be here,' Jenna said, putting the garland boxes into a neat stack.

'So he was,' agreed Mr Sandown. 'He's been knocking

in pins round the walls, and some little hooks so all they decorations'll drape nice. But then he went off to fetch something. He'll be back presently.'

'Right.' Jenna consulted her list. 'I'd better start in the kitchen—checking the fridge temperatures for the caterers. Although I can't think why.'

'That'll be Brussels, that will,' her helper said sourly. 'I dunno what they don't want, with their regulations. Separate sinks for washing hands,' he added with scorn. 'My old mother had one sink and she washed everything there, including the six of us children. And what's wrong with that, I'd like to know?'

'Well, it all looks very nice,' Jenna said soothingly, glancing round. The hall had just enjoyed an extensive facelift, with fresh paint everywhere, smart pale green curtains at the high windows, and a new woodblock floor. Christy's wedding reception would be the first major event there since refurbishment.

The kitchen, too, had been set up in a way that would suit even the fussiest hygienist, she decided, crossing those items off her list with satisfaction.

She coaxed Mr Sandown into putting the old trestles back in store and getting out the brand new tables for the buffet, and although he complied with only a token grumble about his deteriorating physical condition, he made it clear he was prepared to do no more.

'Tis time for dinner,' he announced. 'And the missus will have it ready.'

Jenna stifled a grin as she watched him depart. Mrs Sandown's state of readiness, she knew, counted for nothing when compared with the alternative lure of the bar at the Tinners Arms. And she would bet real money on where he was actually heading.

Still, so far, so good, she congratulated herself, glancing

at her watch. But time was passing, and if Adrian would only come back they could make a start on the decorations.

She glanced appraisingly up at the walls as she began to remove the garlands carefully from their boxes. The fixings were in place, after all, she mused, and it seemed a pity to wait around indefinitely.

There was a pair of steps leaning against a wall, and she dragged them over to the first window and climbed up, a garland draped over her shoulder.

It was not that easy to hang, she soon discovered. These were big windows, and she could only reach Adrian's hooks by gingerly putting one foot on the narrow sill and stretching at full length, while the elderly steps creaked ominously.

She was glad to find herself back again on *terra firma*, and sorely tempted to leave the rest for someone else to struggle with.

But she'd come here to work, and at least she knew what she was doing now, she thought, man-handling the bulky steps to the next window along and grabbing another garland.

But as she struggled to attach it to its fastening she heard a slithering noise, and felt the ladder began to slide. Glancing down, she realised that the frayed cord which held both halves together had given way, and the damned thing was collapsing on to the floor.

Hastily Jenna snatched her foot away, transferring her entire weight to the inadequate support of the window sill instead, and found herself perched there precariously, on tiptoes, clinging monkey-like to the frame.

Too late, she remembered Aunt Grace's warning, and shuddered, closing her eyes. The strain on her calf muscles was already painful, and her white-knuckled hands couldn't gain any real purchase on the smooth frame. If she took the risk, and jumped backwards, she would land on the ladder and undoubtedly damage herself badly.

Perhaps, she thought, opening her eyes reluctantly, she could manoeuvre herself round and jump sideways. She tensed as she saw that the view from the window had suddenly changed, and that Adrian's car was now parked right outside.

There was no sign of Adrian himself, but he couldn't be too far away. She screamed his name, knowing, as she did so, that he wouldn't hear her through the double glazing. And in order to pound on the glass to attract his attention she would have to let go of the frame. Which was impossible.

She was close to panic when the hall doors eventually squeaked open, and cried out again, 'Adrian—help me, for God's sake. I'm slipping.'

She heard running footsteps, the sound of the ladder being kicked away. Then strong male hands clamped on her hips, steadying her, and Ross's voice said tersely, 'Let yourself go, Jenna. Do it now. I'll catch you.'

'I—can't.' Her voice was a whimper, and she was ashamed.

'Yes,' he said. 'You can. Just relax and slide down—don't throw yourself. See if you can get on to your knees. Slowly, now.'

Shakily, gasping for breath, she did as she was told, lowering herself by degrees, her hands slipping down the frame. As soon as her bent knees touched the sill she felt his arms fasten round her like steel bands, lifting her back against him. For one endless moment she seemed to be held there in his arms, and she felt her whole body clench in a sudden agony of yearning. Then, at last, she was lowered to the ground.

Instantly, she wrenched herself free, turning on him. She said between her teeth, 'Don't—touch—me.'

She saw his eyes narrow in disbelief and his mouth tighten. Then he stepped back, raising his hands in a gesture that was almost resigned.

'Well, that has a familiar ring.' His voice was sardonic. 'What was I supposed to do, Jenna? Wait until someone more acceptable turned up? Or let you break your leg and leave Christy to find a substitute bridesmaid as well?'

There was a loaded silence. Jenna felt the throb of tension pulsing between them. Was aware of it building to danger levels and knew she needed to defuse it—and fast.

She stared down at the pattern on the wooden floor. 'I—I didn't mean that as it sounded,' she said at last.

'No?'

'I overreacted, that's all.' Jenna lifted her chin and met his sceptical gaze, her own eyes flashing. 'And I'm sorry. But I was scared—and you—startled me,' she added stiffly.

'I suppose that could be considered an advance on the disgust and contempt I usually inspire in you.' His voice bit. 'Didn't you hear me coming to the rescue?'

She shrugged. 'I saw Adrian's car and thought it was him.' *Relied on it.* She frowned. 'Where is he, anyway?'

'I left him up at Trevarne House. He'll be coming down presently with your uncle. He lent me his car to collect another pair of steps from Thirza's cottage. It was obvious these were going to fall to pieces at any moment.'

'Not to me,' she said. 'Unfortunately. Well—thank you.'

'The pleasure,' he said softly, 'was all mine. But if you're planning any more balancing acts, perhaps you'd save them for when I'm not around. You're not the featherweight you look, and hauling women around wasn't actually part of the treatment my consultant prescribed.'

'Oh, have I interrupted your convalescence?' Jenna

clicked her tongue. 'How remiss of me. Especially when you're trying to build up your strength for your next wedding. Or at least the honeymoon part of it.' She paused. 'Have you decided on a suitably romantic location?'

'Of course I could say it's none of your damned business,' Ross said slowly. 'But, as it happens, we may well dispense with the honeymoon.'

'But convention demands it.' Jenna felt as if she was probing an aching tooth. It hurt badly, yet somehow she was unable to stop herself. 'A private time for the newlyweds. You can't deny your bride that.'

'I don't intend to deny her anything,' Ross told her coolly. 'But honeymoons can be overrated pastimes. I'm already intimately acquainted with my future wife, and she with me, so we don't need a period of seclusion to consummate our vows. I'd prefer us simply to get on with the rest of our lives.'

'And she'll agree with that?'

'Yes,' he said. There was a tenderness in his faint smile that caught at her heart. Caught it—and twisted it in a vice of pure jealousy. 'I'm sure she will.'

Jenna kept her voice even. 'You're really determined to make it work this time—aren't you?'

'Oh, yes,' Ross said quietly. 'You'd better believe it.'

'Yet,' she said, 'if you have this well-nigh perfect relationship, how is it you chose to recuperate from your illness here with Thirza rather than with your fiancée? Or is she not the Florence Nightingale type?'

'I've never asked her,' Ross drawled. 'But she has a lot going on in her life right now, so I decided it would be better this way.'

'And, naturally, you wouldn't want to start off a new relationship from a position of weakness either.'

He shrugged. 'If that's how you want to figure it. I shan't argue with you, Jenna.'

'Nothing new there,' she said tautly. 'The Ross Grantham creed. Never apologise—never explain—never argue. Isn't that how it goes?'

'That may be how it went,' he said. 'But things are very different now.' He paused. 'Do you want to continue this fascinating inquiry into my motivation and philosophy of life, or shall we do something more useful? There are still these garlands to hang up.'

'Just as you wish.' She hunched a shoulder. 'Sure it won't cause a relapse?'

'I'll risk it,' he said. 'But to be on the safe side I'll climb the ladder from now on. I'd hate you to suffer any further mishap. Especially one that might prevent our dance together.'

'Our dance?' Jenna repeated, puzzled, watching him position the new pair of steps, retrieve the garland, and hang it effortlessly. 'What are you talking about?'

He looked down at her as he made a minute adjustment to his handiwork.

'At the reception,' he said. 'The bride dances with the groom. The bridesmaid with the best man. It's one of those conventions you seem so keen on.'

'Well—yes.' *But that was with Tim. I was to have danced with Tim.* She swallowed. 'However, that doesn't apply to us—surely.'

'You'll find it does,' he said, descending to the floor. 'But I'll make it a dance that involves no touching.' His smile was thin-lipped. 'Does that reassure you?'

There was sudden anger in her voice. 'Nothing about you will ever do that. So perhaps we should just—stop talking and work.'

They'd reached the last window when they heard voices

and Mr Penloe came in with Adrian. He checked, looking faintly surprised.

'Jenna, my dear. So this is where you've got to.'

'I thought this was where Aunt Grace wanted me.' Jenna handed Ross the final garland, and watched him place it.

'Well, I'm sure it was,' her uncle said. 'But things have changed—become a little fraught. I think Christy would appreciate some support.'

'Then I'll go,' she said. 'We've finished here, anyway.'

'Yes, indeed.' Her uncle looked round, nodding. 'You've done really well.' He paused. 'The pair of you.'

Ross folded the steps and leaned them against the wall. 'We make a good team.' He glanced at Jenna, and she saw mockery in his eyes.

'Yes,' she said. 'But only in the short term.'

His mouth slanted an acknowledgement. As she reached the door his voice followed her. 'Goodbye for the present, Jenna.' A pause. Then, 'See you in church.'

It was safer not to respond in any way. And particularly not to look back at him. Because he might see the tears in her eyes, and that would be a disaster.

She'd regained a measure of control by the time she returned to the house. She found Christy up in her bedroom, surrounded by cases and tissue paper.

'Running away?' she enquired.

'I'd like to,' Christy said with a sigh. 'But only with Adrian. Do you think it's too late to elope?'

'Do that,' Jenna said, 'and I shall follow—and strangle you with a garland of evergreens.' She made a space on the bed and sat down. 'Uncle Henry thought you might need me.'

'I had a little spat with Ma.' Christy looked contrite. 'She was fussing. I asked her not to, and off we went.'

'Well, that was bound to happen eventually,' Jenna soothed. 'Weddings are always stressful.'

'Yours wasn't,' Christy objected. 'I've never seen anyone so calm and composed.'

'I was probably comatose.' Jenna forced a laugh. 'Numbed with horror at the ghastly mistake I was about to make.'

'Garbage,' Christy said roundly.

'Yet that's what everyone thought—including your parents. And in the end, of course, they were proved right. Ross and I did not belong together.'

'Well, I still can't figure out why.' Christy frowned. 'I've never seen two people so in love. Just being round you both was like entering a force field.' She paused. 'Jen, I've never asked before, but what really went wrong?'

'You know what happened.' Jenna picked up a bikini from the bed and studied it as if it was an alien object. 'Ross had an affair with someone from his past—an Australian blonde called Lisa Weston.'

Christy spoke gently. 'I know she was the effect, darling, but what was the cause? Because something must have led to it.'

Jenna shrugged. 'Perhaps, once the novelty wore off, Ross discovered that monogamy bored him.' She hesitated. 'I don't think she was the first.'

Christy was open-mouthed. 'What are you saying?'

'Oh, there were signs, even before the baby.' Jenna bent her head. 'The phone would ring, and no-one would speak when I answered it. I found a woman's handkerchief that wasn't mine in the pocket of his suit, and another time one of his shirts reeking of some expensive scent in the clothes basket.'

Christy frowned again. 'That's not very clever—encouraging your lady-friends to call you at home and bringing home stray bits of laundry into the bargain. Asking for trouble, in fact. Did you ask him to explain?'

'Yes.'

'And?'

'And, naturally, he denied all knowledge of it. He was very convincing. You'd have sworn he was genuinely bewildered. He said he'd probably picked up the hankie somewhere, thinking it was mine.'

'And the shirt?'

Jenna folded the bikini with infinite care and put it in the nearest case. 'He said that girls were always spraying themselves with scent on the tube, and he must have got in the way.'

'So what did you do?'

'I washed the shirt and threw the handkerchief away.'

'And the phone calls?'

'Ross said they were just someone being a nuisance, so he had the number changed and—they stopped.'

Christy was silent for a moment, then she said, 'He could have been telling you the truth, Jen. He was crazy about you. Everyone knew that.'

'Was he?' Jenna stared down at her bare hands. 'If so, it didn't last. It was like a forest fire. It blazed up, and when it died everything was black and empty. No life. No shelter. Nothing.'

She drew a deep breath. 'Whereas with you and Adrian it's the real thing. A sure and steady flame that will burn for the rest of your lives.'

'Oh, Jen.' Christy's voice broke. 'I'm so sorry. I want you to be happy, too.'

'I will be. I am.' Jenna rose to her feet. 'And no one else knows what I've just told you, so please—please keep it to yourself.'

'I promise,' Christy said gently. 'Not even Adrian.' Her brows lifted as Jenna walked to the door.

'Where are you going?'

'I want to find your mother.' Jenna flashed her a quick smile. 'I expect she's just realised that when you and Adrian leave on honeymoon she's going to have an empty nest. Not easy.'

She paused. 'She's probably taken refuge in the greenhouse, as usual. I'll try and tempt her out with food. Will soup and sandwiches do? I feel we should have something. After all, we don't want you fainting at the altar during the rehearsal. And when we've eaten I'll give you a hand with the rest of the packing.'

But once outside the door she made no attempt to go downstairs. Instead, she leaned for a moment against the wall, aware of the uneven thudding of her heart.

What had brought those particular memories bubbling to the surface? she wondered breathlessly. Did she really need such a potent reminder of what a blind, credulous fool Ross had made of her?

I should have confronted him, she thought. Made it clear that I wasn't deceived. But I was scared—scared of losing him—so I wanted to believe him. Needed to think that he was telling the truth.

Whereas in reality I was setting myself up for the biggest betrayal of all.

And each time I look at him—each time I remember the touch of his hands on my skin, and let the ache, the wanting back into my heart and mind—then I'm simply betraying myself all over again.

And I can't do that. At least, not if I'm ever to know another moment's peace.

And she sighed. Because peace might be all that was left for a one-man woman, doomed to spend the rest of her life alone. Without him.

CHAPTER SEVEN

THE tiff between Christy and Mrs Penloe was soon resolved over lunch, and the bride and her mother even enjoyed a little weep in each other's arms while Jenna tactfully took her sandwiches into the garden.

She was glad to have some time to herself. Her last conversation with Christy had disturbed her more than she wanted to admit.

The cupboard door was open, she thought, and all the skeletons were tumbling out.

Because, if she was honest, she and Ross had been having problems long before Lisa Weston came back into his life. Even before the baby...

Almost as soon as the honeymoon was over, in fact.

It had begun when Ross came home one evening to find her poring over a sheaf of estate agents' brochures.

'What are you doing?' He'd looked at her enquiringly, brows raised.

'Doing some preliminary browsing,' Jenna returned airily.

'But we don't need anywhere else to live,' he said quietly. 'We have this flat.'

'Yes, and it's beautiful.' She smiled up at him. 'But it's a bachelor pad, darling. And we need a home. Somewhere we can put down roots. Expand into.'

He said with a touch of grimness, 'I think I need a drink.' He poured himself a single malt, then came to sit beside her. He said, 'Is this a subtle way of telling me that you're pregnant?'

'Of course I'm not.'

He said quietly, 'Well, God be praised for that, anyway.'

Jenna stiffened. 'Would it be such a bad thing?'

'At this stage in the marriage?' His mouth twisted. 'Yes, Jenna, I think it would. We're still learning to live together. We don't need to take on any more commitment just yet.'

'But you're not against the idea in principle?' she persisted.

'I don't know.' His tone was even. 'I haven't thought about it.'

She stared at him. 'But that's why people get married—isn't it? So that they can be a family?'

'Perhaps,' he said. 'But right now I'm more interested in our being a couple. And I thought you liked living here.'

'Yes.' Jenna bit her lip. 'And—no.'

'Ah,' Ross said slowly. 'Care to explain?'

She shrugged evasively. 'I'd like us to be somewhere that's new to us both—and without—resonances.'

He said drily, 'From my past, presumably.' He was silent for a moment. 'If you're waiting for me to apologise for not remaining celibate all these years, then you're going to be disappointed, my sweet. And, yes, other women have shared the bed that we now sleep in. Hell, if it troubles you that much why don't we just buy another bed?'

She said unevenly, 'You find this really funny, don't you?'

'It's becoming rapidly less amusing with every moment that passes.' He swallowed some whisky, the dark face brooding. 'Why did you never mention this before?'

She lifted her chin, 'Because I wasn't your wife before.'

'No,' he said, softly. 'Of course not. You were just another girl sharing my bed—is that it?'

She flushed, furious that he could read her so well.

'Oh, Jenna.' Ross sighed impatiently. 'Can't you see that

you were never that? That you are the one—the only one. We don't have to buy a house to prove it. It's our relationship that matters, not bricks and mortar.'

She said, 'I thought you'd want to move, too. Make a fresh start…'

'And I believed we'd just done so.' His tone held a touch of bleakness. He drank the rest of his whisky. 'Do you want to go out to eat?'

She shook her head. 'I'm—not very hungry.'

He stared at her, eyes narrowed.

'Really?' he drawled. 'Then it looks as if I'll have to dine alone. See you later.'

He picked up his jacket, slung it over his shoulder, and sauntered to the door.

As it closed behind him Jenna swept the brochures off the low table to the floor in one furious gesture.

He wouldn't even look at them, she raged inwardly. And, to add insult to injury, he'd walked off and left her without a backward glance. Without even one miserable attempt to persuade her to go with him.

She marched into the kitchen and made herself a self-righteous supper of beans on toast, but it wasn't easy to swallow past the lump in her throat, and she threw half of it away.

Aunt Grace's voice came to her. 'Never attempt to discuss anything serious with a hungry man, my dear.'

Good advice, which she wished she'd remembered at the time.

She was in bed when Ross came home a couple of hours later, lying on her side, facing away from the door. She heard him come into the room and walk softly over to the bed.

She was acutely aware of him standing beside her, looking down at her. Then he said quietly, 'Jenna,' but she made no response, lying without stirring and making herself breathe deeply and regularly.

And presently she heard his footsteps going out of the room again.

She opened her eyes then, feeling slightly foolish and a little sorry, too. She was tempted to go to him in the living room, but that would solve nothing, she told herself. They would only argue again.

No, she would wait until he came to bed, and then pretend to wake up, and turn drowsily into his arms, inviting him to make love to her. And when they were both sated and relaxed, lying entwined in the aftermath of pleasure, she would coax him round to her point of view.

Not something Aunt Grace had ever advised, she thought, smiling into the darkness. But deliciously effective just the same.

She stretched luxuriously, her skin warming at the prospect, then burrowed her cheek into the pillow and waited for him to come to her.

Minutes passed and became half an hour. Turned into a full hour, and then another. Only by that time Jenna was asleep, deeply and genuinely.

When she woke the next morning she was alone, and for a moment she thought he hadn't come to bed at all, but spent the night on the sofa. Except that the rumpled pillow on his side of the bed and the covers thrown back told a different story.

It was very quiet in the flat, so it seemed he had already left for the day. Glancing at the clock on the night table, Jenna saw that he'd allowed her to oversleep, and that she was going to be late for work.

'Hell's bells.' She slid out of bed, grabbing her robe. Coffee, she thought, hot and strong, before her shower.

But Ross hadn't gone to work. He was in the living

room, standing silently, a dark silhouette by the sunlit window, looking out at the river.

Jenna skidded to a halt. 'Oh—you're still here. Why didn't you wake me?'

Without turning, he shrugged. 'Because you might still have been playing games.' His voice was flat. 'And this one time I thought I'd allow you to get away with it.'

He paused. 'I've also decided to put this flat on the market, if that's really what it takes to make you happy. Find a house you like, and I'll set the wheels in motion.'

'Oh, Ross—darling.' She would have run to him, but there was something about the set of his shoulders that warned her she might be risking a rebuff, and she hesitated, huddling her robe around her because she felt suddenly cold.

She said, 'But you have to like it, too.'

'This is your game, Jenna, with your own rules. I choose not to play.' He turned and looked at her, the dark face unyielding, his eyes remote. 'But understand this. From now on, you never again pretend to be asleep, or have a headache, or lie about the time of the month, or any of those other shabby little tricks. Our marriage is worth more than that.'

She bit her lip. 'Ross—I...'

'There's coffee in the pot,' he went on as if she hadn't spoken. 'I'll see you tonight.'

She stood once more, watching him walk away from her. Wanting to call him back, yet not making a sound. Realising she'd won. But feeling as if somehow she'd lost.

She threw away the brochures that had sparked off the disagreement, feeling that they were somehow tainted—even unlucky. She wanted to begin her house hunting with a clean sheet. Then laughed at herself for being superstitious.

She did her sums carefully, calculating how much the flat would fetch, and the amount of mortgage they could afford, especially if she had to give up work for any reason and they were reduced to just one income, she thought with a private joyous smile.

At the same time it occurred to her that she had little real idea how much Ross earned, although he clearly liked to live well.

I suppose this is something we should have talked over before we got married, she thought, wrinkling her nose ruefully.

It was certainly something they ought to discuss before she started contacting estate agents in earnest. Although, because of the events of the past eight hours, she probably needed to postpone her enquiries to a more appropriate time.

But when Ross came home that evening, the cool, taciturn man who had departed that morning might never have existed. He swept in, smiling, his arms full of champagne and long-stemmed crimson roses.

'I was a bear—forgive me,' he whispered passionately as he picked her up and swung her round, his mouth warm and hungry on hers. 'Nothing matters but being with you.'

Jenna yielded thankfully, gloriously, as he carried her into the bedroom. 'Love me.' Her voice was husky. 'Ross—love me always, and I won't ask for anything else.'

'You have it.' His hands were tense with desire as they stripped the clothing from her body. There was no time for indulging in tender preliminaries. Their mutual need was too strong, too fierce for anything but immediate satisfaction. As he entered her Jenna cried out, her voice thick with passion. She was aware of nothing but the heat of him filling her, making her complete, and she gave with total recklessness, her body twisting beneath his with unthinking sensuality as she drove towards culmination.

At the height, Ross made her wait for a trembling eternity, then gave her the release she craved, making her body fragment into rapture.

Later, lying entwined, they drank champagne, and Ross poured some of the chilled wine over her breasts, licking every last drop of it from her nipples before beginning the slow, sensuous ascent to pleasure again.

Afterwards, 'If this is making up, maybe we should argue more often,' he murmured, a note of laughter in his voice.

'No.' Jenna was vehement as she nestled closer to him. 'I hated arguing. I've been miserable all day.' She took a deep breath. 'Ross—I've had time to think, too, and we don't need to move anywhere else—not yet. We can wait—save some money first.'

He tipped up her chin so he could look into her eyes. 'Why do you say that?'

'I was thinking this might not be a good time. After all—this flat must have cost a fortune, and there's the upkeep on the Brittany house as well.'

'It's not a problem.' He kissed her mouth gently. 'Have your house, Jenna. I want you to be happy.'

'But I wanted somewhere with a garden—and they're asking ridiculous prices.' She sighed. 'We couldn't afford anything like that.'

'Yes,' he said quietly. 'Actually, we could.'

Jenna stared up at him. 'I don't understand...'

'That's entirely my fault,' he said. 'There are things I should have told you before this. I suppose I was waiting for the right moment, and this seems to be it.' He paused. 'You see, the house in Brittany wasn't my only legacy. My other grandfather also made me his heir, and he left me money—quite a lot of it. Some of it's tied up in trusts, of course, but the rest is available if and when I want to use it. Only I never have before.'

Jenna saw his mouth tighten with remembered pain, and put up a hand to stroke his cheek. 'Why not?'

'Because of the trouble it's always caused.' He sighed. 'Even when I was a small child. I can remember the friction between my father and Grandpa Grantham. He was a financier, and expected his son to follow in his footsteps—become a solid citizen. And that was never going to happen.

'Instead he found himself having to bail him out over and over again, until at last he decided that enough was enough. For a long time there was no contact between them, although Thirza did a lot to heal the breach. She was tough and sensible, and Grandpa recognised that. But, all the same, he made it brutally clear that Dad would never see another penny of his money, or take his place on the bank's board. And that he'd made a new will in my favour, bypassing him completely.'

Jenna gasped. 'And he actually did so?'

'Oh, yes,' Ross said drily. 'And I can't altogether blame him for that. Dad's track record with money did not bear scrutiny. But it created a rift between my father and myself that I've always regretted. Dad was full of resentment and treated me as if I was some kind of robber baron, although we were reconciled before he died—again, thanks to Thirza.

'So, from the first, the money was a burden. And I was sufficiently my father's son to want to go my own way and leave my seat on the board empty, although there's been a certain amount of pressure on me lately to think again.' He pulled her closer, his mouth warm on her skin. 'Perhaps they think marriage has tamed me.'

'How wrong can they be?' Jenna returned breathlessly, feeling the blood leap in her veins.

'They may see my using the money as a concession in itself.'

'You'd rather we didn't…?'

'It's not that.' Ross was silent for a moment. 'I'm always aware of how much trouble it's caused in the past. I don't want it to affect what we have.'

'It won't.' Jenna drew his head down and kissed his mouth. 'It's just a way of finding the home of our dreams, that's all.' She moved against him, softly and sensuously, revelling in his instant response. 'Oh, darling, we're going to be so very happy. And nothing will ever spoil that.'

Even at this distance, the memory of those words—and the wild, unthinking optimism which had inspired them—had the power to make Jenna shiver, as if a cloud had suddenly obscured the brightness of the sun.

Was it really the money? she asked herself with a kind of despair. Did it cast some kind of blight—start the rot? If we'd stayed in the flat would our relationship have been different? Could it have survived?

She got up from the garden seat and walked back towards the house. No, she thought. That was just a fantasy. The reality was Ross being exactly what he'd said—his father's son—restless and unfaithful.

And nothing could survive that.

Over the next few hours she threw herself almost grimly into preparations for the wedding. There was certainly plenty to do. Other family members and friends would start arriving soon, and every bedroom at Trevarne would be in use, so Jenna found herself flying around with armfuls of sheets, blankets and towels under her aunt's direction.

Some of the guests would be staying at the Fisherman's Arms, or in bed and breakfast accommodation in the village. And for the final few, mostly young and male, there would be air mattresses and sleeping bags in quiet corners of the house.

'I hope they'll be comfortable,' Christy said, her forehead creased anxiously as she stuffed yet another pillow into its case.

'Of course they will,' Jenna returned robustly. 'Besides, it's only for one night.'

'Yes.' Christy hesitated awkwardly. 'Jen—I know I should have mentioned this before, but I hope you didn't mind my not inviting Natasha. I know that you're close—flatmates and now business partners—but the guest list was getting out of hand...'

'And, anyway, you've never been her greatest admirer,' Jenna supplied drily.

'Oh.' Christy pulled a face. 'You guessed.'

'I've watched you bending over backwards to be polite and friendly,' Jenna admitted, amused. 'That's usually a bad sign. But don't give it another thought, love. I'm sure it never occurred to Tasha that you'd ask her.'

'I expect it did.' Christy's tone was almost waspish. 'Not a lot gets past that one.'

Jenna decided it was best to ignore that. Christy didn't realise just what a tower of strength Natasha had proved over the past months.

'It's just as well she's not here.' She shook her head. 'I can imagine how she'd have reacted to Ross's presence.'

'Yes,' Christy said thoughtfully. 'So can I.' She paused, sending Jenna an odd glance. 'Are you going to tell her?'

'Naturally. And how I weathered the storm.' Jenna lifted her chin. 'She'll be proud of me.'

'Will she?' Christy shrugged. 'Well, you know her better than I do.' She glanced at her watch. 'Hell, we'd better get changed. It's nearly time. See you downstairs in fifteen minutes?'

'Yes.' Jenna's smile was so wooden her lips had splinters. 'Yes, of course.'

No matter how hard she'd worked, the prospect of the wedding rehearsal had been there all day in her consciousness, like a high wall on an obstacle course.

She was half tempted to go as she was, in washed denim jeans and a sweater, but the vicar was a conventional man, who specialised in pained looks, and finding herself on the receiving end of one of them would only draw attention to her. When what she really wanted was to be invisible.

She'd brought a dress to wear, in her favourite green with a tight bodice and a swirl of a skirt, but that had been when the best man was a stranger, for whom she was prepared to make an effort.

She didn't want Ross to imagine, even for a moment, that she'd dressed to please him.

Unobtrusive was the name of the game, she told herself, sorting restlessly through the clothes she'd brought with her and coming up with a cream linen skirt and a matching round-necked sweater in fine wool.

She pushed her feet into a pair of low-heeled bronze pumps and studied herself in the mirror with dissatisfaction. The shadows under her eyes had deepened, and her entire facial bone structure looked gaunt and haggard.

I look like a ghost, she thought. Or, worse, a woman in mourning.

Grimacing, she got to work with the concealer, then applied a dusting of blusher and a touch of brownish lip colour.

On the stairs, she met Aunt Grace, who was staying behind from the rehearsal to welcome arriving guests.

'Putting a brave face on it all, dear?' She was inspected rapidly and given an approving pat. 'I'm sure that's wise.

I was just coming to find you. You're wanted on the phone.'

Jenna frowned as she continued down to the hall. She hadn't been expecting any calls, but, then, she hadn't been anticipating any of the other things that had befallen her at this wedding either, she reminded herself with a certain tension.

She picked up the receiver. 'Hello?' For a moment there was no response, just an eerie, almost deafening silence, reminding her of all those other unexplained silences. She found she was gripping the carved edge of the telephone table.

She said harshly, 'Who the hell is this? Who's there?'

There was a crackle, then Natasha's voice said, 'Jenna—is that you?'

'Oh, Tasha.' Jenna let out a gasp of relief, then paused. 'What's the matter? Has something gone wrong at the gallery?'

'No—no, everything's fine. But I suddenly found I was thinking about you, and wondering how things were at the wedding of the year?' Even at this distance Jenna could pick up the faint edge in Natasha's voice. 'Is Christy still planning to go through with it, or has she had second thoughts?'

'Christy has never been happier,' Jenna returned with emphasis. 'And the weather is glorious. It should be a wonderful day.'

'And you're coping all right?'

Jenna bit her lip. The correct response, she knew, was, Never better, and that was what she should say, but this was her concerned friend, so why pretend?

She said slowly, 'Not really. When I arrived I found Ross was here.'

'Ross?' She could feel the shock waves reverberating

down the phone. 'Is this some kind of sick joke?' Natasha's
tone sounded harsh, almost aggressive.'

'Unfortunately, no.' Jenna kept her own voice temperate.
'He's staying with Thirza while he gets over some virus.'

'Did you know about this in advance?' Natasha demanded harshly.

'No, of course not.'

'But you've seen him?'

Jenna sighed soundlessly. 'I haven't had a great deal of
choice. He's had to step in as best man.' She swallowed.
'It's—just one of those things.'

'My God—after all you've been through, you're still letting them do this to you. I cannot believe it.' Natasha
paused. 'I knew it. I sensed you were in trouble.' Her voice
quietened, became more persuasive. 'Jenna, listen to me.
Get out of there—now. You don't need to be treated like
this. Tell them all to go to hell, and come back to London.'

'I can't do that. It would upset everyone and everything.
And, besides, it's not as bad as it sounds. Ross and I have
declared a truce.'

'A truce?' Her friend's laugh was shrill. 'You'll be telling me next you've decided to forgive and forget. Or maybe
you've already done so.'

Jenna bit her lip. 'No, but we've agreed to try and behave
decently to each other for the duration of the wedding.'

'Decently?' Natasha echoed derisively. 'Are you crazy?
Ross is incapable of decency. Has it slipped your mind that
he deserted you after your miscarriage? That he proved
over and over again that he was nothing but a serial womaniser? Someone who discarded his lovers like soiled clothing—and that you were no exception?'

'No.' Jenna's voice shook. 'I remember everything that
happened, including a lot of stuff that I must have buried
in the back of my mind and hoped I would never discover

again. Only seeing Ross again has brought it all to the surface.'

'What kind of thing?' Natasha asked sharply. 'What are you talking about?'

'It doesn't matter, because I'm dealing with it.'

'Of course it matters. I can't bear to think of you torturing yourself like this. You've got to tell me...'

'Tasha, I really can't discuss it now. It's the wedding rehearsal, and they're waiting for me.'

'Will Ross be at this rehearsal?'

'Naturally. I told you—he's acting as best man.'

'And your family are allowing this?' Natasha gave an angry laugh. 'My God, they should be shielding you from him.'

'They don't have to, because there's nothing left between Ross and me.' Jenna hesitated. 'And anyway, he's getting married again.'

This time the silence was so profound she thought they'd been cut off.

She said, puzzled, 'Tasha—are you there?'

'Yes,' Natasha said. 'Yes, of course.' She laughed again, an odd, strained sound. 'Ross—does not learn from his mistakes, does he?'

Jenna winced, but kept her voice light. 'Apparently it's the real thing this time.' She caught sight of Christy signalling to her from the front door, and stiffened. 'Look, I must go. We'll talk when I get back, but I'm fine—really. See you soon.'

It was a relief to put the phone down. Sometimes Natasha carried her protectiveness too far, she thought unhappily as she went out to the car. At times during the conversation she'd sounded almost paranoid.

And, far from blaming Christy for failing to invite her

to the wedding, Jenna felt almost grateful to her cousin for the omission.

As for herself—only twenty-four hours to go and she would be free again. And safe.

She waited with Christy outside the church while Uncle Henry went in to make sure everything was ready for the rehearsal to begin.

'He's even arranged for the organist to be there so that we can practise walking up the aisle without falling over,' Christy said, leaning against the side of the car and squinting up at the sun. She sighed. 'The way things are going I shall probably be making the trip on my knees anyway.' She paused. 'You haven't got a cigarette on you, by any chance?'

'No,' Jenna said calmly. 'Because I don't smoke, and nor do you.'

She grinned at her cousin. 'Do I detect a touch of bridal nerves at last?'

Christy shook her head. 'Oh, Jen, it's all so chancy. People get married, but they don't seem to stay married any more. And I don't want us to become another statistic.'

Jenna shrugged. 'Tell me about it.'

'Oh, *hell*.' Christy gave her a rueful look. 'Me and my big mouth. But I swear I wasn't having a dig.'

'I never thought you were. But, if it's any consolation, you and Adrian have looked like a couple from the moment you met. And you're both the product of stable marriages, which they say helps, too.'

Christy smiled reflectively. 'I once asked Ma if she'd ever thought about divorcing Pops, and she said absolutely not—but she'd contemplated murder a few times. I can settle for that.'

And they were both laughing when Mr Penloe came out to summon them into the church.

It was an ancient building, constructed on a site where, it was believed, far more primitive forms of worship had once been conducted. Jenna sometimes found it dark, but today, with the afternoon sun pouring through the windows, dappling the stone floor with pools of colour, and the elderly pews already decorated with lovers' knots in primrose and white ribbons, its dignified beauty was at its best.

As the stately notes of the 'Wedding March' filled the air, Christy walked slowly forward on her father's arm, with Jenna pacing behind them. Tomorrow she would have flowers to carry, but for now she kept her hands clasped in front of her to hide the fact that they were shaking.

Because this was all too reminiscent of everything she needed so badly to forget. Like a slow-motion replay of her own wedding, she thought, her heart thudding unevenly. Except that this time she was cast in a minor role.

Ahead of her she could see the kindly figure of the vicar waiting at the chancel steps. She realised that two tall figures were rising from the front pew and moving to join him. And that they'd both turned to watch the small procession making its way up the aisle. Adrian's face was one broad grin of delight as he saw them approach, but his companion was unsmiling, pale, even gaunt beneath his tan. And he was looking only at Jenna.

Don't look back at him, she told herself, her throat tightening uncontrollably. Look at the back of Christy's head, the vicar, or the cross on the altar. Anywhere but at him...

And yet, as if mesmerised, her gaze was drawn inexorably to his.

It was like being plunged into a furnace, she thought, her steps faltering involuntarily.

Because, in Ross's eyes, she saw anger, bitterness and naked pain. And, transcending all these, a stark and passionate physical hunger that sent her mind and senses reeling out of their strictly imposed control.

You can't—you can't do this to me! The words were screaming silently in her head as she tried and failed to tear her eyes from his. As she felt, shocked, the harsh, pagan stir of her blood in a response as terrifying as it was inevitable.

She realised that Christy was turning to her, pretending to hand her a non-existent bouquet, but passing her, instead, the keys to her car.

And at the same time she became sharply, agonisingly aware that Ross had taken a step nearer to her. That if he put out a hand he could touch her.

Panic rose inside her like nausea. Her hand closed round the keys—the miraculous, life-saving keys—as she took one pace back, and then another. Until she whirled round and fled down the aisle, ignoring the startled voices calling out to her, out into the sunshine and the waiting car.

And escape.

CHAPTER EIGHT

SHE was in no fit state to drive, but she drove all the same, away from the church, away from the village, away from the fool she'd just made of herself. That—that most of all.

She had an abiding inner vision of all those astonished, appalled faces watching her go. And Ross, alone unmoving and unmoved, like a pillar of granite, observing this act of total self-betrayal.

She took a corner too fast and too wide, and a car coming in the opposite direction blared its horn at her, shocking her back to reality.

That was all she needed, she castigated herself. To end up in pieces physically as well as emotionally. Besides, she was going to be in quite enough trouble with Christy as it was. She didn't need to bend her car as well.

She drove on more sedately, hugging the tall hedges for safety, her hands clamped on the wheel as if it was her last hold on sanity, then took a turning totally at random, heading for the ever-present coast.

Here the landscape was wilder and more bleak, with the wind shivering over rocks and clumps of gorse and whining in the ruins of a long abandoned tin mine.

Straight ahead of her the Atlantic heaved itself at the guardian cliffs, then fell back defeated.

Jenna parked a safe distance from the edge, then grabbed the stray fleece Christy had left on the rear seat, huddling it around her against the chill of the strong breeze as she left the car. She stood for a moment, catching her breath, then made her way to a flat boulder and sat down.

To her relief, there was no one else around. She needed to be alone and out of reach for a while, as she sorted out in her mind what had just happened. Because there was every chance that she was going to cry, quite loudly and quite bitterly, and for that she didn't require an audience.

There was no sound but the eternal wash of the ocean, and suddenly the solitary cry of a bird—a curlew, perhaps—sparking an answering wrench of loneliness deep in her gut.

She tucked her trembling hands into the sleeves of the fleece and bent forward, staring sightlessly at the rutted ground at her feet.

It wasn't the anger in Ross that had defeated her and put her to flight, but that searing glimpse of fierce, almost anguished desire.

Because he had no right to look at her like that, his dark gaze stripping away her clothing for his own private satisfaction.

So many times before she'd encountered that particular expression in his eyes—that focussed, almost stark sensuality, combining heated demand with passionate promise.

She would look away, feeling a responsive warmth invade her skin, a swift scald of excitement building within her. Knowing that by the time they were alone together she would be sobbing, half-frantic for him. Which had always been his intention.

There was never time for subtlety or love play. That would come later. There was only the fever of their breathing as they wrenched their clothing apart, desperate for the graze of skin against bare skin. For the mutual filling of their senses.

And afterwards they would sleep, sated, in each other's arms, his hand possessively cupping her breast.

A shudder of pure sensation quivered through her at the memory.

But it wasn't just the pleasure of sex which had enthralled her, binding her to him for ever, although she acknowledged that had been a potent force.

Jenna remembered, too, the laughter, the tenderness, the private jokes, the way he'd reach for her hand as they walked along the street, all the small day-to-day intimacies of a relationship, made all the more poignant because she'd been robbed of them so swiftly and cruelly.

Oh, God, why couldn't she have been enough for him, as he'd been for her?

And why had she been too blind to realise that he was turning away from her?

One last time she would allow herself to ask those questions for which she had never been able to find the answers. Always before she had pushed them away, knowing that she would find such self-interrogation too painful to deal with.

But now she was already suffering more than she could bear, and it was time to examine the failure of her marriage once and for all time.

Not that it would be easy. It would be like trying to piece together the fragments of a treasured piece of crystal that she knew was smashed beyond repair, and that would leave her fingers cut and bleeding.

Yet she owed it to herself to find an explanation. To understand why she had lost him. And, most important of all, to justify her decision to cut him out of her life.

Maybe once this unfinished business had been dealt with she would finally be able to forget.

She lifted her head and stared at the restless, tumbling sea.

She had never wanted to regard herself as any kind of victim, but all the same she had always been certain in her own mind that she was the injured party, and Ross was solely to blame for their divorce.

But over the last few days she'd been faced with the unpleasing fact that others might not totally share her view. Even Christy, who'd always been one of her staunchest supporters.

And this was what she now had to confront. Because simply repeating to herself that Ross had been unfaithful to her because he was his father's son didn't work for her any longer.

When had things started to change between them? she asked herself, biting her lip. Was it when they'd moved into the tall house in Notting Hill she'd found for them, with its spacious rooms and stripped floorboards, and, importantly, the lawned garden at the rear shaded by a magnolia tree?

Jenna had had a secret vision of herself, sitting on a rug under the tree watching her baby kicking happily in the sunlight, and hugged it to herself smiling.

On a more practical level, there had been four bedrooms, two bathrooms, and a brand-new kitchen, so they'd been able to move in right away without needing to carry out any preliminary work.

'There's even a basement which you could convert into a dark room,' she told Ross, bubbling. 'You're going to love it.'

Ross kissed her smiling lips. 'I love you,' he told her softly. 'And that applies wherever we may happen to live.'

Thirza was one of their first visitors. 'My word,' she said with a touch of dryness. 'Playing house, Jenna?'

Jenna, who'd been given free rein with the furnishings, too, and was pleased with her efforts, stiffened. 'Don't you like it?'

'What's not to like?' Thirza looked round again. 'It's— quite charming, if a little large.' She paused. 'So, which room is going to be the nursery?'

Jenna flushed. 'It's far too soon to be thinking of that,' she said, ignoring the fact that she'd already decided on the sunny rear room on the second floor.

'Quite right,' said Thirza. 'Two being company and all that.' She gave Jenna a pleasant smile. 'Is that coffee I smell?'

But Natasha's reaction had compensated for Thirza's lukewarm response.

'It's absolutely perfect. A dream house,' she said. 'You are clever, darling. And it will hold its resale value,' she added practically.

Jenna laughed. 'We're never going to sell,' she said. 'Or at least not until the children are grown-up and gone.'

Natasha's head snapped round. 'Children?' The word was almost shrill. 'Surely you're not pregnant already?'

'Not as far as I know.' Jenna gave her a surprised look. 'But is there some reason I shouldn't be?'

Natasha hesitated. 'None at all.' She gave a smiling shrug. 'I just can't visualise Ross coping with nappies and broken nights, that's all.'

'Nonsense,' Jenna said. 'He'll be a wonderful father.' *Once he gets used to the idea.*

Which, she had to admit, he showed no signs of doing. He was preoccupied more with the agency, frankly unhappy with the quality of the work being sent back. Clearly chafing that he wasn't still in the front line himself.

'You wouldn't go back, would you?' Jenna asked one night as they lay in bed together.

'Would it be so terrible?' He was playing with her hair, twining it round his fingers, brushing it across his lips.

'I don't know.' She tried to speak lightly. 'How terrible is danger?'

He sighed. 'Jenna, I could leave the house tomorrow and be run over by a bus. Or walk into a terrorist bomb. You can't rely on staying safe—not any more.'

'But you don't have to take unnecessary risks either.' She was on full alert, her heart thumping. 'And you're making a great job of running the agency. Everyone says so.'

'Really?' His tone was sardonic. 'Yet I feel as if I've been on an overlong holiday, stranded in some pleasant, undemanding limbo, and it's time to get back to some real work.' He sighed, briefly and sharply, then tipped up her face and kissed her. 'But we won't talk any more about it now. Let's get some sleep.'

He slept, but Jenna did not. She lay awake, staring into the darkness, her mind full of explosions and falling buildings, and the wailing of people in pain and distress. And Ross would be there in the front line—in the thick of it all.

Her throat closed in panic. How could he even think of going back, when he was married—when he had a life with her?

She would have to give him, she thought, a good reason to stay.

In the morning, after he'd left for work, Jenna buried her foil strip of contraceptive pills deep in the garbage sack she was putting out for collection. She wasn't proud of herself, but desperate circumstances called for desperate measures.

Six weeks later, a pregnancy testing kit told her that her ploy had worked.

She left the gallery early, and shopped for a special meal. Flowers, she thought, and wine and candles. The works.

When Ross came home his brows lifted at the sight of the shining dinner table laid for two.

'Are we celebrating something?' he asked. 'Don't tell me I've forgotten some monthiversary?'

'No, nothing like that.' She put a basket of warm toast for the pâté on the table. 'I've had some good news, that's all.'

He was very still for a moment, his eyes narrowing as he studied her, then he said lightly, 'You've been promoted—given a pay rise—discovered some new artist who's going to take the world by storm? All of these?'

'None of them.' She filled the wine glasses. 'I'll tell you after we've eaten.'

'No,' he said, and his voice was suddenly steely. 'You'll tell me now, Jenna.'

She'd practised the words in her head all day—the perfect phrase that would be not too blunt, but not coy either.

But what she heard herself say was, 'I'm pregnant.'

She looked at him, waiting—wanting to see joy explode in his face. Expecting to be snatched up into his arms.

Instead, his head went back, and he looked at her as if she was a stranger. He said quietly, 'But that's impossible. Because we've talked about this. We agreed. And you're on the pill.'

She took a step towards him. Put out her hand. 'But nothing's one hundred per cent reliable. You know that.' She touched the tip of her tongue to her dry mouth. 'I—I had a slight tummy upset a few weeks ago. That can affect things.'

'Did you?' he said. 'How unfeeling of me not to have noticed. Now, I'd have said you hadn't had a day's illness since we met.'

She hugged her arms round her body. It was all going terribly wrong, and she had no idea how to retrieve the situation. Or even if she could…

She tried again. 'Ross, I thought you'd be pleased.'

'Oh, no, Jenna,' he said, too softly. 'You know better than that. And that's exactly why you've forced my hand like this. Bad move, my love.'

He picked up his jacket and walked to the door.

'Where are you going?'

'Out,' he said. 'To think, and probably get very drunk.'

'But I've cooked this lovely meal…'

'Then it's just as well you're eating for two, darling,' he said. 'Isn't it?'

And a moment later she heard the door slam behind him.

She cleared the table, threw away all the careful preparations, then went to bed and cried herself to sleep.

She awoke very early the next morning, and lay for a moment, wondering why. Then two things occurred to her. Firstly, that the bed beside her was still empty. And, secondly, that she was about to be violently sick.

She only just made it to the bathroom. And when, at last, she raised her head groggily from the toilet bowl Ross was there, pale and unshaven, but concerned.

'Where—where have you been?' Her voice was a croak.

'I slept on the sofa.'

He wiped her face with a damp towel, then lifted her into his arms and carried her gently back to bed.

'Would you like some tea?'

Jenna shuddered violently. 'Just some fizzy water, I think.'

'Probably wise.' He paused, then bent and kissed her. His lips were tender, offering reconciliation, and perhaps acceptance.

'Well, you've had the dream, darling,' he whispered wryly. 'Now welcome to the reality.'

That particular reality, Jenna recalled without pleasure, had impinged on her with monotonous regularity over the next two months. The up-side had been that within half an hour she'd felt fine and bursting with energy again, so the nausea, although unpleasant, hadn't caused any major inconvenience.

She hadn't been able to wait to tell everyone, travelling down to Cornwall for the purpose. Her family had been delighted, but clearly surprised.

'A baby—and so soon in the first year,' Aunt Grace pondered, after she'd hugged her niece. 'Can you really afford it?'

'Of course. I'm going to work until the last minute, and Ross is incredibly well paid at the agency. And I told you about his inheritance...'

'Oh,' said Aunt Grace. 'I wasn't actually thinking about money.'

Thirza had received the information quietly, and without any astonishment.

'And how does Ross feel about this?' she asked. 'Coping with the inevitable, I suppose.'

Jenna lifted her chin. 'He's thrilled to bits.'

In truth, she wasn't altogether sure how Ross was dealing with the prospect of fatherhood. He could not have been kinder and more protective. But she was nevertheless aware that his concern was for her rather than the tiny life growing inside her.

He'll feel differently when it starts to show—and to

move, she thought, placing a hand over her still-flat abdomen.

He was also beginning to suggest with increasing frequency that she should give up work, and for the life of her she couldn't understand why.

'Darling, I'm fine,' she assured him. 'And I'd be so bored at home, alone all day. Surely you can understand that?'

'Yes,' he said slowly. 'But, just the same, I think you need to take extra care.' He gave her a taut smile. 'You look—tired sometimes.'

She went into his arms, hugging him close. 'But I really enjoy my work,' she murmured. 'And I've never felt better in my life. Besides, Mr Haville and Natasha keep me wrapped in cotton wool.'

It was no more than the truth. She'd been hesitant about breaking the news of the baby to Natasha, as she hadn't been sure what her reaction would be. But there'd been no need to worry. Rather to her surprise, Tasha had been over the moon, and had fussed round her solicitously ever since. Indeed, right up to the moment when...

Jenna's hands gripped the rock on either side of her. Now she was coming to it—to the terrible, unbelievable thing that had befallen her. The memory she had tried unavailingly to push away ever since.

It had begun like any other day. At the gallery they'd been planning another exhibition, and there had been a stack of canvases up in the office, waiting to go to the framers.

Jenna's offer to help carry them downstairs had been turned down flatly by Natasha. 'I wouldn't dream of it,' she declared. 'You shouldn't be lifting heavy weights, and those stairs are lethal anyway.'

'They're not heavy, just bulky,' Jenna protested. 'And, anyway, I'm not made of glass.'

Natasha paused. 'All right then,' she allowed grudgingly. 'We'll do it between us. But you only carry one at a time.'

It was on Jenna's third trip that it happened. She waited at the top of the stairs for Natasha, who was coming up, then began to descend carefully. But as she reached the fourth step she suddenly lost her footing. She cried out and clutched at the rail, but she was already falling forward, her body rebounding helplessly from step to step, until she reached the wooden floor at the bottom of the steep flight. And the painful pit of darkness that awaited her there.

She learned afterwards that the ambulance had been there within minutes, but she was already bleeding when she arrived at the hospital, and miscarriage had proved inevitable.

She lay in the narrow bed in a private room, physically bruised and emotionally torn into pieces. Yet, oddly, unable to cry.

They'd called it 'an unlucky accident' and 'no one's fault', but Jenna knew better, and blamed herself. After all, she was the one who'd wanted this pregnancy—who'd manipulated it into being, ignoring Ross's wishes. And now she was being punished. Taught in one poignant lesson that it was dangerous to engineer life to suit one's own wishes, because fate could and would hit back.

And her agonised heart grieved for the tiny being she had lost.

'These things happen,' one of the nurses told her, trying to be kind. 'But as soon as the consultant gives you the all-clear you can try again.'

'No,' Jenna said. 'I won't be doing that.'

The woman gave her a bracing smile. 'Your husband may have a point of view on that, dear.'

'Yes,' Jenna said with difficulty. 'I—I'm sure he will.'

And she turned painfully on to her side and faced the wall.

The medication they'd given her allowed her to sleep, and when she woke Ross was there, sitting beside the bed, white-faced and hollow-eyed.

He said, 'I was out of the office and they couldn't find me. Not at once.'

He took her hand and lifted it to his cheek, cradling it there. 'Oh, darling.' His voice broke. 'You could have been killed.'

'No,' she said. 'The baby died instead. In my place.'

'Oh, my love,' he said. 'My love. I'm so sorry.'

'Why?' She shook her head, her eyes almost blank. 'You never wanted this baby. You knew I'd tricked you into it. Didn't you?'

'Yes,' he said. 'But that doesn't matter. It stopped mattering a long time ago. You must believe that.'

'Must I?' She sighed. 'Somehow it doesn't seem very important any more.'

'It's important to me.' Ross paused. 'Can you remember how it happened?'

'I tripped on the stairs. Or slipped. Whatever.' She removed her hand from his clasp. 'It's ironic, isn't it? You wanted me to give up work, but I couldn't. And if I had, I'd still be having the baby.'

'Darling,' he said. 'Don't think about that now.'

'No,' she said. 'There's no point. Because it's all over.' She was silent for a moment. 'Will you tell everyone—my family—and Thirza? And ask them not to fuss. Apparently it happens a lot—with first babies.' She smiled at him politely, almost apologetically. 'And often it's for the best. They said that, too.'

'Oh God,' he said. 'Jenna—*Jenna.*'

A nurse came bustling in, saying it was time Mrs Grantham got some more sleep and that he should come back in the morning.

Ross looked at her coldly. 'I'd like to stay with my wife.'

'No,' Jenna said. 'There's no point. Please go. I—I'm very tired.'

For a moment he looked as if he was going to protest. Then he sighed. 'Very well,' he said, and his voice was infinitely weary. 'If that's what you wish...'

She was kept in for a couple of days, with the small room filling up with flowers and loving, anxious messages. She was also offered grief counselling, but declined.

Mr Haville came to see her, wringing his hands and saying he'd examined every inch of the stairs and could see no reason for her fall—no reason at all.

Later, Natasha arrived, looking pinched and white. 'I can't believe it,' she kept saying. 'I just can't believe it. I keep seeing you lying there, not moving.' She shuddered, then paused. 'Do you remember how it happened?'

'No, it's all pretty much a blank.' Jenna paused. 'I was carrying a canvas, wasn't I? Did it survive?'

Natasha pulled a face. 'Not really, but that's the last thing you should be bothering about. You just need to get strong again.'

Jenna found she needed all the strength she possessed when the time came for her to go home. She sat beside Ross in the passenger seat of the car, taut as a drum, as they drove back to the house. The hospital room had become a refuge, but now she was out in the cold world again.

'Darling.' Ross was watching her, worried. 'Will you be all right? I need to get back to the agency. Something's come up. But Christy's coming over to be with you.'

'Thank you,' she said. 'However, there was really no need.' She summoned a smile. 'I'll be fine—really.'

But she wasn't fine at all. Suddenly the house was like an empty shell, sterile and heartless, where her footsteps rang hollow on the polished boards.

Up in the would-have-been nursery, the pretty chest of drawers she'd bought only a couple of weeks before had gone, and the paint cards and swatches of fabric had also been removed. Making it just another room again.

This had to be Ross's doing, and she knew she should be grateful, yet a blind, unreasoning anger began to stir in her. How easily he'd disposed of all her hopes and plans, she thought. Proving how little they'd meant to him.

The sound of the doorbell was a relief, and Christy's warm and comforting presence a blessing.

As they sat in the kitchen drinking the coffee her cousin had made Jenna said, 'Ross has stripped the nursery. Everything's gone.'

Christy laid a hand over hers. 'I'm sure he's done it for the best,' she said gently. 'He's very concerned about you.'

'Yes.' Jenna looked down at the table. 'But he doesn't really care about the baby. He never did.'

'Oh, Jen, I'm sure you're wrong.'

'Not one word of regret.' Jenna bit her lip hard. 'Not one. He's hardly mentioned…'

'It can't be easy for him either,' Christy soothed her.

'No?' Jenna asked harshly. 'Isn't that why he cleared out the room? What's the old saying—"Out of sight, out of mind"? Everything back to normal as soon as possible?'

'Perhaps it's his way of dealing with it—the only way he knows.' Christy patted her hand. 'Don't be too hard on him, love.' She rose. 'Do you feel up to a trip down to the

Gate for some food shopping? I'll put a casserole in the oven for you for tonight.'

'Aren't you going to stay and have some?'

'Not tonight. I think you two should be alone and do some talking. Besides, I have a date.'

'Oh.' Jenna managed a smile. 'Anyone nice?'

Christy said slowly, 'I think he might be. His name's Adrian, and he works for a merchant bank. But it's too soon to judge.'

'Yes,' Jenna said tautly. 'Because there's another old saying—"Marry in haste, repent at leisure."' She nodded almost fiercely. 'Don't you make that mistake.' And thought, *As I did…*

Ross looked tired and preoccupied when he came home that night, and it was clearly no time for a heart to heart. In fact he said little, apart from enquiring how she felt, praising Christy's casserole, and asking if there was anything she wanted to watch on television.

Jenna went up to bed first, and Ross followed half an hour later. She was propped up on her pillow reading when he came into the room.

As he began to unbutton his shirt she said, quickly and breathlessly, 'Ross, the consultant said I should get as much rest as possible.'

'Of course,' he said. 'For a start, I've contacted a domestic help agency and they're sending someone in the morning.'

'I—I didn't mean that.' She swallowed. 'I really need to get a good night's sleep—without being disturbed.'

Ross was very still for a moment, then he tossed his discarded shirt over a chair and began to unbuckle his belt. 'Meaning?'

'Meaning I've made up a bed for you in the next room.'
She forced a nervous smile. 'Just for a few nights.'

'I see.' He was silent for a moment. When he spoke
again his voice was level, but there was an underlying note
of harshness. 'Jenna, I need to sleep with you—to hold you.
But that's all. You surely don't think I'm so crazed with
lust that I'd force myself on you sexually? I'm your husband, not a monster.'

'That's not what I'm trying to say at all.' She sat up,
pushing her hair back with a defensive hand. 'I just want
the chance of a peaceful night's sleep for a little while. Is
that so much to ask?'

'Peace,' he said slowly, 'is a commodity in pretty short
supply these days. And I'm not sure this is the way to
achieve it. But if you don't want me in your bed, I won't
insist.' His mouth twisted sardonically. 'And I'd better not
kiss you goodnight either—just in case that arouses the
brute in me. So—sweet dreams, my love.'

The door closed behind him and Jenna was alone, which
was just what she'd wanted, so it was stupid to feel so
desolate. And galling to find that she couldn't sleep anyway. She was still too bruised and sore to toss and turn, so
all she could do was lie there in the darkness—and endure.

She found herself wondering whether Ross was finding
sleep equally elusive. She could always find out, of course.
He was only a few yards away on the other side of the
wall, and the temptation to go to him—to feel the welcoming warmth of his arms enclosing her, soothing her, was
almost overwhelming.

Almost, she thought unhappily, but not quite. Because
nothing between them could ever be the same again, and it
was useless to pretend otherwise. However much she might
want him physically, emotionally they were on different

planets, and she was going to need time to come to terms with that.

Gradually her bruises faded, and she began to heal mentally as well as physically. But she and Ross were as far apart as ever, by day as well as night. And the more time passed, the harder it became for her to invite him back into the bedroom they'd once shared.

She realised she was hoping he'd ease matters by making the first move. But he didn't, and she was almost glad when the Penloes invited her down to Cornwall to stay with them.

'Ross says you're still pale, and not eating properly,' Aunt Grace told her on the phone. She paused. 'It's a shame he can't come with you.'

'Oh, well,' Jenna said lightly. 'He'll be all the more pleased to see me when I come back.'

But when her week's cosseting was over, and she returned to London, it was to discover that Ross had given up his desk job and was about to depart on another assignment abroad, thus damning any hopes she'd cherished of a blissful reconciliation.

'You didn't think to discuss it with me first?' She stood helplessly, watching him pack.

He shrugged. 'It's my career—my life, Jenna,' he told her quietly. 'And we rarely discuss very much at all these days. But when I come back we'll talk, if you want.'

She said hoarsely, 'I can't believe that you're doing this. Leaving me on my own after—after what happened.'

His mouth tightened. 'You're not on your own, my sweet. You never have been.' He ticked off on his fingers. 'You have your family, friends, offers of counselling—a whole support system. Including your job at the gallery, which you're about to return to. I doubt very much if you'll notice my absence.'

She wanted very much to plead. To cling to him and beg him not to go. But her pride wouldn't allow that.

He hadn't wanted the baby, she thought, pain closing in on her. And now, it seemed, he didn't want her either.

She, however, missed him achingly, every hour of every day. And when he returned he found the spare bed stripped and his clothes and belongings back in the marital bedroom, in mute acknowledgement that his exile was over.

But even that didn't work out as she'd hoped. When he made love to her she was tense and anxious, and he was almost icily restrained.

At the end, he said bleakly, 'I'm sorry,' and turned away from her. While he slept she lay awake beside him, tears of bewilderment and disappointment squeezing under her eyelids. All her worst fears confirmed. She found herself remembering some anonymous phone calls when they'd first moved in, and other mysteries too—and wondering.

And there was another potent reason why she couldn't relax in his arms. Although the obstetrician had given her the all-clear, she was actually scared of becoming pregnant again. Of displeasing Ross by conceiving another unwanted baby.

Eventually, on the occasions when they did make love, it was swift and almost perfunctory, as if fulfilling some unappealing obligation.

Once she had dreaded him going away, but now it was almost a relief. Or that was what she told herself. But at the same time she was weeping inside, watching her life collapse around her, and bewildered by the speed at which it seemed to be happening.

It was the sudden escalation in the Middle Eastern conflict he'd been sent to cover that finally brought her to her senses. The knowledge that his life was seriously in danger made her realise she wasn't prepared to allow her marriage to slide away, out of control. She had to make a stand.

She watched the television news channels almost obsessively, as well as ringing the agency every day to demand if there'd been any contact with him, only to be disappointed.

But she mustn't worry, they told her. Ross would come out of it all right. He led a charmed life.

But nothing could reassure her. By day she paced the house, unable to concentrate on anything but the next newscast and grim reports of spiralling violence. At night she lay curled into a foetal position, with his favourite sweater wrapped round her.

And when the agency called her, at long last, to tell her they'd heard from him, and that he and another group of journalists and photographers were already flying back, she sat for a long time with the phone cradled against her breasts, tears of relief pouring down her face.

Then she moved into action—filling the house with flowers, making sure the fridge was packed with his favourite food and wine, and putting clean sheets on the bed before setting off to the airport to meet him. Something she hadn't done before.

This time, she told herself, she was leaving nothing to chance. And when she walked into his arms he would know that everything had changed.

His flight had landed when she got there, and she roamed Arrivals like an animal in a cage, mouth dry, palms damp, her eyes restlessly scanning the doorway through which he would emerge.

He was one of the last to come through, and as Jenna saw him she raised a hand to wave—to attract his attention and bring him to her. Then froze as she realised what she was seeing.

He was walking slowly, his head bent, and he was not alone. A woman was walking beside him, slim, young and blonde, and his arm was round her shoulders.

As Jenna watched, shocked and helpless, she saw the girl pause and her arms go up round Ross's neck, drawing him down to her in a long, lingering kiss, her body pressed against his with total familiarity.

Dispelling, once and for all, any last, desperate hope she might have had that their closeness was that of colleagues who'd just shared a common danger.

Jenna heard herself make a sound—hoarse, almost visceral. And then she was turning, running like a hunted creature through the crowd to the exit, intent only on flight. Seeing nothing but the intimacy of the embrace she had just witnessed. Hearing nothing but the rasp of her breathing and her voice silently moaning her husband's name.

CHAPTER NINE

JENNA had been at home for over two hours when Ross returned. Two hours in which her imagination had run riot as she'd visualised Ross and his blonde entwined in some hotel room.

She heard the cab draw up outside, and his key in the door, then the sound of his bags being deposited in the hall. But he did not call out her name, and her throat tightened in fear as well as anger.

And when, a moment later, he came into the drawing room, and saw her standing rigidly by the empty fireplace, he made no attempt to go to her. Instead, he remained by the door, the dark face enigmatic as he watched her in a silence that seemed to echo round the world.

At last she said, 'I—came to meet you at the airport.'

'Yes,' he said, his mouth twisting faintly. 'I thought I saw you—disappearing.'

She threw back her head. 'Who is she, Ross? Your blonde—companion.'

'Her name is Lisa Weston.' His voice was even. 'She's an Australian journalist and she works for the *Sunday Globe*.'

'And is that all you have to tell me about her?'

'I thought,' he said, 'that you'd have worked out the rest for yourself.'

Her lips parted in a soundless gasp. She'd expected him to deny it, to come up with some explanation. Some reassurance. She realised how desperately she'd been relying on this.

She said hoarsely, 'You've been—sleeping with her?'

'Sleep,' he said, 'didn't feature highly on the agenda.'

The brutality of it sent her reeling mentally, as if he had raised his hand and struck her across the face.

She stared at him, searching his face for some sign of softening—some remorse. A touch of regret. Something she could use, even now, to build a bridge between them. But the cool mask was impenetrable. Merciless.

She whispered, 'How could you? Oh, God, *how could you*?'

'Because she wanted me, Jenna.' His voice seared her to the bone. 'And that made a refreshing change, believe me.'

Her legs were shaking under her. Her mind was shuddering into denial, telling herself that this was the man she loved—the man who'd taught her to want him to the point of oblivion. The man she'd planned with such excitement to welcome home again into her heart and her arms.

And who could not be saying these things to her.

She was dying inside, but she managed to find a voice from somewhere.

She said, coldly and clearly, 'Then maybe you should make the change a permanent one.'

His brows lifted. 'Of course, if that's what you wish.' He paused. 'Have I time to pack the rest of my things, or would you prefer me to leave at once?'

He sounded polite, even matter of fact. He might have been asking if she wanted some coffee, Jenna thought incredulously. She stiffened, her nails digging viciously into the palms of her hands.

'Yes,' she said. 'Please go—now.'

She couldn't bear, she thought, for him to glimpse all the pathetic arrangements she'd made to please him. To signal that she wanted them to make a fresh start together.

And that she'd hoped, stupidly, innocently, that their reconciliation would begin in bed.

She turned away, staring down blindly at the cold hearth. Even now, she realised in stunned disbelief, she was still waiting for him to speak her name—to step across the abyss that divided them and come to her. To hold her while he apologised. While he offered some kind of excuse for his betrayal of their marriage and begged for her forgiveness. While he told her that the pressure they'd all been under had driven him momentarily crazy...

Tell me anything, she thought, anguished, and I'll cling to it like a drowning man to a rope.

But there was nothing. Just the sound of his footsteps receding into the hall. And then the door closing behind him as it had done so often before. Only this time it was for ever.

The anger which had sustained her went with him, leaving a vacuum into which pain began to pour in suffocating waves.

And she sank down on to her knees, her numbed lips repeating, 'It's over. It's all over,' again and again, as if it was some mantra that she relied on for her ultimate salvation.

So, she had done it. She had confronted her most agonising memories. But had she managed to exorcise the demons that had stalked her ever since? Could she now, sanely and rationally, put the past behind her?

Because she had to face the fact that, in spite of what he had done,

Ross was still there, entrenched in her heart and mind. Whereas he had moved on. Found another woman—another life.

The irony was that she'd been telling herself constantly

over the past few days that once the wedding was over she would never have to see him again. Now she was faced with precisely that situation and it was wrenching her apart. Repeating, all over again, the agony of betrayal—of desertion.

And what kind of a fool does that make me? she asked herself, shivering.

Even now she wasn't sure how she'd survived the days immediately following Ross's departure. Her anger had carried her along as she'd packed up his clothes and other possessions, erasing every trace of him. And before she'd closed the last bag she'd placed inside, on top of everything else, so it was the first thing he would see, the small velvet case containing her wedding ring. And then she'd put it in the hall with the other bags and boxes to await collection. Giving him, she had told herself, no excuse to linger.

But he hadn't needed any excuse. In the end he'd removed his things while she was at work, leaving his key on the hall table as a sign that their separation was complete and he would not be returning.

But, all the same, acting on Natasha's advice, she'd had the locks changed.

Over the next weeks she had begun to discover what loneliness meant. The house on which she'd pinned so many hopes had become just another piece of real estate, cold and without heart. She'd hardly been able to bear to spend any time there, remembering what used to be. And mourning for what might have been.

Without Ross, she thought, her life had become soulless and meaningless, and she might have drifted for ever but for Natasha, who'd found her a divorce lawyer, and an estate agent, and urged her forward into her new single life.

She'd been a wonderful friend, of course, but Jenna had wished sometimes that she wouldn't be quite so obsessively vitriolic about Ross. She'd felt quite raw enough without having his sins detailed to her on a daily basis.

I wonder why she dislikes him so, she thought, with a little sigh, then paused as the sound of an approaching car engine alerted her to the fact that she was no longer alone. That she was going to have to share her sanctuary. But it was time she was leaving anyway, she acknowledged, rising reluctantly from her rock. Time she went back to Trevarne House and grovelled to Christy for messing up the wedding rehearsal.

She turned to walk back to the car, and paused, dismayed, as she realised the vehicle parked next to it seemed all too familiar.

Oh, God, she thought, swallowing. It's Thirza's Alfa Romeo.

Not only that, but Ross and Adrian were climbing out of it and walking towards her, both of them unsmiling.

Jenna stood her ground, her chin lifted defiantly. 'Hi,' she greeted them with an assumption of nonchalance. 'Come to enjoy the view?'

'On the contrary, I see very little to admire,' Ross returned harshly. He held out his hand. 'I'll have Christy's keys, if you don't mind. Adrian's going to drive her car back.'

She hesitated, suddenly wary. 'Then I'll go with him.'

'No,' he said. 'You're staying with me. Because it's time we talked. Got a few things out into the open.'

'And if I don't want to?'

'You have no choice in the matter.' His tone was brusque. 'And we've wasted quite enough time searching for you as it is. So hand over the keys, unless you want me to shake them out of you.'

For a moment Jenna considered defiance, then, as their

eyes met and she read the purpose in his gaze, she decided discretion was best.

'How very macho of you.' Reluctantly she produced the keys and dropped them into Adrian's waiting hand. 'And I thought you were supposed to be convalescing. You seem to have made a lightning recovery from your mysterious illness.'

He shrugged, the dark eyes still hard. 'It's astonishing what effect a few days' serious aggravation can have on the constitution.'

'Well, fortunately for both of us, it won't last much longer,' she said tautly. She turned to Adrian. 'Is Christy very angry with me?'

'You know better than that,' Adrian said quietly. 'She's—concerned.'

'That I'll spoil the actual ceremony by running off in front of everyone?' Jenna shook her head. 'I shan't.' She tried a smile. 'You know what they say—bad dress rehearsal, good performance.'

'So they tell me.' Adrian turned and began walking towards Christy's car. 'See you both later.'

'Adrian.' Jenna started after him. 'Please, take me with you…'

But Ross caught her easily, his arm going round her like an iron bar, preventing any further attempt at flight. 'Don't you listen?' he asked coldly. 'I said you were going with me.'

'Leave me alone, damn you.' She struggled unavailingly to free herself, realising with disbelief that Adrian was driving off, apparently deaf and blind to her predicament. 'I'm going nowhere with you.'

'You're planning to walk back to Trevarne?' Ross shook his head as he released her. 'I don't think so. Which doesn't leave you many options, unless you intend to jump off the cliff. Now, there's a thought,' he added mockingly. 'Why don't we jump together? They could call this place "Lovers' Leap" and run bus tours out here.'

'We are not lovers.' Her voice shook. 'And I mean to keep my feet firmly on the ground. Anyway, you wouldn't jump,' she added defiantly. 'In spite of the risks you've always taken in your work, you're not the suicidal type.'

'No,' he said softly. 'I have a strong sense of self-preservation. Yet there have been plenty of moments in the past couple of years when I'd have happily opened a vein.'

Their eyes met, and Jenna felt her skin shiver, as if his hand had brushed her, as she encountered the intensity of his gaze.

'But not any more,' she said, recovering rapidly. She adopted a mocking tone of her own. 'Not when you have so much to live for.'

'Why, yes.' His smile was cool. 'Off with the old and on with the new. I can recommend it.'

'Is that all you came here to say?'

'It isn't even part of it.' His hand closed on her arm. 'Let's go for a walk.'

She wrenched herself away. 'I can manage that without help.' Her voice was mutinous. 'You don't need to touch me.'

'Don't I?' The dark brows lifted. 'Perhaps that's something we should include in our discussion.'

'I don't think so.' She looked past him, suddenly not wanting to meet his gaze, aware that her pulses had quickened. 'Just say what you have to and get it over with,' she added curtly. 'I should be getting back to Trevarne. Christy might be needing me.'

'Oh, you're all heart,' Ross said gently. 'Was it Christy you were thinking about when you did your spectacular runner a short while ago?'

'I shall apologise to her for that, naturally.' Jenna took a firm grip on her dignity. 'I—I had a panic attack. It—happens.'

'All you had to do was follow your cousin up the aisle and stand there.' He paused. 'Not too onerous.'

She glared at him. 'The circumstances were—unusual, to say the least.'

'For both of us,' he acknowledged, his mouth twisting. 'Yet I managed to stand my ground.'

'Yes,' she said. 'But you don't have my memories.'

'Of course not,' he said softly. 'You are Jenna the victim, Jenna the vulnerable, Jenna the fragile flower. Don't you think you're rather over-playing that particular role, my sweet, and it's time for a change?'

'You—bastard.' Her voice was thick. 'I wasn't the one who was unfaithful.'

'Not in the conventional sense, perhaps,' he came back at her harshly. 'But you stopped being a wife long before I had a mistress. And you know it.'

She came to a halt, turning on him, her eyes blazing. 'What the hell are you saying?' Her voice rose. 'That somehow it was all *my* fault?'

'No,' Ross said, unmoved by her surge of anger. 'But it wasn't all mine either. It takes two to make a marriage, and two to break it. And that's what we need to talk about, before it's too late.'

She hauled herself back under control. Managed a shrug. 'Too late has come and gone. We're divorced.' She took a breath. 'So none of this actually matters any more.'

'No?' he said. 'Then if it's all so unimportant why did you run away this afternoon? And why have you been dancing around me like a cat on hot bricks since our first meeting?'

'I—I don't know what you're talking about.' It was a feeble response at best.

'Stop playing games,' Ross said harshly. 'And try to be honest. You ran away today because you were suddenly confronted by a truth you couldn't deal with, and that has to stop if there's any hope for us.'

She said breathlessly. 'Us? There is no "us". And I'd like to go back to Trevarne, right now.'

'I'm sure,' he said. 'But it's not going to happen, Jenna. Not until we've looked at our marriage and established where it went wrong. And that wasn't during my brief fling with Lisa, either,' he added harshly. 'The rot had set in long before that. Even before you shut me out of your life when you lost the baby.'

'The baby you didn't want,' she threw at him.

He was white under his tan, his mouth a compressed line. When he spoke his voice was like ice. Ice that burned. 'Don't ever say that to me again, Jenna. I admit that the news of your pregnancy wasn't the most welcome I'd ever had, but that was because I already knew I'd be going back on the front line, and it was an extra responsibility I didn't need right then. Also, I didn't appreciate the way I'd been manipulated into it,' he added bitingly. 'Suddenly love and laughter had been translated into house and baby, whether I was ready for that or not. And I had no say in the matter. You were determined to conceive, at all costs, and I was presented with a *fait accompli*.'

He paused. 'But I couldn't stay angry for long, Jenna, and you must have known that. You were far too precious to me. And so was the child we'd made together. Because I realised that was just another part of the love and laughter that I treasured so deeply. God, I cared so much that I wanted to keep you safe and cherished for the whole nine months. I'd even have had the baby for you, if I could.'

He shook his head. 'When you had the miscarriage I felt as if the sun had gone out for ever, but I knew what you were suffering, and that I had to be strong for you. Or that's what I was told on all sides. But it never seemed to occur to you, or anyone, that I could be hurting, too. That I would have given my soul to weep and have the comfort of your arms around me.'

He took a breath, his face stark—remote. 'Instead, you didn't want me anywhere near you. I wasn't even allowed in your bed, but banished to another room.'

She was trembling. 'The consultant…'

'To hell with that,' he said roughly. 'I talked to him, too, remember. He said that you'd need love to help you through the grieving process. He took it for granted that would be mutual, and unstinting. He also said that once you'd recovered, we should try for another baby.

'But the wall you built between us, Jenna, wasn't just bricks and plaster. It was an emotional barricade with no way through for me. So you stayed in your private world and I was left to mourn alone. Have you any idea how hard—how bloody impossible—that was?'

She said 'I—I didn't know—I didn't realise…'

'You didn't ask,' he returned, more gently. 'And I began to wonder if you even cared. Whether you'd ever really wanted a husband at all, in the fullest sense of the word— or just someone to father your children and provide a roof of your choosing for them.'

Her head went back in shock. 'That's—unfair.'

'Perhaps,' he said. 'But you don't think very clearly when your life is falling apart. When the wonderful shining girl that you love has become an aloof stranger who only permits sex on sufferance.'

He sighed sharply. 'In many ways, snipers and bombs seemed easier to deal with.'

She drew a deep, painful breath. 'And Lisa Weston?'

'She was kind,' he said. 'At a time when kindness seemed like a forgotten dream. And when I was lonely, and scared witless most of the time, although I'm not offering that as an excuse.

'We talked one night—when, admittedly, I'd had too much to drink—and we ended up in bed. That was it, and that was all of it. Afterwards the guilt cut in, and the self-hatred, because I'd used her, and it didn't solve a thing and never would.'

She swallowed. 'Are you telling me that—it only happened once?'

'Yes,' he said. 'Although that makes it no better. It was still weak, selfish and unpardonable.'

She said in a low voice, 'Ross, I—I can't believe you're telling me the truth. Don't forget I saw you together, and it clearly wasn't over for her.'

Ross's mouth tautened. 'No,' he said slowly. 'I don't think it was. And that was another good reason to feel guilty—to hate myself. Because, as I'd always known, there was only one woman in my life that I would ever want and need, and I resolved that when I got back to London I wouldn't leave again until I'd put things right between us. Until I'd persuaded you that our life together was worth saving.

'Only you came to meet me at the airport,' he added quietly. 'And I knew then that you'd seen me saying goodbye to Lisa. And that I'd ruined everything. Taken the dream we had, and smashed it.'

Jenna stared down at the ground. 'It didn't look like goodbye,' she said in a low voice. 'And you went to her after you left me.'

'No,' he said. 'I did not. I went to a hotel for a couple of nights, and then I moved in with Seb Lithgow while I got a flat sorted out. But there was never any question of being with Lisa. I didn't feel that way about her, God forgive me.'

She began, 'But I was told…' then paused awkwardly.

He said softly, 'I wonder by whom? Or could I hazard a guess that it was your best friend and business partner?'

Jenna flushed. 'She meant it for the best. She told me about a rumour she'd heard, because she didn't want it to reach me from anyone else.'

Ross's mouth twisted cynically. 'Now, that I do believe,' he drawled.

She bit her lip. 'You've never had any time for Natasha,' she accused.

He shrugged. 'That cuts both ways.'

'She's always been there for me. I don't know what I would have done without her.'

'You might still be married.'

The shock of that held her mute for a moment. She said hoarsely,

'What is that supposed to mean?'

He was also silent. Then he said, 'I don't imagine she was upset when we split, or that she did anything to bring about a reconciliation.'

Jenna tilted her chin, ignoring an inner suspicion that this was not what he'd originally meant to say. 'She was never your greatest admirer. You're right about that.'

'And wrong about everything else?' he queried softly. 'Is that what you're saying?' He paused, his eyes fixed on hers gravely, searchingly. 'That panic attack, for instance, Jenna? Let's get back to that for a minute. What inspired that, I wonder?'

'I don't want to discuss it.' She made a play of looking at her watch. 'I really should get back. We have a houseful of people…'

'And your aunt can't cope without you, naturally.' His tone was sardonic. 'It won't work, Jenna. I promised myself I wouldn't let you run out on me again.'

She sank her teeth into her lower lip. She said hoarsely, 'What—what do you want from me? Absolution? All right—you have it.' She swallowed. 'I'll even admit that I was to blame, too. I see that now. I—I've made myself look back at everything that happened between us—and it was a shock. Because I realised I didn't like myself very much—not the self-absorbed, obsessive creature I was then. Thirza once accused me of playing house, and I hated her for it, but I think she was right.'

She paused. 'No one could have been sweeter to me than Uncle Henry and Aunt Grace, but they weren't my real parents. They were lost to me, and I think what I was trying to do was recreate them in ourselves—the father, the mother, the loved child.'

She tried to smile and failed. 'The perfect set-up. Only it was all a fantasy. It had nothing to do with us, or our marriage, and it's taken me all this time and all those tears to see that. And later I—I was too caught up in my own misery to think what you might be enduring. And I shouldn't have shut you out. Driven you away as I did. It was stupid—and cruel. And I was duly punished for it, as I deserved to be.'

She spread her hands helplessly. 'So, there you have it. Now—will you let me go?'

He was smiling. 'Not a chance, my love.'

'What else can I say? What would satisfy you?'

He said with sudden roughness, 'To hear you tell me that you love me, that you always have done and you always will. That every minute we've spent apart has been a living nightmare. And that when you saw me in church today you realised that, in spite of everything, we still want each other as desperately as ever. And that's what scared you. That's why you ran.'

She was shaking. 'Ross—don't do this to me. To either of us. We—we're not the same people any more...'

'That's what I'm counting on.' He turned her to face him, his hands gripping her arms, his face intense. 'We got married, my darling, because nothing could keep us apart. But that wasn't enough. We both had things to learn—about ourselves, and each other—and we learned them in the hardest possible way, and were almost destroyed in the process. But now we have another chance, and it's not going to pass us by. I won't let that happen. Because I need you, Jenna, like I need food to eat and air to breathe.'

He shook his head. 'In a way, going down with that virus was a blessing in disguise, because it gave me time to think, instead of racing round the world, using work to blot out the past, as I'd been doing. There were moments in the hospital when the treatment wasn't working, and it wasn't certain that I was going to survive. I realised then that I didn't care. That life without you was no life at all. And I swore that if I recovered I would get you back somehow.

'And that's why I decided to stay on, even when I discovered I'd be around for Christy's wedding. Because I knew it would bring you, too, that I'd eventually get a chance to talk to you—discover if you still cared, even a little.'

'Oh, I care,' she said unevenly. 'I just didn't realise how much. But I didn't want to admit it.'

'You fought me every step of the way,' he said. 'I tried needling you—making you jealous—and you brushed me aside every time. I was almost beginning to despair. Until I saw you in church today, walking towards me, and I remembered how you looked on our wedding day, my beautiful wife. And I wanted you so much it nearly tore me apart.

'And in that moment, like a lightning flash, I saw you wanting me, too. And when you turned and ran it actually gave me hope. Because you were admitting that you knew it wasn't over between us. And that a dozen divorces couldn't alter the way we still feel about each other. Now, deny it if you can,' he added passionately. 'And if you do I swear I'll walk away and never trouble you again.'

The tears that she'd managed to dam back for so long began to trickle down her white face.

'Ross—if that's how you feel, why did you let the divorce go through? Why didn't you come to me—ask me to think again—give our marriage another chance?'

'Because I knew how badly I must have hurt you,' he said. 'And I was ashamed. Besides,' he added drily, 'it seemed as if you couldn't wait to be rid of me, which confirmed all my worst fears -that you'd actually stopped loving me long before I'd been unfaithful.' He paused. 'If I had come to you, what would you have said?'

'I—I don't know.'

'Then maybe we needed a breathing space,' he said quietly. 'Time to reflect and get our priorities sorted out. To reach a stage where we could let our love for each other heal the wounds of the past.'

She was suddenly very still. 'But you have other priorities, Ross. You said so. You're planning to get married again. You can't just—cut her out of your life.'

'I've no intention of doing so.' He reached into his jacket pocket and took out a small jeweller's box. 'Remember this?'

Jenna swallowed. 'My wedding ring? You mean—the woman you were talking about—that you were going to marry—was me?'

He nodded. 'No one else. Give me your hand, my love.' When she obeyed, he slid the gold band back on to her finger. 'Will you marry me, Jenna?' he asked in a low voice. 'Will you now, at last, be my wife, and the mother of my children? I swear I'll never betray your trust in me again.'

'And I promise I'll never again turn away from you,' Jenna whispered, and lifted her face for his kiss.

At first he was gentle, as if her lips were the petals of a flower he was afraid to bruise, and then, as she responded with unguarded, passionate ardour, he cast his own restraint aside, kissing her with all the pent-up hunger that the long months apart had engendered.

His hands were shaking as they explored her body, pushing aside the fleece and sliding under her thin sweater to find the warm swell of her breasts, to stroke the hardening peaks into a glory of erotic pleasure. And she sighed her delight and longing against his mouth.

Her starved body was coming to life again under his caress, melting and burning as his touch became more intimate, more demanding. The long fingers traced a familiar, sweet path down her spine to her flanks, then pulled her to him, his hands on her hips, so that their bodies ground together. Making her know, beyond question, how deeply and hotly he was aroused. And how completely she was desired.

She swayed in his arms in a kind of sensuous intoxication, her mouth a heated seduction under his, her hands as seeking and as urgent.

She would have given herself to him there and then. Would have sunk down to the short windswept turf, drawing him after her.

But Ross pulled himself away from her, with a sound

between a groan and a laugh, standing with his hands on her shoulders as he recovered his breath.

His eyes swept her face, lingering on the fever-bright eyes, the flushed cheeks and parted, faintly swollen lips. He said unsteadily, 'I think it's time we went home.'

'But where can we go?' Jenna's voice was husky. 'What are they all going to say if we show up together.'

'If Adrian's done his work well, they'll have said most of it already.' He took her hand, tugging her back towards the car. 'And, anyway, I only care about you.'

She hung back. 'Darling, maybe we should wait—for each other—until we get back to London.'

'No way,' Ross said firmly. 'I've never been a fan of cold showers, and I'm damned if I'm going through the next twenty-four hours with this kind of ache in my guts. We've both spent too many lonely nights already, my love. But that ends right now.'

'Yes, Ross.' Her voice was demure, but the look she sent him combined mischief and passion in a mixture that quickened his breathing.

She expected him to drive back to Trevarne House, but instead he stopped outside Thirza's cottage.

'Oh, God,' Jenna said, appalled. 'Ross—we can't. She never approved of your marrying me in the first place. You know that. She'll be furious...'

'Have a little faith,' Ross said, as he took her up the path. 'You may get a surprise...'

They found Thirza in the sitting room, sitting beside a crackling log fire and studying a book on ancient embroidery.

She glanced up, her brows rising questioningly as she looked from one to the other.

Ross said quietly, 'Thirza—I've brought my wife home with me.'

'This time to stay, I hope,' his stepmother said with a touch of her old austerity. 'If you've both decided to stop behaving like fools.'

Jenna gave an unsteady laugh. 'I think we have.'

'I'm delighted to hear it.' Thirza got up briskly from her chair. 'Well, Grace has invited me to dinner at Trevarne tonight. I'll make your excuses, shall I?'

'Please.' Jenna nodded, feeling suddenly absurdly shy.

'And as your bedroom won't be occupied I think I'll spend the night there,' Thirza added meditatively. On her way to the door, she patted Jenna's flushed cheek. 'You'll find a spare pillow in the linen cupboard, my dear, if you need it. But I dare say you'll make do with one.'

At the door, she paused, looking back at them.

'And bless you both,' she said. And went out, leaving them alone together.

CHAPTER TEN

THEY went up the narrow stairs hand in hand, past the linen cupboard where the spare pillow would wait in vain, and into the long, low room at the back with the wide bed under its snowy quilt.

In many ways, Jenna thought, it was like their first time together. She stood, shaking, as he undressed her, his face absorbed, his hands and mouth magically gentle as he adored each inch of skin that he uncovered.

'Oh, God.' His voice was ragged when she was finally naked. 'You're so lovely.'

Jenna looked into his eyes and saw his hunger for her. Saw too that it had made him vulnerable—even a little uncertain.

She reached up, pulling his head down to the sudden fierceness of her kiss. 'Then love me!'

Their bodies were fierce, too, as they rose and fell, entwined and urgent, their mutual need driving them on. Later there would be time for tenderness, but now there was shallow hectic breathing, and little feral cries. There was the rasp of sweat-dampened skin, and the cling of mouths that had been starved of kisses for too long. There was a burning compulsion to possess and be possessed, and thereby to transcend all known heights.

There was a sheer physicality that was also spiritual.

There was a yielding and a taking that somehow became one and the same. And at the end, before they were even aware, there was a soaring, almost brutal rapture that left them drained, half weeping in each other's arms.

'I love you,' Ross said hoarsely, when he could speak. 'God, but I love you.'

'Oh, Ross—oh, darling.' She was weeping, partly from joy, partly from the depth of sensual fulfilment she had just experienced. 'I'm sorry. So sorry. All the time we've wasted…'

'Hey, now.' Ross tipped up her face, wiping away the tears with a gentle hand. 'We're together now, and that's all that matters. Isn't it?'

'Yes,' she said. 'That's all.'

He said, 'I also think, my sweet, that we have to stop beating ourselves up over the past. Because we can't change a thing.'

'I know that,' she said. She kissed his shoulder. 'I'm so happy that it scares me. Because in my heart I don't feel I deserve it.'

'You mustn't say that, my love. Perhaps we didn't treat each other very well, but we'll do better in the future.'

He kissed her slowly and very thoroughly. 'I told you once that I wasn't going to make the same mistakes again,' he murmured. 'And I meant it. But I'll make others, and so will you, and we'll have rows, and shout and bang doors. But we'll also remember how very nearly we lost each other, and that will be our salvation.'

She said, 'I'm sorry I cut my hair. I know you hate it.'

'Actually, I think it suits you.' He brushed a few damps strands away from her forehead. 'It was the reason why you had it cut that I hated.' He paused. 'On my way back, that morning, I went into the hairdresser's and persuaded her to give me a long strand of it as a keepsake.'

'Stella did that?' Jenna propped herself up on an elbow. 'What on earth must she have thought?'

'At first that I'd escaped from somewhere. Then I explained, and she melted.' Ross stretched luxuriously. 'Tell me, Mrs Grantham, are you hungry?'

'I suppose I should say, ''Only for you, beloved'',' Jenna said ruefully. 'But the truth is I'm starving.'

Ross grinned at her and threw back the covers. 'So am I. Let's eat.'

He pulled a dark red silk robe from a chair and put it on.

'My God.' Jenna studied it, frowning. 'That looks familiar.'

'It should. You gave it to me our first Christmas together.'

She wrinkled her nose. 'Actually, our only Christmas together. I'm amazed you kept it.'

'I kept everything that had the slightest connection with you,' he said quietly. 'I think my worst moment was finding your wedding ring, pushed into a bag. It was like hearing my own death knell being sounded. Yet there it is—back where it belongs.'

Jenna lay back against the pillows, folding her arms behind her head. 'So,' she said, giving him a deliberately provocative look from under her lashes, 'what am I going to wear?'

Ross laughed. 'Do I get to choose? Because what you have on now is incredibly becoming.'

'Not if I'm covered in goosebumps,' she retorted. 'These old cottages can get very chilly in the evenings.'

'I could supply a remedy for that, too.' Ross gave her a mock leer, then reached into the wardrobe and produced one of his shirts. 'But as an alternative will this do?'

There were two fillet steaks in the fridge, which they grilled and ate along with tiny new potatoes and a tomato salad. They drank Rioja.

Afterwards they made coffee, and drank it in the living

room, sitting on the rug next to the fire, which he had coaxed back to life.

And later, as she sat in the circle of his arms, watching the flames and listening to Debussy's *La Mer* on the hi-fi system, she said softly, 'I'm still hungry.'

'For food?'

'No.'

'Ah,' he said, and began, without haste, to unfasten the buttons on the shirt.

This time his lovemaking was unhurried, too, as he attended to all her wants with exquisite and tantalising finesse, his own pleasures subjected to hers, bringing her over and over again to the brink of climax before he allowed her the ultimate release, muffling her sobbing, enraptured cry with his kiss.

And then it was her turn to please him, using her hands and mouth with voluptuous joy, as she knew he liked her to do. Reviving a thousand passionate, sensuous memories. Until he lifted himself over her and entered her again, to take them both soaring to a new universe that was theirs alone.

Afterwards Ross wrapped his arms around her. He said softly, 'Would you think me very unromantic if I suggested we went up to bed and got some sleep?'

'Not at all.' Jenna burrowed against him. 'I haven't had a full night's rest since I saw you on Trevarne Head.'

She felt him smile against her hair. 'Now, that's a pattern I intend to continue,' he said. 'But for more enjoyable reasons.'

'Really?' Jenna trailed a fingertip down his chest. 'Would you care to provide details?'

'I'd be delighted,' Ross said courteously. 'At some more convenient moment. In the meantime, we have a wedding to attend tomorrow, and it won't look good if we suddenly keel over and start snoring in the middle of the ceremony. Apart from mortifying Christy, we'd probably give Betty Fox a heart attack.'

'I expect she'll have one anyway., when word gets out. You realise we'll be her sole topic of conversation for the foreseeable future?'

'Well,' he said, 'we won't be around to hear it.'

'You don't want us to remarry in the parish church.'

'I want to marry you,' he said, 'with a special licence, in London, as soon as it can be arranged. But we'll come back here for the christening.' He ran a questing hand the length of her body and sighed regretfully. 'Now, up with you, minx. Put the spark guard in front of the fire while I lock up.'

'Yes, my lord,' Jenna said demurely, doing a little questing on her own account, then jumping up and running off, laughing as he reached for her.

Once they were in bed Ross went to sleep almost at once, one arm thrown protectively across her body. But Jenna stayed awake for a little while, for the sheer joy of feeling his weight next to her and hearing his quiet, steady breathing.

It was true, she thought, marvelling. Love did conquer all. It had fought pain and bitterness and recrimination, and won triumphantly. And she and Ross were both the victors.

When she did finally close her eyes, her rest was quiet and dreamless.

Even through the waves of sleep that still engulfed her, Jenna was aware that something was wrong. That a noise was intruding upon her consciousness.

She forced open unwilling eyelids and listened. Someone, she realised without pleasure, seemed to be knocking on the front door.

Thirza must have decided not to stay at Trevarne House after all, she thought, making use of Ross's shirt again and buttoning it more decorously this time.

He hadn't stirred, of course, and she bent, dropping a wry kiss on his hair before treading barefoot out of the room and down the stairs.

The pounding on the door hadn't abated at all. Indeed, it seemed to have increased in impatience.

'Hold on, I'm coming,' she called, as she took the key from its hook and turned it in the massive lock.

As the door opened her brows snapped together in a frown of sheer incredulity as she saw who was standing on the doorstep.

'Natasha?' She shook her head in bewilderment. 'What are you doing here?'

'I drove down. I was worried about you—about the situation here. And how right I was.' Natasha's eyes, burning like hot coals, travelled over Jenna's half-clad body. 'Very fetching.' She used the words like daggers. 'I was on my way up to Trevarne when I met this man coming away— Adrian something. Christy's intended, I suppose. He told me you were down here—and why.' She paused. 'Well, aren't you going to invite me in? I've had a hell of a journey.'

'Tasha.' Jenna hesitated, feeling embarrassed and self-conscious. 'This isn't my house. I can't really invite you to stay here.' She wanted to feel sorry about that, because Natasha really did look tired, her face strained and her skin sallow. She knew she should be more welcoming, but somehow it was impossible.

'I don't want to stay,' Natasha said curtly. 'I want you to get in the car and come back to London with me. Now. Before you make an even more abject fool of yourself over Ross Grantham.'

Her mouth twisted contemptuously. 'I see he's managed to get you into bed. But, then, that's his speciality, isn't it? Giving women a wonderful, unforgettable time sexually. A one way ticket to Paradise. And I suppose it's a novelty—doing it with his ex-wife. But don't fool yourself, Jenna. The novelty will soon wear off, and he'll be on to the next lucky girl in line.'

She was in the hall by this time, pushing the heavy door shut behind her, and Jenna found herself wanting to take a step backwards.

Don't be stupid, she adjured herself silently. You're half awake and off-balance, that's all.

Aloud, she said gently, 'Natasha—it isn't what you think.'

'Wrong.' Natasha walked past her into the living room, switching on the wall lamps and undoing her trench coat. 'Wrong. It's exactly what I think. Because you have that look about you again—that sleek, cat-that-got-the-cream look that I always hated. There were times when you came sneaking back at dawn when I swear I could smell him on you.'

She drew a breath, eyes half closed. 'That unique clean scent of his skin, mixed up with that cologne he always used.'

Jenna began to feel cold in a way that had no connection with her admittedly scanty covering, or the temperature of the room.

This was a deep, bone-aching chill that she knew of old. And it was called fear.

'I suppose I can't really blame you,' Natasha went on, almost conversationally. 'You have been celibate for some time, and Ross is a marvellous lay. Why shouldn't you indulge yourself—have some fun? But now it's time to wake up to reality again, my pet. You finished with Ross.

You divorced him because he was blatantly and cruelly unfaithful. As he's always been. And as he always will be.' She shrugged. 'I don't think he can help himself.'

Jenna made a small sound and Natasha stared at her. 'Why, Jenna, sweetie, you've gone quite pale.' She giggled. 'What's the matter, pussy cat? Has your cream suddenly gone sour?'

Jenna steadied herself. Any moment now, she thought, I'm going to wake up and find this whole thing has been a nightmare.

She said quietly, 'I'm not going back to London until after the wedding, Natasha. And when I do Ross will be with me. We're getting married again.'

'Why, yes.' Natasha sounded amused. 'Adrian, the bridegroom to be mentioned something of the kind. But it's all nonsense, you know, Jenna. Ross and marriage simply don't work. And you can't take him back just because he's fabulous in the sack. All serial womanisers are. It's their stock in trade.'

'Thank you,' Ross said politely, 'for the unexpected testimonial. But then, Natasha, you're always so—unexpected.'

Neither of them had been aware of his approach. He was also barefoot, wrapped in the red silk robe, leaning against the door frame. He was smiling, but his eyes were black ice.

He said, 'To what do we owe this—signal honour?'

'Jenna is my best friend,' Natasha flung at him through taut lips. 'Also my business partner. I came to rescue her.'

'How very dramatic of you,' Ross drawled. 'I wasn't aware that she needed rescuing.'

'Oh, but she does,' Natasha said, nodding. 'She really does. From a love rat like you.'

'You have a nice turn of phrase,' he said. 'If the art game
ever palls, you could get a job on a tabloid newspaper.'

'Don't you laugh at me.' Her voice shook with some
suppressed emotion. 'Don't you dare laugh.'

'Please believe that I find nothing even remotely amusing
in this situation.' Ross straightened and took a step into the
room, tightening the sash of his robe. He said, 'Jenna, darling, haven't you offered your best friend and business partner some refreshment after she's driven all this way in the
middle of the night?' He tutted reprovingly. 'How remiss
of you, when she's been to all this trouble. And on your
behalf, too.' He paused. 'Or did you ask her to come?'

Jenna said tonelessly, 'I didn't invite her, and I don't
know why she's here.'

His brows lifted. 'You mean she just—turned up?'

'She telephoned this afternoon just before the rehearsal.
I—I told her that you were here, and that it had brought
back a lot of memories I'd thought buried. But I never
asked her for help.'

She hesitated, then went on, her voice faltering a little.
'Ross—she's been saying—hinting at—things. I need you
to tell me they're not true.'

'Only hinting? You surprise me.' He looked at Natasha,
his face hardening. 'You have your captive audience. Why
not open the whole can of worms? Or are you waiting for
me to tell Jenna that we once slept together?'

Jenna took a step backwards, her hand flying to her
mouth. 'Oh, no.' It was a moan. 'Please—no.'

'Unfortunately, yes. But it was before I met you again.
And I had no idea that she was your flatmate, or that she
even knew you.'

'Why—why did you not say—something?'

'Because I don't kiss and tell. Also, I didn't see what

possible good it would do. I thought she would feel the same, but I was wrong.'

'Oh, yes,' Natasha said huskily. 'Wrong about so many things. You really thought you could become my lover, then drop me—*me*—when something better came along?'

'Natasha,' he said. 'We had sex together—once. Not a raging affair.'

Natasha swung round to Jenna, her face gloating. 'I was there first, Jenna. How does that make you feel? I was before you in that beautiful riverside apartment of his. Before you in his bed.'

'Oh, God,' Jenna whispered. 'Oh, dear God.'

Ross came over to her. He took her hand and held it tightly. 'Jenna, listen to me. I met Natasha at a party. We started talking, and as we were leaving I asked if she'd like to go for a drink. We went to a bar, and then back to my place. She said all the right things, made all the right moves, but I already knew it was a mistake.

'So I made noises about a heavy day tomorrow and offered to get her a cab. She asked if she could use the bathroom. She was gone for such a long time I thought she'd been taken ill. I found her in my room, stretched across the bed without a stitch on. She looked spectacular, and it seemed—churlish to disappoint her. Another big mistake. When it was over I called the cab and she disappeared— out of my life, I thought. But I was wrong.'

'Don't listen to him,' Natasha said, smiling. 'He seduced me. He couldn't keep his hands off me. He wanted me to stay the night.'

His voice was ice. 'Believe me, Natasha, that was the last thing I wanted.'

He turned back to Jenna. 'She hadn't wasted her time in the apartment. She'd taken my phone number, mobile number, and even the name of the agency.' He sighed impa-

tiently. 'I began to get daily calls. She wanted to come
round and cook me a meal. She had theatre tickets. There
was this film she was dying to see. A couple of times I
came out of the agency and found her outside. She said she
happened to be passing, but I began to feel hunted—as if
I was being stalked. And I was beginning to run out of
excuses as to why I couldn't see her.'

'But you did see me again,' Natasha said. She sounded
complacent, almost triumphant, as if nothing he'd been saying had impinged on her. 'I asked you to the private view
at the gallery and you came.'

'Yes,' he said. 'I planned to take you to dinner afterwards
and tell you as gently as possible that it wouldn't work in
a hundred years, to ask you not to call me again.'

He looked at Jenna, his eyes softening. 'But then I saw
you, my love, and everything else went out of my head.
Everything but the need to be with you, and you only.'

He paused. 'I intended to call Natasha, to apologise and
explain, but she called me first. I'd expected her to be angry, but I wasn't prepared for the tirade of hysterical abuse
that hit me. She'd got it into her head that we were into
some on-going relationship and that I'd jilted her.

'And then it stopped, as if she'd thrown a switch, and
she was all sweetness and light and being incredibly understanding about me being a man who couldn't keep his
bloody zip fastened. I think she even forgave me at one
point, and said we'd start again. I told her that we wouldn't.
That I was involved, and in love. And she went very quiet.
When she spoke again, she said it was far from over between us, and that unless I accepted it she'd make me sorry.

'I told her I was already sorrier than she could have ever
dreamed, and rang off.'

Jenna said, 'But that wasn't the end of it—was it? I heard

her on the office phone once. She must have been talking to you.'

'Probably,' he said. 'Unless she had a whole series of us staked out across London.' He put an arm round Jenna and drew her close. He said, 'And then the anonymous calls started. And all that other stuff.'

Natasha said thickly, 'You can't prove a thing.'

'It was your scent on the handkerchief, and the shirt,' Ross said. 'I recognised it at once, because it was one I'd never liked and you were wearing it at that party.'

'Tigresse,' Jenna whispered. She stared at Natasha. Her friend. Her business partner. A woman with a stranger's face. 'Your special occasion scent. Why didn't I recognise it?'

'Because you had no reason to make the connection,' Ross said grimly. 'But I did. And you worked with her, invited her to the house, so it was easy for her to plant the evidence.'

'Oh, Natasha.' Jenna's voice broke. 'How could you?'

'Because I wanted him.' The older woman's voice throbbed with bitterness. 'I could have made him happy if he'd just given me a chance, and instead I had to stand there and watch him walk off with you. I swore I'd make you both sorry, and I did.'

The look she sent Jenna was sly, almost gleeful. 'Even I never imagined how successful I'd be at that.'

'So what brought you here tonight?' Ross asked quietly. 'The need to make more trouble—to convince Jenna that I was just a worthless, womanising bastard who'd break her heart all over again? Or did it go deeper than that? Was it her admission that being with me had stimulated all kinds of lost memories that made you come running?'

Natasha threw her head back haughtily. 'I don't know what you're talking about.'

'I think you do,' Ross said. 'I've always thought so. Always had this terrible suspicion that maybe Jenna's fall in the gallery that day wasn't as accidental as it was made out to be.' He studied her with narrowed, inimical eyes. 'After all, you were alone together when it happened.'

'Ross,' Jenna intervened, troubled. 'I think that's taking things too far. Tasha was nowhere near me when I tripped.'

'Is that what you did?' He held her shoulders, looking deeply into her eyes. 'On one of the few occasions I could get you to talk about it, you said you'd slipped. That's a very different thing. So which was it, Jenna?'

'You want her to remember that?' Natasha spat at him. 'The worst day of her life? Don't do this, Jenna. You'll only distress yourself.'

'I think it's a little late for you to worry about that,' Ross said harshly. 'But that's why you're here, isn't it. Because you're terrified that among all the other memories she might recall just how she came to fall that day.'

Jenna was very still. 'I didn't trip,' she said. 'I was going down the stairs, carrying a picture, and I stood on something—something that rolled under my foot—and I—went forward.'

'A pencil?' Ross said. 'Or a pen, perhaps? Which was it, Natasha?'

She stared at him, her eyes glittering. 'Are you completely mad? I was the one who looked after her. Who got the ambulance when I realised she was bleeding.'

'By which time it was too late, of course.' Ross sounded bleak, and unutterably weary.

Jenna detached herself gently from his clasp and went over to Natasha. She said, 'Tell me—please tell me you didn't do this. That you didn't put something on the stairs, hoping that I'd fall.'

'Pride always comes before a fall.' Natasha was

breathing hoarsely, her breasts rising and falling swiftly. 'And you were so proud, Jenna, so pleased that you were carrying that bastard's child. Everything you needed to make your happiness complete, you said. Everything I was never going to have.

'And I hated you for that. For making him love you. For taking him away from me—*me*. And for having his baby.' She shook her head slowly. 'I—really couldn't allow that…'

She smiled almost reminiscently. 'It wasn't anything that I'd planned. I could see you were having trouble on the stairs, and I decided to help that on a little. There was a piece of dowel in the office, and I put it one of the steps.' She shrugged. 'After that, it was in the lap of the gods.

'You could have missed it completely. And there was a moment when I almost stopped you. Because I always liked you, Jenna. It was only Ross that came between us. Once he was out of the way, we could be friends again. And we were.' Her smile was placid, almost childlike. 'Weren't we?'

'Yes,' Jenna said, breaking the appalled silence. She was shivering. 'Yes, we were. You were—good to me.'

'I needed to make amends,' Natasha said, making it sound totally reasonable. 'It's a terrible thing to lose a baby.' Her face seemed to shrink, become much older. 'Almost as bad as never having one.'

'Natasha.' Jenna's voice rang with pain. 'Don't. You'll meet someone—who'll love you…' And she faltered into silence, because she knew it wasn't true.

Natasha was too damaged, too unstable ever to sustain a relationship. She needed help, and maybe had done so for a very long time.

'But I wanted Ross,' Natasha said simply. 'And now you have him—again.'

Her hand came out of her pocket, holding a small sharp knife, and she lunged towards Jenna, her face twisted, almost unrecognisable. Only Ross was there first, grabbing her, seizing the hand that held the knife and forcing her to drop it. Holding her until she stopped struggling.

For a moment there was silence, then a new sound filled the room—the noise of weeping, huge tearing sobs interspersed with small animal cries, and Natasha sank down to the carpet, curling herself into a small, defensive ball, her hands covering her face and her whole body shaking.

Ross looked across at Jenna, who was standing, white-faced and wide-eyed, her hand pressed to her throat, still trying to comprehend everything she had seen and heard.

He said gently, 'Darling, you have to ring for an ambulance—and the police. Can you do that? I think I should stay here—keep an eye on her.'

She stirred, said in a low voice, 'Does it have to be the police?'

'Yes,' he said. 'This whole thing has gone far enough. She's a danger—not just to us, but to herself. We can't let it pass.'

When the emergency services arrived Natasha was relatively calm again and sitting in a chair. 'It's so kind of you all,' she kept saying. 'So kind of you to help me.'

Jenna couldn't bear to watch her being taken away, so she escaped into the kitchen. Where Ross found her, sitting at the kitchen table, her hands folded in her lap, staring into space.

She said, 'I was going to make some coffee, but I couldn't open the jar.'

'I'll do it,' he said. 'And I'll get us both some brandy, too. I think we need it.'

'Yes,' she said. She swallowed. 'Ross—that was so awful. Because that was the vegetable knife she had with her.

Something I've used myself in the kitchen when we shared a flat.' She shuddered. 'I—I still can't really believe any of this. That she could do these things...'

'Nor I,' he said quietly. 'Even though I did have my suspicions about her from the first. There was something odd about her—something that warned me to steer clear. I know Seb felt it, too, when we had them over for dinner.' He shrugged, his face cynical. 'But she had a beautiful body, and I was fool enough to be tempted.'

'Why didn't you tell me that you knew her?' Jenna asked quietly. 'That you'd been to bed with her?'

His mouth tightened painfully. 'I meant to—and I should have done, as soon as I realised how close you were to her. But we had only just got together, darling, and what we had was all so new—so fragile. I was afraid of damaging our own relationship. And later—it never seemed the right time, apart from being a pretty unsavoury incident.

'I hoped, you see, that I was wrong about her. That she'd find herself a man of her own and the whole thing could be quietly forgotten.' He shook his head. 'Only she had other ideas.'

Jenna shivered. 'What will happen to her?'

'I've no idea. I suppose the whole mental health machinery will swing into action. We'll have to make statements at some point.' He paused. 'Did she have any family?'

'I don't know,' Jenna said slowly. 'She never talked about them. I suppose I should have realised that was—strange.' She sighed. 'And I shared a flat with her—a place of work. I should have known. I feel as if I'm to blame...'

'No, Jenna.' Ross knelt beside her chair, capturing her hands firmly in his. 'You must never think that. I am certain that whatever was wrong with Natasha began a long time

ago, before she met either of us, although I suspect I might
have been the catalyst.'

She said quietly, 'Poor Natasha.'

'You can say that?' Ross's brows snapped together. 'My
darling, she could have killed you that day in the gallery.
And tonight she tried to stab you—do you serious damage.
And you can still feel sorry for her?'

'Yes.' She freed one hand, so that she could touch his
face. Stroke his hair. Reassure herself that her own personal
miracle had really happened.

Her smile was wavering, but it was a smile just the same,
and her eyes were shining with everything she felt for him.
'Because we have everything. And she has nothing.'

Ross bent his head, and put his lips against her bare knee.
'Yes,' he said. 'My one and only love. We have everything.
Poor Natasha.'

It had been a wonderful wedding. Everyone was agreed on
that. The weather was perfect, the bride looked radiant, and
the reception was going with a swing.

The bridesmaid, it was felt, looked a little pale, but there
were rumours flying about some fuss in the village the previous night.

'One of they stalkers,' Betty Fox said with relish. 'Terrible, they are, by all accounts.' Her tone suggested it would
provide valuable material to chew over in the days to come.
'Still, no harm done,' she added with faint regret.

Ross had dealt with the celebratory messages with charm
and aplomb, and now he was rising with a glass in his hand.

'Ladies and gentlemen,' he said. 'This is the moment
when it's my duty as best man to propose the health of the
bridesmaid. But on this occasion I'm combining it with
another toast. So, will you please rise and drink with me
to Jenna, and to the happiness of my once and future wife.'

Jenna sat, flushed and laughing, amid the surprised cries and smug smiles. Christy and Adrian were the first on their feet, glasses raised. Further down the table she could see Thirza nodding wisely, and Aunt Grace dabbing at her eyes with a lace handkerchief.

And when the dancing began she and Ross were applauded warmly as they followed the bride and groom on to the floor.

'Happy?' Ross whispered, holding her closely.

'More than you will ever know.' She looked into his eyes, afraid no longer. Knowing what she would see there. Glorying in the passion, the tenderness and the need.

And in the certainty of a love that would last for the rest of their lives.

The Token Wife

SARA CRAVEN

PROLOGUE

WHEN Alex Fabian was displeased, his annoyance invariably radiated from him like static electricity, alerting the wary to keep their distance.

Tonight, entering his grandmother's Holland Park house, he was crackling like an approaching storm, although he managed a brief smile for the elderly manservant who admitted him, and who'd known him since childhood.

'Barney—you're well? And Mrs Barnes?'

'Both fighting fit, thank you, Mr Alex.' Barnes paused. 'Her ladyship hasn't come downstairs yet, but you'll find Mr Fabian in the drawing room.'

'My father?' Alex's brows snapped together. 'I thought they weren't speaking to each other.'

'There has been a rapprochement, sir.' Barnes' tone was sedate. 'Last week.'

'I see.' Alex shrugged off his overcoat, and cast a fleeting but critical glance at his reflection in the big gilt-framed mirror before crossing the wide hall to the double doors which led into the drawing room.

He supposed he should have fitted in a visit to the barber, he thought, raking an irritable hand through the tawny hair which brushed his collar.

But the charcoal suit he was wearing, set off by a silk waistcoat in a paler shade of grey, the pristine white shirt, and discreetly striped tie acknowledged that this was a formal visit.

That he'd been sent for.

And his tight-lipped expression and smouldering green eyes indicated that he suspected what was behind the summons.

He found George Fabian seated on one of the sofas that flanked the fireplace, glancing through a newspaper.

He said, without looking up, 'Good evening, Alex. We have been instructed to help ourselves to a drink.'

'Thank you, sir, but it's a little early for me.' Alex glanced pointedly at his watch. 'I wasn't sure whether I was being invited for dinner, or nursery tea.'

'I suggest you ask your grandmother that,' his father advised curtly. 'This little family gathering was her idea, not mine.'

'And its purpose?' Alex walked to the hearth and gave the logs that burned there an impatient kick with a well-shod foot.

'I understand to discuss the arrangements for her birthday party.' George Fabian paused. 'Among other things.'

'Indeed?' Alex's brows rose sardonically. 'And am I permitted to speculate what those "other things" might be?'

His father gave him a dry look. 'I imagine your position as chairman in waiting at Perrins Bank might come up for discussion.'

There was a silence, then Alex said, with a touch of hauteur, 'Are you implying that it could be in some doubt? I wasn't aware that my ability to run the bank was being called into question.'

'It isn't, as far as I know.' George Fabian folded the paper, and tossed it aside. 'It's more a matter of image.' He pursed his lips meditatively. 'Too many pictures in the wrong sort of paper. Too many pieces in the gossip columns. And too many girls,' he added flatly.

'I wasn't aware that I required a vow of celibacy to work at Perrins.' Alex kept his tone light, but his fingers beat a restless tattoo on the edge of the mantelpiece. The fact that he'd been expecting this made it no less unwelcome, he thought, his edginess increasing.

'Then think again,' his father said brusquely. 'Perrins is an old-fashioned bank, run by conservative people, and they don't like the kind of adverse publicity you've been attracting.'

He shook his head. 'The customers want to know that there's someone solid and reliable at the top, whom they can trust. Not a playboy.' He paused. 'You're a high-flyer, Alex, but you're getting perilously close to the sun. Take care you don't come crashing down.'

'Thank you,' Alex said with dangerous politeness. 'Have you been asked to pass on these words of wisdom, or was it all your own work?'

George Fabian sighed wearily. 'Don't be so damned prickly, boy. I'm your father, so I think I have the right to be concerned. I don't want to see you throw away the potential for a brilliant career.'

'If the worst happens, there are other banks besides Perrins,' Alex said tautly.

'Indeed there are,' his father agreed. He gave the younger man a long, steady look. 'Unless, of course, you become too hot for any of them to handle.'

There was a silence, then Alex said quietly, 'Maybe I will have that drink after all.' He went over to the side-table, where decanters and glasses were set out, pouring himself a single malt whisky. 'So.' He turned back, glass in hand, his expression challenging. 'What's the rumour on the piazza?'

'This and that.' Mr Fabian paused. 'I gather Peter Crosby is going to be promoted in the next government reshuffle,' he added almost inconsequentially.

Alex stiffened. 'And?'

'And that means he'll become of increasing interest to the tabloids.'

George Fabian drank some of his own whisky. 'I gather the *Daily Mercury* is already on red alert. And that a news team has been detailed to keep a close eye on his wife.'

There was another, longer silence. Then, 'I see,' said Alex, his voice expressionless.

'In addition,' Mr Fabian went on, 'there's an unconfirmed report that Crosby has consulted a lawyer, and is considering hiring a private detective to follow Mrs Crosby, and monitor her calls.

'There are no children, of course, and he may be preparing to dump the beautiful Lucinda before she jeopardises his triumphant march to power by some further indiscretion. You're not the first, you know.'

'I am aware of that.' Alex's look and tone were icy.

'And it's by no means certain he would go for a simple, no-fault divorce. He has the reputation of being a vindictive bastard.' He gave his son another steady look. 'He could decide to name and shame.'

'It's a pity the bloody gossip-mongers haven't something better to do.' Alex threw the whisky down his throat with a jerky movement.

'They have their uses,' his father returned placidly. 'Perhaps you should be grateful to them. Featuring in a messy, high-profile divorce is something that the Perrins board would never stand for in their chairman.'

Alex's smile glittered. 'Gratitude is not my overriding emotion at the moment.'

George Fabian looked concerned. 'I hope you're not going to tell me that Lucinda Crosby is the love of your life.'

'Certainly not.' His son gave a cynical shrug. 'I doubt if such a creature exists.' He'd been thoroughly enjoying his liaison with Cindy Crosby who was not only beautiful but also sexually voracious, he thought with an inward grimace. But he'd been planning to end it anyway, married women not being entirely to his taste.

He gave his father a stony look. 'I hope that reassures you.'

'Don't congratulate yourself too soon,' Mr Fabian cautioned. 'You're not out of the woods yet.' He paused. 'Have you ever heard your grandmother talk about a cousin of hers who went off to South Africa just before the war—Archie Maidstone?'

Alex frowned. 'Yes, she's mentioned him. I got the impression she'd been very fond of him at one time, and then he got himself into some kind of trouble, and had to be shunted out of the country.'

'That's the one.' George Fabian nodded. 'He had a job with Perrins, and embezzled some money. The family closed ranks and made good the loss, apparently, but he was warned never to come back to England.'

'And has he?' Alex gave a faint whistle. 'He must be a hell of an age.'

'Actually, he's dead,' said Mr Fabian. 'But his grandson isn't, and he's been over here visiting. Building bridges. Seems to have made an excellent impression on your grandmother, too.' He paused. 'He even got her to invite him down to Rosshampton for the weekend.'

Alex's attention was suddenly, sharply focused. 'Go on.'

'He's married,' said George Fabian. 'And she's asked him to come back for her birthday, and bring his wife so that he can show her Rosshampton too.'

Alex went on staring at him. 'Meaning?'

'Just that your inheritance may not be as secure as you thought,' his father said bluntly. 'There's an alternative claimant.'

'I'm her only grandson,' Alex said. 'What is this guy —a second…third cousin? And she's always said that Rosshampton will ultimately come to me. You really think that's in doubt?'

'I don't know,' George Fabian admitted. 'But she's very taken with him—and the fact that he's married…stable. She likes that—and she may have been drawing a few unfavourable comparisons.'

Alex's mouth had firmed into a steely straight line. 'I see.' He glanced up at the picture on the wall above him, a water-colour that he had commissioned for Lady Perrin's eightieth birthday. He saw the elegant grey stone house sheltering among the ancient trees; the sunlight falling in swathes across the sweeping lawns, and, in the distance, the gleam of water.

He thought, with a pang, of how many of the happiest weeks of his childhood had been spent there. How, over the years, it unerringly drew him back to its rock-like security. How it had always seemed enshrined in his heart, timeless and unchanging, waiting for him to become its master.

And his grandmother had encouraged that, he thought with a pang of disquiet. Had deliberately fostered his love for the house, and let him think that it would one day be his.

And now, for the first time, there was a doubt in his mind. A shadow in the sunlight that disturbed him perhaps more than any of the other unpalatable things that had been said to him tonight.

This unknown South African, he thought, his hand tightening round his empty glass. This grandson of a man who'd been sent away in disgrace, but for whom Selina Perrin might cherish tender memories. This man was going to steal Rosshampton from him? Over his dead body!

Then the door opened, and Lady Perrin came in. She was wearing one of the elegant long black dresses she favoured for the evening, and her snowy hair was piled on top of her head in an imperious knot.

Alex saw that she was using the silver-topped cane she usually despised as a sign of weakness, and realised that she must be in real pain from her arthritis to give way like that. The anger and unease within him was replaced by a swift compassion he dared not show.

His father received a brief inclination of the head, and, 'Good evening, George.'

Then she was turning to himself, the fierce eyes beneath their arched brows sweeping him from head to foot, the carefully painted mouth stretching in a wintry smile.

'My dear Alexander. Quite a stranger.'

Alex took her hand, and kissed the scented cheek. 'Never to you, Gran dear.'

'Hmm.' Selina Perrin made her way to the other sofa, and sat with an effort, accepting the dry sherry that Alex brought her with a word of thanks. 'Now, come and sit with me, and tell me everything you've been doing—apart from what I read about in the papers, of course. There's quite enough of that.'

'Ah,' Alex said lightly. 'You should never believe all the papers say. But I've always thought that if you work hard, you should be allowed to play hard too.'

'I have no objection to that,' she said. 'Just to your occasional choice of playmate. And don't glare at your father,' she added calmly. 'He didn't tell me about the Crosby woman. I already knew.'

Alex bit his lip. 'What a pity you never worked for MI5, darling.'

'There weren't the same openings for women in my day.' She paused. 'Isn't it time, Alexander, that you left other men's wives alone, and found a decent, respectable girl of your own? Settled down?'

He'd expected a sly ambush over dinner, not this frontal attack, and had to make a swift recovery.

'How dull you make it sound, Gran,' he said lightly. 'Besides, I'd be the last man on earth a girl like that would want to marry.'

'Specious nonsense,' Lady Perrin said contemptuously. 'And you know it. You're doing the family no credit, Alexander, and it has to stop. And I refuse to allow the bank to be affected by your rackety behaviour. You're—what? Thirty-three?'

'Thirty-two,' he said, instantly cross with himself for rising to the bait.

'Precisely. You should have sown your wild oats by now.'

He was seething inwardly. 'Perhaps you'd like to suggest a suitable candidate?'

'I could suggest dozens,' his grandmother said calmly. 'But I certainly wouldn't jeopardise their chances by naming them.'

In spite of himself, he found his lips twitching. 'Gran, you're impossible.'

'I'm also serious,' Lady Perrin returned implacably. 'It's my birthday in three months' time. I shall expect you to attend it with your bride.'

Alex was shaken to the roots. From the opposite sofa, he could see his father staring at them both in open incredulity.

He said quietly, 'Darling, that's quite impossible. You must see that. How could I possibly meet someone...persuade her to marry me in that sort of time frame?'

'You are wealthy, clearly attractive to women, and blessed with far more charm than you deserve.' Selina Perrin's tone was resolute. 'It should be entirely within your capabilities.' She paused. 'I would not wish to be disappointed.'

The warning was there—implicit—staring him in the face.

He said, with a touch of desperation, 'Grandmother...'

'Besides,' she went on, as if he had not spoken, 'Rosshampton is a family house—a home waiting to be occupied. I must warn you, Alexander, that I should not wish it to become a bachelor pad. Or, indeed, permit that to happen. Do I make myself clear?'

Alex stared at her, the colour draining from his face, the blood drumming in his ears.

He said hoarsely, 'Clear as crystal.' And saw her give a brief, satisfied smile.

Reaching for her cane, she rose purposefully to her feet. 'Then let us go into dinner. I hope you're both hungry.'

He couldn't speak for his father, Alex thought grimly as he followed her to the door, but his own appetite had been killed stone dead.

He'd come prepared for disapproval, and instead been presented with an ultimatum.

But he wasn't going to let Rosshampton go without a struggle, he told himself. And, although she was infuriating, he did love his grandmother.

If his inheritance depended on him finding a girl to marry in the next three months, then a wife he would have.

But a wife on my own terms, he thought as he took his place at the dining table. Not yours—my dear, clever Gran. And we'll see, shall we, who has the last laugh?

CHAPTER ONE

'LOUISE—are you up there? What on earth are you doing?'

Louise Trentham, on her knees in the loft, surrounded by open trunks full of elderly clothing, heard her stepmother's querulous tones from the landing below, and grimaced faintly.

'I'm looking for thirties evening dresses,' she called back. 'For the Village Players.'

'Well, come down, please,' Marian Trentham said sharply. 'I can't conduct a conversation peering up into a hole.'

Lou sighed inwardly, but made her way over to the hatch, and swung slim, denim-clad legs onto the loft ladder.

'Is something wrong?' she enquired as she made her way down. 'I made up the rooms as you told me, and did the flowers. And all the food is in the refrigerator, ready for Mrs Gladwin.'

'That's the trouble,' Mrs Trentham said crossly. 'She's just telephoned to say her eldest child is ill again, and she won't be able to cook dinner tonight. And she knows how important this evening is.'

Lou reflected drily that there probably wasn't a soul in the known universe who wasn't aware that Alex Fabian was coming for the weekend. And why.

She said, 'It's hardly her fault. Tim can't help being asthmatic.' She paused. 'Why don't you have dinner at the Royal Oak instead?'

'At a public house?' Mrs Trentham reared back as if her stepdaughter had suggested a visit to a burger joint.

'A very upmarket one,' Lou pointed out. 'With a restaurant in all the food guides. In fact, you'll be lucky to get a table.'

'Because it's intended to be a quiet family meal,' Marian Trentham said tartly.

'Offering Alex Fabian a preview of domestic bliss?' Lou's cool face relaxed into a sudden grin. 'From what I hear, he'd prefer the Royal Oak any day of the week.'

Her stepmother's lips thinned. 'Please don't be more irritating than you can help, Louise. On an occasion like this, the right atmosphere is essential.'

'Shouldn't he and Ellie create their own ambience?' Lou enquired mildly. 'Especially when he's sweeping her off her feet into marriage?'

'Well, I don't intend to stand here arguing about it,' Marian Trentham said with finality. 'I simply came to say that you'll have to stand in for Mrs Gladwin, and do the cooking.'

Lou had seen this coming a mile off, and she had no real objections. But the word 'please' would not have come amiss, she thought wryly.

'Shouldn't Ellie do it?' she suggested straight-faced. 'Convince him that she has all the wifely virtues?'

'He's more likely to run out of the house, screaming,' Marian said, with one of her rare glimmers of humour. 'Ellie could burn boiling water. Not that it matters, of course,' she added, reverting to briskness. 'When she's married, there'll be staff to attend to that kind of thing.'

'Of course there will,' Lou murmured. 'Silly me.'

There's staff here too, she thought. And I seem to be it.

'So that's settled, is it?' said Marian. 'You'll cook tonight's dinner? I thought you might do that mushroom soup you're so good at—and an orange sauce with the ducks.'

'Fine,' Lou said equably. 'And, having done so, am I expected to join this quiet family party?'

Marian hesitated for a micro-second too long. 'But of course. If you'd like to. It's entirely up to you, naturally.'

Lou took pity on her. 'Actually, I think I'll pass. Odd numbers and all that. And anyway, I have to go out. There's a rehearsal at the village hall, and I need to get these costumes settled.'

Marian's eyes took on that slightly glazed look which appeared when village matters were under discussion. Marian was a big-city woman. She liked the idea of a weekend country home—something to mention casually in conversation, and invite people to—rather than the reality of it. And she took a minimal part in local activities.

'Well, just as you please,' she said, adding, 'Lou, dear,' as an afterthought. 'And see if you can find something for Ellie to do, would you?' She attempted a silvery laugh. 'She's getting absurdly nervous, silly girl.'

Left to herself, Lou replaced the loft ladder thoughtfully. She didn't mind being part-time caretaker in the house where she'd been born and keeping it pristine for the occasional descents from London by the rest of her family. But sometimes she felt a flicker of resentment at being taken so much for granted.

But it wouldn't be for much longer, she thought, giving herself a mental shake. Because she too was getting married, and would be moving to the tall Georgian house in the main square which belonged to David Sanders, her future husband, who would be furious if he discovered she was acting as head cook and bottle-washer again.

'They're just using you, darling,' he told her over and over again. 'And you're too sweet to mind.'

Lou had never regarded herself as particularly sweet, but it was nice to hear, she acknowledged contentedly.

She shrugged. 'It's no big deal. And it gives me something to do when you're away.'

David worked for the regional office of a national firm of auctioneers and valuers. A recent promotion had involved him in a lot more travelling, and attendance at a series of courses in London, which had left Lou to her own devices more than she cared for, if she was honest.

Her own day job was working as a paralegal at the leading firm of solicitors in the nearby market town. The plan was that she would go on working until they started a family.

She loved the sound of that. Loved the thought of the future they would have together. It seemed to her that there had never been a time when David had not been a part of her life. They'd played as children, fought and made up again as teenagers, and rediscovered each other when he came back from university. And for the past year they'd been unofficially engaged.

It would have been put on a formal footing with a party for family and friends but for the sudden death of David's father, and his mother's subsequent refusal to cope with anything that approximated to 'happy'.

'She will come to the wedding, won't she?' Lou had asked at one point, with a faint irony that was lost on David.

'Of course,' he'd said, kissing her. 'She just needs time, that's all. Be patient.'

Secretly, Lou found patience difficult with David's mother, whom she suspected to be milking widowhood for all it was worth. For one thing, it provided her with an excuse not to leave the family home, which now technically belonged to her son, and move to the bungalow in Bournemouth that she was to share with her sister. Something which had been planned forever, but which now seemed to have been shifted to the back burner.

But it would have to happen sooner or later, Lou assured herself. Because she was congenitally unfitted to share a roof with Mrs Sanders, and David knew it.

So, for the time being, she occupied Virginia Cottage in peace, most of the time, occasionally allowing herself memories of the time when she'd lived there with her mother, enjoying much the same placid existence, with her father coming home at weekends from Trentham Osborne, the independent publishing company which he ran in Bloomsbury.

But following Anne Trentham's shocking and unexpected death after a two-day illness from a strain of viral pneumonia, Lou's whole life had changed. She had been sent away to boarding-school, and her holidays had been spent with Aunt Barbara, her mother's only sister, her big farmer husband and their rowdy, kind, loving family.

But no sooner had she become adapted to this new set of circumstances than they changed too. Her father, his eyes sliding away in embarrassment, had told her that he was getting married again, and she would have a stepmother and sister.

Ellie would be going to the same school, and the rest of the time would be divided between the flat in London and Virginia Cottage.

In retrospect, Lou could see that her father had been involved with Marian long before her mother's death, and that Ellie might well be her half-sister, but by the time she was old enough to realise this, it no longer seemed to matter that much. Marian could be kind enough when she remembered. And Ellie—well, Ellie truly deserved David's epithet 'sweet'.

She was blonde like her mother, but lacked Marian's statuesque build. She was small, blue-eyed and shy, with a pretty, heart-shaped face, in total contrast to Lou, who was taller, and thin rather than slender, with a cloud of unruly dark hair. Lou had pale, creamy skin, and long-lashed grey eyes that were undoubtedly the best feature in a face that she herself dismissed as nondescript. And she had learned, over the years, to appear calm and self-contained.

At school she had soon found herself Ellie's unofficial protector, and she seemed to have carried this role into their adult lives, although, admittedly, she didn't see as much of her stepsister these days, as Ellie lived and worked in London as a copy-editor for Trentham Osborne.

And now, with amazing suddenness, Ellie was going to be married, and someone else would be looking after her. Someone called Alex Fabian.

'I met him at the office,' she'd confided to Louise only a few weeks before. 'Apparently he's a banker, and Daddy and he were doing some kind of business deal.' She frowned. 'I didn't think he'd really noticed me, but he rang the next day and asked me to go to the theatre.'

'Terrific,' Lou said absently, focusing rather on the words "business deal". 'Is Dad looking to re-capitalise?' she enquired.

Ellie shrugged. 'I don't know. But we are bringing out the new art and architecture list, and they say times are hard for independents in publishing.'

'They always were,' said Lou.

Gradually, through Ellie's artless disclosures, she began to build up a picture of this Alex Fabian. He was, it seemed, absolutely gorgeous. There wasn't a club where he wasn't a member, or a restaurant where he couldn't get a table. He was usually seen out with models, actresses and rich girls-about-town. Everywhere they went, he was recognised.

Why, only the other evening they'd gone to the launch of a new brasserie, and this stunning woman, tall with red hair and a fantastic figure, had come up to their table. Alex hadn't seemed very pleased to see her, but he'd called her 'Cindy' and she'd asked him if this was the sacrificial lamb.

Ellie had mentioned this later, and Alex had said that Cindy had a sense of humour all her own, and Ellie wasn't to worry about it. But wasn't it strange?

'Weird,' Lou had agreed with total sincerity.

As she went downstairs she found herself wondering yet again what someone like Alex Fabian was doing with Ellie, who was gentle to the point of naïveté, and certainly no party animal. In fact, she still lived at her parents' flat under Marian's watchful eye.

And what was Ellie's slant on all this? She talked about fabulous meals she'd eaten, and celebrities she'd met. She mentioned the opera, and the ballet, and private viewings at art galleries.

But she said nothing about Alex Fabian himself, the man who was providing all these earthly delights. And demanding—what, in return? Just, it seemed, the pleasure of Ellie's company.

Maybe he'd recognised her intrinsic innocence, and decided to respect it, although that kind of consideration seemed unlikely from someone who clearly lived his life on the fast track.

So, perhaps it was just the attraction of opposites. Whatever, he was coming down this weekend to become formally engaged to Ellie, having apparently first sought the permission of her mother and stepfather.

Very dear and old-fashioned of him, Lou thought, wrinkling her nose in a faint unease she was unable to explain.

And it had resulted in a string of frenetic instructions from Marian, who wanted Virginia Cottage at its quaint and sparkling best, to provide the perfect setting for such a momentous event.

Lou found Ellie in the drawing room, curled up in the corner of a sofa. She didn't fit her mother's description of 'silly' at all. Instead she looked remarkably serious—rather like a small creature caught in the headlights of an oncoming car.

'Hey there,' Lou said gently. 'Come and peel some potatoes for this man of yours. I thought I'd do rosti with the duck.'

'OK. Fine.' Ellie summoned a wan smile as she followed her to the kitchen. She sat at the table, staring without enthusiasm at the bowl of vegetables awaiting her attention.

'Isn't this a little early for bridal nerves?' Lou enquired, surveying her with concern as she handed over an apron and a paring knife, then began swiftly and deftly to prepare the mushrooms for the soup. 'You aren't even engaged yet.'

'No, but I will be in a few hours' time.'

'But only if that's what you want,' Lou countered, frowning. 'So—is it?'

'Of course.' Ellie tilted a charming chin. 'How could it not be?'

'You tell me,' Lou said wryly. 'You look like someone under sentence of death.'

'Don't be absurd,' Ellie said shortly. 'Alex is an incredible man, and I'm going to have an amazing life with him. No one in her right mind is going to turn that away.'

Lou reached for another mushroom. That, she thought, didn't sound like Ellie at all. More as if she was repeating something she'd been told. Something that had been impressed upon her.

I detect Marian's fine white hand in this, she told herself grimly.

She said quietly, 'Ellie—you do love him, don't you?'

'Naturally.' Ellie hacked the skin from an inoffensive potato. 'It's all happened a little fast—that's all.'

'Then tell him you need more time. If he cares for you, he'll understand.'

Ellie shook her head. She said, 'Time is something I—don't have.'

'Oh, God.' Lou came to an apprehensive halt in her preparations. 'Ellie—you're not pregnant, are you?'

Ellie stared at her in astonishment. 'Of course not. How could I possibly be?'

Lou shrugged uncomfortably. 'People in love are usually—lovers too,' she suggested. 'And accidents happen.'

Her stepsister flushed. 'Well, not in our case. Because we—don't...'

'Oh,' Lou said, adding mendaciously, 'I see.'

Although she didn't know why she should be so surprised, she thought, turning back to the mushrooms. After all, sex before marriage wasn't obligatory. And in a sharp-eyed village, where any kind of privacy was at a premium, and your beloved still resided with a mother who tracked his every move, it was virtually impossible, as she knew to her cost.

But, as David had said ruefully, there was no real hurry when they had the rest of their lives together. And what could she do but reluctantly agree?

However, Alex Fabian didn't live his life under the spotlight of parental disapproval, she thought. On the contrary. So, why this uncharacteristic restraint?

She said, 'Then what's the matter? Because there's clearly something.'

Ellie was silent for a moment. She said, 'He—he scares me a little. To be honest, he always has.'

'Then why on earth did you go out with him?' Lou demanded, bewildered.

Ellie shrugged. 'Oh, I wasn't very happy at the time,' she said evasively. 'I thought it might—take my mind off things.'

'And did it?'

Ellie's laugh sounded a little forced. 'Well, of course. Alex demands—total concentration at all times. And now we're going to be married,' she added brightly. 'So everything's worked out for the best.'

'In this best of all possible worlds,' Lou murmured with

irony. 'And maybe you should leave the potatoes to me, love. There'll be none left at the rate you're going.'

'Oh, Lou, I'm sorry.' Ellie looked with contrition at the results of her labours.

'Don't worry about it.' Lou rinsed her hands. 'The future Mrs Fabian will never have to bother with such mundane tasks, anyway. So go and make yourself look gorgeous for him.'

'Yes,' Ellie said slowly. 'I suppose so.' She looked up at the clock, her expression blank. 'He'll be here soon. Time's running out.' And she wandered off, leaving Lou staring after her, perplexed, and frankly worried.

Ellie, she thought, bore no resemblance to a girl about to say 'yes' to the man she adored.

She wondered if she ought to talk to Marian about it, then dismissed the idea, knowing that it would be seen as interference rather than intervention.

And Ellie wasn't a child any more. She had to work out her own salvation. And whether that would include Alex Fabian was entirely her own decision.

Left to herself, she worked steadily, and competently. Soon the ducklings were waiting on their rack, the vegetables prepared, the soup simmering, and a bowl of Chantilly cream whisked up to accompany the dessert of fresh local strawberries.

As David's wife, she might always have to do her own cooking, she thought with faint amusement, but she didn't have one iota of envy for Ellie's carefree future. David was her rock, and she'd never entertained the slightest doubt about him.

Dinner was to be served at eight o' clock, so she now had a breathing space to go back into the loft and choose the dresses to take down to the village hall later.

It was a fascinating task. Like most lofts, it was crammed with remnants of the past, including a lot of old photograph albums, and Lou was constantly being sidetracked.

'Oh, hell,' she muttered as she glanced at her watch. 'It's time those ducklings were in the oven. I'd better get cracking.'

She picked up the armful of dresses she'd chosen. They were

too bulky to manage safely on the ladder, she decided. Much better for them to go first.

She dropped them through the hatch, and was about to follow, when a startled cry reached her from below.

Glancing down in sudden apprehension, Lou saw the dresses seemed to have taken on a life of their own. Were, in fact, on the move. And under their concealing folds a muffled male voice was swearing angrily.

'Oh, God.' Lou scrambled down the ladder at neck-breaking speed. She grabbed a handful of satin, and hauled it away. 'I—I'm so sorry. I didn't realise anyone would be there.'

Her victim shook himself free, his impatient glance flicking over her. 'Really?' he drawled. 'I thought it might be some bizarre rite of passage.'

And Lou realised, horrified, she was taking her first look at Alex Fabian. In the flesh, she thought, swallowing.

He was tall and lean, with broad shoulders and endless legs. His hair, dishevelled from its close encounter with several pounds of fabric, was thick and tawny, and curled slightly. Lou remembered Ellie once saying that his nickname in the City was the Lion King, and could understand why.

He was not conventionally handsome, but he was arrestingly, dynamically attractive, with high cheekbones, glinting green eyes under heavy lids, and a firmly sculpted, almost insolent mouth.

And he was frighteningly, effortlessly sexy. A man who did not have to try, she thought instantly, and wondered how she could possibly know.

A shiver traced its way down her spine. And she thought, 'Poor Ellie.'

Alex Fabian was looking at her too. Lou recognised with shock that she had been stripped, assessed and dismissed in one devastating and totally male glance. A conditioned reflex, she told herself angrily. That's all it was. See a woman—imagine her naked. He probably can't help himself.

But all the same she resented it, even as she realised he was speaking to her again.

He said softly, 'And who are you?'

Lou gave him a bland smile. 'The cook.'

'Indeed?' His brows lifted. He stirred the mass of shimmering cloth at his feet with the toe of a polished shoe. 'Is it part of the job to dress for dinner?'

'No,' she said. 'These are for the local drama group. They're doing a revue—*An Evening with Noël Coward.*'

'Dear God,' said Alex Fabian, and his lips twitched into an appreciative grin. 'A little ambitious, wouldn't you say?'

Lou had thought exactly the same when the idea was first mooted, but she stonily refused to share his amusement. Particularly when his smile had sent his attraction quotient soaring into some sexual stratosphere.

'Don't worry,' she said crisply. 'You won't be expected to buy a ticket.'

'Ah,' he said. 'I've just realised. You're Louise, Ellie's stepsister. How do you do? I'm Alex Fabian.'

Lou dived to pick up the dresses, pretending not to have seen his outstretched hand. It occurred to her that she did not want to touch him. That even a polite handshake might carry some inherent risk, like making contact with a force field. And that she could not afford to find out.

'Yes,' she said. 'I'd gathered who you were.' She hoisted the pile of silks and satins into her arms, using them as a barrier. 'Now you must excuse me. Duty calls.'

'You mean you really are doing the cooking?'

'Well, don't sound so surprised. Someone has to.' She gave him a swift, taut smile. 'Reliable staff is hard to come by round here. But I promise not to poison you.'

'I'm completely reassured.' He paused. 'Before I was booby-trapped,' he said, 'I was looking for the guest bathroom.'

'Second door on the left.' She edged round him.

'One moment,' he said, and a sudden tremor went through her as she felt his hand brush her hair.

She practically jumped backwards, nearly flattening herself against the wall. She said breathlessly, 'Just—what do you think you're doing?'

'Relax,' he advised, a sudden glint in those amazing eyes. 'You had a cobweb in your hair. See?' He showed her its remains on his fingertips. 'Some poor spider is now homeless.'

'A banker with a caring side,' she said. 'I'm impressed.'

'Now, why do I find that so hard to believe?' Alex Fabian said musingly. 'But I won't detain you now for any further discussion. You have your pots and pans to get back to. So, as Noël Coward himself would have put it, Miss Louise Trentham, I'll see you again.'

No, she thought with relief. No, you won't.

Tonight she would be at the village hall, and tomorrow she would persuade David to take her out for the whole day. And on Sunday she'd invent a headache, and stay in her room until they'd all gone back to London.

She muttered something unintelligible into the pile of dresses, and headed off to her room.

Once safely inside, she leaned back against the door panels, and whispered, 'Phew.'

So that was Alex Fabian, she thought weakly. Hell's bells, he should carry a government health warning. No wonder Ellie was becoming flaky at the prospect of marriage with him.

Nor was he a picture of the eager suitor. He was a cool operator. She had seen no kindness in that smiling mouth, no warmth to soften the sensual speculation in the green eyes. For Alex Fabian, women were no more than a commodity to be enjoyed. And what happened when a particular commodity began to pall?

Did Ellie really have the emotional and mental stamina to cope with someone like him? Or was she too glamoured—too beguiled by his looks, charisma and money to care?

She should turn him down, she told herself vehemently. Instantly, and without a second thought. It was a question of survival—pure and simple.

A description which could never be applied to the bride-groom-to-be, she added, her mouth twisting wryly.

She left the dresses on her bed. As she turned away she caught sight of herself in the mirror, and realised there was a smudge of dust on her cheek that Alex Fabian had not seen fit to mention.

Thank God he didn't try to remove it as well, she thought caustically as she went down to the kitchen, or I'd probably be a gibbering wreck by now.

She was concocting the orange sauce for the ducklings when Marian came in.

'Is everything under control?' she demanded, glancing sharply around her.

'In here, it is.' Lou added a dash of Cointreau. 'I can't speak for the rest of the house.'

Marian stared at her. She was elegant in amethyst jersey, with pearls at her throat and in her ears, and her blonde hair was drawn back into an elaborate chignon. 'What is that supposed to mean?'

'I met Ellie's intended,' Lou returned. She paused. 'Are you really going to let her marry him?'

Marian's brows lifted haughtily. 'I think that is a decision that we can safely leave to them.'

'I don't agree.' Lou met her gaze calmly and directly. 'I think it's like handing a lamb over to a tiger.'

'What a dramatic turn of phrase,' her stepmother said mockingly. 'Perhaps you should be writing melodramas for your little village group.'

'Better melodrama than tragedy,' Lou said curtly. 'Marian, she's not in his league. You must see that.'

'I see that she's marrying a very successful man, who will soon be chairman of Perrins Bank,' Marian retorted.

'So you're not pretending she loves him.'

Marian laughed. 'Oh, I think she'll find it very easy to love him—in the ways that matter to a man. After all, she'll have an expert teacher.' She paused. 'Are you quite sure, Lou, dear, that you're not just a tiny bit jealous?

'No,' Lou said steadily. 'Because I have a man that I can love in all the ways there are. Not just those that happen in the bedroom.'

'You're really a little prude, aren't you?' Marian drawled. 'I'm sure you and David will suit each other admirably.' She glanced at her diamond watch. 'Are you leaving yourself enough time to change?'

'I'm going to a village-hall rehearsal, not Glyndebourne.' Lou tasted her sauce, and nodded with satisfaction.

'But you can't serve the dinner in jeans and an old sweater.'

'I've no intention of serving it at all,' Lou retorted curtly. 'I said I'd cook, and that's it. You and Ellie can manage the rest between you—unless, of course, you want Alex Fabian to end up with a lap full of mushroom soup,' she added menacingly. 'No? I thought not. And I presume you know how to load the dishwasher as well,' she called after her stepmother as Marian flounced out.

A minor victory, she thought, but what did that matter when the war was already lost?

Up in her room, she went across to the window to close the curtains against the gathering twilight, and paused, alerted by a movement in the shrubbery below her. To her surprise, she saw it was Ellie, pacing up and down, and talking on her cell-phone.

What on earth is she doing out there? Lou asked herself in bewilderment. 'I'd have thought Marian would have had her chained to Alex Fabian's wrist by now.'

She was about to rap on the window—attract Ellie's attention—then held back. Even in the poor light, she could see that her stepsister looked strained. Every gesture, every restless movement betrayed her agitation.

Maybe she's decided she can't go through with it, she thought. But who is she talking to? The Samaritans?

She went back to the bed and began shaking out the dresses, folding them with care and placing them in large carriers.

On her way out to the car she would have a word with Ellie, she decided. Tell her that she, at least, was on her side.

But when she got outside, there was no one about. As she went past the dining-room window she glanced in, and saw Ellie sitting next to Alex Fabian at the candlelit table, talking and laughing as if she didn't have a care in the world.

The Samaritans must do a wonderful job, Lou thought with a resigned sigh, and went to her rehearsal.

The carrier bags were seized on joyfully by the female cast members and taken off to the women's dressing room. Lou found a chair and sat down to watch while she waited for David to arrive. He didn't act in any of the village productions but he helped with scenery and lighting, and he was coming to discuss the design of the set with Ray, the producer.

Lou hadn't attended any rehearsals for a couple of weeks, and she was amazed to find what progress they'd made. Even Ray who was also playing Noël Coward, was far better than she'd expected.

Then the girls came back in the evening dresses she'd brought, and paraded them on stage for Ray to make a final choice, and it was only when she was re-packing the rejected ones that she realised how late it was getting.

'Where on earth is David?' she asked Ray.

For a moment he looked blank, then, 'Oh, he phoned earlier, just before you got here, love. Said something had cropped up, and he couldn't make it.'

Lou frowned. 'He didn't call me.'

'He probably took it for granted I'd tell you,' Ray said peaceably. 'Which I now have.'

'He didn't say what the problem was?'

'No,' Ray admitted. 'But I expect his mother's thrown an-other wobbly. He'd hardly want that generally known.' He paused. 'You haven't got any tailcoats or top hats in that loft of yours, by any chance?'

She forced a smile. 'I didn't notice any, but I'll have a good look tomorrow.'

She took the long route back to Virginia Cottage, going through the square, but David's house was all in darkness, so she drove on without stopping.

Perhaps Ray had been quite right about his mother, she thought. And once David had managed to get her calm again, he'd decided to have an early night. Well, she couldn't blame him for that, and nor would she.

But all the same, it was disappointing not to have seen him, and she wished very much that he'd rung her to explain. No doubt he'd ring in the morning, and they'd arrange to spend the day together then.

To her surprise, all the lights were out at Virginia Cottage too. She'd expected to find a party going on, but perhaps there was nothing to celebrate after all.

She parked at the rear, beside the low, sleek sports car that looked so alien in the cobbled yard, and went in through the back door. Her immediate intention was to make herself a hot drink, but that was before she saw the state the kitchen was in.

Clearly Marian had decided the dishwasher was unknown territory after all, she thought grimly, because all the plates, cutlery, dishes and pans used for the meal were piled haphazardly on every surface.

She was half tempted to leave them there, except for the knowledge that they would still be waiting for her in the morning, and she hated that.

David is quite right, she thought, smouldering. They do use me. But this is the last time.

She filled the kettle and set it to boil, then began the dreary task of rinsing the crockery, and putting it in the dishwasher.

The running water disguised the sound of the kitchen door opening behind her, and she only realised she was no longer alone when Alex Fabian said, 'Good evening, Cinderella. Did the ball end early?'

He was standing just behind her. Close enough, she thought, to touch.

Her whole body clenched in sudden, uncontrollable panic, and the dish she was holding slipped from her hands, and smashed into fragments on the quarry-tiled floor between them.

Then there was silence.

CHAPTER TWO

A SILENCE that Alex Fabian was the first to break.

He said, 'I seem to have startled you. I'm sorry. I hope the breakage won't be stopped out of your wages,' he added smoothly.

Lou glared at him. He'd discarded the jacket and tie he'd been wearing at dinner, and his white shirt was half-unbuttoned, revealing more than she wished to see of a brown, muscular chest. His cuffs were undone and turned casually back over equally tanned forearms.

She said, 'What the hell do you think you're doing—creeping around at this time of night?'

'This time of night?' he echoed derisively. 'Lady, in London the evening would just be beginning.'

'Well, we don't go in much for big-city nightlife round here,' Lou said curtly.

'I gathered that,' he said drily. 'On the stroke of midnight, everyone turns back into pumpkins.'

'You should have made it clear you wanted to be entertained.' Lou went over to the broom cupboard in the corner, and extracted a dustpan and brush. 'I'm sure my family would have turned cartwheels for you.'

Alex Fabian whistled softly. 'I get the distinct impression, Miss Trentham, that you don't like me very much.'

'Fortunately, I don't have to.' She began to sweep up the broken pieces. 'We inhabit totally different worlds, Mr Fabian.'

'Worlds which seem to have collided,' he said. 'I'm about to become part of the family. Aren't you going to congratulate me?'

She emptied the dustpan into the rubbish bin with a clatter. 'On having got what you want? I imagine that's the norm for you. Besides, with all you have to offer, how could Ellie possibly resist?'

'I admit I thought she'd respond better to the carrot than the stick.' He seemed amused, rather than offended. 'I'm glad you agree.'

'Well, I'm not glad about any of it. And where is Ellie, anyway?'

'She opted for an early night, and the others followed,' he said. His mouth twisted. 'I think the excitement was all too much for her.'

Lou went on loading the dishwasher. She said in a low voice, 'I think you're too much for her. Don't you know that she's frightened of you?'

'No,' Alex Fabian said quietly, after a pause. 'I didn't realise that. But she truly has nothing to be scared of. Maybe I didn't make that as clear as I should have done.'

'Ellie's a beautiful girl, but she's also fragile. She needs kindness, Mr Fabian. I'm not sure you have much of that to spare.'

'Then maybe that's a trait we share, Miss Trentham.' His voice was suddenly harsh. 'You're very ready to condemn on very little evidence. I promise you on my word of honour that Ellie has nothing to fear from me. That I will look after her as my wife, and treat her well. Does that satisfy you?'

'Perhaps it's her that you should reassure.'

His mouth tightened. 'I would have done, if I'd had the chance to be alone with her before she scuttled off to bed. As a matter of fact, I tapped on her door just now and spoke to her in case she was still awake, but there was no answer.'

'She probably thought you wanted more than conversation.' The words were out before she could stop them.

'Oh, God,' Lou muttered under her breath. 'I've done it now.' And she bent swiftly to put the detergent tablet in the machine to disguise the fact that she was blushing.

He said quite mildly, 'Now, why should she think any such thing? As you're so much in her confidence, you must know I've made no demands of that kind.'

'Yes, but you're engaged now. Officially. That—changes things.' Lou, having dug the hole and fallen into it, was now sinking rapidly. She shut the machine door, and switched on the programme. Anything not to have to look at him. Or hear him. Or even share the same universe with him, she thought detachedly.

'Does it indeed?' he said, and she could hear the unholy amusement quivering in his voice. 'Well, I've never been engaged before, so I bow to your superior wisdom. Should I rush upstairs and ravish her now, do you think, or can it wait until tomorrow night?

'You see, I'd actually planned to make myself some coffee, and do a couple of hours' work on my laptop, but I'm prepared to make the sacrifice, if necessary,' he added piously.

'This is all a big joke to you, isn't it?' Lou swung round and faced him stormily.

'Think what you want.' He shrugged. 'If I told you the truth, you wouldn't believe me. And the kettle's boiling. Shall I make us both some coffee?'

'I'm having herb tea.' If it was an olive branch, Lou didn't want it. 'I don't drink coffee at this hour. It keeps me awake.'

'How naughty of it,' Alex Fabian said gravely. 'Of course, there are a lot of far more pleasurable activities that have exactly the same effect, but perhaps you haven't tried those.'

Helplessly, Lou felt her face warming again. She went over to the cupboard, produced two beakers, set them on the worktop, and pushed the coffee jar towards him without a word.

'Before you flounce out of the room, slamming the door behind you,' Alex Fabian said pleasantly, spooning granules into his beaker and adding boiling water, 'I should tell you that was a magnificent dinner you gave us tonight.'

'Thank you.' The beguiling aroma of coffee seemed to fill the kitchen. Biting her lip, Lou dropped a camomile tea bag into her beaker, and let it infuse.

'Have you ever thought of cooking professionally?' he went on. 'Private lunch and dinner parties in people's homes? I should think you'd make a fortune.'

'On the contrary,' Lou said. 'In future, I intend to cook only for my husband.'

He gave her bare left hand a fleeting glance. 'Does this fortunate guy exist, or is he simply an erotic fantasy in your caffeine-free dreams?'

'Of course he's real. I—I thought you knew I was engaged.' Her flush deepened.

'Ah,' he said. 'Our brief debate on sexual etiquette. I thought you knew that was a wind-up.'

'And Ellie didn't tell you?'

'Ellie,' he said, 'has told me very little. But I haven't exactly been forthcoming myself, so I can hardly complain.' He paused. 'So, who is he?'

'Someone I've known forever. He lives in the village, and works for Galbraiths in their regional office.'

'Does he have a name?'

'He's called David Sanders.' Her tone was short. 'Why do you ask?'

'So that when I come to your wedding I'll know what to call the groom,' Alex Fabian said calmly. 'I presume, as Ellie's husband, I'll receive an invitation.'

Ellie's husband, she thought. *Ellie's husband?* If she lived to be a thousand, she could never see him in any such role.

She said slowly, 'I suppose so.' She fished out the tea bag and disposed of it. 'Do you want milk in your coffee?'

'I take it black,' he said. 'It helps me stay awake.'

'Of course,' she said. 'You have work to do. Please don't let me keep you.'

'I am working,' he said, and smiled at her with faint mockery. 'Building bridges, I hope, with my future sister-in-law.' He leaned against the kitchen table and took a meditative sip of coffee. 'Tell me, how is it you don't work for Trentham Osborne as Ellie does?'

'Because publishing never appealed to me, and London certainly didn't. I was always happiest here, so I moved back permanently and got a job with a local law firm.'

'You're a solicitor?'

She bit her lip. 'No, a paralegal. I went to the same school as Ellie, and they weren't geared up for university grades, just…' She hesitated.

'Just grooming the girls to make suitable marriages?' he prompted softly.

'Actually—yes,' Lou acknowledged ruefully. She shook her head. 'You wouldn't believe that it could still go on.'

'No?' He drank some more coffee, watching her over the rim of the beaker. 'Yet it seems to have worked for you.'

'David isn't "suitable" in that sense,' she said. As her step-mother never failed to make clear, she thought wryly. 'Just—the right man for me.'

'How fortunate you are,' he said softly. 'To be so certain so early in your life.'

'Yes,' she said. 'I think I am.'

She finished her tea, and rinsed her beaker briskly under the tap. She gave him a bright, meaningless smile. 'Well—good-night. Will you switch off the lights as you go up?'

At the door, she paused. She said haltingly, 'And I'm sorry for the way I spoke earlier. I—I hope that you and Ellie will be very happy together.'

The green eyes met hers, cool and enigmatic.

'I feel sure,' he said, 'that her old school would be proud of her. Goodnight—sister-in-law.'

She was suddenly aware that her heart was thudding quickly—unpredictably. She smiled uncertainly, and went swiftly upstairs to her room. She closed the door behind her and drew a deep breath.

For a moment there, she'd allowed her guard to drop. And had been made aware, in a few devastating seconds, how disturbing a man Alex Fabian could be.

Bad move on her part, she thought. And lesson duly learned. From now on she would take more care. And keeping out of his way was just the first step.

Lou was tired when she climbed into bed, but sleep proved elusive just the same. She found her mind was churning, going over her encounter with Alex in the kitchen, and trying to analyse what had been said, and what else had been implied.

Oh, this is ridiculous, she adjured herself at last. Forget about the wretched guy, and concentrate on tomorrow.

She supposed, glumly, that if Mrs Gladwin failed to arrive again she would be expected to cook the breakfast, and she would do so, but after that they could forage for themselves, because she was going to the coast with David.

They would have a seafood lunch in a pub, then walk along the beach, and talk seriously about fixing a date for the wedding. It had hardly been mentioned in recent weeks.

Three months ahead, she thought contentedly, would surely give Mrs Sanders plenty of time to move to her sister's place.

When eventually she slept, it was to dream that her wedding day had come, and she was walking up the aisle of the village church on her father's arm to her bridegroom, waiting at the altar.

But as she got nearer he turned his head, and she saw, instead of David's ruggedly familiar and beloved face, a mask, blank and featureless. And, crying out with fear and grief, she fled, alone, back the way she had come.

The dream was still vivid in her mind when she woke. Nasty, she thought, shivering, then threw back the bedclothes. Nothing, especially a nightmare, would be allowed to cloud this lovely day.

She showered, and dressed casually in a knee-length denim skirt and a white short-sleeved top, then brushed her hair into a silky cloud on her shoulders.

Because she would soon be seeing David, she accentuated her eyes with grey shadow and mascara, and coloured her mouth with her favourite dusky rose lipstick before she went downstairs.

When she got to the kitchen she found to her relief that young Tim had recovered from his asthma attack, and Mrs Gladwin was there ahead of her, already assembling the ingredients for the kedgeree and cutting the rind off the bacon rashers.

'I took Mr and Mrs Trentham's tea up to them,' Mrs Gladwin reported. 'But I had to leave Miss Ellie's tray outside her door, as I couldn't make her hear me. And I didn't know what to do about her visitor.'

'I think he'd prefer coffee.' Lou found the small cafetière and filled it. But she had no intention of taking Alex Fabian coffee in bed, she thought, her mouth tightening. That was Ellie's task, and she could wake up and do it.

While she was waiting for the coffee to brew, she popped out into the yard and called David on her mobile, only to discover that his was switched off.

She pulled a face as she returned indoors. If she used the ordinary phone his mother was bound to answer, and be plaintive at the prospect of her boy spending time with anyone else.

But maybe David would call her instead before that happened.

When she went upstairs, she found Ellie's tray still untouched outside her door.

Puzzled, she set the coffee down beside it and knocked. 'Ellie—Ellie, wake up. Your tea's getting cold.'

There was no answer, and, after a moment's hesitation, she opened the door, and looked in.

But there was no blonde head lifting sleepily from the pillow. The bed was empty, and the room unoccupied.

And no prizes for guessing where Ellie was, Lou thought, feeling oddly embarrassed. That neatly made bed was a total giveaway. She must have decided to celebrate her engagement in the arms of her fiancé after all.

'Everyone's still asleep,' she told Mrs Gladwin as she carried all the things back to the kitchen. 'I'm going into the village to get the papers.'

She followed the previous night's detour on the way back. The curtains were still firmly closed on the first floor of David's house, but his car was missing from its usual parking spot outside.

He must have gone to the cottage to find me, Lou thought, her heart lifting. 'We can have breakfast together.'

Yet there was no sign of his blue Peugeot at Virginia Cottage either. Instead, there was Alex Fabian, walking alone in the garden. He was the last person she'd expected to see so early, under the circumstances. And the last person she wanted to see, she amended quickly.

She hesitated, feeling strangely awkward, wondering if there was some way to evade him, but he had already seen her, so she had to reluctantly stand her ground.

'Good morning,' he said as he came up to her. 'Did you sleep well?'

'Yes—thank you.' She stared down at the gravel. 'And—you?'

'Not particularly,' he said. 'The coffee did its work too well.'

She gave a quick, forced smile. 'I'm sure Ellie wouldn't agree.'

'Oh,' he said. 'And how does it concern her?'

'I took her some morning tea,' she said. 'And her bed hadn't been slept in. I—I drew the obvious conclusion.'

His hand closed on her arm. 'Look at me,' he commanded harshly. 'What the hell are you talking about?'

She stared up at him, bewildered. 'Ellie wasn't in her room this morning. I—I thought she was with you.'

'I haven't seen your sister,' he said, 'since nine-thirty yesterday evening, when she decided to have that extremely early night. And the last place she would ever be likely to spend the night is in my bed.'

He set off towards the house, taking Lou with him, whether or not she wished to go.

She tried to hang back. 'I'm sure there's a perfectly logical explanation.' She tried to think of one. 'Perhaps she got up early, and went for a walk.'

'Walking,' he said, 'is not one of her pastimes. Your sister believes in taxis, when chauffeur-driven cars aren't available. I think you know that.'

'Maybe there's been some emergency at the office, and she's had to go back to London.' Lou clutched at a passing straw.

'If so, I think they'd probably have sent for your father,' he said. 'And he's still here.'

In the hall, Marian greeted Alex, all smiles. 'Breakfast is ready, if you'd like to come into the dining room.'

He said, 'Have you seen Ellie this morning, Mrs Trentham? Because Louise says her bed has not been slept in.'

Marian's hand went to her throat. 'Oh, what nonsense. I expect she was just too happy and excited to sleep.'

'All the same, with your permission, I'd like to look in her room.'

Lou tried to detach herself from his grasp. 'I'd rather not…'

'I'm afraid you must,' he said. 'You can tell me if anything's missing.'

My God, Lou thought as she followed him unwillingly upstairs. She's done it. She's decided she can't go through with the engagement, and she's run away. And, if that's so, I should be delighted for her. So why do I feel so scared suddenly?

'Well?' Alex demanded as they stood in the middle of Ellie's bedroom, looking round them.

Lou swallowed. 'The case she brought down with her has gone.' She opened the wardrobe, and looked in the drawers. 'And she seems to have taken underwear and some clothes.'

'And left these.' His voice was suddenly grim.

Lou turned to see him holding two envelopes. 'Where did you find them?'

'Propped against the lamp on the night table,' he said. 'One for each of us.' He paused. 'Are you sure you want to open yours?'

'Of course,' Lou said indignantly. 'I'm worried sick about her. I need to make sure she's all right.'

'I think you underestimate her sense of self-preservation,' Alex Fabian said drily as he handed her the envelope.

Her name was a mere scrawl on its surface. Inside was a single sheet of paper. She could barely decipher the writing. 'Lou, darling,' she eventually translated, 'I'm so terribly sorry. Please try to understand and forgive me.'

'What does it say?' Alex's level voice reached her.

She turned and looked at him. He was holding his own letter, two pages of it, between thumb and forefinger as if he found it distasteful.

She said, 'She wants me to forgive her—but for what? For running away?'

'Not just for that, I'm afraid.' He paused. 'You see, she didn't go alone.'

She saw something in his eyes that she had never expected to find there. Compassion. And it frightened her more than any coldness—any anger.

She tried to say 'What do you mean?' But, although her lips moved, the words would not emerge.

She heard a sound from the doorway, and looked round swiftly, praying it would be Ellie standing there. Ellie, saying it had all been a silly mistake, and here she was, safe and sound.

Only it was her father, his face like thunder.

'Louise—Mrs Sanders has telephoned. Will you come and speak to her, please? She's hysterical—out of control. I can't make out what she's saying. She keeps repeating "David and Ellie" over and over again. I think she must have gone mad.'

'It would be convenient to think so.' Alex Fabian stepped forward to station himself between Lou and her father. Shielding her white face, trembling mouth and wide, bewildered eyes.

'But I'm afraid her hysterics are justified. My erstwhile fiancée has run away with her son, and they're going to be married. She's left me a letter, confessing everything.'

'I don't believe a word of it,' the older man said harshly. 'It must be some sick joke. Good God, man, it was only last night she became engaged to you.'

'Apparently that was the final straw,' Alex told him calmly. 'She and David Sanders had been in love for some time, but they'd tried to behave nobly for Louise's sake—or some such maudlin nonsense. She went out with me to try and forget him, but when she realised marriage was on the agenda she decided she couldn't go through with it after all, and appealed to Sanders to rescue her.

'And—they eloped last night.'

Louise felt totally numb. Presently, she knew, there would be pain. But now there were images passing through her mind like some nightmare slide show. Ellie's frantic phone call. Click. The dark house. Click. The empty space where David's car should have been. Click. Until she wanted to scream.

'Well, they won't get away with it.' Mr Trentham's voice shook. 'I'll have them found. Make her come back.'

'I hope you won't do anything of the kind,' Alex Fabian said coldly. 'She's not a young child. She's a woman, and quite capable of making her own choices. Something we overlooked in our negotiations.'

'Ellie?' Marian Trentham had joined them now, her face ashen, her eyes blazing. 'My beautiful girl with that—that buffoon? It can't be true.'

Lou made a small sound in her throat, and Alex glanced at her sharply. He said, 'Mrs Trentham, I think you've forgotten that Louise was engaged to David Sanders.'

'I haven't forgotten a thing,' the older woman said shrilly. 'It's all her fault—encouraging him to hang round here, where he could meet my lovely Ellie. Of course he preferred her. What man wouldn't?'

'No,' Alex said, studying her with cold dislike, 'according to her letter, they met up in London when he was on some course. So Louise can't possibly be blamed. In fact, she's been subjected to the worst kind of betrayal by both of them.'

Betrayal. The word made Louise shiver, but it brought her back to life. And to unpleasant reality.

She heard herself say, 'Mrs Sanders must still be waiting on the phone. I'd better go and talk to her.'

'No.' Alex halted her, his hand on her arm. 'Your father can do that for you. Or your stepmother,' he added curtly. 'There's no reason why you should be exposed to any more recriminations.'

Her father said hoarsely, 'Yes, of course. I'll go now. Though God knows what I can say...'

As he departed, muttering distractedly, Marian Trentham moved forward, her hands outstretched. 'Alex, my dear.' Her voice throbbed. 'What you must be suffering.'

'I don't appreciate being made a fool of,' Alex said tersely. 'And your daughter's defection is going to cause me immeasurable trouble and inconvenience. But please let's drop the pretence that Ellie and I were ever in love with each other.'

For a moment she faltered, then she returned to the attack, forcing a smile.

'You're hurt,' she said. 'As you have every right to be. I do understand. But all is not yet lost. I think we should go downstairs and have some breakfast, and decide what to do next.'

'I know exactly what I'm doing next,' Alex said coldly. 'I'm going back to London, and I'll forgo your kind offer of breakfast. I'd prefer to be on my way as soon as possible.'

'But there are matters outstanding,' she said rapidly, her voice beginning to shake. 'Things we need to discuss.'

'You mean the re-financing plan? But that was dependent on certain conditions being met, so there is really very little to talk about.'

Louise could hear the words, but she could not grasp what they meant. They seemed to float past her. The room, too, suddenly seemed to be swimming.

She said in a stifled voice, 'I—I think I'm going to be sick.'

During the miserable and humiliating minutes that followed, Louise was dimly aware of an arm supporting her as she retched violently into the lavatory bowl, of a hand smoothing back her hair, and wiping her face with a damp flannel.

'You,' she said shakily as she sat up at last, the tiles on the bathroom walls still swooping dizzily around her. 'Oh, God, it's *you*.'

'Well, who else would it be?' Alex Fabian retorted crushingly. 'Your father's still on the phone, being screamed at, and your stepmother's shut herself into her bedroom. You needed help.'

'You're the last person I'd turn to for that.' She got painfully to her feet. 'If you hadn't pressured Ellie to marry you, none of this would have happened.'

'It would have eventually. A different set of circumstances, perhaps, but the same result.' He shrugged. 'They're in love. They were always going to end up together. I was just the catalyst.'

She glared at him. 'Is that supposed to make me feel better?'

'That's up to you. But I'd say it would be a pretty refined kind of hell to find you'd married a man who wanted someone else. Here, drink this.'

Unwillingly Lou accepted the glass of water he held out to her. She'd just caught a horrified glimpse of herself in the bathroom mirror—her ghost-white face streaked with mascara, her lipstick smeared. The pretty, confident picture she'd painted for David totally ruined. Like her life.

Not only did she look like hell, she thought, writhing inwardly, but she'd just thrown up in front of a man she detested.

She said stiltedly, 'I think I'd like to be alone now.'

'Just as you wish.' He paused. 'I'll have some tea brought up to you.'

'Tea?' Her voice rose. 'My heart is broken, and you offer me—bloody clichés.'

'It's also the classic remedy for shock,' he returned, unperturbed. 'And hearts are more resilient than you think. Would you like me to help you to your room?'

'No,' she said. 'And stop behaving like someone out of a medical drama. Because the best thing you could do for me would be to get out of my sight, and my life.'

'I think,' Alex Fabian said quietly, 'that's something that could be open to discussion. But possibly not at this moment.'

'Not ever,' Lou said fiercely. 'So—please go.'

She turned away, and began to run hot water into the basin, and when she glanced around again she was alone. Which was something she would have to get accustomed to, she realised, wretchedness stabbing her as she washed her face.

With the worst ravages removed, she went back to her room

and threw herself across the bed, digging clenched fists into the coverlet.

Love must indeed be blind, she thought, because she'd never had the slightest idea that David might be looking elsewhere. She'd always felt so happy and comfortable with him, and on the surface everything had seemed just the same.

Yet, she supposed, there had been clues for anyone with a suspicious mind. The fact that David no longer talked about the wedding had been one. And he'd been more preoccupied than usual lately, although he'd blamed problems at work for that.

And Ellie hadn't been the same either, dating Alex Fabian with such feverish, determined enjoyment. As if trying to convince herself that they could have a life together.

You fool, she told herself. You complacent, trusting idiot.

She could sense the tears gathering inside her, threatening to fill the ache of emptiness. And pain was prowling, too, waiting to sink its claws into her heart and mind.

The tap at her door sent her bolt upright, looking apprehensively over her shoulder. But it was only Mrs Gladwin bringing the threatened tea. Her face was solemn, but her eyes, understandably, were sparking with curiosity.

'No one wanted any breakfast,' she said. 'So I've had to throw all that lovely food away. It seems a wicked waste.' She paused. 'I've cleared up the kitchen, so if I'm not wanted for anything else…?'

Lou realised wearily that she was asking to be paid. She forced a smile. 'That's fine, Mrs Gladwin, and thank you.' She found her bag, and handed over the cash.

Mrs Gladwin lingered. 'Next weekend, Miss Louise? Will the family be down?'

Lou looked at her blankly. 'I—I really don't know.' Nor did she care, she thought. And how absurd to think that life could just—go on. For anyone to assume that she would go on living in this house—in this village—with all the dead hopes, dead memories. When everyone must know that was quite impossible.

When she knew, beyond all doubt, that she had to get away—and fast. Leave it all behind her, and escape.

She said quietly, 'I'm sure my stepmother will be in touch over the arrangements. Thank you for the tea.'

'The cup that cheers,' said Mrs Gladwin, nodding portentously, and departed.

Louise looked at the tray, with its snowy lace cloth and the pretty flowered crockery. Another act of kindness, she thought, amid the personal desolation that was beginning to tear at her. But, again, from the wrong person. She did not want Alex Fabian's kindness. She could not bear the thought of it.

She went on staring until the outlines of cup, saucer, jug and teapot lost their separate shapes, and became oddly blurred. Until the first scalding, agonised tears began to sear their way down her face, falling faster and faster.

She began to sob, making small, desperate, uncontrollable noises, pressing her hands over her eyes so that the salty drops squeezed through her fingers. She could feel grief burn in her throat, and taste it on her icy lips.

At some moment, still weeping, she stripped off the skirt and top and threw them across the room, shuddering as if they were rank—rancid. Knowing she never wanted to see them again as long as she lived.

She went to the wardrobe, dragged out a pair of black jeans and a round-necked sweater in fine grey wool, and pulled them onto her body.

She found her soft leather travel bag, and began hurriedly to fill it with underwear, more trousers and casual tops, flat shoes.

Escape, she thought, the word echoing like a mantra in her brain. Escape...

But where could she go?

There was Somerset, she thought. She could stay with her aunt and uncle, and find kindness with them. Use their farm as a sanctuary while she tried to decide what she could do with the rest of her life.

On her way downstairs, she paused outside the main bedroom and tapped on the door.

Her father opened it. 'What is it?' He looked at her bag. 'Is it Ellie? Has she come back?'

'No,' she said, wincing. 'That's—not going to happen, Dad. But I'm going away for a while.'

'But she must come back,' he said. He looked past her. 'You don't realise how serious all this is. It was part of the deal with Fabian, and he's walked out on us. We need that injection of capital, or the business could go under. We could lose everything.'

Lou stared at the man in front of her, and wondered when he had first become a stranger.

She said, 'I think you already have lost everything. At least everything that matters.' She paused. 'I'll be in touch—some time.'

She went out of the cottage the back way, feeling fresh tears springing up as she realised how much of her life she was leaving behind. Yet knowing at the same time that she had no other choice.

She'd expected—hoped—maybe even prayed that Alex Fabian would be long gone. But there was to be no respite for her on this merciless day.

Because, as she came out into the yard, he was there, loading his own bag into the boot of his car.

She checked instantly, wondering if she could duck back into the house before he saw her. But it was too late.

He was already straightening, turning to look at her, the green eyes curiously intent.

'So there you are,' he said softly. 'I've been waiting for you.'

CHAPTER THREE

SHE knew, of course, what he was seeing. The drenched eyes, the trembling mouth, and the pale face smudged with tears. She couldn't even hide behind her hair, because her final act before leaving her room had been to drag it back and confine it at the nape of her neck with an elastic band.

Oh, God, she thought desperately. Why did this man of all men have to be around when she was at her most vulnerable?

She lifted her chin. Kept the betraying quiver from her voice. 'I'm sorry if I've detained you, Mr Fabian, although I can't imagine why that should be. We've said everything that needs to be said, and now we can go our separate ways.'

'Not quite,' he said. 'Where are you going?'

'None of your damned business.' She reached into her shoulder bag, found her sunglasses and jammed them on her nose. One small barrier to shelter behind, she thought, searching for her car keys. 'Will you please leave me alone?'

'No,' he said. He walked across, picked up her travel bag and slung it into the boot of his car next to his own case.

'How dare you?' Lou's voice cracked with outrage. 'What the hell do you think you're doing?'

'Taking over,' he returned tersely. 'Someone needs to. Most families are hell at times, but you seem particularly unlucky in yours. Your sister runs off with your man, and your father and his wife are too caught up in the financial ramifications of it all to notice that you're falling apart.'

'Thank you.' She was shaking again, but this time it was with temper. 'But I can manage on my own.'

The green eyes swept her dismissively. 'Well, you certainly can't drive in that state,' he said. 'You'd kill yourself within a mile.'

She glared at him. 'Do you think I'd care?'

'Suicide may have its attractions,' he said, meditatively. 'And the news might well put a temporary blight on married bliss for the happy couple, although I wouldn't count on it. But it also tends to drastically reduce all future options. So I think you should consider living. And living well. That's a far better revenge on your ex-fiancé.'

'Do you think that's what I want—revenge?' Lou was gasping.

'Well, I hope you don't want him back,' he said. 'I should be very disappointed in you, if so.'

'And we couldn't possibly have that, could we?' Her voice dripped scorn. 'Why can't you just get out of my life, Mr Fabian?'

'Because fate seems to have thrown us together, Miss Trentham.' He closed the boot, and walked round to open the passenger door. 'Are you going to tell me where you'd like me to take you, or shall I make it up as I go along?'

'Anywhere—as long as it's away from here.' Lou stayed where she was. 'And away from you,' she added stormily. 'Can't you see that you're the last person I want to have around?'

'That's unfortunate,' Alex drawled. 'Because I really seem to be all you've got. And you must have some destination in mind. You can't have been planning to simply drive until you ran out of petrol.'

'No.' She bit her lip. 'I'm going to Somerset—to stay with my aunt and uncle,' she offered unwillingly.

'Well, that's a first step,' he said. 'And afterwards?'

'I don't know,' she admitted. 'I—I can't seem to think that far ahead. But I can't ever come back here. Everyone in the village knew I was going to marry David. Half of them would have been coming to the wedding. I—I just can't face them all.'

'Don't be a fool,' he said. 'Do you seriously imagine anyone would blame you for what's happened?'

'No.' Her voice broke. 'But they'd feel sorry for me. And that would be the worst—the unbearable thing. To be pitied...'

'I agree,' Alex said briskly. 'Which brings us back to my original suggestion that you should take life by the throat and use it to your own best advantage.'

She gave him a mutinous look, swallowing back the tears which threatened again. 'And you, of course, are full of bright ideas about how I can do that.'

'Perhaps,' he said. 'When you're prepared to listen. In the meantime, get in the car, and I'll take you to Somerset.'

She was suddenly too weary to argue any more. Besides, her bag was shut in his boot, and she suspected it might take an undignified scuffle to retrieve it.

She moved reluctantly towards his car, then halted. 'But you were going back to London,' she objected. 'Won't people wonder where you are?'

'You forget,' Alex said sardonically. 'I'm away for the weekend getting engaged. No one's expecting me back until Monday.' He saw her into the passenger seat, then moved round to the driver's side. 'And a little sympathy for me wouldn't go amiss,' he added. 'I'm also an injured party in this, if you remember.'

'Yes,' Lou said. 'I can see you're totally devastated.'

'I'm actually bloody angry,' he said. 'I just hide it well. Fasten your seat belt.'

'Why—is it going to be a bumpy ride?' Lou's voice held an edge as she complied.

His mouth slanted in a faint smile. 'I'd say that was entirely up to you,' he said softly, and started the engine.

There was a produce market in the village each Saturday morning, so their progress was slowed to a snail's pace.

Lou had expected Alex Fabian to become swiftly impatient at the delay. A powerful man in a powerful car could be an explosive combination, but he seemed cool and relaxed, lost in his own thoughts.

A powerful man, she thought, prepared to play a waiting

game, and bit her lip, realising that she found the idea
disturbing.

By now, she knew, she was bound to have been noticed. At
any moment, someone might tap on the window and ask where
David was—and, by implication, why she was driving through
the village with a complete stranger.

A question that she would find it quite impossible to answer.
Because she still couldn't believe that she was actually doing
this. That she was meekly allowing Alex Fabian to take her all
the way to Somerset, with the awful prospect of being cooped
up in this car with him for at least two hours.

And he'd made it seem as if it was her only choice, she
thought, savaging her lip again.

She sat staring rigidly ahead of her, her nails cutting into the
palms of her clenched hands, as they edged along. She didn't
want to see familiar faces—familiar landmarks. She was being
torn up by her roots, and it was hurting badly. Her future had
seemed settled—secure—yet now it was in chaos, and she
would have to go to some strange place, and begin all over
again. But how could she? she asked herself in agony. Where
could she go, and what could she do?

By the time they'd finally won free of the village, and were
heading through the lanes towards the motorway, Lou's throat
muscles were aching with misery, but she wouldn't allow herself to cry any more. Not yet. And certainly not in front of
Alex Fabian.

As if he could read her thoughts, he said quietly, 'Things
will get better. You are going to come through this.'

'I don't want to,' she said fiercely. 'I want my old life back.'

'Really?' His tone was caustic. 'You like skivvying for your
family, do you? You enjoy being betrayed by people who are
supposed to love you?'

'No,' she said. 'And stop making me sound like some kind
of pathetic victim. After all,' she added, darting a burning
glance in his direction, 'I'm not the only one who's been made
a fool of.'

He sighed over-heavily. 'Sad, but true.'

Lou's lips tightened. 'I'm glad you can treat it all so lightly. To you, it's just a minor glitch on the surface of your untroubled life.'

'It's rather more than that,' he said. 'In fact, it's a major inconvenience, but I'll recover.'

'I'm sure you will,' she said with intense bitterness.

He sent her a faint smile. 'And, believe it or not, so will you—given time.' He paused. 'What are you going to do about your job? I presume you'll have to give notice.'

'It's normally a month,' she said tightly. 'But I have some holiday owing.' *Holiday that she'd hoped and planned to use for her honeymoon.* 'I—I'll write to the partners, and explain. I'm sure they'll understand—the circumstances…'

Her face worked suddenly, and all the tears she'd tried to dam back came welling inexorably to the surface again.

She said chokingly, 'Oh, no,' and pressed clenched fists to her streaming eyes.

Alex pulled the car into a convenient lay-by and stopped. Lou sat beside him, head bent, her shoulders shaking with the sobs she was trying hard to suppress. Even through the misery that overwhelmed her, she was aware of anger and shame at betraying herself like this in front of him.

She could only be grateful in a confused way that he did not look at her, or speak. Or touch her. That, she thought, most of all.

As she began to regain her self-control, however, she found herself being handed an immaculate white linen handkerchief.

'Thank you,' she mumbled. Then, stiffly, 'I'm sorry.'

'You don't have to apologise,' he said. 'Or explain.'

Lou mopped her face, and blew her nose. Still snuffling a little, she said, 'I'll have it laundered and returned to you.'

'Don't worry about it. I have plenty of others.' He closed the book of maps he'd been studying, and tossed it onto the rear seat. 'Shall we go on, or do you want to change your plans?'

The truth was she had no other plans, but she didn't want to admit that. She said, 'I'd just like to get to the farm, please.

I've already taken up too much of your time,' she added stiltedly.

'I can take the tears,' Alex said as he started the car. 'But not the humility. It's not your thing, darling. Just keep reminding yourself that I'm the heartless swine who's caused all your problems, and you'll be fighting fit in no time.'

She sent him one brief, fulminating glance, then transferred her attention ostentatiously to the passing hedgerow. Which was fine until they reached the motorway some fifteen minutes later, and all she had to stare at was other traffic.

'Why did you want to marry Ellie?' She'd meant to sit beside him in stony and unbroken silence for the duration, but curiosity eventually got the better of her.

'I didn't,' he said. 'I had no intention of getting married at all, but suddenly I needed a token wife, and Ellie seemed a likely candidate. That's all.'

'All?' Lou echoed, wonderingly. '*All?* How did Ellie feel about that?'

'Oh, she didn't want me either,' he said blandly. 'I—er—tested the waters quite early on to make sure.'

'Really.' She sent him an inimical glance. 'That must have hit you right in the ego.'

'On the contrary,' he returned, unmoved by her hostility. 'It convinced me that she was ideal for the part. After all, the last thing I wanted was someone who might fall in love with me.'

'Is this some weird, sophisticated game?' she asked coldly. 'Marrying people you don't give a damn about?'

'No, of course not,' he said. 'And I did give a damn about Ellie. While we were married I'd have made sure she got everything she could ever want in the way of comfort, plus a quick, no-fault divorce at the end of it all, with a generous settlement. Is that so bad a deal?'

'I'd say it was a cold-blooded nightmare.' Lou shook her head incredulously. 'I can't believe that Ellie would ever agree to such a thing.'

'But then,' he said softly, 'you didn't know Ellie as well as you thought—did you?' He let that sink in for a moment. 'And she certainly knew it was a business arrangement, and not a real marriage,' he added evenly. 'Although I admit we hadn't got around to discussing the small print.'

'No wonder she ran away,' Lou said bitterly. She was silent for a moment. 'But I still don't understand why you picked Ellie. You're a rich man. I'd have thought there would have been plenty of other more willing candidates around.'

'Too willing,' he said. 'That was the problem. Because they might not have wanted to leave after they'd outlived their usefulness.'

She said scornfully, 'Do you really think you're that irresistible?'

'I might be.' He slanted a swift grin at her. 'Under the right conditions.'

Well, she thought, biting her lip, she'd walked right into that.

She said coldly, 'To some women, perhaps. But not to me.' She paused again. 'If you really hate the idea so much, why get married at all?'

'I wouldn't,' he said. 'Only I'm being blackmailed.'

Lou became aware that her jaw had dropped, and hastily adjusted her face. 'By an irate husband, no doubt.'

'Wrong sex.'

'My God,' she said. 'Some woman you've refused to marry?'

'I doubt if she'd have me,' he said, deadpan. 'She'll be eighty-five in a few weeks, besides being my grandmother.'

'Your grandmother?' Lou echoed, then shook her head impatiently. 'Oh, I don't believe one word of all this. Are you involved in some insane practical joke?'

'I only wish I were,' he said, a note of grimness in his voice. 'Unfortunately it's no laughing matter. She wants me married, and she's in a position to apply pressure.'

'How?'

'By disinheriting me.'

'My God,' she said contemptuously. 'Are you really so desperate for cash? I thought you were supposed to be a wealthy man.'

'It's not a question of money.' His tone was curt. 'It's a house.'

She stared at him. 'And it means—that much to you?'

'I was born there,' he said. 'And so was my mother. I spent a lot of my childhood there, too, and I've always loved it—always known it would be mine one day.' He paused. 'And I'll do whatever it takes to ensure that it comes to me and no one else.'

'You mean that there's someone who could cut you out?'

'Some distant cousin,' he said, 'who's turned up from South Africa, complete with bride. And my grandmother has a bee in her bonnet about Rosshampton being a family house.' His mouth twisted. 'So, she's given me an ultimatum. Unless I put my neck on the wedding block, she's going to change the arrangements. Only I have no plans to change my way of life. Or not on any permanent basis.'

'You're saying you want someone to pretend to be your wife until your grandmother dies?' Lou said indignantly. 'But that's ghoulish.

'Nothing of the kind,' Alex said briskly. 'For one thing, Selina has no intention of dying—ever. For another, she's always meant to make a gift of the house in her lifetime, to avoid death duties.'

'You have no compunction about making her give up her home?' she queried acidly.

'No one has ever made Selina do anything,' he returned. 'In any case, she finds life livelier in Holland Park these days,' he added sardonically. 'So ditch the image of the forsaken pensioner.'

She flushed. 'It's really none of my concern. But no wonder Ellie wanted nothing to do with such a crazy scheme. Who in her right mind would even consider it?'

'Actually,' Alex said calmly, 'I'm hoping that you might.'

Shock made it suddenly difficult to breathe. She twisted in her seat, staring at him in total incredulity, her flush spreading—burning over her entire body.

'You—have to be—joking,' she managed at last.

'On the contrary,' he said. 'I'm deadly serious. On your own admission, you need a job and a home. Step into Ellie's shoes, and I'll provide you with both. And as soon as Rosshampton belongs to me, you'll be completely free again, with a cash settlement, to go where you please, and make a new life. Is that really such a bad deal?'

'It's nauseating.' She was gasping. 'Monstrous.'

'A slight exaggeration,' he said. 'I prefer "practical". Because you must admit it would solve major problems for both of us. I'd have a wife to dangle in front of Selina. And you would have somewhere to lick your wounds. Get your head together again.'

She said thickly, 'Living with you? I don't think so.'

'But you wouldn't be living with me,' he said gently. 'Not in any real sense. We'd simply be sharing a roof. I thought I'd made that clear.'

He paused. 'You'd have all the space you need, Louise, with the added bonus that no one would feel sorry for you. Money has that effect.'

'You disgust me.'

'I'm sorry about that.' He sounded infuriatingly unmoved. 'I dare say your father will also have his regrets, now that the future of Trentham Osborne is seriously in question once more.'

'You mean you're going to cancel the re-financing?' Louise stared at the cool profile. 'But you can't do that.'

'Actually I can,' he said. 'Because it was always conditional.' He lifted a shoulder in a faint shrug. 'And the conditions are not being met.' He paused. 'You could, of course, change your mind—and persuade me to think again, too.'

There was an endless, tingling silence. Lou found she was counting the seconds in her head, as if she'd seen the lightning flash and was waiting for the inevitable crash of thunder.

At last, she said huskily, 'Your grandmother must be very proud of you. Where blackmail is concerned, you're a chip off the old block.'

'You don't have to accept my terms,' he said coolly. 'Considering the way your family appear to treat you, I think you'd be perfectly justified in allowing Trentham Osborne to go under.'

'But you know that I won't,' she said, bitterly. 'That I can't.'

'Yes,' he said. 'I know. In fact I was counting on it.' He shot her a swift glance, assimilating her pale, set face. 'So, you accept my proposition? You'll marry me—in name only? Until I get what I want?'

It was her turn to shrug, hunching a defensive shoulder. 'I don't seem to have a choice.'

'I'll take that as an acceptance of my honourable proposal.' He sounded amused. They were approaching a motorway junction. Before Lou knew what was happening, he'd signalled, changed lanes and was driving up the slip-road.

'What are you doing?' she demanded tensely. 'This isn't the exit we want. We're miles away.'

'Are your aunt and uncle expecting you?'

'No—not exactly...'

'Then we needn't trouble them,' Alex said, as he negotiated the roundabout. 'I think we should go straight back to London, and make the necessary arrangements.'

He paused. 'Under the circumstances, I suggest a special licence, and a private ceremony with just a couple of witnesses. Present our friends and relations with a *fait accompli*. What do you think?'

Her hands gripped each other so tightly in her lap that the knuckles turned white. 'You—you don't want to know what I think.'

He had the audacity to laugh. 'No—probably not.' He became brisk. 'We both missed breakfast, so I suggest we stop and have an early lunch. There's quite a good place a few miles from here.'

'I—I'm not hungry,' Lou denied swiftly.

'All the same, you need to eat.' He was civil but inexorable. 'You'll feel better after a meal.'

'I shall feel better,' she said, 'when your grandmother hands over the deeds of your precious house. And not before.' She shook her head. 'I still can't believe I'm doing this. It's madness.'

The restaurant he'd chosen was part of a country hotel set deep in its own grounds. There were a number of vehicles already parked on the gravel sweep that fronted the pillared portico, and Alex slotted his own car neatly into a vacant space.

'It's busy,' he commented. 'I'll go and make sure we can have a reservation.'

'It looks lovely,' Lou admitted, peering up at the mellow brick façade. 'I didn't even know it existed, so how did you find out about it?'

'I stay here sometimes, at weekends.' His tone was casual. 'It's comfortable, discreet, and the food is excellent.'

He was telling her obliquely that this was somewhere he brought his girlfriends, Lou realised, her face warming slightly, as he walked away. And no doubt he would continue to do so, after their farce of a wedding had taken place. He'd warned her, after all, that he was not going to alter his way of life.

And she didn't want him to, she hastily reminded herself. In fact, as far as she was concerned, he could take a different lady to a different hotel every weekend that their non-marriage lasted. Anything that would spare her his company had to be welcome.

He was only gone a few minutes, and when he returned he was holding a key card. 'I've taken a room for you,' he said. 'I thought you might like to freshen up a little—wash away the tear stains at least. I don't want people to think I've been ill-treating you.'

'Of course not,' she said. 'After all, what's a little blackmail and deception between friends?'

'I'm glad you consider us friends,' Alex said silkily. 'That's a step in the right direction at least.' He paused. 'Do you have a skirt in that bag of yours, because if so you might change into it?'

'No.' Lou faced him with a militant sparkle in her eyes. 'I don't. I was going to stay on a farm, remember.'

He shrugged. 'It doesn't really matter. You'll need a whole new wardrobe, anyway. We'll deal with that next week.'

'No,' she said, '*we* will not. If I need clothes, I'll buy them myself.'

'You're going to be dressing for a completely different life,' he said. 'And you're going to need guidance. Not negotiable,' he added swiftly, as her lips parted mutinously. 'Oh, and you can get rid of that band round your hair, too. I prefer it loose.'

Lou was quivering with temper. 'And why should I pay any attention to your preferences?'

'Because from now on, sweetheart, I'm calling the shots,' he said. 'And don't you forget it.' He gave her the key card. 'When you look less like an orphan of the storm, you can join me in the bar.' He paused. 'What can I get you, by the way?'

'If you're calling the shots,' Lou said icily, 'then you should know.' And she marched past him, up the shallow stone steps, and through the double glass doors, furiously aware that, if she looked back, she would find him laughing.

It was a beautiful room, she had to concede unwillingly, with its wide, canopied bed and elegant furniture. And the bathroom was the height of luxury with its gleaming tiles and marble surfaces. The roomy shower cubicle was constructed in a pretty hexagonal shape, and the tub was enormous, and clearly intended for dual occupation.

The perfect love nest, Lou thought with irony, inspecting the array of scented oils and lotions on offer as she dried her face and hands on one of the fluffy towels. Except that love would have very little to do with it.

For a brief moment she had a sharp, disturbing image of that bed in the other room occupied. Of Alex Fabian, his mouth smiling as he bent over some naked, sinuous beauty.

She closed her eyes swiftly, blotting the picture from her mind, bewildered at its sudden potency.

Wondering why she had thought of Alex and not David, who was probably entwined with his Ellie in a similar room somewhere.

She leaned against the cold edge of the marble for a moment, recovering her composure, then opened her eyes. She barely recognised the white, strained face looking back at her from the mirror. Her eyes were still slightly reddened, in spite of the cold water she'd splashed onto them, and her lips were pale and vulnerable.

Reluctantly she took her cosmetics purse from her bag, and made use of the concealer and compressed powder before adding a soft pink lustre to her unhappy mouth.

Finally, she took the band from her hair and shook it free, the dark, waving strands forming a silky aureole round her face.

It was a slightly braver picture than before, she thought, but no more than that. The inner fire which had once lit her eyes and flushed her cheeks had been quenched.

In just a few hours, she'd been transformed into a quiet grey shadow of her former self.

And no one in this world, especially a shrewd, manipulative old lady, was going to believe that she would ever be the choice of a man like Alex Fabian. Not in a month of Sundays. Because she hadn't even been enough for David, whom she'd loved.

Ellie, the golden, the glowing, would have convinced everyone, of course. And she would have enjoyed spending the money, and having clothes and jewellery lavished on her. She'd relished the glimpse of the high life that Alex had shown her, and she had the charm and prettiness to make her mark in the circles he moved in. She'd have made him a trophy wife, rather than the token variety.

He might even have fallen in love with her, given time, Lou thought, replacing her comb in her bag. But there had been no time. Instead there had been David...

She drew a deep, painful breath, then turned away from the mirror. It was time she went down to the bar before Alex came looking for her.

The long, low-ceilinged room was filled with people enjoying their aperitifs and looking at leather-bound menus, but she saw him at once, sitting at a table in the window, her gaze drawn to him like a magnet.

And she wasn't the only one. As she threaded her way towards him, she was aware of other glances targeting him with open avidity. Of women's fingers nervously playing with their hair, their jewellery, as they watched him. Of laughter that was pitched a fraction too high.

But why should she even be surprised? Alex Fabian was always going to be a man who would attract female attention without even trying, she thought. And he wasn't trying now, just lounging on the cushioned seat, and staring out of the window.

He rose politely as she reached him, the cool eyes scanning her, their expression unfathomable. 'Did you find everything you needed?'

'Thank you—yes.' There were no spare chairs around, so she took her place beside him on the window-seat, maintaining a deliberate and cautious distance.

Alex lifted a hand in a silent signal, and a waiter appeared from nowhere with an ice bucket containing a bottle of champagne, and two glasses.

Lou's brows drew together as she watched the man remove the cork with a flourish and fill the glasses. 'What is this?' she demanded in an indignant undertone, as soon as he'd departed.

'Bollinger,' Alex said. 'Conventional, I know, but we do have our engagement to celebrate.'

'I fail to see why.'

'Then just regard it as a much-needed tonic,' he said softly. 'The wine for all seasons and all times of day.' He raised his glass. 'To us.'

Then, as she made no move, he added mockingly, 'Or would you prefer—absent friends?'

'No,' she said between her teeth, 'I would not.'

'Then choose your own toast,' Alex said. 'But drink to something—anything. People are beginning to look.'

'Yes,' she said with quiet fierceness, 'because they're wondering what the hell you're doing with a—a nonentity like me.' She took a deep breath. 'I'm sorry, but I've realised that I can't do this after all. It just won't work. We—we wouldn't fool anyone. Your grandmother will pick up in seconds that I'm not in your league.' She swallowed. 'That we don't care for each other.'

He shrugged, his face suddenly hard. 'She specified marriage,' he countered. 'Not a love match. And it's too late for second thoughts, Louise. Our bargain stands. Now pick up your drink, and smile at me nicely for the audience. You need all the rehearsal you can get.'

The wine was cold and clear, the bubbles exploding in her head as she obeyed him.

And he smiled back at her, tiny, glittering devils dancing in his eyes, and reached for her hand, raising it to his lips and pressing a light, sensuous kiss into her palm.

Shock ran through her like a flame. She tried to snatch her hand back, but his clasp tightened.

'What—what do you think you're doing?' she demanded breathlessly.

'I felt the occasion called for a gesture,' Alex drawled. 'That was it.'

He paused, his gaze even as it met hers. 'Understand this, sweetheart. Whatever does not happen between us in private, in public we're the couple of the decade. I expect you to pretend—and pretend well.

'You will smile at me. You will not pull away when I touch you, or shudder if I should feel obliged to kiss you. You're getting well paid for a service, and that's the service you'll provide.

'And if you find physical contact between us difficult, then that's your problem,' he added with a touch of harshness.

She drank some more champagne quickly, trying to ignore the fact that her fingers were entwined with his, and that he was stroking the soft mound at the base of her thumb.

She said in a low voice, 'Is it—absolutely essential?'

'We'll be newly-weds. People will expect the occasional demonstration of affection. So what are you so uptight about?'

She took another frantic sip. 'Perhaps I'm not sure that—I can cope—with this kind of—intimacy.'

'Really?' His grin was cool and cynical. 'But I'm not irresistible, darling. You told me so yourself—remember?' He paused. 'However, if the going gets tough, just keep reminding yourself of the money. That should provide some consolation.'

'Yes,' Lou said softly and stormily. 'Because, one day, it will enable me to tell you to go straight to hell. And that will make it all worthwhile.'

'I'm sure it will,' he said silkily. 'And I'm also beginning to think that married life won't be nearly as dull as I expected.'

He allowed her to absorb that for a startled moment, then passed her a menu. 'Now—shall we order lunch?'

CHAPTER FOUR

LOUISE had ordered more or less at random, convinced that she would be unable to eat a thing, but discovered that the chilled cucumber soup and the perfectly poached salmon with its accompanying watercress salad were exactly what she wanted, and too delicious to resist anyway.

She found herself, somewhat defiantly, ordering a *crème brûlée* to follow.

Alex asked for cheese, after his choice of vegetable soup and rare roast beef sliced from the joint on the trolley.

Lou had to admit, as coffee was brought, that the meal hadn't been the nightmare she'd envisaged. Under other circumstances, she might even have found Alex pleasant company. He'd chatted lightly about the food, a film he'd seen, a book he'd recently read, a concert he'd attended, and while doing so, she realised afterwards, had managed to extract a fair amount of information about her own tastes.

They would never be lovers, they might not even be friends, but there was a faint possibility that they could manage a certain level of coexistence, she told herself, trying to feel hopeful.

'You're very quiet,' he said. 'I hope that's not a bad sign.'

'No.' She played with her coffee spoon. 'I was just—thinking.' She made herself look up, meet his quizzical gaze across the table. 'Thinking that I'll want the whole thing in writing—a proper contract between us.'

His brows lifted. 'Naturally,' he said with faint hauteur. 'Do you want your father's lawyers to act for you over the financial arrangements, or do you plan to conduct your own negotiations?'

'I—I wasn't talking about the money,' she said jerkily. 'But the rest of it. About it not being—a real marriage.'

'Ah,' he said meditatively. 'You mean you don't trust me to leave you in peace?'

'Not—precisely.' She drank some coffee. 'But I think it's better that the lines should be drawn. That we both know exactly where we stand.'

'About a thousand miles apart, by the sound of it.' He studied her with a faint frown. 'I have no plans to seduce you, Louise. I thought I'd made that clear.'

'Yes,' she said. 'But all the same...'

'All the same, you intend to hedge yourself round with rules and regulations,' he said softly. 'Tell me something, my sweet. Which of us don't you trust? Is it me? Or could it possibly be yourself?'

She bit her lip. 'Don't be ridiculous.'

'I ask,' he went on, 'because when I was holding your hand in the bar just now, your pulse was off the scale. And I found that—interesting.'

Lou put her cup down with a bang. 'You've never heard of stress?' she came back at him. 'I imagine I'm allowed some kind of reaction to the worst day of my entire life.'

'Or the first day of the rest of it,' he said equably, 'depending on your point of view.'

'Thank you,' she said. 'But the Pollyanna outlook has never appealed to me.'

'But if you're really so stressed,' he went on, 'the room is still ours for the rest of the afternoon, and I know something that might help.'

For a moment, the only sound to break the taut silence between them was her own indrawn breath. Then she rallied, her voice low and husky with anger.

'How dare you—how dare you even suggest...'

'A shoulder rub,' he supplied. 'It works for me every time.' He gave her a mocking grin. 'And I won't even make you take your clothes off—unless you insist, of course.'

Her throat muscles were tightening, and she was shaking inside, but she forced herself to lift her chin and confront him.

She said, 'Kindly don't talk to me like that. Not now, not

ever again, or the deal's off, and to hell with Trentham Osborne.'

'Hell,' Alex said, 'is going to be extremely crowded at this rate.' He paused. 'I suppose that's going to be Clause Three, subsection B of the contract. The party of the first part—me— will not tease, wind up or joke with the party of the second part—you. Especially on any subject even remotely connected with sex.'

She said stiffly, 'No doubt you find this very amusing...'

'No,' he said. 'I find it sad. But you're not the only woman in the world with a sense of humour bypass, so I'll get by.'

Lou saw just in time the pitfall in telling him in a dignified way that there was nothing wrong with her sense of humour.

She said coldly, 'Perhaps we could go now, please. The sooner we begin this nauseating charade, the sooner it will be over.'

'Not necessarily,' Alex said drily. 'But I catch your drift.'

His fingers clasped her arm lightly as they walked to the door.

'It's a statement,' Lou whispered silently, forcing herself not to flinch. 'Only a statement...'

And halted as she found their exit suddenly blocked.

'Why, Alex, darling.' The woman confronting them was beautiful, her vibrant red hair expertly layered, and the deep blue eyes fringed by impossibly long lashes.

She was wearing a knee-length black dress which hugged her spectacular figure, topped by a jacket in exaggeratedly large checks of black and white.

There were black onyx studs surrounded by pearls in her ears, and a matching pendant at her throat.

And the voice that issued from the smiling red lips was throaty and undeniably sexy. 'How utterly lovely to see you.'

'Lucinda,' Alex responded with cool civility. 'What a surprise to find you here.'

She laughed. 'Hardly, darling. This has always been one of my favourite places. And I rather fancied a trip down memory lane.'

'By yourself?'

'Of course not. Peter's parking the car. He's bribing me with lunch before we visit his elderly aunt. Practically gaga, but loaded.' A shrug. 'You know how it is.'

She turned her gaze to Louise, who found herself assessed and dismissed in one lightning glance. 'Aren't you going to introduce me to your friend?'

'To my fiancée, actually,' Alex drawled. 'Louise—this is Lucinda Crosby. Lucinda, I'd like you to meet Louise Trentham, who has just promised to become my wife.'

'Well,' Lucinda said softly, her eyes narrowing. 'How very surprising—and marvellous for you both, of course. And I thought...' She broke off artistically with a little laugh. 'My best wishes—and congratulations, especially to you, Alex, darling. I hope you'll be blissfully happy together.'

'I'm sure we shall.' Alex's arm slid round Lou's shoulders, and remained there. She felt herself quietly drawn against him, and fought the immediate impulse to resist.

Just another statement, she told herself. But this time she had the impression that it mattered.

It occurred to her at the same time that this was the closest she had ever been to him physically. That this was the kind of contact she would have to accustom herself to. And that it was never going to be easy.

The arm that held her was strong. The shoulder she leaned against was hard with muscle. She could smell the faint drift of some cologne he was wearing and feel the heat of his body through the layers of his clothing.

And in one blinding flash of revelation she knew exactly what the warmth—the scent of him would be like if he was naked and she was in his arms, naked too.

She felt the shock of that certainty deep in her bones—in the sudden surge of her blood. She felt the fine hairs rise along her spine, and her nipples harden helplessly against the thin wool of her sweater.

And thought, This is impossible. This *cannot* be happening to me.

Dazed, and trying desperately to hang on to her composure, she heard Lucinda say, 'But you're not rushing off, surely. You must wait for Peter, and then we can all have a drink together—to celebrate.'

'It's a kind thought,' Alex said smoothly. 'But perhaps some other time. We really have to go. We're getting married very soon, and we need to make a start on the arrangements. I'm sure you understand.'

'Of course.' Lucinda's smile widened. 'I shall be able to tell Peter all about your charming bride-to-be over lunch. I'm sure he'll be delighted for you.' She turned to Lou. 'Goodbye, my dear—Laura, is it?'

'Louise,' Lou supplied woodenly.

'Of course—and I'm Cindy. I know we're going to be great friends. Be sure and invite me to the wedding.'

Hell, Lou thought, smiling politely, will freeze over first—on both counts.

As they crossed the foyer to the reception desk, she was aware of the other woman's gaze boring into her back. She waited quietly while Alex paid the bill, getting herself back under control with a rigorous act of will, subduing her flurried breathing and the scamper of her pulses.

She could find no excuse or explanation for that totally animal reaction, and she was ashamed that she could be so easily beguiled. But it was one thing to recognise that Alex Fabian possessed a powerful sexuality. She'd known that since their first encounter. It was a different thing to find herself exposed to it—and at the mercy of her senses—when he hadn't even been trying.

Heaven help me if he ever did try, she thought, her mouth suddenly dry. Dear God, I shall have to be so very careful.

'Peter Crosby,' she said as they went out to the car. 'Isn't he in the government?'

'Yes.' His tone did not invite further enquiries.

Nor did she really need to ask. But something—some small, strange pain deep inside her—drove her on.

She said, 'Living in the country does not make me stupid, Alex.'

'I hope it doesn't make you over-curious about things that don't concern you either,' he returned curtly.

'No,' she said. 'You can live your life exactly as you wish. I can put that in the contract, too, if you like.'

'That,' he said, 'will not be necessary. And that particular episode is in the past, anyway.'

That's not what she thinks, Lou thought.

Aloud, she said, 'She met you with Ellie, didn't she?'

'She's met me with a lot of people.'

'And she meant me to know, didn't she? That you'd stayed here together?'

'God knows,' he said. 'Possibly. Probably. I never figured out how Lucinda's mind worked.'

'But then,' she said, 'I don't suppose her mind was ever her chief attraction.'

'Ouch.' He sounded amused. 'You have sharp claws, country mouse.'

And I suspect I'm going to need them, Lou thought as they drove off.

It was a quiet journey. Alex found a classical channel on the radio, and she lay back, eyes closed, letting the music wash over her, deliberately making her mind a blank.

She did not want to contemplate what lay ahead of her in London. She did not want to think about the choice she had made, or the risks she was taking. And how serious those risks were had become only too apparent in the past hour.

The past was too painful to remember. The future was a leap in the dark. It was better to let herself drift. She might even have dozed a little.

But Alex's voice telling her quietly that they were coming into London brought her sharply back to full awareness of the difficult present.

She struggled to sit upright, pushing her hair back from her face, hoping that her mouth hadn't dropped open, or that she hadn't—oh, God—been snoring.

She cleared her throat. 'I—I've just realised that I've no idea where I'm being taken. A hotel, I suppose.'

He said, 'We're going to my flat.'

'Oh?' She stiffened. 'Why?'

'Because we have a lot to talk about,' he said. 'And being under the same roof makes conversation easier, somehow.'

'Yes,' she said, 'I—I see that. It's just that I didn't expect to move in with you before—the marriage.'

'For God's sake.' He was half amused, half exasperated. 'I'm not asking you to share a bedsit. There are two bedrooms in the damned place, and the doors lock.'

He paused. 'And it's the norm for lovers to live together. It might be found extraordinary if we didn't.'

She swallowed. 'We are not—lovers.'

'In the eyes of the world we are. So carried away by our feelings, in fact, that we can't wait to tie the knot. You might care to remind yourself of that from time to time,' he added sardonically. 'It could add depth to your performance.'

'Did you take Ellie there?' She couldn't remember it ever being mentioned.

'I hardly had the opportunity,' Alex drawled. 'No sooner had she agreed to marry me than she was disappearing over the horizon. But I planned to show her the place—ask if she was prepared to live there. After all, she might have hated it.'

Lou lifted her chin. 'And I might too.'

'Of course,' he said. 'And if so, you must tell me, and we'll start house-hunting. Find something that will suit you better.'

She gasped. 'You mean you'd be prepared to give up your home for this—non-relationship?'

'Firstly,' he said, 'it's not my home in any real sense. It's just a flat. The only place I care for, as I've made clear, is Rosshampton. Which is why we're involved in this ''non-relationship'', as you so eloquently describe it.

'Secondly, you're doing me an immense favour,' he added levelly. 'And the least I can do in return is make sure that you're as happy as I can make you, which includes your immediate surroundings.'

'Well,' Lou said awkwardly, 'thank you—I think.'

'I have to tell you,' he said, 'that after your stepsister's wide-eyed compliance with everything I said and did, you come as something of a shock to the system, Miss Louise Trentham.'

She hunched a shoulder. 'Don't despair, Mr Fabian. I may dwindle into compliance myself, given time, and the gratification of my every wish. And Ellie wasn't the pushover you thought, either.'

'I stand corrected,' he said, the ghost of a laugh in his voice.

She hated it when he did that, because it made her want to smile back at him.

'So what else does this flat have besides its two bedrooms with the lockable doors?' She made herself sound brisk and businesslike.

'Two bathrooms, a dining room, and a drawing room with a balcony which leads up to a private roof garden, where you can sunbathe in the nude if you wish.'

'I don't,' Lou said coldly. 'But I gather that makes your flat the penthouse. I suppose I should have guessed.'

'You make me feel as if I've failed some basic test.' The amusement in his tone deepened. 'Besides, someone has to live up there, and I thought the garden might actually appeal to you. It has some nice tubs and things.'

'Sent round from Harrods each spring, no doubt,' Lou said. 'I can't see you up to your elbows in compost.' She paused. 'You didn't mention a kitchen.'

'There is one,' he said. 'I'm almost sure I've seen it.'

'But it doesn't get much use.'

'The kettle works,' he said. 'And the microwave. And I have an excellent corkscrew.'

'Well,' she said, 'what more could one want?'

'But then,' he said, gently, 'you'd hardly expect me to spend my leisure hours grinding up pesto, or perfecting my soufflé.'

Lou found she did not want to consider how Alex Fabian

might occupy his leisure. She said rather hurriedly, 'Do you have a housekeeper?'

'No, because the flat is fully serviced. The maid comes in every day, and laundry and dry-cleaning is back in twenty-four hours. There's a gym, sauna and swimming pool in the basement, underground parking, and a good restaurant on the first floor, which also delivers.' Alex sent her a lightning glance. 'Am I selling you the idea?'

'It sounds quite attractive,' she admitted sedately.

'You overwhelm me.'

'Oh, no,' she said. 'I don't aspire to that.' She considered. 'I think I'm going to aim to be unobtrusive. If I move into the kitchen, we'll probably never meet at all.'

'Let's cling to that thought.' He spoke cordially, but there was an odd note in his voice, almost like suppressed anger.

And that, thought Lou, was ridiculous.

Part of her wanted to hate the flat, but she couldn't. It was too spacious, and the views from its windows too spectacular. It had soft carpets, subdued lighting and furniture to sink into.

But it certainly wasn't a home. Alex had been right about that. It looked as if it had been tastefully assembled by a good designer, she thought, looking round her, but there were no personal touches. Nothing to give a clue to the character of the owner. Even the flower arrangement in the hall looked as if it was too correct to shed a petal.

'What do you think?' Alex propped himself in the doorway of the drawing room, watching her move round.

'You don't spend much time here, do you?'

'No,' he said. 'I thought you'd find that a point in its favour. But can you bear to live in it?'

She bit her lip. 'Yes,' she said. 'As far as the situation itself is bearable.

'Then perhaps you'd like to come and look at the bedrooms. Decide which one you want.' He paused. 'At present, I'm using the master bedroom myself, but if that's the one you'd prefer I'll move out. It's not a problem.'

'No,' Lou said hastily. Even if he moved to another planet, it would still be his bed she was using, and the mere thought made her throat tighten. 'The other one will be fine,' she added with an attempt at lightness. 'It's not important, after all. Just a place to sleep in.'

'As you say,' Alex agreed rather too gravely. 'So shall we just toss a coin?'

'No.' She smiled resolutely. 'There's no need. I'll have the spare bedroom.'

'Very well.' He picked up her bag, and started down the passage. He threw open a door, then stood aside to allow her to precede him.

It was a large room, with tall windows hung with long cream curtains. The tailored bedspread on the wide bed was cream also, and the carpet was a soft blue.

'The bathroom's there.' Alex pointed. 'And the door next to it is the dressing room, although it's more of a walk-in closet.' He looked around him, grimacing slightly. 'It's very much a guest room, isn't it? I hadn't realised.'

'Well,' Lou said, 'I'm a guest.'

'Look,' he said, 'do whatever you like with it. Have it re-decorated—change the furniture—anything you want.'

'There's really no need,' she said. 'I shan't be staying that long.'

'I can't guarantee that,' he said. 'There's no set time limit. My grandmother is a law unto herself, and she'll act when she's ready, and not before. In the meantime, there's no reason why you shouldn't be comfortable.'

'I shall be.' Lou squared her shoulders. 'It's actually a very nice room.' She hesitated. 'Where do you sleep?' She tried to sound casual.

'Across the passage.' He indicated the door behind him, and gave her a quizzical look. 'I hope that's a sufficient distance.'

This time her hesitation was fatal, and his brows snapped together.

'Clearly not,' he commented coldly. 'And I'm beginning to find the role of potential rapist a little wearing. I wonder what they did with the stones from the Berlin Wall. I could find a use for them.'

Lou bit her lip. 'I'm sorry,' she said with constraint. 'I didn't mean...' She stumbled to a halt. 'This isn't easy for me.'

'It isn't what I'd have chosen either,' Alex came back at her, his frown deepening. 'I didn't realise I'd be sharing my life with a professional virgin. No wonder your fiancé cleared out. You must have frozen him away.'

'You—bastard.' Lou almost choked on the word, wrapping her arms defensively round her body. 'Don't you dare say that. I loved David, and I wanted him—wanted to belong to him.'

'Then why didn't you?' he challenged. 'Instead of—saving yourself for marriage like some Victorian miss.'

'We agreed to wait. It was a mutual decision.' She drew a deep breath. 'And anyway, it's not that easy, not in a village where everyone knows everyone else's business. Besides, there was his mother...'

'Those are excuses—not reasons,' he said. 'There are ways and means. You could have gone away together somewhere. That hotel where we had lunch—how many of those couples do you think were married?'

She gasped. 'You think that's what I wanted? To be taken off for some—sordid weekend?'

'Why should it be sordid,' he said, 'if you love each other? Why couldn't it be passionate, and exciting—and fun?'

'You speak from the depth of your own vast experience, of course,' she said scornfully. 'But I'm talking about real love. The sort that lasts a lifetime—not casual sex with other people's partners. So don't lecture me about love, because you—you don't know the meaning of the word.'

'Perhaps not,' he said slowly. 'But I know there's an imperative that drives men and women together through fire and flood. And your romance sounds a pretty tepid affair to me. Perhaps David thought so too. Perhaps he wanted more than safety and domesticity, and sex on Friday nights when there was an ''r'' in the month.'

'You have no right to say these things.' Lou flung her head back. 'No right at all.'

'No,' he said unexpectedly, 'I haven't. But maybe someone needs to tell you a few home truths about this deathless love of yours, before you wrap it round you like a security blanket and end up strangling in it. Because there's no safety in love. It's the ultimate risk, not a soft option with a wedding ring and roses round the door.'

'Have you—quite finished?'

'Almost.' He paused, then said more gently, 'It's probably too late to say I didn't mean to hurt you, but it's true. Maybe I shouldn't have said what I did. But the fact is they made fools of us both. And it riles me to think that neither of them had the guts to stand up and admit what was going on. Tell us to our faces that they wanted more than we had to offer. And in your heart, you must feel that too.'

She stared at him. 'Don't you dare tell me what's going on in my heart.' Her voice rose stormily. 'You know nothing about me—nothing.'

'You're right,' he said, 'I don't. But during the course of our short marriage, I plan to find out.' He turned away. 'I'll leave you to unpack.'

'What makes you think I'll stay here another minute?' she flung after him.

Alex sighed. 'Louise—you have nowhere else to go. And we have a deal.' The green eyes were cool, direct and implacable. 'Stay with me—marry me—and Trentham Osborne get another chance. Otherwise they don't. Jobs will be lost. Good books will not be published, and your father and his wife will lose their home. But it's entirely up to you. As it always was.'

He glanced at his watch. 'I'm going out for a while. If you're still here when I return our deal goes ahead, with no more arguments or recriminations. A business decision, no more, no less. So, think about it.'

The door closed behind him.

Lou sank down on the edge of the bed, still hugging herself protectively, staring ahead of her with eyes that saw nothing.

The silence pressed down on her, surrounded her. She was shaking inside, her mind in freefall.

He was vile, she thought. Vile, disgusting and heartless. The things he had said seared her memory, and she would never forgive him—never.

But, at the same time, she could not ignore the tiny voice in the corner of her mind that whispered he was right. That her relationship with David was never strong enough to stay the course. That if they had loved ardently enough, nothing could have kept them apart. That what she'd thought was consideration had merely been a warning signal that all was not well.

After all, he had had no such qualms about running away with Ellie, she acknowledged sadly.

Her overwhelming impulse was to pick up her bag, and leave. Find a hotel for the night, then make her way to Paddington in the morning. She could be at the farm by lunchtime. And Alex Fabian would not follow her. He'd made that clear.

If she left—it was over. And the fate of Trentham Osborne would be sealed. And, as her father had said, they would lose everything. Undoubtedly, both the London flat and Virginia Cottage had been used as collateral to raise money in the past, and would be snatched away if the company collapsed.

And, while she might not have had the easiest of relationships with Marian and her father, she could not wish to see them destitute—especially when she had the power to prevent it.

And when Alex Fabian had achieved his purpose, she would be totally free to do whatever she wished—go wherever she wanted.

Machu Picchu, she thought. Ayers Rock. The temples of Cambodia. So many places in the world that she'd thought she would never see, because David wasn't keen on foreign travel. And soon she would have the time and the money to explore them all.

If her life had to change, then she would make sure it was a change for the better.

She would earn Alex Fabian's money, she told herself with steely determination. Earn it—and ultimately enjoy it, in the certain knowledge that she would never have to set eyes on him again.

And she would not come cheap. He would pay, and pay again for her services. He might even be sorry their paths had ever crossed.

She got to her feet and took her bag into the dressing room, which had one wall lined with shelving and drawers, and another occupied by fitted wardrobes. Her few belongings looked lost and lonely in all that space. Rather as she herself felt, she thought wryly, then paused.

That was negative thinking, and whatever happened she was going to emerge from this situation as a victor not a victim.

And tried to ignore that small, aggravating voice now whispering an insistent reminder that Alex Fabian was someone who also expected to win. And generally succeeded.

She said aloud, 'But not this time.' And made it sound like a vow.

CHAPTER FIVE

LOUISE was sitting curled up in a corner of a sofa, trying hard to concentrate on the paperback thriller she'd brought with her, when Alex returned several hours later.

She raised her head slowly, and looked at him standing motionless in the doorway, aware that her heart was thudding unevenly. And that it had occurred to her more than once that he might not come back at all...

There was a long silence, then he said quietly, 'Thank you.'

'Don't be too grateful,' she returned with an assumption of coolness. 'I fully intend to take you to the cleaners.'

'I can accept that.' He walked to the sofa opposite, removing his jacket and tossing it over the padded arm. 'And I'm sure it will be very good for my soul.'

He leaned back against the cushions, closing his eyes briefly. For the first time since she'd met him, he looked weary—even strained—and Louise had detected the faint tang of whisky as he walked past her.

She said, 'Where have you been?'

'That's a very wifely question, darling,' he drawled. 'Getting into your role already?'

'Isn't that what you wanted?'

'Of course.' He opened his eyes and met her gaze. 'Actually, I walked for a while, and then I went to the bank, and did some work.'

'At this time—on a Saturday?' Her voice lifted in disbelief.

'Why not? I've never been a nine-to-five man, and I like to know I won't be interrupted. Besides, there were some things I needed to get out of the way.' He paused. 'I called your father, and told him that the re-financing of Trentham Osborne would go ahead as arranged.'

'You did?' Louise's eyes widened in bewilderment. 'But how did you know I'd still be here?'

'I didn't.' His tone was laconic. 'I just decided that if you were going to stay, I'd rather it was of your own accord rather than any threat I could hold over you.' He paused. 'Which, in turn, means that you're free to leave, if you want, and I won't stop you.'

She swallowed. 'That's—good of you. But I've decided to remain—to stick to my side of the deal, as agreed.' She hesitated. 'Did you tell my father where I was?'

'Yes.' She detected a faint chill. 'I told him.'

'What did he say?'

Alex shrugged, his mouth twisting. 'He seemed to take it in his stride.'

Louise bit her lip. 'I expect he was too relieved about the company to understand properly.'

'That's certainly the charitable way of looking at it,' he said drily. 'I wonder what he'll do next time he needs a daughter to sacrifice.'

She bent her head. 'Has there been any word,' she asked in a low voice, 'from Ellie?'

'Apparently not,' Alex returned. 'But plenty of words from the bridegroom's mother, who's been haunting the place all day, having acute hysterics. As a result, your stepmother has retired to bed with a severe migraine.'

'Oh, poor Marian.' Louise found herself suppressing a giggle. 'I can imagine. Mrs Sanders is the ultimate monster.'

'Then she should find Virginia Cottage a home from home,' Alex retorted caustically. He shook his head. 'How the hell did you ever get lumbered with such completely selfish relations?'

'We just inhabit different worlds, that's all.' Louise moved uncomfortably. 'And I think I remind my father too much of my mother.' She sighed. 'He's always felt guilty, I'm sure, that he wasn't there when she died—among other things.'

'And handing you over to me will somehow assuage his guilt?' There was a scornful note in his voice.

'I don't know,' she said. She tried to muster a smile. 'But it will certainly get me out of the way.'

'So,' he said, 'what made you decide to keep to our bargain, after all?'

She shrugged. 'As you've pointed out, I'm homeless and jobless.' She lifted her chin. 'I need the money you're going to pay me to kick-start my life all over again.'

He linked his hands loosely behind his head as he watched her. 'And how do you propose to do that?'

'Well,' she said, 'first, I shall go round the world. And when I've done that, I shall come home and train properly for a career.'

'In the law?'

'Perhaps,' she said. 'Or teaching. I shan't decide anything immediately.' Her smile was wintry. 'I have to survive the next few weeks and months before that.'

'You might, of course, fall in love and get married instead.'

'Oh, no.' Louise shook her head with determination.

'You seem very positive about it.' His voice was faintly amused.

'While you were out, I had a lot of time to think—about what you said to me earlier about my affair with David being…tepid.'

He moved sharply, almost defensively. 'If you remember, I did apologise for that.'

'Yes, but it occurred to me there could be an element of truth in it, all the same. That maybe David started seeing me because we were the right age, and knew the same people, and it was—convenient. But that's not good enough—is it? I should have realised when he kept finding excuses not to make the engagement official, or fix a date for the wedding.'

She smiled wanly. 'It was all supposed to be out of consideration for his mother, but I bet he hasn't given her a second thought since he left.'

He said quite gently, 'Louise, don't punish yourself like this.'

'Is that what I'm doing? I thought I was being realistic.

Facing up to a few things.' Her hands gripped each other in her lap. 'And just think how much worse it would all have been if we'd been properly engaged—or even married.'

He shrugged. 'Nothing lasts forever—least of all marriage, these days,' he added cynically.

'Mine would have lasted,' she said. 'I'd have made it work.'

'How ferocious you sound.' His own voice held amusement. 'And now you can concentrate all that determined will of yours on the job in hand—pretending to be my wife in front of my grandmother.'

She stared down at her clenched hands. 'Couldn't we keep it like that—just a pretence, rather than actually getting married? It would make things so much easier—later on. When it's all finished with.'

'Alas, no.' Alex gave a wry shrug. 'If I know Selina, she'll demand to see the marriage certificate. There has to be a wedding, but it will be quick, quiet, and as painless as I can make it.'

'Yes.' She bit her lip. 'Actually, I thought that was where you might have gone—to see your grandmother, to tell her…'

'She's not around.' He smiled faintly. 'Every year at this time she goes on a kind of royal progress to visit all those of her friends who are still standing. You'll have to wait to meet her at her birthday party—at Rosshampton.'

His voice seemed to caress the word.

Oh, God, Louise thought. This means so much to him. Suppose it all goes horribly wrong.

He was speaking again, more briskly. 'Have you learned your way round the flat yet?'

'As much as I need to do.' She forbore to mention that his bedroom had been the only no-go area. 'You certainly weren't joking about the kitchen. The cupboard's bare—and the fridge.'

'Damnation,' he said. 'You've had nothing to eat. I should have shown you how to use the internal phone—order from the restaurant. Would you like them to bring up some sandwiches?'

'Oh, no, I'm fine,' she assured him hastily. She paused.

'Would you mind if I got some food in—stocked up a bit on basics?'

His brows lifted. 'Trying to domesticate me already, darling?'

'I was thinking of stuff like milk and bread,' Louise said steadily. 'Not dinner for two.'

He shrugged. 'This is your home for the duration,' he said. 'Buy whatever you need. Just make sure there are always plenty of my favourite coffee beans, as well as your herbal stuff.'

'I'm not totally committed to camomile,' she said lightly. 'Sometimes I ring the changes with hot chocolate.' She got to her feet. 'If you don't mind, I'd like to go to my room now.' She tried to smile. 'It's been—quite a day.'

'And this,' he said softly, 'is only the beginning.'

He rose too, and she had to control an impulse to step back. 'Have you everything you need?'

'Oh, yes,' she said quickly. 'I'm sure I'll be very comfortable.'

'Well, if you think of anything, let me know,' he said. 'I'm going to watch television for a while.'

There *was* something, of course. The lock on her door had no key, after all, but she felt, absurdly, that this was not the most appropriate moment to mention it.

It can wait till morning, she told herself.

'Fine.' She sounded cheerful to the point of inanity, she realised crossly. 'Goodnight, then.'

'Sleep well,' he said, smiling faintly. 'And—sweet dreams.'

Unlikely, Louise thought as she escaped. Although screaming nightmares were a definite possibility.

Her head was aching slightly, and her eyes still felt sore from weeping as she let herself into her room. She had no aspirin with her, but maybe a hot bath would take away some of the stress.

It wasn't going to be acting a part in front of his grandmother which was going to present the major difficulty, she acknowledged as she began to run water into the tub, adding a splash of the lily-scented bath oil which stood with the array of other expensive toiletries on the tiled surround. It was the ordinary day-to-day living under the same roof. Trying not to jump when he entered the room, or overreacting whenever he came within three yards of her.

I wish, she thought drily, that there was a crash course I could take in becoming used to having him around.

I'd really like to be able to take it as easily for granted as he does himself. Although, of course, he's had infinitely more practice.

And found herself grimacing at the thought with something very like real pain.

The bath helped. She lay back in the warm, fragrant water, eyes closed, her head resting on the small pillow provided for the purpose, letting herself drift above the confusion of emotion within her. Telling herself there would be a time when none of it would matter any more. And hoping desperately that it was true.

She dried herself slowly on one of the thick, luxurious bath sheets, then rubbed creamy, scented body lotion into her skin before putting on the simple white lawn gown with its low-cut bodice and narrow straps, which was the only nightdress she'd brought with her.

Altogether too bridal, she thought, pulling a critical face at her reflection. Red flannel pyjamas would have been more appropriate.

She felt relaxed but not particularly drowsy as she climbed into bed, so she piled the pillows behind her and reached for her book. Considering she'd been reading it for most of the evening, she could remember very little of the plot, she thought, turning back to the beginning again.

She'd just started the second chapter when she heard it. The quiet but definite sound of a knock on her door.

The book slipped from her hands. 'Who—who is it?' she called, her voice strangled.

'Who do you think?' He sounded irritable rather than

amorous, she noted thankfully. 'There's hardly a cast of thousands out here. May I come in?'

'I'm in bed.' It was a feeble protest and she knew it.

'Really—in a bedroom?' His tone was caustic. 'How bizarre. This I must see.'

The door opened, and he walked in, carrying a tray on which reposed a steaming porcelain beaker. And a plate of biscuits.

Louise's eyes widened incredulously. 'What is this?'

'You said you liked hot chocolate.' He placed the tray on the night table. 'I ordered some for you.'

'Oh,' she said, touching the tip of her tongue to dry lips. 'That was—kind.'

'Well, make the most of it.' He slanted a grin at her. 'It doesn't happen very often. It's also practical,' he added. 'Lunch was a long time ago, and you could have problems trying to sleep on an empty stomach.'

'Yes,' she said. 'Yes—I suppose so.'

'Is the bed all right?' He tested the mattress with an experimental hand, then sat down on its edge. 'I've never slept in it.'

Well, that at least was a comfort, Louise thought, her apprehension increasing with every second. She tried unobtrusively to move further back against her pillows.

'And I've no immediate plans to do so,' he went on mockingly. 'Unless you insist, which seems unlikely. I hope that sets your mind at rest.'

'I'm really not concerned.' She tried to sound nonchalant. 'I hardly think you'd be stupid enough to jeopardise our deal.'

'No,' he said, 'but—to seal it perhaps.' And he leaned forward and kissed her lightly but sensuously on her parted lips.

She wanted to leap away, shuddering—to scream her outrage—to hit and claw at him, but that would only suggest that it was important to her. That it mattered too much. And she could not let him think that.

So by a superhuman effort she forced herself to remain still and passive under his brief, but telling, exploration of her mouth.

And when, at last, he lifted his head and looked at her, his green eyes shadowed and speculative, she spoke with cool derision. 'Just testing the waters again, Mr Fabian?'

'As you say, Miss Trentham,' he murmured. 'And they were just as icy as I expected—and as you could wish.'

She said crisply, 'I'm delighted to hear it—if it means I'll be spared any more of your unwanted advances.' She turned, and gave one of her pillows a thump. 'And now, if I could have some privacy?'

And only realised as she saw his gaze sharpen and focus that her sudden movement had caused the thin strap of her nightgown to slip down from her shoulder, revealing, as it did so, far too much of the rounded curve of her breast.

Alex tutted reprovingly, then leaned forward and hooked a finger under the errant strap, lifting it back into place with exaggerated solicitude, breathing in, as he did so, with smiling and quite deliberate appreciation, the warm fragrance of her skin.

'Careful, darling,' he said softly, 'or I might think you were coming on to me—and that would never do. Would it?'

He got to his feet and sauntered to the door, whistling quietly under his breath. Then turned.

'Enjoy your chocolate,' he said, and disappeared.

Her hand was already reaching for the tray, to send his damned chocolate crashing after him, when some instinct halted her. Warned her that was just what he'd be expecting. And that, more than anything else, she needed to keep her cool.

To demonstrate her total indifference to the kiss that still seemed to be burning on her lips—and to that stroking, too-knowing finger that had left its indelible brand on the bare skin of her shoulder. To his intimate enjoyment of the scent she'd rubbed into the smoothness of her skin.

Not shaken, she thought, ignoring the fact that her heartbeat was going crazy. Not stirred, either, in any way that he would ever discover.

Because Alex Fabian was a sexual predator *par excellence*.

One sign of weakness—one drop of blood in the water—and he would be circling on her. Moving in for the kill.

She could no longer doubt that he believed it would happen. Not immediately, as he'd said himself. But eventually. Not 'if' but 'when'...

When time and enforced proximity had done their work.

When the ring on her finger, allied to the indisputable fever in her blood, gave her no reason to resist him any longer.

Because, she realised with an odd sense of detachment, he would make her want him. He had that power, as she'd probably recognised in the first moments of their meeting. Recognised and feared...

And, if she was honest, the lingering touch of his mouth on hers had already done its damage. Because there had been a brief, shocking moment when she'd felt the sharp pang of desire. When she'd longed for more, and it would have been so easy to put her arms round his neck and draw him down to her. So easy—and so fatal, she thought, shivering.

She swallowed. Well, if he was the irresistible force, she would have to be the immovable object, adamant and unyielding in spite of him. Keeping him rigidly at much more than arm's length.

And causing him to experience failure for once in his spoiled, self-indulgent life. A rejection that would register on the Richter scale for a man who regarded women as his legitimate prey.

Because it was nothing more than a game to him, she acknowledged bitterly, and one that he confidently expected to win. Her inexperience would be a challenge to him, and he'd regard seduction as a bonus while he set out to acquire the house of his dreams.

Pass 'Go', she thought, her mouth curling, and collect whatever was available.

Only she wasn't playing. She was deadly serious. And she wasn't available either.

Alex Fabian was her ticket to the new life she needed to build for herself. But that was all he was, she cautioned herself.

And she could not allow herself to consider him in any other way.

Otherwise, she would just be another name on the long list of sad women who'd mistaken his lovemaking for love.

Not, she thought sorrowfully, that she knew a great deal about love either, or she would not be here now—a puppet dancing to Alex Fabian's strings…in every way but one.

And tomorrow she would start again—guarded, wary. Armoured against the involuntary pull of her senses in response to his wickedly male allure.

And, in the meantime, she still had the solace of hot chocolate and biscuits. A much safer consolation at bedtime, she told herself, her mouth twisting wryly, as she leaned across to reach for the beaker.

And noticed for the first time the metallic glint of what was lying beside it. A key. *The* key to her bedroom door, in fact.

And offered, she thought with sudden fury, in the full and certain knowledge that her pride would not allow her to use it. That she would use her own force of will to keep him away, rather than cowering behind locks and bolts.

And that what had happened between them was merely a preliminary skirmish, with the real battle to follow.

'So be it, then,' she said aloud, her voice shaking. 'I'm ready for you.'

And, for no reason she could ever explain, she burst into tears.

When she awoke the next morning, she felt drained and almost disorientated. But maybe that last bout of weeping had been exactly what she needed, because she seemed to have slept deeply and dreamlessly.

Overslept, in fact, she realised, glancing at her watch. And she had better get up and dress before Alex came to find her.

She showered rapidly, then dragged on close-fitting cream trousers that hugged her slim hips and long legs, topping them with a matching crew-neck sweater.

As she walked along the passage to the sitting room, she

realised that her hands were balled tensely into fists, and thrust them into the concealment of her pockets.

Alex was lounging on one of the sofas, reading the financial pages of one of the Sunday broadsheets, a cup of coffee beside him, the paper's remaining sections scattered at his bare feet.

He was wearing, Louise saw with a nervous leap of her pulse, a black silk robe, and apparently nothing else. His tawny hair was still damp from the shower, and she was breathlessly aware of the faint scent of some enticing citrus-based fragrance in the air.

He said, without looking up, 'Good morning. There's more coffee in the kitchen if you'd like some, although you'll have to take it black.'

'It doesn't matter.' She needed a shot of caffeine to energise her. Get her focused. Also an excuse to get away from the sight of all that brown, muscular chest and long, tanned legs exposed by the inadequacies of his dressing gown.

This, presumably, was how he chose to spend his Sunday mornings, she thought with a mental shrug. And he was signalling quite clearly that her presence would not change a thing.

When she returned, he was putting down the white internal phone.

'I've ordered scrambled eggs and smoked salmon to be delivered in about fifteen minutes. I hope that suits you.'

'Yes—thank you.' She hesitated. 'But it seems crazy to order something from a restaurant that I could easily make for us both.'

'Wanting to cook for me, darling?' He came back to his seat, shaking his head reprovingly. 'That's the first step on the slippery slope. Next, you'll be offering to have my babies.'

'No,' Louise said between her teeth, 'I will not.'

'I'm relieved to hear it,' he murmured unabashed, and continued his scrutiny of the paper.

When the scrambled eggs arrived, they were accompanied by Buck's Fizz, brown toast, curls of butter in a small dish and

Seville marmalade. And a further tall pot of coffee, with, this time, a jug of cream.

Louise, discovering she was ravenous again, ate and drank everything she was offered.

Breakfast over, she said stiltedly, 'Can you tell me where I'll find the nearest supermarket?'

'No,' he said. 'But my driver will undoubtedly know. If you can curb your housewifely impulses for twenty-four hours, I'll send him to pick you up tomorrow.'

'Is that strictly necessary?'

'You'll certainly find it more convenient.' He paused. 'Do you plan to question everything I say?'

Louise flushed. 'I'm just not used to having my decisions made for me.'

He shrugged. 'Then that's something you'll have to deal with. Although I promise to try and curb my natural arrogance,' he added drily. 'And any—suggestions I make are only intended for your benefit. Why struggle with buses or cope with the rush-hour on the underground when you don't have to?'

Louise's mouth tightened in irritation. 'How do you always manage to sound like the voice of sweet reason?' she asked crisply.

He grinned at her. 'Years of practice. And as you're cross anyway, may I wind you up further by suggesting that you turn your mind to forgetting the past, and start looking forward to the future?'

'Not easy,' she said, 'when I've no real idea when I'll be free to enjoy it.'

'Then don't think about that aspect,' Alex said softly. 'Concentrate instead on the prospect of seeing the Taj Mahal at sunset, or exploring the Great Barrier Reef.'

'And what do I do about the current situation?' She lifted her chin. 'Simply—grit my teeth?'

'I don't think a bride with her jaw permanently set would give a convincing picture of wedded bliss,' he said reflectively. 'You'll need to do better than that.'

'How much better?' Her tone held misgiving.

He considered for a moment. 'Primarily, you need to relax more. At the moment you're vibrating like some high-tension cable whenever I'm around.'

It might help if you were actually wearing some proper clothes. She permitted the thought, but didn't dare utter it aloud. Because she could not let him see that anything he said or did mattered. Or that his lack of attire allied with the beguilingly clean scent of his skin had the least effect on her.

She drew a breath. 'So what do you want me to do?'

The green eyes studied her dispassionately. 'You need to be able to smile, to walk with your arm in mine, and to talk without spitting my name out like cobra venom. At some point at my grandmother's party we'll be expected to dance together, without you turning to stone in my arms.'

He paused. 'And, of course, we're going to have to kiss each other as if we meant it,' he added silkily. 'To behave, in fact, as if we were physically and mentally attuned.'

She said harshly, 'The perfect couple.'

'You've got it in one,' he returned coolly. 'Pretend it's the next production of your village drama group, darling, with costumes and script supplied, and you'll be fine.' He studied her rigid expression, his mouth twisting wryly. 'And in return I promise to keep the kisses to a minimum, although I suspect the opposite course of action might yield better results.'

'On the contrary.' She took a quick, uneasy breath, anxious to move the conversation to safer ground. 'Do you really think your grandmother will be fooled by this nonsense?' She shook her head. 'I—I can't believe that.'

'Maybe not,' he said. 'But whatever she suspects about my motivation, she can't deny that I've fulfilled her requirements to the letter. And all you have to do, my sweet, is behave, in public, like a girl who's been swept off her feet, and hasn't touched earth since.'

'I see.' She swallowed. 'May I ask, in turn, how you plan to behave? In public?'

He said slowly, 'Like a man who, against all expectation,

and to his own astonishment, has finally met the only woman in the world for him. And is totally bewildered by his undeserved good fortune.'

'Tricky,' she said, 'for someone who clearly believes he's merited all the good things in life.'

He said gently, 'If I ever believed that, Louise, then meeting you would soon have made me think again.'

He got to his feet. Stretched lazily, making her disturbingly conscious of the strength of bone and play of muscle beneath those few yards of silk. Raked back the tawny hair with a careless hand as he strolled to the door.

The Lion King, she thought nervously, *on the prowl.*

In the doorway, he paused and looked back at her. 'While I'm getting dressed, decide how you'd like to spend the day,' he told her casually. 'I'm at your service.'

'Oh, but…' She paused, swallowing. 'There's really no need for you to bother. I—I'll be fine on my own.'

'I don't doubt it,' he said courteously. 'But this is all part of the familiarisation process I mentioned. Persuading you to loosen up.'

She met his gaze. 'Aren't you afraid that familiarity may breed contempt, Mr Fabian?'

'The cobra strikes again.' His mouth smiled but his eyes were hard. 'And the name is Alex—remember. Keep saying it over and over and you'll soon get the hang of it. Just as you'll have to steel yourself to enduring my company for the rest of the day.'

'It seems I have little choice,' she said stiffly. Adding, 'For the rest of the day.'

'Good,' he said mockingly. 'You're learning.' He paused. 'I've arranged to take some time off in the week to spend with you too.'

Louise's eyes widened in dismay. 'Is that strictly necessary?'

'Your enthusiasm flatters me,' he said. 'But there are arrangements to be made. Also, as I've already mentioned, I plan to take you shopping. For one thing, I'd prefer my bride to wear something other than jeans at our wedding,' he added, his eyes flickering over her.

She flushed stormily. 'I'm perfectly capable of choosing something appropriate. I don't need—supervision.'

'No,' he said. 'But you need a trousseau, and I thought some guidance might be helpful.'

'Of course,' she said. 'I'm sure you're an expert on women's clothing.'

'I tend to confine my interest to how easy it is to remove,' he said silkily, and unforgivably. 'But my PA Andie Crane has a more than working knowledge of Bond Street and designer shops and she'd love to show you around. I'll confine myself to buying the ring—if you can spare me the time.'

'Bond Street?' Louise echoed, her face flushed, her mind flinching from the wedding ring and its connotations, among other things. 'You can't be serious. It's ridiculous to spend that kind of money on a—a temporary arrangement.'

'You're going to be my wife,' he said. 'And, for the duration, you will dress accordingly. No chain-store gear, or stuff from a trunk in the attic. Primarily, Andie will help you find a dress for my grandmother's party, and something to wear when you're invited for lunch at the bank.'

'You think I will be?'

'I know it,' he said. 'Because I'm going to be the chairman, and the directors will be forming a line to meet my new bride.'

She said shakily, 'Oh, God—it just gets worse all the time.'

'Don't be scared, darling,' he drawled. 'They won't eat you—unless I give the word. And maybe not even then.'

He added casually, 'Ask Andie to recommend a hairdresser, too, and somewhere to get your nails done.'

Louise stiffened. 'What's wrong with my hair?'

'Nothing,' he said. 'And it would look beautiful spread across my pillow.' He heard her indignant indrawn breath, and grinned. 'But, as that's doomed to remain a private fantasy,' he went on, 'maybe you should have it trimmed a little.'

'Certainly,' she said icily. 'Perhaps I could have a nose job too. Or a breast enlargement. Complete the transformation.'

Alex looked her up and down again, more slowly, his eyes lingering quite deliberately on the rounded curves revealed by the cling of her sweater.

'No,' he said gently. 'No other enhancement is required, believe me.'

Well, I walked into that one, Louise thought, the realisation failing to improve her temper by one iota. I'll have to learn to think before I speak. Or not speak at all...

She mastered herself. Made herself look back at him coolly. She said, 'I'm not a total country mouse. I have been in London before, and I don't need a minder, or a personal shopper. You won't have any reason to feel ashamed of me, whatever the occasion.'

'As you wish,' Alex said after a pause. 'Then let's return to the subject of how we should spend today. I thought of a walk in the park followed by lunch by the river, but I'm open to counter-suggestions.'

'Good,' she said. 'Because you don't need to lead me around the place either. I'm not a visiting tourist.'

'No,' he said softly, 'you're my future wife, and as I've explained I'm simply trying to create a slightly more relaxed situation for us to get to know each other better.'

He paused, leaning against the door frame, his smile thin and suddenly dangerous, setting off alarm signals in her own awareness.

'But we don't have to go out,' he went on cordially. 'We can stay here and—further our acquaintance just as well. A quiet day at home might be just what we need, because who knows where it might lead?' He registered her sudden tension, her widening eyes and lips parting in shock, and his smile widened sardonically. 'And it has the added bonus, of course, that I don't even need to get dressed,' he added gently.

There was a silence that seemed to stretch out, screaming, into infinity.

Then Louise said quietly, huskily, 'On second thoughts, maybe I'd rather go out after all.'

'You have wisdom beyond your years,' Alex said silkily. 'And I shall just have to control my disappointment.'

'I'm sorry.' Her eyes and voice were stony. 'But I'm sure you won't lack for consolation.'

'Well,' he said, 'there's a lot of it about. I won't be lonely.' He paused. 'But you, my sweet, might be. Have you thought of that?'

'No,' she said, with great clarity. 'Because my consolation will be the thought of all the money you're going to pay me.' She took a quick breath. 'And the exquisite certainty that I'll never have to see you again.'

For a brief moment his eyes narrowed, and she thought her words might just have got under his guard.

But the next second he was grinning at her, apparently unmoved. 'In that case,' he told her, 'I'd better make the most of you, darling, while you're around.'

And left her staring after him, her arms wrapped round her body in sudden, uneasy defensiveness. Knowing that it was her own guard, in fact, that was under the real threat.

She thought, Oh, God, I'm going to have to be careful—so very careful...

CHAPTER SIX

IN SPITE of the misgivings which tormented her, Louise found herself forced to admit that a walk had been exactly what she needed. And, traffic fumes notwithstanding, she could not help responding to the warmth and charm of the sunlit day.

There was a real holiday atmosphere in the park, with live music from the bandstand and people sprawled on the grass, with children playing around them and the air filled with voices and laughter.

And, when Alex held out his hand to her, she obeyed his unspoken imperative, after only a brief hesitation, and yielded her fingers to his light clasp.

He was looking good, she acknowledged reluctantly, in pale chinos and a light blue shirt, open at the throat and its cuffs turned back to show off his tan. She was aware of female glances following him with wistful curiosity as she walked at his side.

They'll be wondering how I managed it, she thought with an inward sigh. My God, if they only knew…

Alex took her to lunch at a floating restaurant on the Thames, and the novelty of that, with the sun dancing on the water around them, and the sights and sounds of the great river absorbed her attention satisfactorily until the waiter brought his lamb cutlets and her salade niçoise.

They exchanged a few polite comments about the food, then silence descended again as they ate. Louise found, to her disquiet, that she could not help watching Alex covertly across the table as the meal proceeded. He had classic bone structure, she admitted without pleasure, and incredibly long, gold-tipped eyelashes that might have seemed almost effeminate on someone less confidently male.

In addition, she could remember with terrifying exactness how that coolly humorous mouth had felt when it brushed hers, too, and guessed it was a recollection that would haunt her for a long time.

He had no right to be so attractive, she thought sombrely. Why couldn't he have had an absurd straggly beard, a cast in one eye, or an unsightly mole? Something—anything—that she could have used as a physical focus for her dislike. And which would have made him infinitely easier to resist.

She took a sip of the mineral water she had asked for instead of the wine Alex was drinking, telling herself she needed to keep a clear head.

So far, she thought, her resolve had not been seriously tested. In fact, she found it hard to judge whether or not he'd simply been teasing her with the veiled threats of seduction that she'd found so disturbing.

Which in turn led her to question what might or might not have happened if she'd decided to call his bluff, and spend the day at the flat instead. Recalling, as she did, his comment about seeing her hair spread across his pillow...

And permitting herself to wonder, just for a brief moment, what it would have been like to find herself in his bed, his robe discarded, and Alex intent on his pleasure. And hers.

She thought of his voice, whispering. The late-afternoon sun glinting through drawn curtains onto smooth brown skin. Her own pale by contrast. His weight against her. On her...

'Is it too warm in here?'

She looked up with a guilty start at the sound of Alex's voice, to find him observing her, brows raised quizzically.

'No.' She took another swift gulp of water. 'Everything's— fine. Why do you ask?'

'Because you look rather flushed.' He drank some of his wine, the green eyes speculative. 'What are you thinking about?'

She shrugged, trying to appear insouciant. 'Just that I'm going to need something to do,' she improvised hastily. 'After all, the occasional lunch or party won't fill the time available. And shopping till I drop has never held any attraction for me.'

His brows drew together. 'What are you saying? That you plan to get a job?'

'Would you object?' The forbidden images were beginning to fade. Her breathing to steady.

His frown deepened. 'I do not expect my wife to work,' he said brusquely.

'Then how am I supposed to spend my day?' Louise spread her hands, glad to find they weren't shaking. 'I have no home to run—even the cooking and laundry is done for you. I have no friends here. I can't sit staring at four walls from breakfast to bedtime. I'll get cabin fever.

'Or go mad,' she added. 'They don't let you out of a padded cell to visit the Taj Mahal.'

He didn't smile. 'A lot of people get involved in charity work.'

Louise bit her lip. 'I don't think I'm ready for that yet.' She paused. 'It occurred to me that there might be an opportunity for me at Trentham Osborne.'

'There's certainly a vacancy,' he agreed sardonically. 'I'm not sure you're the right person to fill it.'

'How difficult can it be?' She stopped herself just in time from saying 'Ellie's not that bright', realising that it would almost certainly be interpreted as pure spite, instead of a family truth, always understood but never spoken aloud.

'I wasn't referring to your undoubted abilities,' Alex played with the stem of his glass, 'but the advisability of stepping into your sister's shoes.'

'Why not?' she said harshly. 'She did it to me first.'

'Precisely.' He reached across the table and took her hand, stroking, she realised with shock, the hollow of her palm with his fingertips. Making her catch her breath. Prompting a corresponding curl of sensation to uncoil slowly in the pit of her stomach.

Oh, no, she thought, appalled. This isn't fair. I'm still in recovery.

He said softly, 'Take my advice, darling. Don't do this. Let it go.'

She said hoarsely, 'I can't just—forget...'

'Can't you?' His eyes met hers, smiled into them. 'Why not—try?'

'For one thing it's too soon.' She bit her lip. 'May—may I have my hand back, please?'

'Not yet,' he said. 'But don't worry. I'm not trying to turn you on—even if I believed for one moment that I could. I do have a good reason for this, which I can explain, but not right now.'

'Let me guess,' she said. 'You've seen someone you know. And this is your less than subtle way of letting them know we're an item.'

'If you like.'

'I don't,' she said shortly. 'Wouldn't a simple introduction be better than this—charade?'

'I said it was someone I knew,' he told her. 'I did not mention we were friends.'

He raised her hand to his smiling mouth, his lips tracing the faint blue veins.

His eyes caressed her, openly stripping away the concealing sweater, and the lacy fragment beneath it, making desire an invasion. Sending it running like fire through her blood.

Louise could feel her nipples lift and harden. Instinctively. Involuntarily.

She felt confused suddenly, almost light-headed. Because he was good at this. Oh, God, pretence or not, he was good, and she was no longer in control of her responses.

How—with such little effort—could he make her believe...anything? she asked herself in bewilderment bordering on distress. And, even more dangerously, how could he make her dream?

The arrival of the waiter to remove their empty plates and offer the dessert menu was an intrusion—a shock to her senses.

She felt outraged, as if this polite man, who was only doing his job, had seen her naked. And yet all that had really happened, she thought, was that Alex had released her hand. So really, she ought to be grateful for the interruption.

She heard herself ordering a white peach parfait. Not that she was still hungry, but she needed something to say and do. And asking for food was the simplest option. It restored normality.

'Have some chocolate mousse.' Alex was proffering some on his spoon, and she made herself lean forward and smile and accept it, her still raw senses wincing at the implied intimacy.

'Aren't you going to give me some of yours?' he asked.

'Feeding each other with pudding,' she muttered as she complied. 'I can't believe I'm doing this.'

'It's the kind of absurdity lovers indulge in,' he said quietly. 'And you do it very well. Thank you.'

They lingered over coffee and brandy, and when Alex suggested taking a cab back to the flat, Louise demurred.

'I need to walk again,' she said brightly. 'Work off some of those calories.'

'Oh, God,' he said. 'Promise me you're not obsessed with some non-existent weight problem.'

Her smile was unforced. 'I swear I'm not. It just seems a pity to be indoors on such a lovely day,' she added quickly.

'That's one viewpoint,' he said, his glance enigmatic. 'There are others.'

It seemed safer not to pursue that. 'Has your non-friend gone?' she asked instead as they went ashore.

He nodded. 'Some time ago.'

'So you can tell me who it was.'

His mouth tightened. 'It was a journalist,' he said, 'from a particularly sleazy tabloid newspaper. It's not the first time I've been aware of his presence.'

'But why should someone like that be interested in you?' she began, then paused abruptly. 'Or is it your choice of female companion?'

'Clever girl,' he approved sardonically. 'Go to the top of the class.'

She was astonished at the stab of sheer pain that assailed

her. Astonished and ashamed, because she had no right to be feeling like that about anyone when her tears for David were scarcely dry.

And particularly not about Alex.

I despise myself, she thought, wincing.

She braced herself to speak normally as they began to stroll along the Embankment. 'But how did he know where to find you?'

'It's recognised as one of my haunts,' Alex said, shrugging. 'I imagine one of the staff tipped him off.'

'Does it happen often?'

'I'm hoping it soon won't happen at all,' he said drily. 'Once I'm happily married, the gutter Press will cease to trouble about my activities. Or that's the plan, anyway.'

Louise gave a small, wintry smile. 'I didn't realise how useful I was going to be.'

But, of course, he was using her, she told herself as she walked at his side. That was precisely what she'd agreed to.

But there were limits. And she could not afford to let him amuse himself with her with a casual seduction.

It did not help that Alex Fabian was the most physically desirable man she'd ever encountered in her admittedly limited experience. But that was no excuse for her total overreaction just now.

The greatest risk she faced was not Alex's attraction, she thought unhappily, but her own weakness, and she would have to find some way of dealing with it.

Because she needed to emerge from this situation with her pride intact, not as just another notch on his already over-crowded bedpost, she reminded herself tautly.

She was recalled from her troubling thoughts to the equally tricky present by Alex, who came to a sudden halt, muttering a soft but pungent curse under his breath.

'What is it?' Puzzled, Louise turned to look up at him, and saw his mouth twist ruefully.

'Just—this,' he said, and took her by the shoulders, pulling her into his arms, any protest she might have made immediately crushed under the pressure of his lips.

For a moment she was stunned, frozen in disbelief, unable to think—barely able to breathe.

If he'd been brutal she could have fought back, but the searching mouth was gentle as it moved on hers, caressing the soft, trembling contours with slow, enticing patience.

So that, at last, it seemed natural—inevitable—that her lips should part in obedience to his insistence.

The noise of the traffic shrank to a distant murmur. If people turned to look at them, and smile, Louise was oblivious to their stares. The sunlight dazzled her eyes, and permeated her entire body with its golden warmth. Or was it simply the heat of his body, closer to hers than it had ever been?

One hand lifted to stroke her cheek, the line of her jaw, then twined in the soft coils of her hair, making dissent impossible. The other moved down her spine to the small of her back, propelling her forward, their bodies grinding together as if the layers of clothing between them did not exist. His kiss deepened passionately, and she felt the hot, sweet invasion of his tongue exploring the moist inner recesses of her mouth.

She gasped silently, her body arching involuntarily, intimately against his, her hands sliding up to hold his shoulders as the real world began to spin slowly out of control. As she gave way at last to her clamouring instincts and offered her first unguarded response to the demands of his mouth.

And then, as suddenly and shockingly as it had begun, the kiss ended. Not only that, but Alex was also putting her gently but firmly away from him and stepping back, the green eyes narrowed, his expression dispassionate—almost cool. And, she realised with bewilderment and pain, seemingly unmoved by what had just taken place.

When he spoke, there was even faint amusement in his voice. 'Well, he's persistent. I'll give him that.'

Louise found she was taking a pace backwards too, grateful for the support of the stone parapet behind her because her legs were shaking under her.

She said, 'I don't understand. What—who are you talking about?'

'Ed Godwin,' he said. 'The journalist I mentioned. He was following us. Clearly our holding hands over the lunch table didn't convince him that my intentions were serious.'

Hurt twisted like a knife in the pit of her stomach. Dear God, she could still taste him—still bore the imprint of his touch on her body. And it was all pretence. The tenderness she'd sensed—the passion—all a sham. And herself only a fraction away from making an abject fool of herself.

Somehow she snatched at the fragments of her control, her self-respect, and lifted her chin.

She said quietly, 'Then I'm sure your recent performance will have put all his doubts to rest.'

'I certainly hope so,' he said. 'And, if so, he could be useful, keeping the rest of the vultures at bay.'

'You think there'll be more?' She managed to sound politely interested, no more.

He shrugged. 'For a while—until they accept the fact that I'm a married man, and of no further interest to them. That I plan to feature on the financial pages from now on, instead of in the gossip columns.'

'Until our divorce, anyway,' she pointed out.

'Perhaps,' he said. 'But I'll deal with that when I have to.'

'So, what happened to our stalker?'

'He hailed a black cab, and pushed off.'

And you, she thought, couldn't wait to push me away...

She said, 'Then I suggest we do the same. I think I've had enough fresh air for one day.'

'As you wish,' Alex said equably. He paused. 'Louise, I'm sorry if I took you by surprise just now, but I could hardly warn you in advance.'

'Please,' she said, 'you don't have to apologise—or explain.'

'Naturally I'm concerned,' he said. He hesitated again. 'I hope you didn't find my ardour—a little excessive.'

'A little, maybe.' She even managed a smile as cool as his

own. 'But I can hardly complain. After all, that's what you're paying me for. Isn't it?'

And she turned and walked away from him, head high, and her shaking hands thrust safely out of sight in her pockets, leaving him staring after her.

Two weeks later they were married in a ceremony so brief and formal that Louise could almost have thought it a fleeting dream, but for the sudden presence of Alex's wedding ring on her hand.

She supposed there would come a time when its golden gleam would not seem so alien, but, in a way, it was the least of her problems.

After the incident on the Embankment, she had decided that her only recourse was to treat the whole situation as a game. And a game with strict rules from which there could not be the slightest deviation.

And it seemed that Alex must have had similar thoughts during that silent taxi ride back to the flat, because ever since they had behaved with almost rigorous civility on the occasions when they were together, walking round each other as if they were treading on eggshells.

To her surprise, he had kept his word about the written contract she'd demanded.

'Here.' He'd tossed it into her lap. 'I hope this is the reassurance you wanted about my good intentions.'

Louise had read it, her eyes widening. 'Generous isn't the word,' she had said when she'd caught her breath. 'I feel as if I've won the lottery.'

'I'm glad you're pleased,' he'd said politely. 'However, if you're looking for the non-molestation clause, forget it. My lawyer's eyes were popping out of his head as it was. So I'm afraid you'll just have to take my word that I won't touch you—or not without your express invitation, anyway.'

She had stared down at the typed words until they blurred. 'Then I'll just have to rely on that.'

But so far she had no real complaints. She had to admit that

Alex had made things easier by spending a minimum of time at the flat, and she was managing to accept his appearances as well as his prolonged and unexplained absences with apparent equanimity.

She was slowly becoming accustomed to her new environment, too. The weather had been mainly fine and warm, encouraging her to spend a lot of time in the roof garden. She even sunbathed sometimes in the black bikini she'd bought for that very reason. She could even indulge her passion for reading as never before, and she'd also purchased a portable CD player so that she could listen to music and drama on disc while she relaxed.

It was, she thought, almost a life. And if her heart leapt painfully when she heard his key in the lock, then that was a secret she kept well-hidden, desperately ashamed of her own weakness.

Besides, if she seemed awkward or withdrawn at any time, she could always imply she was still heartbroken over David and Ellie. And only she would know it was a lie.

However, she supposed, they would both have to lower their guard a little for his grandmother's birthday party—the next ordeal to be endured—if she did not count the forthcoming wedding celebration at the Savoy.

'It was not my idea,' Alex had told her flatly the night before. 'My father insisted.'

Louise bit her lip. She had met George Fabian only once, a difficult rather stilted encounter at the Ritz. He had concealed his astonishment at his son's choice of wife with smiling good manners, but Louise was tautly aware that he knew the exact reason for this amazing mismatch. Knew it—and disapproved.

'Well,' she'd said, 'I'm sure he means to be—kind. And you did ask him to be one of our witnesses.'

'Yes,' he'd said. 'I thought one of us at least should have a blood relative present.'

Louise flushed. Her visit to Trentham Osborne to inform her father that the wedding date had been set was not a treasured memory. But neither was reporting on it later to a cynical Alex.

'Belated guilty conscience, darling?' he'd inquired pleasantly, after she'd stumbled through her explanation that a long-planned trip to the States would prevent her father from attending their marriage. 'Could he be feeling bad about selling you to me?'

'No,' she denied defensively. 'He has all these meetings set up that he can't postpone.' She forbore to add that she had no chance of any kind of job with the family firm, her father having stared at her in disbelief before impatiently brushing her tentative enquiry aside. She did not want to hear Alex say that he'd told her so.

She paused. 'And Marian is still down at the cottage, waiting to hear from Ellie. So that's that.' *And in London, her father was doing exactly the same thing, and she knew it.* She tried to smile. 'Anyway, I'm glad that you invited Andie instead. I—I like her.'

She had not expected to do so. In fact, she'd been angry when Alex had ignored her protests, and insisted on his PA acting as her guide and mentor round the London fashion houses.

But Andie Crane had proved to be a slim blonde, whose high-powered chic had been set off by her merry face and insouciant manner, and who had clearly no intention of forcing her own tastes or opinions on her boss's bride.

She herself had been married for less than a year, she'd confided, and had found the run-up to her own wedding positively nerve-racking. 'And I had months to spend on the planning,' she said, laughing. 'Whereas you've had days rather than weeks. Although maybe it's better that way,' she added more thoughtfully. 'Less time for second thoughts.'

Second, third, fourth and fifth, Louise thought wearily. With more to come.

She said quietly, 'I don't think Alex would allow them, anyway.'

Andie's eyes twinkled. 'Probably not.'

She must have been burning to know the story behind this

unholy dash into matrimony, but was far too discreet to ask questions or attempt to invade Louise's confidence.

And the hairdresser she recommended was a revelation, expertly layering Louise's unruly dark curls into an altogether sleeker and more manageable style that also gave her, she felt, a much needed edge of sophistication.

While shopping, she soon discovered, could be fun with a knowledgeable companion—and, admittedly, when money, too, was no object.

Andie's idea of a trousseau ranged from outfits for every conceivable occasion down to the prettiest, sexiest lingerie that Louise had ever possessed. Gossamer stuff, primarily designed to appeal to male senses, she realised, biting her lip. And totally wasted on her.

A visit to a beauty salon resulted in a make-up lesson, which she enjoyed, and a pastel leather case equipped with co-ordinated replacements for her own hotchpotch of cosmetics, which Andie advised her to ditch.

The pale pink sheath Louise wore for the much dreaded lunch at Perrins Bank had been bought on Andie's advice, too.

'Men love pink, especially the older ones,' she said. 'You'll wow them.'

A slight exaggeration, perhaps, Louise thought, but the lunch had went better than she could have hoped, her obvious shyness doing her no disservice at all.

'Well done,' was Alex's laconic comment when it was over, and she was disconcerted to find herself beaming as if she'd received some accolade.

Even the search for a wedding dress that was not too overtly bridal proved simplicity itself in the end. A small boutique in Knightsbridge produced a slender shift in ivory silk, high-necked and sleeveless, topped with a matching hip-length jacket, narrowly edged in gold, which floated as she moved. Plain kid court shoes and a tiny bag on a long gold chain completed the ensemble.

It was a far cry from the billowing white gown and veil she'd always envisaged, but then nothing about this marriage was like anything she'd ever contemplated—not even in her wildest nightmares.

And now it was done. She'd made her promises in a small, calm voice, and become Mrs Alex Fabian, currently on her way to lunch at the Savoy in the chauffeur-driven car which had also, somehow, become part of her everyday life. Proof, if proof were needed, that Alex was a man who liked his own way, and expected to get it—even in minor matters.

He had kept his word about taking her to buy the wedding ring.

They'd gone to a discreetly exclusive jewellers, where they were shown into a private panelled room, offered a glass of excellent sherry, and where Louise's finger was ceremoniously measured.

Tray after velvet-covered tray was then brought out for their inspection. So many shades of gold—Alex having decisively rejected platinum—in so many styles. Wide or narrow, plain or chased, no two rings seemed the same.

Louise had expected that the whole thing would only take a few minutes. That Alex, conscious that it was only a temporary measure, would make a swift selection, pretty much at random.

She was embarrassed too by the kindly smiles of the middle-aged jeweller, who so obviously believed they were happy lovers choosing a ring that would last their entire lives long.

I'm a fraud, she wanted to tell him. And we might as well use a brass curtain ring.

But she said nothing, and when Alex picked out a plain, elegant ring in a medium width, she smiled as he slipped it onto her other hand, and murmured truthfully that it was beautiful.

Now, seated beside him in the car, she stared down at the flowers she was holding—tiny cream and gold roses, their petals just unfurling, and tried not to think about the inevitabilities of the future. About the strain of maintaining the pretence, the topics of conversation that, for safety's sake, remained strictly taboo. And, of course, the strict avoidance of all physical contact when they were alone. So that they seemed like two people trapped in separate vacuums. Isolated. Unreachable.

But that was the way she wanted it, she reminded herself, and the way it had to be. Because anything else would be unthinkable.

Alex had kissed her when they were pronounced man and wife, because it was expected of him. A swift, formal brush of his lips on hers that meant nothing, and would cause no restless, unhappy dreams. Or so she could only hope, she told herself as the car drew up in front of the famous Savoy façade.

George Fabian had reserved a table overlooking the river, where champagne was waiting, expertly iced. And, although she could not decide whether it was the wine, or the fact that she was finally married—committed, with no way back—that was the cause, she found herself able to relax a little and almost enjoy herself as her health was drunk.

The food was delicious too, with tiny asparagus tartlets being followed by poussins in a wine sauce, with straw potatoes and tender French beans. A rich confection of raspberries whisked into thick and alcoholic cream ended the meal.

Louise would have lingered over the coffee and petits fours, but to her surprise George Fabian was glancing at his watch and murmuring about appointments, and Andie, in a blue linen dress that matched her eyes, was saying briskly that she too needed to get back to Perrins.

Oh, God, Louise thought, staring at the tablecloth as if it fascinated her. They're being tactful. Even his father, who knows precisely why we went through that ceremony this morning, thinks that Alex will want to be alone with me. That, now I'm his wife, he has a right to take full advantage of the circumstances, and won't hesitate to do so.

She groaned inwardly, realising that Andie, who worked for him, and presumably knew his reputation, would imagine her as a more than willing bride, eager to respond to his expertise as a lover.

She made herself look up, swallowing, and found Alex

watching her, the green eyes hooded and enigmatic, and her heart lurched in a kind of panic mingled with excitement.

'It's such a pity that your honeymoon has to be postponed,' Andie sympathised quietly as they all made their way to the main entrance. 'But there's so much going on at Perrins now that Alex has definitely been confirmed as the next chairman. He really can't afford to take any time off just now.'

Louise bit her lip. 'It's—not a problem. Really.'

'No?' Andie's expression was faintly puzzled. 'Well, I expect Alex will choose somewhere extra-glamorous and romantic to make up for it,' she added cheerfully. 'When the time comes.' She gave Louise a swift hug. 'Enjoy the rest of your day,' she added with a wicked grin.

Louise stood beside Alex, waving goodbye as the cabs containing George Fabian and Andie went off in their different directions, and smiling so determinedly that it hurt.

Alone at last. The words came into her mind, along with Andie's mischievous, knowing smile, and would not go away. She felt a faint shiver—half dread, half longing—run along her nerve-endings.

As she turned away Alex's hand closed on her arm, and she glanced at him, her eyes blank with sudden alarm.

'Don't worry,' he said softly. 'I don't think the Savoy rents rooms by the afternoon.' He paused. 'Although I could always ask.'

She hated herself for blushing. She said coldly, 'Please don't be absurd.'

'It's a fairly absurd situation,' he returned shortly. He paused. 'I have a meeting to go to in the City. Have you any plans for the rest of the afternoon? May I drop you somewhere?'

She shook her head slowly. Suddenly, she felt that she was the absurd one here, all dressed up with, patently, nowhere to go. And no one to go with.

She said, 'You mean you're going back to work?'

'You have some objection?'

'None,' she said swiftly. 'Only Andie didn't mention it.'

'Andie doesn't know,' Alex said shortly. 'I arranged this meeting yesterday, after she'd left for the day.'

It was her wedding day, and she was being left totally to her own devices. And he hadn't even said she looked nice, she thought childishly. Not even when she'd stood beside him in front of the registrar. Just one brief, unsmiling glance as he took her hand.

She sighed inwardly, soundlessly. 'I think I'll go back to the flat.'

'As you wish.' He signalled and the car drew up in front of them.

He was clearly impatient to be off. To be rid of her, and that hurt. Yet another absurdity, she thought.

She said carefully, as they emerged into the Strand, 'Alex— is there anything wrong? Have I—done something?'

'No, my sweet.' His mouth twisted. 'Your behaviour has been faultless throughout.'

'Then what is it?' She tried to smile. 'If you've decided you don't want to be a married man, after all, you've left it rather late.'

'But that's exactly it,' he said, and she could hear the faint throb of anger under his even tone. 'You see, I discovered there in the registry office that marriage doesn't suit me, Louise. It doesn't suit me at all. Yet here I am, the condemned man hearing the doors of the prison cage slam behind him—and knowing that he's trapped.'

Pain tore through her. She managed, just in time, to suppress a little, shocked gasp.

She said stonily, 'Then it's a trap entirely of your own making. I just hope you think your precious inheritance is worth it.'

'At the moment I have my doubts,' he returned bleakly.

They didn't exchange another word until they arrived outside the block of flats.

'Do you want me to come in with you?' He was frowning faintly, not looking at her, as if his mind had already leapt ahead to his City appointment.

'No,' she said, 'thank you. Let's just get on with the rest of our lives—shall we? And don't look so furious,' she added, striving for lightness. 'Play your cards right, and you might get time off for good behaviour.'

She slammed the door of the car, and stalked across the pavement to the massive glass doors which the commissionaire was holding open for her, and went inside.

She was shaking with anger as she rode up in the lift. She was helping him, and he couldn't even be bothered to make the day special for her.

He thought he was in prison? she thought, seething, as she let herself into the flat. Well, this was her cage too. It was luxurious—gold-plated even—but the bars were there just the same. And she was in solitary confinement.

But in her case, this was a cage she did not want to leave—ever...

She came to a stunned halt halfway across the living room, standing white-faced and motionless, staring into space, as she considered the implications of this unwanted revelation.

As she recognised, with a silent scream of anguish, that—somehow and unbelievably—she had fallen in love with Alex. No—more than that. That she loved him, and that was why he filled her thoughts by day, and haunted her dreams in the long, lonely nights.

Alex, she thought, shivering, who cared nothing for her. Who was already resenting his lost freedom, and, indeed, planning to discard her at the earliest opportunity.

He doesn't want me, she reminded herself with swift, searing desolation. He never did, and he never will. And I have the written contract to prove it.

And—God help me—there isn't a thing I can do about it.

CHAPTER SEVEN

SHE sat for a long time in the corner of the sofa, twisting the wedding band on her finger, while the slow, scalding tears trickled down her face and dripped off the end of her nose.

She was being ridiculous, and she knew it, but all other choices had been removed in the light of her recent self-revelation.

She might argue with herself that it wasn't love but simply physical attraction, triggered by that kiss, and that, left untended, it would wither and die of its own accord. But a female instinct she'd never known she possessed told her otherwise.

Suggested that she'd actually been fighting her awareness of him from day one. That there'd been a moment when that awareness had transmuted into an aching need. When he'd become part of the essence of her day, and to see him, and hear his voice brought their own meagre satisfaction. Because that might be all that she would ever have of him.

After all, Alex had married her purely for convenience. Because he needed a token wife as a weapon in this private battle he was waging with his grandmother. It was a financial transaction, as he'd made clear. A solution to their mutual problems. A business deal, offered and accepted without emotion, or so she'd convinced herself.

Well, she'd been half right. Because the only emotion on his side was clearly regret. He'd married her in haste, and repented instantly.

He'd chosen her in the first place because she was not attractive to him, and therefore easily expendable when her usefulness to him was at an end.

His attempts to seduce her had never been wholly serious, she reminded herself painfully. Just another conditioned reflex from a man who was accustomed to having a girl in his bed, and because she was there—in his life, on the premises. A little enjoyable lust without commitment.

Most of it had simply been sexual teasing anyway, used solely to catch her off-balance—to flurry her into doing precisely what he wanted. And it had worked, she admitted ruefully, because she'd never been brave enough to call his bluff, and he knew it.

But even if he'd been genuinely tempted to amuse himself with her for a night or two, instinct would probably have warned him that she wasn't the type for casual sex. That her lack of experience would soon pall. And that she might not want to 'kiss and part' when it was over.

That was why he chose me, she thought wretchedly. Because my demands were going to be financial, not emotional, and he could handle that. Because I wouldn't make a nuisance of myself.

Looking back, she could see that perhaps her unguarded, ardent response to his kiss had set alarm bells ringing. Hinted that maybe she wasn't as indifferent as she pretended. And this was why he'd avoided her so studiously ever since.

Louise drew a long, trembling sigh. She could hardly believe what was happening to her. What she was allowing to happen. Or what she was thinking. Because, on the face of it, Alex Fabian was the last man in the world she should ever want, and she knew it.

Her ideal man had always been someone quiet, rugged and totally dependable. Someone who was ready to settle down, in some quiet backwater, and be happy.

Someone like David...

That same David, she derided herself bitterly, who'd run off with her stepsister. Well, good thinking, Girl Wonder!

Whereas Alex, who lived his life unashamedly in the fast lane, and who found even the prospect of monogamy boring, was at least honest about it. Too honest at times, she thought, smearing away her tears with her fingers, as she recalled his coldness in the car, his anger at the pit he'd unthinkingly dug for himself, blinded by everything but his obsession with a house.

As the love of her life, he promised to be a complete disaster, she thought, an unwilling smile quivering on her lips.

But love, when it came, wasn't sensible or realistic. Nor did it wait to be invited, as she'd so ruinously discovered. It took possession, mind, soul and body, and stretched you on the rack of your own senses and emotions.

With David, however mistakenly, she'd felt safe. But loving Alex was like falling from the high-wire without a net. The ultimate risk, as he'd once warned her himself.

And, as a result, she could well end up in pieces that would never mend.

If she allowed it to happen...

Because there was no need for him to feel trapped, she told herself. Contract or not, he could afford the best lawyers in the world to free him from this non-marriage which had so quickly turned sour. Surely they could arrange an equally speedy annulment?

But why hadn't he spoken while they were standing in front of the registrar? she wondered. Just 'I can't do this' would have been enough to stop the whole thing in its tracks. It would have been cruel, but kinder in the long term. And better than this terrible limbo where she now found herself.

She got up wearily, and went down the corridor to her bedroom. She paused for a moment, staring at her wan reflection in the long wall mirror. So different from the hopeful girl in the shimmering, floating silk who'd looked back at her that morning. Who, without realising why, had expected—longed for—her bridegroom's approval.

It was one of the conventions that you cried at weddings, she thought, her mouth twisting ruefully, but not usually your own.

In fact, her primary instinct, fired by the blind rush of anger that had carried her up in the lift, had been to strip off her wedding dress and hack it to pieces with her nail scissors.

Obliterate it, just as the marriage itself would eventually be erased.

Now she took it off and put it carefully on a hanger, placing it at the back of one of the fitted wardrobes where it would be lost among all the other clothes.

It was so lovely, but it hadn't changed a thing, she thought, although that was hardly the dress's fault. When she could bear to look at it again, she'd donate it to a charity shop.

She rescued her bouquet from the living room floor where she'd dropped it, gently unwiring the roses and placing them in a vase beside her bed. Because Alex had bought them for her. Stupid, she knew. Pathetic, but she couldn't help herself.

Then she ran a bath scented with geranium oil, and sank down into it, emptying her mind, and letting the warm water do its healing, washing away the marks of her tears.

Recriminations were useless, she thought as she padded back into her room, wrapped in an enormous, fluffy bath sheet. After all, she knew the conditions. She'd walked into this situation with her eyes wide open, and now she had to deal with the consequences.

And, whatever else happened, Alex must never know that she loved him. She was heading for heartbreak as it was, so total humiliation might just be more than she could bear, she thought with irony.

Therefore, when Alex returned, all traces of the unwanted bride would have been removed, and cool practical Louise would be in place again, neutral in her jeans and T-shirt. The girl who made no demands, and invaded no space. Calm and casually friendly.

And if he'd decided in the meantime that he still wanted to go on with this charade, and needed her to play the role he had assigned to her, then she would adhere strictly to the script from now on. In particular, the lines for his grandmother's party, which would take place next weekend.

Louise winced. That would prove an overwhelming test for their fragile bargain, she thought apprehensively. And if Alex was still in resentful mourning for his lost bachelor status then

they wouldn't deceive a child of three. This was just one of
the points she needed to raise with him when he returned.

When he returned...

Louise said the words aloud, and sighed, knowing that she
had never felt so entirely alone in the whole of her life.

The hours dragged slowly past. At some point in the evening
Louise went into the kitchen and cooked the seafood risotto
she'd planned originally as a celebration dinner, in the forlorn
hope that Alex would be there to share it with her.

And how sad is that? she asked herself impatiently, pouring
herself a glass of the crisp white wine she'd chosen to accompany the meal.

When they'd first met, he'd praised her cooking. He'd even
suggested she was good enough to be a professional. Yet, since
she'd been living with him, the only thing she'd been allowed
to prepare was coffee.

But, as the doors of Trentham Osborne were closed to her,
she could always try to get a job in catering—providing corporate lunches, perhaps, like the efficient, smiling girls in the
smart blue uniforms who'd served the meal at Perrins that day.

It was something to consider anyway. Because she couldn't
spend her life cooped up in the lap of luxury. For one thing,
it would give her too much time to think.

She ate her risotto with due appreciation, glad that she did
not appear to be losing her touch. She allowed herself two
glasses of wine only with her meal, because she needed to keep
a clear head, as never before. There were matters she needed
to settle with Alex, and the sooner the better. Preferably tonight.

Dishes washed, and the kitchen tidied, she went back into
the living room and watched some television, only half concentrating on the images in front of her, more concerned about
what she would say to Alex—when he returned. And how she
was going to be able to hide her true feelings for him.

It was only when her eyelids drooped and she began to doze
that she realised how late it was. That midnight had come and

gone, and there was still no sign of him. Surely he'd be back soon, she thought, trying to soothe her own anxiety.

But when another hour had passed she finally admitted defeat, and went to bed.

But she couldn't rest. Although she was tired, she was still listening for some sound that would tell her that Alex had come home at last.

And she could never be sure when she made herself face the fact that he probably hadn't been whisked to hospital with a mystery virus, or knocked down by a bus.

No, the truth was undoubtedly far simpler, she thought, her heart thudding painfully against her rib cage. Because she had to accept that Alex was almost certainly celebrating the first night of his marriage in the arms of some other woman.

A little moan rose to her lips, and she turned over, burying her face in the pillow to muffle the sound and blot out the troubling—the unbearable—images invading her mind.

And when she eventually fell asleep she dreamed she was running through a wild and rocky world, endlessly calling his name, but receiving no reply.

She awoke the next morning feeling jaded, a faint, nagging ache lodged above her eyebrows.

I need coffee, she told herself, wearily reaching for her dressing gown.

On her way to the kitchen, she paused by Alex's bedroom. The door was open, and one glance showed the wide bed still unused and pristine. He had truly been gone all night, she thought, her heart dropping like a stone.

She filled the cafetière, and carried it into the living room. She'd filled her beaker, and taken her first cautious sip, when she heard the front door open and close. She stood very still, the colour draining from her face, and a moment later Alex appeared.

His tie was missing, his waistcoat unbuttoned and his shirt open at the neck, but he was still in the same clothes he'd worn for the wedding. His eyes were bloodshot, and there was a shadow of stubble on his chin.

He looked, she thought, as if he had been drinking, too.

She said quietly, 'You're home.'

'Is that how you think of this place?' Alex glanced around him, his brows lifted cynically. 'How quaint.'

Louise decided it would be better to ignore that.

She said, 'You—didn't come back last night.'

'Obviously,' he said coolly. 'I thought you'd probably be glad to be spared my presence—it being our wedding night.'

His smile did not reach his eyes as he registered the sudden defensive stiffening of her slim figure.

'Such an evocative phrase, that, don't you think, darling?' he drawled derisively. 'So full of—resonances. Only I really wasn't in the mood to deal with them. Or not in any way that you would have wished for anyway,' he added.

Louise looked down at the floor. She said in a low voice, 'I was—worried. I didn't know where you were.'

'Do you really want the details?' he asked mockingly. 'Of where I spent the night? In what bed?'

Her immediate impulse was to wrap her arms round her body in self-protection. But that would be instant self-betrayal—letting him see that he had the power to hurt her. And she was in agony, even though he'd merely confirmed her own worst suspicions.

Instead, she lifted her chin, facing him again.

She said crisply. 'It's really none of my concern. In future, I'll simply take it for granted that you'll be staying elsewhere.'

His mouth twisted. 'You are gracious beyond my desserts.'

'No,' she said. 'Just indifferent.' She paused. 'So what happens now? Am I supposed to make you a free man again by divorcing you? If that's the plan, I imagine your tabloid friend will have a field-day, and you'll lose any remaining chance of claiming Rosshampton.' She shrugged. 'But it's your choice.'

'How could I possibly want to rid myself of such an understanding wife?' There was a faint jeering note in his voice. 'No, my sweet, we'll let the marriage stand.'

She bit her lip. 'Very well.' She surveyed him stonily. 'You look terrible.'

'Thank you,' he returned courteously. 'But a bath and a shave will soon restore me. And no one is going to be surprised if I look as if I didn't sleep much last night.' His smile glinted. 'Under the circumstances, they'll expect it.'

To her fury, Louise felt her face warm. Worse still, she was aware of the sudden bitterness of tears in her throat.

With a superhuman effort, she kept her voice steady. 'Please help yourself to coffee. You look as if you need it.'

She picked up her beaker and started towards the door, desperate to get to the sanctuary of her room.

As she passed him, Alex put a detaining hand on her arm. 'Louise—listen…'

Coffee splashed onto the floor as she shook him off, her eyes blazing. 'You don't touch me when we're alone, remember?' she said hoarsely. 'Not now, or ever. And in public only when strictly necessary. That's the deal, Alex, and if you break it I will go. I swear it.' She drew a swift, uneven breath, wanting to hurt him in turn. 'Don't you understand? You make me feel—contaminated.'

He was very pale suddenly, his mouth taut. 'And, of course, we can't have that, my little plaster saint.' There was icy bitterness in his voice. 'I just hope you won't get too lonely up there on your self-righteous pedestal.'

She gasped, anger surging up inside her, overwhelming the pain, the bewilderment, and the aching, desperate need. Before she could think, her hand swung back, and the remains of her coffee were sent showering over him.

For a second she stood transfixed, watching his expression change from astonishment and disbelief to something altogether more dangerous. Then she dropped the empty beaker and fled to her room, slamming the door and turning the key in the lock with clumsy fingers.

She leaned against the panels, listening tensely, half expecting him to come after her, but after a moment or two she heard him go into his own room, and close the door.

And later still she heard him leave, presumably for the bank. It was weak and self-indulgent to feel relief, but she did. She sank down to the carpet, her back against the door, her clenched fist pressed to her quivering mouth.

A small sound between a laugh and a sob escaped her. So much for calm, she thought, not to mention casually friendly.

'And welcome to married life,' she whispered, staring dry-eyed and unseeing into space.

The flowers arrived during the afternoon. More roses—deep crimson this time—and carnations and lilies in an exquisite, heady arrangement, filling the room with their scent. The card said simply 'Alex'.

A peace-offering, Louise wondered as she placed them on the coffee table, or a wreath?

Even more surprisingly, he arrived himself not long after six p.m. Louise had been curled up on the sofa, watching the television news, prepared for another solitary evening, if not an action for assault.

As he came in she pressed the mute button on the remote control and got to her feet, eyeing him apprehensively.

But his face was cool, unreadable. 'I see you got the flowers.'

'Yes,' she said. 'I thought they might be wired to a bomb.'

'And I expected to find them splattered all over the pavement.' He propped a shoulder against the door frame, watching her.

'Why did you send them?'

His mouth twisted wryly. 'I felt some gesture was called for. But I'm not into grovelling. And I thought the thing with the coffee wouldn't work so well a second time,' he added, dead-pan.

Louise flushed. 'No.' She swallowed. 'I—I don't usually do things like that.'

'You mean like losing your self-control,' he said. 'I've noticed.'

Wiser not to respond to that, she decided.

Instead, she said, 'I hope I didn't ruin your beautiful suit.'

'The dry-cleaners tell me it will live.'

She lifted her chin. 'I'm sorry.'

'Why? I asked for it.' He studied her for a moment. 'I didn't even tell you how lovely you looked yesterday,' he added unexpectedly. 'I was the envy of every man at the Savoy.'

Lovely, she thought, *but not lovely enough...*

'I doubt that very much,' she said. 'But—thank you, anyway. I know how appearances matter,' she added stiltedly.

Alex reached behind him and produced a carrier bag. 'To make further amends, I've brought food. I thought we might have dinner together.'

'Dinner?' Louise echoed, stunned. 'You want me to cook you dinner?'

'I hoped we could make some kind of fresh start.' He shrugged. 'But if you'd prefer not to, I shall understand. It's nothing too outrageous—just a couple of fillet steaks and some salad. I could probably manage that myself.'

In spite of herself, she found her mouth trembling into a smile. 'I bet you didn't go out and buy all that yourself. I bet you sent Andie.'

His own face relaxed too. 'Considering we live as strangers,' he drawled, 'you're getting to know me too damned well.' He paused. 'Do you want me to cook dinner?'

'No,' she said. 'I'll do that, and you can pour the wine. That sounds like a fair division of labour.'

That was friendly and casual enough for anyone, she thought as she went into the kitchen. But calm was nowhere within reach. Her heart was going like a triphammer, and there was an odd trembling in the pit of her stomach.

She had spent a wretched day, trying and failing to dismiss from her mind the unwanted images of Alex with some unknown woman that kept constantly invading her consciousness, and tormenting her. It was, she thought, like mistakenly finding herself at the showing of some erotic movie, and being unable to leave.

Nor was there any guarantee that the woman he'd been with was unknown to her. Because, ever since their brief meeting,

Cindy Crosby's beautiful face and voluptuous figure had never been far away from her mind.

She had realised almost at once that it must be that particular liaison which had attracted the attention of the gutter Press. The Crosbys were news, his political career seriously on the move. Not long ago, there'd even been a full-colour spread about them in one of the gossip magazines, showing them in their Surrey home, the picture of marital devotion, complete with manicured lawns and the obligatory Labradors.

'Lucinda's my rock,' her husband had gushed. 'Always there for me.'

Except, Louise thought cynically, when she was elsewhere, and not alone.

Alex's sudden marriage might have thrown Ed Godwin and his like temporarily off the scent, but one hint that he was still involved with the lovely Cindy would bring them back in full cry, and Louise could only imagine the kind of scandal that would ensue—and its ruinous consequences.

But she had told Alex to his face that she did not care what he did, or where he went, and now, somehow, she had to live up to those brave words, whatever the personal cost. Hide the fact that the vividly sensuous pictures in her imagination were tearing her apart, giving her no peace. Present a façade of indifference when her entire being seemed to be one silent scream of jealous misery. And fear…

She moved round the kitchen like an automaton, trying to put these thoughts from her mind, collecting the ingredients for a salad dressing from the store cupboard she'd begun to build during her shopping expeditions.

'Is there anything I can do?' He appeared beside her so quietly and suddenly that Louise jumped, nearly dropping the mustard on the floor.

'Everything's under control.' She mustered a taut smile. 'Andie's done us proud. There are baby new potatoes to go with the steak, and a tarte au citron for pudding.'

He leaned against the refrigerator. 'May I watch, or will it disturb you?'

Everything about you disturbs me, she thought with sudden, savage longing. Even when you're unshaven, hung-over and exhausted, as you were this morning. Even when I know you've just climbed out of another woman's bed. And I can't help myself.

The way your hair grows back from your forehead disturbs me. The line of your jaw. Your hands. The way you move. How you laugh with your eyes when your mouth stays solemn. Your mouth—oh, God—your mouth most of all…

Aloud, she said, 'Be my guest.'

'Can we talk, or do you want me to keep quiet?'

'Not at all,' she said. She paused. 'Is there anything particular you want to say?' *Or confess?*

'No,' he said, 'I don't think so.'

She summoned a forced smile. 'Then why don't you tell me about Rosshampton?'

'What do you want to know?'

She began to mix the dressing. 'Maybe—why you love it so much.'

He said slowly, 'I suppose because it's always represented comfort, safety—and security.'

'All the things I wanted from David.' She reached for the olive oil.

'True,' he said. 'But bricks and mortar tend to be more reliable.'

She bit her lip. 'Why did you spend so much time there?'

'My parents had a fairly chequered marriage.' His tone was brusque. 'My father was abroad a great deal on business when I was young. Although he loved my mother, he never regarded fidelity as a major issue, which did not endear him to Selina. My mother did, so she decided it was safer to travel with him. Therefore I stayed at home with my grandmother at Rosshampton.'

'That must have been hard on you,' Louise said in a low voice, her mind wincing away from this confirmation that unfaithfulness was a Fabian trait.

'Please don't regard me as a lonely waif.' Alex spoke with

a certain asperity. 'Believe me, I never lacked for a thing, including affection. Even when my mother died, Selina was there for me, like a rock, although she must have been dying inside herself at the loss of her only child.'

'Yes,' she said slowly. 'I—I'm so sorry.'

Alex stared at the floor. 'It was a brain haemorrhage,' he said too evenly. 'She was only ill for a couple of hours. They were in New York, and my father had just come back from the pharmacy with some painkillers for the headache she'd complained of, and she smiled at him and simply—went...'

He shook his head. 'He was very withdrawn for a long time. Eventually, he started going out—meeting up with friends and, of course, seeing women. Everyone said it was only a matter of time before he married again. But they were so wrong. She was the one—the real thing in his life. Everything else was just a trivial diversion. And still is, as far as I know.'

She said quietly, 'Thank you for telling me.'

There was a silence as she rinsed the potatoes, and placed them in the steamer.

'Is that new?' Alex enquired.

'Well, yes,' she admitted. 'I hope you don't mind.'

His brows lifted. 'Do I look as if I mind?'

No, she thought bitterly, the breath catching in her throat. He looked as he always did—tanned, tawny and too damned sexy for his own good...or hers.

She said hurriedly, 'Tell me something about the house itself.'

He shrugged. 'It's just a big country house, surrounded by trees. Said to date from Queen Anne's time, but much added to since. Has a ballroom at the rear and ten bedrooms, not including the Royal Suite.'

'Royal?' Louise turned the salad leaves into a bowl, and added the dressing. 'That sounds very imposing.'

'It's extremely comfortable,' he returned. 'Two bedrooms, with a sitting room in between, plus dressing room and bathroom. Apparently Queen Victoria stayed there once or twice with Prince Albert.'

'Then why two bedrooms?' Louise lit the grill for the steaks. 'I thought she was crazy about Albert—couldn't get enough of him.'

'Perhaps he liked the occasional night off,' Alex suggested blandly. And, heaven help her, he was doing that thing with his mouth and eyes again. 'Whatever, that's where we'll be sleeping. Selina always puts me in there when I stay—which is convenient.' He paused. 'Shall I set the table?'

'All by yourself?' Louise asked dulcetly. 'Or will you ring for someone?'

'You, my sweet,' he said softly, 'are asking for trouble. Less of it.'

When she carried the food to the dining room, she found to her surprise that the dining room looked a picture, the polished table set with linen place-mats, gleaming cutlery and glassware, and lit by tall candles in polished silver holders.

She whistled. 'Isn't this a little OTT?'

'Perhaps,' Alex said. 'But it could be the first and last time we ever do this, so let's go for it.'

She flashed him a too-bright smile. 'You're right. Let's.'

She would never forget this evening as long as she lived, she thought later as she sat across the table from Alex in the candlelight. The food and wine were delectable, but, even better, she found suddenly that they were chatting like old friends. In a strange way, even the occasional silences were companionable.

'Do you realise,' she said, 'that I don't even know when your birthday is?'

'It's not a closely guarded secret.' Alex finished his slice of tarte au citron. 'Try August the fifth.'

'Ah,' she said. 'Leo. I should have known.'

He sighed. 'I see someone's told you my nickname.'

'Does it bother you?'

'Not in the slightest.' He paused. 'Do you like the wine?'

'It's wonderful,' she said. 'I can taste cherries.'

'Well done.' Alex smiled at her. 'Maybe I should take you on a tour of the French wine regions.'

'You forget,' Louise said. 'I already have my future itinerary all mapped out.'

'Yes,' he said, 'I almost did forget. But thanks for reminding me.' He was silent for a moment. 'Would you like brandy with your coffee?'

She shook her head. 'Nothing more for me, thanks. I'll clear away, and then I think I'll have an early night.'

'You're allowed to stay up until midnight, Cinderella.'

Not, she thought, when you're trying to catch up on last night's sleep.

She shrugged. 'All the same…'

'As you wish,' he said. 'But don't worry about clearing away. I'll do it.'

'You will?' Louise regarded him with suspicion. 'Or will you just stack it up in the kitchen for the maid?'

'My name,' he said gently, 'is not Marian Trentham.' He shook his head reprovingly as he refilled his glass. 'One of these days, I'm really going to have to teach you to trust me.'

She offered a constrained smile. 'Well—I'll be off, then.' And rose.

'Run away, if you must.' He raised his glass. 'Sweet dreams, Louise.' He paused, looking at her meditatively. 'I suppose you do dream?'

She halted in the doorway, looking back at him. He was leaning back in his chair, his face in shadow. 'Of course,' she said. 'Every night. I believe everyone does.'

'And what do you dream about?' he asked softly. 'Or is it a secret?'

Yes, she thought. My deepest, most intimate secret. Because I dream about you, Alex. About your arms around me, and your lips on mine. I dream that our marriage is a real one, and we're happier together than we could ever have imagined.

I dream that you want me, passionately.

And I know, at this moment, that if you were to give me just one sign—hold out your hand, speak my name—then I'd come to you here and now—tonight—and give myself forever.

But I also know that's the last thing on earth that you would

ever want. So I am indeed running away. Away from temptation. And heartbreak. Away from you.

She gave him a cool smile. 'I dream,' she said, 'about the
Taj Mahal. At sunset. What else? Goodnight, Alex.'

And went, not hurrying, down the corridor to the solitude
and safety of her own room.

CHAPTER EIGHT

'ARE you really sure about this?' Andie asked dubiously.

'If you mean—have I discussed it with Alex, then no,' said Louise, composedly tucking the card from the catering company in her bag.

'Well, don't you think you should?' Andie frowned a little. 'After all, he might not be too pleased to find his wife going round the City serving food to rival banks. Or even Perrins itself, God forbid. And he could have a point.'

Louise sighed. 'I have to do something,' she objected. 'I can't sit around all day wondering whether to have nail extensions or Botox.'

'Especially when you don't need either of them,' Andie agreed cordially. She paused. 'Of course, if you really want a time-consuming occupation, you could always take a leaf out of my book.'

'And become someone's PA?' Louise shook her head. 'I don't think I'm cut out for that.'

'It wasn't what I meant either.' Andie sat back in her chair, smiling. 'I wouldn't mention your proposed career in cooking to Alex until next week,' she added musingly. 'He's jumpy about this party you're going to tomorrow for some reason, and he's had one piece of bad news today already. We don't want an explosion, do we?'

'Bad news?' Louise was signalling to the waiter to bring the bill for their lunch. 'Why, what's happened?'

'I handed in my notice.'

'Oh, no.' Louise's distress was genuine. 'I thought you liked working for him. And, anyway, what am I going to do without you?'

'I do like working for him, and nothing's changed there. And

126

I hope you and I will continue to see each other.' Andie's sudden smile was shy and impish at the same time. 'Especially if you agree to be godmother.'

'Godmother,' Louise repeated on a rising note. 'You mean you're having a baby. Oh, Andie, that's wonderful.'

'I think so,' the other girl agreed. 'All I have to do now is convince Alex. I mean—he congratulated me and everything, but he looked as if he'd been poleaxed, and he's been really quiet all morning.' Her smile widened. 'Perhaps he's never associated marriage with babies before.'

'Probably not,' Louise agreed quietly.

'But now that he has, maybe he'll have his own ideas about your career path.'

Louise flushed at the other girl's teasing tone. 'Are—are you leaving the bank very soon?'

'Not really. I just thought I ought to warn him, so he can start looking for someone new. He is notoriously picky about close staff.' Andie glanced at her watch. 'I'd better get back before he fires me.'

'And I need to go home,' Louise added. 'My dress for the party is being delivered later on.'

'You sound as if they were bringing your shroud.' Andie patted her shoulder. 'You'll have a great time. After all, Alex is showing you off to the second most important woman in his life.'

'Really?' Louise smiled with an effort.

But who is the first? she asked herself with a pang as they emerged into the street, and the mini-heatwave that London was sweltering under. The one who shared our wedding night with him? Or someone else completely?

Aloud, she said brightly, 'Oh, good, there's a taxi coming. Shall I drop you at the bank?'

She chatted and laughed with Andie about her wonderful news until they reached Perrins, but once she was alone again Louise sank back into the corner of her seat, her face and thoughts equally wistful.

Lucky Andie, she told herself wearily. Married blissfully to a man who adored her, and now expecting his child.

The contrast between that and her own situation was almost too wretched to contemplate.

She had hoped so much that things might ease between Alex and herself after the night they had dinner together. That they might even be able to enjoy some kind of tenuous friendship. It wasn't what she wanted, of course, but it would have been better than nothing at all.

Yet, it seemed, she saw even less of him than before. He went out early each day, and came back very late each evening. But at least he did come back, she thought wryly.

And when their paths inevitably did cross, he was politely, even charmingly aloof. He could hardly have told her more strongly that there was no place for her in his life. That the rapport she'd thought was developing between them was simply a figment of her imagination.

I was a fool to hope, she thought with a silent sigh.

However, she might soon be put out of her misery. If things went well at the party this weekend, she might not even be around to be godmother to Andie's baby. She could instead be on the other side of the world, trying to put her life back together.

And her friendship with Andie would be another tie she would have to sever, she realised with real regret.

'Traffic's a nightmare, love,' the driver called back to her suddenly, breaking into her unhappy reverie. 'I'm going to try a short cut.' And he swung the cab down a narrow street lined with antique shops, and small galleries.

It was as the taxi slowed to negotiate its way round a delivery van that Louise caught sight of Alex.

For a moment, she thought she was dreaming. That he was so much in her thoughts that she could, apparently, conjure him up at will.

And then she saw he was not alone. That a woman was beside him, smiling up at him, her hand on his arm. And that they were standing on marble steps under the shade of a striped awning belonging to a hotel called the Belmayne, discreet and clearly exclusive.

It was like living through her worst nightmare, Louise thought, her throat contracting, as she recognised his companion's red hair. Registered the beautiful face with its confident, self-satisfied smile. And realised that her most terrible fears were finally being confirmed.

He said it was over, she thought with anguish. And I wanted to believe him, in spite of all the evidence to the contrary. Yet here they are together. And I can't fool myself any longer, or dream that I'll ever be of anything other than marginal importance to Alex.

Because he can't give Cindy Crosby up, no matter what the risk. Which proves how much he must care for her.

She wanted to cower down in her seat as if she was somehow the one in the wrong. The one who needed to escape attention.

He mustn't see me, she thought frantically. I can't bear it if he sees me. If he knows that I know...

It was a ludicrous reaction, and she knew it, but it was also totally instinctive.

She didn't want to provoke a confrontation in which she would almost inevitably come off the worst. In which she might break down and cry, or be guilty of some other act of self-betrayal.

After all, he had never promised to be faithful. Nor was he aware that he had the power to break her heart, she thought, swallowing back the tears burning in her throat. So at least she still had a measure of pride to sustain her through the remainder of their marriage. Which, she could only hope, would be mercifully brief. Because she was no longer sure how much more she could take.

She was thankful when her cab turned the corner, resisting the temptation to take one last look back.

Now she had to find the strength of will from somewhere to get through the coming weekend. To smile and pretend she was a happy, fulfilled wife. And the better she played her part, the sooner she might have her freedom, she reminded herself and paused, pain slashing at her.

Because she knew all too well that, no matter how many miles or months she was able to put between Alex and herself, she would never really be free of him.

That her unhappy, thankless love would keep her in his thrall for the rest of her life. And that was the secret burden she would have to bear, now and always.

Quite apart from the fevered state of her emotions, Louise felt unbearably hot and sticky when she got back to the flat.

Something cold to drink, she thought, kicking off her high-heeled sandals. And after that she'd take a shower.

She wandered barefoot into the kitchen and extracted a bottle of mineral water from the fridge, uncapping it and drinking thirstily, then placing the chilly glass against her forehead.

However much she was dreading the coming party, it would still be good to get out of the stifling city and breathe some country air, she thought, leaning against the counter-top. Maybe it would help her to think more clearly too.

She still wasn't sure what reception she would get from Lady Perrin. Alex had formally told his grandmother he was married, but so far there had been no reaction, and she wasn't sure if that was a good sign or bad. In fact she wasn't sure of very much at all except her own unhappiness, she thought, her heart like a stone in her chest.

As she tossed the empty bottle into the bin the door buzzer sounded, signalling that her dress had arrived, which was one less thing to worry about, she told herself, starting up the passage.

She had fallen in love with the deep red taffeta confection with its boned strapless bodice, and smooth bell of a skirt, as soon as she'd seen it. Its classic lines enhanced her slenderness, and the colour lent warmth to her pale skin, giving in turn a much-needed boost to her confidence.

She would never be Alex's wife in any real sense, she thought, but at least, for one night, she would look the part. And, if nothing else, she would make him proud of her.

She threw open the door, confidently expecting to see a messenger carrying a beribboned box. Instead she found herself taking a step backwards, her hand going to her throat.

She said, her voice sharp with disbelief, 'David?'

'Hello, Lou,' David Sanders said awkwardly. 'It's good to see you.'

She wished she could say the same, but it was impossible. She'd never expected to see him again. Never wanted to either, she realised.

She swallowed, taking a firm hold on herself. 'What are you doing here? How—how did you find me?'

'Ellie still had Fabian's address in her organiser,' he said. 'May I come in?'

She'd already responded with automatic politeness, standing to one side to admit him, before it struck her forcibly that it was the last thing she really wanted and that she should, instead, have told him to get lost.

Biting her lip, she followed him to the living room, where he stood looking around him appraisingly.

'Well,' he commented, 'you've certainly fallen on your feet.'

Louise was astounded to hear a faint note of injury in his voice. She gave him an inimical look. 'As opposed to flat on my face?' she queried. 'Or was that what you intended?'

'No, of course not,' he protested uncomfortably. He paused. 'Oh, God, Lou.' He shook his head. 'It's all such a bloody mess.'

'Is it?'

'You must know that it is. I've been such an idiot.'

Louise moved restively, regretting even more that she'd allowed him into the flat. And this was the man that, only a short time before, she had planned to marry. Now his presence was an embarrassment—a thorn in her side. How quickly things could change.

Anxious to be rid of him, she said, 'David, I have things to do. What do you want exactly?'

'I need to apologise,' he said intensely. 'To tell you that

going off with Ellie was the biggest mistake of my life, and beg you to forgive me.'

She shrugged. 'Consider yourself forgiven,' she told him curtly. 'Now, perhaps, you'll go. You should never have come here in the first place.'

'But we can't just leave it like that,' he objected. He sounded almost startled. 'You can't be happy, married to that bastard. And Ellie and I are through, or very nearly,' he added despondently. 'She and my mother can't stand the sight of each other, and she says my present salary is a joke, so she's insisting that I sell the house and get a job in London so that she can go back to work at Trentham Osborne.'

He sighed. 'She's changed completely. When we first met, she was so sweet—so fragile. I just fell—headlong. Now all she seems to think about is money. I suppose that's the result of associating with someone like Alex Fabian,' he added, giving his surroundings a look that combined envy with loathing.

Louise frowned. 'But she certainly didn't want to marry him,' she pointed out. 'She told me herself that he scared her.'

David shrugged. 'Maybe she's decided she'd rather be scared than bored,' he countered wanly. 'Or perhaps she was just miffed because Fabian had his own agenda, and wouldn't dance to her tune. Anyway, she certainly misses the high life. And she despises me because I can't afford to take her to the places he did.'

'I find that hard to believe.' Louise frowned. 'Although Alex has always said I didn't know Ellie as well as I thought.'

'Did any of us?' David asked glumly. 'Life's been sheer hell since we got back. My mother never stops complaining. Half my friends won't speak to me.'

'Am I supposed to feel sorry for you?'

'I can't expect that,' he said heavily. 'But hearing that you'd married Fabian was simply the final straw. Something—died in me, I think.'

'That sounds like a line from the drama group's last production,' Louise told him coldly. 'And my marriage is no concern of yours.'

'But you're so wrong.' He gave her a pathetic look. 'We had a good thing going for us, Lou. We could have made it. Besides,' he added, with a startling shift in direction, 'what are you going to do when Fabian gets tired of you, and you're kicked into touch?'

'Oh, that's all settled,' she said over-brightly, resisting the impulse to wrap defensive arms round her body and howl. 'I shall travel the world as a rich divorcee.'

'But not alone,' he said quickly. 'You'll never need to do that, Lou.'

She stared at him open-mouthed. 'You surely can't be suggesting yourself as travelling companion?'

'Why not?' His voice was eager. 'I've admitted I've been a fool, and that must count for something. So, Lou—darling Lou—why shouldn't we make a fresh start?'

She said wearily, 'For more reasons than I care to enumerate. And my name is Louise. My husband prefers it.'

'Husband,' he said with contempt. 'He's no more a husband to you than he would have been to Ellie.'

'And you,' Louise flashed back, 'know only what Ellie's told you.' She went to the door. 'David, I think you should leave. Now.'

'I've upset you,' he said. 'Just turning up like this. I should have written to you, or rung first, but I was just so desperate to see you—to put things right. Because I know that, if you give me the chance, I can make you happy.'

'On the contrary,' Louise said coldly. 'I think we've both had a lucky escape.' She paused, adding levelly, 'You need to remember, David, that you and Ellie were sufficiently in love a few weeks ago to run away together. You may just be going through a bad patch at the moment.'

'It was just a silly infatuation,' David said. 'I see that now.'

Louise moved restively. 'Whatever,' she said. 'I'm really not interested.'

'Sweetheart,' he said coaxingly, 'you don't mean that. You can't have forgotten what we were to each other.'

'A habit,' she said, 'that is now broken. So let's leave it like that.'

'But how can I,' he demanded, 'when you're the only woman I'm ever going to want? Please don't send me away, Lou. I should never have let you go, and I know that, given the chance, I can make it work. You look amazing,' he added huskily.

'The only amazing thing about me is that I'm actually listening to this drivel.' Louise marched to the front door and flung it open, standing beside it, stony-faced.

'My God,' he said. 'I never thought you could be so hard. That's what he's done to you, isn't it?'

'A few other factors were also involved.' She lifted her chin. 'Goodbye, David.'

He gave her one last sorrowful look, and left. Louise closed the door behind him with deliberate firmness, and stood for a moment looking at its blank panels.

I should be in a terrible state, she thought. *The man I planned to marry has just grovelled to me, and begged me to go back to him. And, in view of what I know about Alex, I should be at least—torn. And yet I know beyond all doubt that I wouldn't have David back, if he came gift-wrapped, with a cash bonus.*

She began to unzip her pale yellow linen dress as she walked down to her room. She adjusted the shower temperature to cool, then stripped off her underwear and stepped under the refreshing torrent of water, letting it cascade over her hair, and down her body.

David wanted her, and Alex never would. There was a terrible irony in that, she thought, lifting her face so that the power-driven droplets mingled with the tears she could no longer hold back. Standing motionless until she had regained some measure of control.

When she'd dried herself, and given her hair a swift towelling, she slipped on her white broderie-anglaise robe. *It was pointless trying to alter the immutable,* she thought. *She would only become more hurt than she was already.*

Far better to devote herself to practicalities like packing for the weekend. And telephoning the shop about her dress, which should be here by now, she reminded herself.

Still barefoot, she went up the hallway to the living room, only to come to an abrupt halt in the doorway. It was a day for shocks, she thought, swallowing. Because Alex was there, standing on the other side of the room by the window, his back towards her.

She was all set to beat a retreat, convinced she hadn't made a sound, but he turned instantly, his brows snapping together as he surveyed her.

Louise returned his gaze, her chin lifted. She had no idea what could have brought him back at this time in the afternoon—unless, of course, he'd come to tell her that their token marriage was over. That he and Cindy Crosby could no longer bear to live apart.

Please God, don't let me grovel like David, she whispered silently. Don't let me beg for mercy. Isn't it bad enough that I'm standing here with bare feet and damp hair?

That too potent image of them standing together on the steps of the hotel where they'd been making love flashed into her mind, and flooded her face with indignant, painful colour.

But anger was good. Anger was infinitely safer than hurt—and need.

The green eyes narrowed. He said softly, 'Hello, darling. You seem—surprised to see me.'

'I was having a shower. I didn't hear you come in.' She hesitated. 'And you're quite right. I wasn't expecting you.'

'I hope my return hasn't inconvenienced you in any way.' His tone was silky.

'This is your home,' Louise returned. 'You're entitled to come and go as you please. I thought we'd established that.'

'Do you usually take showers in the middle of the afternoon?'

'Sometimes, when it's as hot as this.' Absurd to feel defensive, yet she did, just the same. 'Why do you ask?'

He shrugged, his smile glittering at her like ice. 'Just natural curiosity, my sweet, about how you spend your time when I'm not around.'

'I could ask you the same thing,' she countered.

'Then why don't you?'

She bit her lip. 'Perhaps because I already know the answer.' She was on thin ice, but she couldn't help herself.

'I wonder if you do,' he murmured.

There was an odd silence, and a tension in the air that made her skin tingle suddenly.

Could he actually be feeling concern about telling her his decision? she wondered. Yet the vibrations she was picking up seemed in some strange way to be more angry than anxious. As if he was controlling his temper with immense effort.

Louise felt as if she was on the scaffold waiting for the axe to fall, and decided she couldn't bear it any longer. That she had to force an open confrontation, whatever the cost.

She swallowed. 'Did—did you come back for a particular reason?' She paused, trying to read his expression and failing. 'You—you have something you want to say to me?'

'Perhaps,' he said. 'But it will keep for another time.'

He walked across the room, tossing his discarded jacket over the arm of a chair, loosening his tie. He sat down on one of the sofas, stretching long legs in front of him with apparent indolence. But still, she realised, watching her with that hooded, enigmatic gaze. Making her suspect that, under the relaxed pose, he was really as tense as a coiled spring.

He said, 'Is that a new dressing gown?'

'I bought it last week.' *And why are we discussing trivialities like this? Why don't you tell me what's really on your mind?*

'Ah,' Alex said. 'I thought I hadn't seen it before. Because I'm sure I should have remembered such a charming—and seductive piece of nonsense.'

He was smiling as he spoke, and she had to fight an impulse to tighten the sash round her slender waist, wishing with all her heart that she were fully dressed. Because his smile, and the cool, watchful intensity of his stare, was beginning to alarm her.

'But then,' she returned with a creditable assumption of calm, 'you're here so seldom these days.'

'Yes,' he said softly. 'And that has clearly been a mistake which I shall have to rectify.' He paused. 'And, as I'm here now, why don't you sit down and let us enjoy a pleasant marital chat, the way that husbands and wives do?'

'Because we don't really fall within that category.' Louise tried to speak lightly. To ignore the fact that she was shaking inside. 'Also, I have things to do.'

'Ah,' he said, his brows lifting. 'And, no doubt, places to go, and people to see.'

'I'm going away with you,' she said. 'To meet your grandmother, and assure her that you've turned into a model husband. So I need to pack.' She touched her dry lips with the tip of her tongue. 'Also to call the shop and ask why my dress for her party hasn't arrived yet.'

'Nothing too urgent, then,' he said. He pointed to the sofa opposite. 'So, join me.' His smile glinted at her. 'Or do I have to fetch you?'

No, she thought. He certainly did not have to do that.

She obeyed reluctantly, sitting bolt upright, carefully arranging her broderie-anglaise skirts around her legs with nervous hands.

Alex leaned back, lacing his fingers behind his head. 'You seem on edge, my sweet,' he remarked. 'Do you find my presence so daunting?'

She shrugged defensively. 'No—I'm still a little taken aback to find you here in the middle of a working day.'

'Perhaps I felt in need of some female company,' he drawled. 'Is that so surprising?'

Hurt wrenched at her. If that was indeed the case, why hadn't he stayed with Cindy Crosby, as he'd had every opportunity to do?

She sent him a burning look. 'Astonishing, frankly.' She paused. 'I can't imagine I'd be your first choice for that, or even on the A list.'

'You do yourself an injustice, darling.' He looked back at her meditatively. 'So—tell me about your day.'

Louise fidgeted with a fold of her skirt. 'I hardly think you'd be interested.'

'Try me,' he invited softly. 'Run through some of the highlights. The key moments.'

Oh, God, Louise thought, her throat tightening. He must have spotted me in that taxi. He knows that I saw him—that I'm well aware he's still Cindy Crosby's lover, and he wants to know what I'm going to do about it. He needs to check my reaction, in case I'm planning to be trouble.

She ticked off on her fingers. 'I got up after you left. I had breakfast. I put on a yellow dress that you also haven't seen. And I had lunch with Andie.' She forced a smile. 'It's great news about the baby, isn't it?'

'The best,' he said. 'And after lunch?'

'I came home.' No, she thought, in truth I came back to this expensive, luxurious shell which merely masquerades as a home. 'And the rest you know,' she went on, trying for insouciance. 'Not exactly world-shattering, is it?'

'That might depend,' Alex said slowly, 'on how you see your world. But is that really all, my sweet? You're sure you haven't forgotten something? Some—encounter, maybe?'

She could not believe he was being so cruel. That he could actually taunt her with the knowledge that he was still Cindy Crosby's lover.

Her hands clenched together in her lap, as she fought an inward battle for calm, and courage. 'If I have,' she said, keeping her voice level, 'it's because it's really not important. Because it doesn't alter the essence of the bargain we made.'

She lifted her chin. 'We—we are both free agents, at least in private. And nothing that's happened is going to change the way I behave towards you in public this weekend. I promise you that. I'll—play my part, as agreed. You'll have nothing to complain about.'

There was a long, deafening silence, then Alex said quietly, 'I see. Then may I suggest that next time you decide to entertain your lover for a little afternoon delight, you warn me in advance? I'd hate to be guilty of some tactless intrusion—as I might have been today.'

'My lover?' Louise repeated, stunned. 'What are you talking about?'

'I saw the lift come down from the penthouse,' he said, 'and David Sanders leave it. And please don't tell me I made a mistake, because I recognised him from the photograph in your bedroom at the cottage.

'He was naturally far too preoccupied to notice me,' he added bitingly. 'But then I'm certain you'd assured him I was safely at work a few miles away, so he wouldn't have expected to see me. Any more than you did, my sweet.'

He paused. 'A word of advice. Avoid taking a bath or shower in the middle of the day. It tends to arouse suspicion.' His smile was hard. 'Besides, it's not essential. I'm hardly likely to taste him on your skin, am I, darling?'

Her head fell back in shock, as if he'd struck her.

'You—you are daring to accuse me?' Her voice was low and trembling. 'You think David came here—for that?'

'It's a fair assumption,' he said coldly. 'When I find you here, the picture of guilt, and next-door to naked. Did you choose the dressing gown specially, my sweet? Does he prefer the virginal look—especially when it only consists of a layer of fabric?'

The anger was out in the open now. The words bitter—corrosive.

Louise bit her lip. 'Believe what you wish,' she returned equally icily. 'But I was fully dressed when David arrived. And there was no prior arrangement, either. I thought he was the messenger delivering my dress, or I wouldn't have opened the door.'

'You're claiming he simply turned up out of the blue?' Alex asked with derision. 'How did he know where to find you?'

'Apparently he looked up your address in Ellie's organiser.' She hesitated. 'He came to tell me—things hadn't worked out between them.'

'What a bloody surprise,' he said contemptuously. 'Was that all he said?'

'No.' Louise stared at the floor. 'He—he wants me to go back to him.'

'How touching,' Alex said blightingly. 'So when's your next assignation? And please don't have him in my bed, darling, because I wouldn't find that amusing.'

'I wouldn't dream of it,' Louise hurled back at him, riled beyond endurance. 'I was thinking we might try the Belmayne Hotel instead. Would you recommend it?'

The sudden silence seemed to stretch into eternity.

At last he said grimly, 'What the hell are you talking about?'

'About your damned hypocrisy.' She was on her feet, shaking like a leaf. 'I saw you, Alex. I saw you with your friend, Mrs Crosby. Your love nest is on a cab drivers' rat run. And I know the name of the rat!'

'Why, Louise,' he said softly, 'if I didn't know better I'd say you were jealous.' He paused. 'So what happens now? I expect the gutter Press would pay handsomely for the information.'

'I'm sure they would,' she hit back. 'But I prefer to make you pay—when all this is over. When I'm free, and you're sharing Rosshampton with the beautiful Mrs Crosby. She already has a country house, so a mansion is clearly the next logical step.'

She turned abruptly, making the broderie-anglaise skirts swirl around her, and marched to the door. 'And now I'm going to my room, to pack for our weekend of wedded bliss. Please let me know when my dress arrives.'

She was at the door when his voice reached her, quiet, but with an odd raw note. 'Louise—tell me the truth. Is David Sanders your lover?'

She looked back at him over her shoulder, her mouth twisting. 'Why, Alex.' She kept her own tone light, even mocking. 'If I didn't know better, I'd say you were jealous.'

She left the room, her head held high. And only she knew that her heart was weeping.

CHAPTER NINE

THEY drove down to Rosshampton the following afternoon, having reached what Louise could only wearily suppose, was a state of armed neutrality.

She had gone to her room, the day before, and stayed there, and he had made no attempt to follow. And she hadn't cried, because she couldn't allow herself to do that. Not again. Not yet.

But one day soon, when she was finally and completely alone, she would let herself grieve for a love that had never been hers.

Instead she had begun to pack for the weekend, moving like an automaton, trying to recall what Alex had told her about its format.

They would be expected to arrive in time for tea, and in the evening there would be a small dinner for family and a few close friends.

The real celebration would be the birthday party on Saturday night, when she would dance in Alex's arms for the first and last time, wearing her new dress, which had finally arrived an hour later.

Alex had tapped on the door. 'There's a package for you.'

'Oh, thank you.' She took a deep breath, then walked to the door and opened it. He handed her the flat striped box, but as she made to close the door again, he stopped her, his expression faintly quizzical.

'Don't I get to see it?'

'Don't you trust my judgement?' Louise parried.

He shrugged. 'Trust hasn't played a great part in this relationship so far.'

'We don't have a relationship,' she said. 'We have a deal.'

'Just the same,' he said. 'May I look?'

Reluctantly Louise lifted the lid of the box, parting the sheets of protective tissue. She took out the shimmering folds of dark red taffeta, and held them against herself, briefly and self-consciously.

'Will it do?' She didn't look at him.

'Yes,' he said, after a pause. 'It will do very well. Thank you.'

He turned and walked away, and she closed the door behind him and leaned against it, aware that her breathing had quickened.

A short while later, she heard him go out, and she had not seen him again until this afternoon, when he had returned to collect her for the journey down to Rosshampton.

She had assumed that Alex would be driving himself, as he'd done when they first met, and had to hide her disappointment when he told her that he had decided to use the limousine and his driver as he had work to do on the journey. This meant that there would be no real chance to talk, and maybe even reach some much-needed rapprochement before they arrived for the party.

Harry, Alex's driver, was polite and pleasant, and she liked him. She also knew there was no way he could overhear any passenger conversations, but that did not prevent her feeling absurdly self-conscious when he was present.

Besides, she thought with an inward sigh, there was no guarantee that she and Alex would discuss the events of the past twenty-four hours any more calmly and rationally than they had done already, and it would only take Harry one glance in the mirror to see they were having a row.

So maybe it was better this way, she thought, sitting on opposite sides of the car and concentrating on anything except each other.

He'd courteously offered her the *Financial Times*, and she'd declined with equal politeness.

Now, while Alex studied the papers he'd taken from his briefcase, Louise turned away from his cool, uncompromising profile and stared resolutely out of the window at the passing scenery, reviewing in her mind what he'd told her in the past about the South African connection.

Cliff Maidstone, she thought, grandson of a man that Selina Perrin might once have wanted to marry, but who'd been sent abroad to avoid prosecution after some trouble over money. Accompanied by Della, his wife of less than a year and a former model. Described himself as an investment adviser. No apparent shortage of funds, or charm. Loud in his praise of Rosshampton, which had been lovingly described to him, as a small child, by his grandfather. Had numerous memories to share with Lady Perrin of times when Archie Maidstone had stayed at the house himself.

'The man's clever,' Alex had commented tersely. 'Apparently, he's mentioned his grandfather's lifelong regret for the "stupidity" that drove him away from everything he held dear. Which, of course, includes Selina.'

He gave a sigh of exasperation. 'What woman wouldn't like to think she was some man's lifelong regret?'

'It's not something that would appeal to me,' Louise said.

But then, she thought sadly, she had her own regrets that might very well last a lifetime.

She cleared her throat. 'How—how have you found out all these things?'

He shrugged. 'Major rule in business. Know your enemy.'

'And presumably,' Louise said quietly, 'your enemy also knows you.'

'Ah,' Alex said with a swift, crooked grin. 'But I have a secret weapon in you, my sweet.'

But will I be enough? Louise asked herself, remembering the exchange. Supposing his grandmother doesn't like me—or has already put two and two together and realises this marriage is simply a put-up job?

She realised suddenly that the car was slowing and turning in between two tall stone pillars, and on, up a long sweep of drive.

Then the house was in front of them, a gracious sprawl of

grey stone and mullioned windows, and she forgot everything else as she had her first view of Rosshampton.

It looked, she thought with sudden wonder, as if it had been there forever, framed by trees, as ancient and mellow as the landscape itself that surrounded it. The lawns seemed almost sculptured in their perfection, and the waters of the lake sparkled with blue and gold in the distance.

It was a house totally at ease with itself, and with its past, and she could understand for the first time why Alex loved it so much and desired it so fiercely that he was prepared to go to any lengths to acquire it.

Could understand—and almost sympathise.

She knew, too, that she would move heaven and earth to help him achieve his dream, if it was at all possible. That it would be her gift of love to him. The first, and also the last.

'Well?'

She started a little at the sound of his voice. Turned to see him regarding her with a faint smile.

'It's so beautiful,' she said slowly. 'I never thought it would be like this.' Or that I—I'd want it too, she added silently. Because that was something he would not want to hear. There was no place for her in Alex's future plans. So much so that he was prepared to pay a fortune for her to go away, she reminded herself, straightening her shoulders and reaching for her bag. And she could not let herself forget that even for a minute.

The car drew to a halt in front of an imposing main entrance, where a man neatly dressed in a dark suit was waiting to greet them.

'That's Gillow,' Alex told her in an undertone as they left the car. 'He and his wife run the place, with additional help when they need it. They've been with Selina for years, and meeting you is going to be a big moment for them. Mrs Gillow has been asking for years when I'm going to meet a nice young lady. Almost from the time I left school, in fact.'

She winced. 'Now, why does that make me feel no better about all this?'

'Want to pull out?'

'No,' she said, lifting her chin. 'I came to do a job, and I'll do it.'

He said, 'Then it begins.' He took her hand, and she walked beside him, smiling, into the house.

Lady Perrin was in the drawing room, seated in a corner of one of the brocaded sofas that flanked the fireplace.

'Grandmother,' Alex said, leading her forward. 'This is Louise—my wife.'

Lady Perrin's shrewd gaze swept over her, taking in every detail of the plain taupe dress, the dark brown patent shoes and bag, the gold studs in her ears and, more particularly, the plain band on her wedding finger. She gave a slight nod.

'So,' she said, 'you're the girl who's managed to tame my grandson at last.'

'Oh, no, Lady Perrin,' Louise said serenely. 'I wouldn't even attempt to do that. I think he's pretty wonderful just the way he is.'

'Then you must be very easy to please,' the older woman said tartly. She patted the sofa beside her. 'Sit down, child, and tell me something about yourself. Alexander has been distressingly reticent. I think he wanted to surprise me, and he has.'

She turned to him. 'You need not wait, Alexander. Gillow will have taken your bags up to the Chinese Room.'

'The Chinese Room?' Alex repeated, an odd note in his voice. 'Not the Royal Suite?'

'I've given that to the Maidstones on this occasion,' his grandmother told him affably. 'I knew you wouldn't mind.'

'No, of course not.' Alex's face and tone were expressionless. 'The Chinese Room it is, then.'

'I'll send your wife to you when we've had our little chat.' She gave him a thin smile. 'You have better taste than I thought, grandson.'

Louise sat down, folding her hands in her lap, drawing on every atom of composure she possessed.

She was expecting the latter-day equivalent of the Spanish Inquisition from this formidable old lady, but once they were alone Lady Perrin became far more friendly. Her questions about Louise's family, education and former career were certainly probing, but they were also kind, and she appeared genuinely interested.

And she seemed to accept without demur Louise's calm explanation that she'd met Alex while he was negotiating a finance deal with her father.

'It's almost the truth, after all,' Alex had pointed out. 'So why invent another story?'

'It's no wonder that he snapped you up with such indecent haste,' Lady Perrin was saying. 'I did wonder—but no matter.' She paused. 'Tell me, my dear, does he make you happy?'

Louise hadn't been expecting that. The older woman had slipped it under her guard, and for a moment she almost faltered, then she made herself look up, and meet Lady Perrin's eyes. She even managed to smile.

She said calmly, 'He's made me love him more than I dreamed I would ever be able to care for anyone.'

'That is not,' said Lady Perrin, 'what I asked, but never mind. Alexander is a very fortunate man.' She glanced at her watch. 'Now go upstairs and join him. Mrs Gillow will show you the way. Tea will be in half an hour, when the Maidstones return from their walk in the garden.'

And Louise found herself dismissed.

On the way upstairs, a clearly delighted Mrs Gillow regaled her with stories about Alex's boyhood. At any other time Louise would have gobbled them up, but a slight feeling of uneasiness was stirring inside her. Alex had been so definite that they would be given the Royal Suite, yet it seemed they'd been put somewhere else. And what were the implications of that? she asked herself, remembering his reaction.

She did not have to wait long to find out. Mrs Gillow opened a door with a flourish, and Louise stepped forward into the Chinese Room.

She could see at once how it had acquired its name. It was a large room, overlooking the lake, its walls covered in a charming oriental paper, and the eastern theme was repeated in the tall porcelain vases that graced the mantelpiece. There were washed Chinese rugs on the polished wood floor, and the window hangings were dull gold, as was the quilted coverlet on the room's only bed.

It was that which caught the eye of course. Focused her appalled attention. It was a very wide bed—kingsize or even larger—but it stood in solitary splendour, everything about it suggesting double occupation.

Which was not, and never had been, part of the deal, Louise thought, her throat tightening uncontrollably.

As she heard the door close behind Mrs Gillow, Louise looked across the room to where Alex was standing by the window.

She said huskily, 'What is this?' Her voice rose. 'You said two rooms. You promised me...'

He shrugged. 'You heard what Selina said. She's given the Royal Suite to the Maidstones. A great mark of favour,' he added drily.

'But she can't.' Louise wrapped defensive arms round her body. 'And we can't either—share this room, I mean.'

'Unfortunately, we don't have a choice,' Alex drawled. 'But it's a very big bed and, although I don't have a naked sword to place between us in the true spirit of chivalry, a couple of those pillows should provide sufficient deterrent.'

'No,' she said, her heart thudding unevenly. 'No, I won't do it.' She pointed to a door. 'What's in there?'

'A bathroom.'

'Problem solved,' she said. 'You could sleep in the bath.'

'Indeed, I could,' he said cordially. 'I could also dangle from the light fitting. But I'm not going to. I intend to spend the night in that bed.'

There was a chaise longue in the window alcove, with a gilded sleeping dragon curled along its back. She pointed to it. 'You can use that.'

'Forget it,' he said tersely. 'Quite apart from being seriously uncomfortable, the damned thing is only about five feet long.

I, on the other hand, am over six feet tall, in case you hadn't noticed,' he added witheringly.

She lifted her chin angrily. 'Then I shall sleep there myself.'

'Fine.' He shrugged. 'That's your decision—and your funeral.' His mouth slanted. 'Or you'll wish it was after a few hours on that bloody couch.'

She was close to furious, frightened tears. Her voice shook. 'You planned this deliberately, didn't you?'

'Oh, sure,' Alex said derisively. 'I can just hear myself. ''Oh, Gran, my wife won't sleep with me, so can you—throw us together somehow? If we're in the same bed, I can maybe talk her round.''' He snorted. 'Get real, Louise.'

'But there must be something we can do.'

'There is,' he said. 'We can accept the situation. And I've already started.' He pointed to the wardrobe. 'I hung up your dress.'

'Thank you,' she said stonily.

'Think nothing of it,' he returned. 'As I'm sure you already do.' He paused, then said more gently, 'I'll try and make the situation as easy as I can for you. Ensure that you have privacy while you're changing. Take care not to walk into the bathroom without knocking. And make sure that the lights are off when I come to bed,' he added drily. 'Because I don't wear pyjamas.'

She stared down at the polished floor, aware that her face had warmed. 'Very well.' Her voice was muffled as she tried to erase from her mind an unwanted image of how Alex would look without his clothes.

'And after all,' he added, 'it's only for a couple of nights. Then you'll have all your own space again.' He gave her a brief smile. 'Now, we'd better go down and have tea with Selina.'

The Maidstones were already in the drawing room when they got there. He was tall and broad-shouldered, with dark hair and hot brown eyes in a ruddy face. Della Maidstone was a willowy blonde with a kittenish expression. They smiled lovingly at each other, showing very white teeth, and touched a lot, too, and Louise found herself quite irrationally disliking them intensely.

Surely Lady Perrin couldn't really think that they were suitable custodians for Rosshampton, she thought in bewilderment.

Yet she seemed to be surveying their antics benignly enough. Cliff Maidstone treated her with a combination of flirtatiousness and respect that she seemed to enjoy, and Della talked brightly about the celebrities she'd met during her modelling career.

Louise was almost certain that Lady Perrin had no idea who most of them were, but she listened to Della's revelations with an air of keen interest.

'I do miss my career,' the younger woman admitted eventually, with a sigh. She looked at Louise. 'Do you have a job, Mrs Fabian?'

'Not at the moment,' Louise responded. 'But I'm thinking of going into corporate catering,' she added, avoiding Alex's swift, narrow-eyed glance.

Della's blue eyes widened. 'You mean complicated cooking and stuff.' She shook her head. 'I can burn boiled water, can't I, Cliffy?'

He laughed heartily. 'You're not that bad, sweet thing.' He turned to Alex. 'So your wife's a great cook, is she?'

'My wife does everything well,' Alex returned silkily. 'She manages to surprise me on a daily basis.'

Louise selected a cucumber sandwich, and bit it—hard.

'Of course, you two are still on your honeymoon,' Della put in suddenly. 'Did you have a wonderful, romantic wedding? I loved every minute of mine,' she went on, fortunately not waiting for an answer, and launched herself into a detailed description, involving yards of tulle, number of layers on the wedding cake, average age of bridesmaids, multitude of guests in attendance, and the hilarious thing her sister's child had said at the evening barbecue and dance which had rounded off the celebrations.

Louise, brain reeling, met, unwisely, the glint of unholy

amusement in Alex's eyes, and was almost betrayed into a giggle.

She was thankful when Della eventually ran out of steam, and the awkward meal came to an end. She found herself left to her own devices, Lady Perrin having stated imperiously that she wished a private word with Alex in the library, prompting the Maidstones to exchange uneasy glances.

Louise made haste to escape to the garden. It was still slumberously warm, the bees industrious in the flower borders, birdsong muted with the approach of evening.

This was what she needed, she told herself, drawing in lungfuls of fragrant air as she headed for the lake.

The prospect of the night ahead was hanging over her like a deep shadow. Sleeping with him just across the hallway at the flat had been a disturbing enough experience. The thought of having to share a room, however platonically, was almost unbearable.

But only to me, she thought. It clearly doesn't worry him in the slightest. And if I needed proof of his total indifference to me, then I have it now.

There were no visible marks, of course, but she was hurting—bleeding—just the same. And she would carry the hidden scars forever.

As she reached the edge of the lake, a pair of swans emerged from the reeds and began to move slowly and gracefully across the sunlit water.

She stood watching them for a while, shading her eyes with her hand. They mate for life, she thought, which is something I don't need to contemplate right now. And she turned her back on them, and walked swiftly on.

If tea had been difficult, dinner proved to be a nightmare. Louise found herself seated next to Cliff Maidstone, and had to endure some heavy-handed joshing on Alex's reputation as a playboy—'Let's hope he's reformed, eh?'—before he moved on to the subject of Rosshampton.

'Of course, I regard the place as almost a second home now,' he told her with open satisfaction. 'Lady Perrin has been extremely gracious with her invitations, and I knew she'd take to my little Della right away. In fact,' here he lowered his voice confidentially, 'I have to say she's treated us as if we were her guests of honour.'

'So when are you planning to go back to South Africa?' Louise asked coolly, as soon as he paused for breath.

He gave her a smug grin. 'Let's just say my plans are—fluid at the moment. The old lady and my grandfather were pretty close at one time, and I guess I remind her of him.

'The family didn't want to know about him, of course. They were pushing her to marry another cousin—a Perrin, naturally. One of those convenient business mergers, and to hell with the bride's feelings. Incredible, eh?'

'Amazing,' said Louise.

The food was delicious but it was turning to ashes in her mouth, she reflected, watching Della bat her long eyelashes at Alex on the other side of the table.

Most of Lady Perrin's other guests were on the elderly side, so once coffee had been drunk in the drawing room they began to make their excuses and drift away home. Then the Maidstones, who'd been concealing their yawns for half an hour, said their goodnights and went upstairs.

'You look tired too, child.' Lady Perrin gave Louise a penetrating look. 'Run off to bed. I promise I won't keep your husband away from you for too long.' She lifted a scented cheek. 'You may kiss me, my dear.'

Louise, obeying, realised that she had no choice but to accept her dismissal, and went reluctantly up to the Chinese Room.

She had cornered Mrs Gillow earlier and asked for an extra blanket, much to the good woman's surprise, and this was now lying neatly folded on the bed.

Louise took the blanket, and one of the pillows, and transferred them to the chaise longue. She had considered sleeping fully dressed, but knew that this would merely subject her to derisive remarks from Alex, so she had no alternative other than to change into the nightdress in primrose voile which was the only night attire she'd brought with her.

But at least she'd be wearing something, she thought, biting her lip.

Her make-up removed and her hair brushed, she came back into the bedroom, eyeing her makeshift bed with misgivings. Perhaps some air would help her sleep, she thought, and went to the window. As she pushed the casement open she heard the sound of voices from the terrace below, and realised Alex must be walking there with his grandmother.

At that moment, Lady Perrin's precise tones came floating up to her with total clarity. 'The Crosby woman, Alex. I trust that she belongs completely in the past.'

There was a pause, then Alex's voice, quiet, almost sombre, reached her too. He said, 'I'm afraid, Gran, I'm not finding it quite that simple.'

What was it they said about eavesdroppers? Louise thought desolately, closing the window noiselessly again. She would rather do without fresh air than listen to any further revelations about the woman Alex loved, and his inability to give her up. And she was astonished that he should be making them to his grandmother, anyway.

Unless of course she'd guaranteed that Rosshampton would be his, and he'd decided he ought to be frank about the identity of its future mistress.

She lay down on the chaise longue, wrapping the blanket awkwardly round her and trying to find a comfortable position. Alex, she thought, had not been joking about this horrid piece of furniture.

She'd wanted very much to be asleep when he came to bed, but she was still wide awake when he came softly into the room half an hour later.

True to his word, he switched off the lights, but Louise closed her eyes tightly just the same, and lay like a stone. The rest of her senses seemed curiously heightened in the darkness. She could hear, she realised, the rustle of his clothes as he removed them. Could remember the taste of his mouth on hers.

Could feel the rougher texture of the blanket grazing her skin through the delicate fabric of her nightgown as if it did not exist, and the swift, involuntary hardening of her nipples in response.

Her whole body seemed alive, stirring—curious.

And suddenly he was there, beside her, standing over her in the shadows. The warm, clean scent of his skin was all around her, making the breath catch in her throat.

Because she knew that he was waiting for some sign. That all she had to do was open her eyes—reach out a hand to touch him.

No, she thought, *I won't—I can't...*

Tiny sparks danced behind her desperately closed lids. She made herself breathe slowly and evenly in a pretence of deep sleep.

And heard him say quietly, 'Goodnight, Louise.'

Telling her plainly that she hadn't fooled him for a second. Then he was gone, and she was aware, even from across the room, of the slight sound of the mattress dipping beneath his weight.

And she turned over, dragging the recalcitrant blanket with her, and buried her burning face in the pillow.

CHAPTER TEN

LOUISE was aware, even before she opened her eyes the next morning, that something was wrong.

That her body was no longer aching from the effort of trying to adapt to that unrelenting couch, or her skin being scratched by the blanket.

That she was, in fact, almost blissfully comfortable. Even though she did not seem to be lying on a pillow.

Very slowly and carefully she raised her eyelids, and paused, her body shuddering into shocked tension. Because the chaise longue was empty and abandoned on the other side of the room. And she was lying in the bed, in the curve of Alex's arm, with her head on his shoulder.

'Oh, no,' she whispered in silent horror. 'It can't be true. It *can't*. Did he come and take me, or did I go to him? Oh, God, why can't I remember?'

At any rate, she appeared to be still wearing her nightgown. And surely she'd know if—anything had happened between them?

Alex seemed to be deeply, genuinely asleep, so she began to ease herself away from the compelling warmth of his body. To extricate herself from the situation while she could.

Only to have him murmur a drowsy protest and scoop her back into his embrace.

Louise decided she was finished with subtlety. She had to get out of this bed right now.

She resolutely removed the hand that was clasping her hip with such dangerous intimacy, and was wriggling across to the edge of the bed when he lifted his head from the pillow and focused sleepy eyes on her.

'Good morning,' he said, yawning. 'I hope you slept well.'

'Exactly what am I doing here?' Her voice was husky.

'You were crying out in your sleep,' he said. 'A bad dream, perhaps. And you'd kicked off the blanket, so you were freezing too. I thought you'd be better off sleeping with me.'

He paused. 'And sleep you did, my love.'

'Do you really expect me to believe that you brought me here for my own good?' Her voice shook.

Alex propped himself on an elbow. He said levelly, 'Louise, you were in trouble—even sobbing at one point. You seemed to need something—someone. And I was all there was.'

'I need to know exactly what happened between us last night.'

His smile glinted at her. 'You were a tigress,' he said softly. 'A revelation.'

For a heartbeat, she almost believed him, then she saw the smile slide into a grin of pure enjoyment.

'Darling,' he said, 'if I'd made love to you last night, you'd have been well aware of the fact this morning. As it was, you curled up against me as if you belonged there.'

'I had no idea what I was doing,' she countered.

'No?' His brows lifted. 'And yet when I was carrying you across the room, you said my name.'

Louise's heart skipped a beat. 'Well,' she said, 'I only have your word for that.' She paused. 'What happened next?'

'We slept,' Alex said. 'Nothing more.'

He stretched, powerfully, lazily, making her vividly aware of the strong play of muscle under the smooth skin. She found she was watching him as if mesmerised, her mouth suddenly dry.

'Although that could always change,' he added casually, 'if you wanted. And right now,' the green eyes met hers, 'do you—want?'

'No.' She remembered, with a pang, the snatch of conversation she'd heard the night before. She bent her head. 'I—I suppose that's where men and women differ. A man can want sex even if he's in love with someone else.'

'What pigs we all are,' Alex said cordially. 'But you, of

course, being female and therefore purer and nobler, could not compromise your principles. Tell me, is it lonely up there on the moral high ground, sweetheart?'

Hurriedly, Louise began to push back the covers. 'I must get up now.'

'No,' he said. 'Not yet. It's still very early, and there are a few matters we need to discuss.'

'Then can we postpone the conversation until later, when we're both dressed?' she asked tautly.

'On the contrary,' he said. 'We can enjoy some pillow talk like other couples, even if a little recreational sex is out of the question. So don't run away, Louise, because I'd only come after you, and who knows where that might lead?' he added mockingly.

She flushed mutinously, but remained where she was. It seemed safer that way, even though her whole body was still tingling in half-shamed excitement at the thought of having spent the night in his arms, and common sense suggested she should distance herself from him, and fast.

She felt suddenly vulnerable in her flimsy nightdress, so she drew the coverlet over her body again. 'What do you want to say?'

'I need to apologise to you,' he said. 'So listen carefully, because it won't happen often.' He paused. 'I made certain accusations yesterday about your behaviour. These were purely circumstantial, and obviously had no basis in fact. Because I know quite well that David Sanders is not, and never has been your lover.' His mouth twisted ruefully. 'But appearances can be deceptive, so I lost my temper, and I'm sorry.'

'Then why did you?' Louise looked down at her tightly clasped hands. 'After all, why should you care what I do? It's not part of the deal.'

'Some atavistic instinct, maybe,' Alex drawled, 'connected with the word "wife". Or maybe I didn't like to think of you wasting yourself on an idiot who didn't have the wit to appreciate you the first time around. You could do better than David Sanders, Louise.'

'I'll bear that in mind,' she said, 'for the future. Is that all? May I go now?'

'Yes,' he said. 'Unless, of course, there's something you want to discuss with me?'

She hesitated. 'Has your grandmother given you any indication about the house? Her plans for it?'

'Yes,' he said. 'I'm afraid the weasely Clifford is going to be disappointed.'

'Good,' Louise said with sudden fierceness, although her heart sank within her like a stone. Her usefulness, it seemed, was at an end.

Alex grinned at her. 'How unkind of you, darling, especially when he's taken such trouble to ingratiate himself with you.'

'Not to mention the number his wife was doing on you during dinner,' Louise countered waspishly.

He laughed. 'Why, Mrs Fabian, are you implying the lady was up for it? You shock me.'

She smiled reluctantly. 'That will be the day. Now, I'd really better go and have my bath.'

She slid from under the covers and walked to the bathroom, wishing that she'd chosen a less revealing nightgown, fully aware that Alex was lying back, watching her go with undisguised appreciation.

Taking the usual unfair advantage, she thought bitterly.

As she reached the bathroom he said her name, and she looked back at him, her brows lifting in cool enquiry. Inwardly steeling herself.

'You've spent the night in my bed, and survived,' he said softly. 'So—was it really such an ordeal?'

'I don't know.' Against all the odds, Louise found her lips curving in sudden mischief. 'Luckily, I slept right through it.'

And she dodged, laughing, into the bathroom and slammed the door shut just as Alex's pillow thudded into it.

It had proved to be a day and a half, Louise thought wryly as she dressed for the party that evening.

Alex had disappeared after breakfast, having been commanded by his grandmother to take Cliff Maidstone to play golf. Della spent most of the day in a deckchair under one of the trees on the lawn, endlessly filing her nails and reading fashion magazines.

'And Louise can help me,' Lady Perrin announced regally.

This turned out to be no sinecure. Although all the arrangements for her birthday were in place, and had been for weeks, she kept having last-minute changes of plan, which Louise was detailed to relay to the staff.

But she found them placidly inured to their employer's vagaries.

'Don't worry, madam,' Mrs Gillow assured her. 'She's always liked things just so, has her ladyship, but she'll have thought again by this evening and want it all back as it was.' She sighed. 'Sad to think she's giving up the house, and this is the last party she'll have here.'

'What will happen to you and your husband?' Louise asked hesitantly. 'Will you stay on afterwards?'

'Bless you, no, madam,' Mrs Gillow said comfortably. 'Gillow and I are retiring, as planned, with a good pension that Mr Alex set up for us a while back. They've been good years here, but nothing lasts forever.'

No indeed, Louise thought sadly.

But Lady Perrin kept her too much on the run to allow time for too many recriminations or regrets.

She enjoyed the buzz engendered by the caterers and florists when they arrived, and was fascinated to see how everything came together, but secretly she found it daunting, too, and was almost relieved to know she would not be called on to organise a similar occasion at Rosshampton. No doubt it was the kind of thing Cindy Crosby would take in her stride, she thought tautly.

Alex had bathed and changed on his return from the golf course, to enable her to have all the privacy she could desire as she dressed for the party.

A long, scented bath refreshed her, and she spent time applying nail polish to her toes and fingers in the same rich red as her dress, and making up her face with extra care. The design of the dress called for nothing but a pair of ivory silk briefs beneath it, and strappy high-heeled sandals, also in red, added an elegant touch.

Louise took a deep breath, then slowly slipped the folds of gleaming taffeta over her head, and zipped them into place. Then she stood back and looked at herself in the long, old-fashioned mirror of the dressing table.

A stranger stared back at her. A girl with exotically shadowed eyes and glowing mouth, whose low-cut, tightly boned bodice cupped her small breasts like the hands of a lover. The passionate red of the dress emphasised the delicacy of her pale skin, and the graceful skirt swung like a slender bell as she moved.

For once in her life she seemed to have got it right, she thought.

There was a tap on the door, and Alex's voice said, 'May I come in?'

She took a deep breath. 'Yes—yes, of course.'

He came to a total halt as he saw her, his lips parting in a soundless whistle.

He said huskily, 'You look—very beautiful.'

He looked pretty amazing too, she thought. Black tie formality suited him. Thought it, but dared not say it.

She felt her face warming helplessly under his regard. 'Thank you, but I think we both know that's an exaggeration.' She paused. 'If you're going to tell me that your grandmother doesn't want the buffet in the dining room after all, I'm going to kill myself.'

'I've come to say that people are starting to arrive, and Selina needs us downstairs.' He produced a flat velvet case from his pocket. 'And to give you this.'

She gasped when she saw what lay on the satin bed inside. A diamond choker, with one magnificent ruby at its centre.

'It—it's wonderful. But I can't accept it.'

'You're my wife, Louise,' he told her quietly. 'I have every right to make you a gift. And you'll wear it for me tonight.'

He lifted the lovely thing from the box. 'Allow me,' he said, and fastened it round her throat.

She raised a hand and touched the gleaming stones almost with disbelief. Alex stood behind her, watching her reflection in the mirror, and she realised with shock that the hands that lightly clasped her shoulders were trembling. That in the lamplight his face looked stark, pared down to the bone. That the green eyes were suddenly hotly, broodingly intense.

The breath caught in her throat. She said hoarsely, 'I think we'd better go down. Your grandmother's waiting.'

He said, 'There's a little hook undone here on your dress.'

'I—I couldn't reach it.'

'Then I'd better.' Alex smiled at her in the mirror. 'Because it would be disastrous if this amazing creation were to slip even an inch—don't you think?'

She was beyond thought. She felt his fingers brush her naked spine, and had to bite the soft inside of her lower lip to control the small moan rising inside her.

She said, 'Yes.' And, 'Thank you.' She turned away, and picked up her evening purse, the taffeta rustling like dried leaves as she made her way to the door.

When they reached the top of the stairs Alex offered her his arm, and they descended together.

Selina, elegant in pale grey lace with pearls, was waiting in the massive hall. Beside her was Cliff Maidstone looking sullen, and Della in layers of blue tulle.

'Do you think she dyed that damned veil?' Alex muttered out of the corner of his mouth, and she was shaking with laughter, her feeling of tension evaporating fast, as they reached the foot of the stairs.

The evening became a blur of faces, young and old; some friendly, some curious. A murmur of names she would never remember, and Alex's voice saying quietly, 'This is Louise, my wife.'

When the music began Alex led his grandmother onto the dance floor, and Louise found herself partnered by a tall grey-haired man, who turned out to be the lord lieutenant of the county.

Someone else seemed to be in charge of her. Someone who smiled her acceptance each time a voice said 'May I have the pleasure of this dance, Mrs Fabian?' Who chatted animatedly with complete strangers, and ate cold salmon, and smoked chicken puffs and caviare, and drank champagne.

And who bore no relation to the shy girl caught up in a maelstrom of unfamiliar emotions, whose gaze scanned the crowded rooms for every glimpse she could garner of a tall, tawny-haired man, only to find him looking straight back at her, a smile in his eyes that set her heart pounding.

'What a nightmare,' Della muttered discontentedly at some point in the evening. 'Call this a dance? Where's the disco?'

'My grandmother doesn't like them.' Alex appeared suddenly beside them. 'Darling, I think this is our dance.'

She said breathlessly, 'Isn't there someone else you should ask?'

'I've done my duty,' he told her. 'Now it's time for pleasure.'

The music was slow and dreamy. He drew her into his arms, and they began to move to its gentle rhythm, his cheek resting against her hair. There was a space around them which gradually grew larger as people drew to the side of the floor to watch Alex Fabian dance with his new bride.

When the music ended Alex leaned forward and kissed her lightly on the cheek, then took her hand and raised it to his lips.

It was an elegant and courtly gesture, and it brought a ripple of laughter and applause from those looking on.

But his eyes, as they met hers, told Louise a very different story. They were sensuous—heavy with desire.

And they said, more plainly than any words could do, that tonight she would cease to be merely a token wife—and that he would not take 'no' for an answer.

She was trembling inside, her body suddenly weak with yearning. She was afraid too. Scared of her own inexperience, and a little ashamed too, because it was ridiculous for a grown woman to be still a virgin.

It wasn't the physical surrender she feared, anyway, but the emotional commitment. The certainty that, once taken, she would be his forever.

She stood beside him, shaking hands, saying the right, polite things as, eventually, people began to leave. She heard him decline his grandmother's offer of coffee and sandwiches when everyone had gone. And knew that there was nowhere to run—nowhere to hide.

She said her goodnights, quietly, and went with him, her hand clasped firmly in his, up to their room.

Where reality waited for her, and the possibility of heartbreak. And where the dreamlike state which had encompassed her all evening was no longer any protection.

She stood in the middle of the room, hugging herself with folded arms, as Alex removed his jacket and tie, and began to unfasten his dress shirt.

She said huskily, 'I—I need some time.'

'Take all you need,' he said. 'While I undress.'

'You're going to do that—here?'

'Yes,' he said. 'But you don't have to watch,' he added with a touch of dryness. 'It's not obligatory, and I'd hate you to be turned to stone.'

She turned away, and went across to the dressing table, her fingers nervously playing with the silver-backed mirror and the trinket boxes on its polished surface.

At last he came to stand behind her, his hands clasping her shoulders as he'd done earlier. The lamplight revealed the sheen of his skin, suggested the planes and angles of his chest, and hinted at the long, supple line of hip and thigh. She could feel the warmth of his naked body through the thin taffeta.

Her voice shook. 'Alex—please. Don't do this…'

'Do what?' he questioned. 'This?' He stroked her hair aside, and kissed the nape of her neck. 'Or this?' He bent his head and pressed his lips to her bare shoulder, forcing a shiver of response from her.

'Because I hear what you're saying, my reluctant wife,' he told her softly. 'But all evening I've seen your eyes. Felt the way you've touched me—how you went into my arms. And you know it's true.'

His fingers released the tiny hook at the back of her dress, and began to slide down the long zip.

The bodice fell away from her body like the petals of a dark red flower, baring her breasts.

For a moment she tried to cover herself with her hands, but he took her wrists and drew them gently away.

'Do you know how long I've dreamed of this?' There was a raw note in his voice. 'Of seeing you like this?' He eased the whispering taffeta down over her slender hips, and let it pool round her feet. She stepped out of it, and he picked up the mass of gleaming fabric and tossed it over the dressing stool.

He said softly, 'Now tell me you don't want me.'

His arms went round her, drawing her back against the heat of him, and she went pliantly, leaning her head on his shoulder, because her legs were shaking so that she could barely stand.

She watched herself in the mirror. Watched him as his lean fingers cupped one rounded breast, stroking gently, making the helpless breath catch in her throat, while his other hand slid down her body to curl possessively round the curve of her hip, pushing away the ephemeral protection of the ivory silk.

A stranger looked back at her. A girl with half-closed eyes, and parted rosy mouth, the erotic charge of her nakedness heightened by the blaze of diamonds at her throat, and the crimson flare of the ruby, like a drop of captured blood. A girl whose body moved restlessly under the first sensual caresses of a man's hands. Who arched against him, gasping as his straying fingers reached the shadowed cleft between her thighs. And paused.

Alex dropped to one knee beside her, undoing the strap on one sandal, then the other, and removing them. He caressed each foot, kissing the instep, then her ankle, his hands and lips moving upwards until they reached her thighs. Coaxed them apart.

His mouth was gentle, skimming over the soft skin like the brush of a butterfly's wing. Tantalising without satisfying in a way that was beyond all imagining.

She heard herself moan softly, languorously—pleadingly.

And he stood, lifting her into his arms and carrying her across the room to where the bed waited, its covers stripped away, lit by a single lamp.

Alex put her down on the mattress, and lay beside her. For a moment he was very still, looking at her, cradling her face between his hands, then his mouth sought hers with passionate, overwhelming hunger.

Louise yielded totally, her arms sliding round his neck, her fingers twining in the crisp tawny hair she'd longed so often to touch, as she tasted the sweetness of his tongue exploring her mouth.

And she returned his kiss with feverish ardour, her body melting into his, gasping as she felt the stark heat of his arousal. Pressing against him. Longing to absorb and be absorbed.

He raised his head and looked down at her, his smile crooked. 'Hey,' he whispered. 'There's no hurry, my love. I want to make this good for you. Something you'll remember.'

I'll remember, she wanted to cry out to him. Every moment of this night is going to be etched on my memory in blood—along with every word you've ever said to me, each kiss, your lightest touch.

Alex began to kiss her body, his mouth lingering on her breasts, his tongue flickering provocatively against the rosy peaks.

His hand explored gently, smoothing the slender curve of her hip bone, the slight concavity of her belly, the passage of his fingertips lighting small trails of fire in her racing blood.

Her head fell back blindly onto the pillow, her body arching up to him in mute yearning as he stroked the smooth line of her thigh, circling lightly on her flesh, pausing, then circling again, oh, so slowly. Making her wait a trembling eternity for the caress she wanted. For the intimacy of the long, clever fingers discovering the secret, molten core of her.

When he touched her, at last, as she desired, his fingers cool as they explored with exquisite precision the white heat of her need, a long, trembling sigh escaped her.

His mouth tugged on her nipples, coaxing them erect, as his fingers teased her tiny hidden bud to an equal pitch of arousal.

Deep within her, she was aware of the thrumming of a tiny pulse. Felt it strengthen—then tauten endlessly, unbearably, stretching her on some breathless rack, her senses screaming.

She made a small, stifled sound in her throat, then the tension broke, like the snapping of a wire, and her astonished body was carried away, lifted to some unknown height by wave after rippling wave of a pleasure so intense she thought she would faint—or even die of it.

And when the storm passed there were tears on her face, and Alex was kissing them away, whispering that she was his darling, his heart's delight, his beautiful, clever girl.

For a while she lay quietly, cradled in his arms, then, obeying an instinct she had never known she possessed, she moved slightly but with definite purpose, smiling up at him, her whole body a silent invitation.

He said her name softly, and slid his hands under her hips, lifting her towards him. There was no pain as he entered her. Her body was too relaxed in its own delight to offer any resistance to the smooth, fluid thrust of his possession. She was filled, completed, amazed by the reality of their union.

He paused. 'Darling.' His voice was shaken. 'Is it all right? Have I hurt you? Do you want me to stop?'

In answer, she reached up and drew him down to her, offering him the sweetness of her parted lips, and eager tongue meeting his.

He had promised her a night to remember, she thought. Well, he was going to remember it too—forever.

She caressed him in turn, running her hands over his muscled shoulders and down the strong back, forcing a smothered groan from him.

And as he began to move inside her, slowly at first, even carefully, then with increasing power, Louise found herself responding in the same way, lifting her slender legs and locking them round his hips.

Gasping, damp with sweat, she realised suddenly that her body was reacting fiercely to these new sensations, her own urgency building all over again with his, strong and inexorable. Threatening, almost before she knew it, to spiral out of control.

Knowing that Alex knew it too.

'Yes.' His voice was husky—almost fevered. 'Yes, my love—my angel.' And, 'Now.'

She felt his body convulse scaldingly in hers. Heard him call out to her. Then she was overtaken, swept away in turn, her body wrenched and shuddering in an agony of rapture.

When it was over they lay together quietly, exchanging kisses, sated and at peace.

At last, Alex propped himself up on an elbow and looked down at her, his hand gently playing with her breast.

'Well, Mrs Fabian,' he said, his voice quivering with tender amusement, 'let me congratulate you on passing your aptitude test. May I recommend you register for the advanced course?'

She stretched languorously. 'How soon does it start?'

He groaned. 'God, darling, don't tempt me.'

'You mean I could?'

He captured her straying hand and kissed it. 'Yes, you Jezebel. But it would be very selfish of me to let you.' He retrieved the covers from the floor, and arranged them round her, before pulling her back into his arms. 'You need to sleep for a while. Let your body adjust.'

'To sex?' How could anything so natural and glorious need any kind of adjustment? she wondered in bewilderment.

'No,' he told her softly. 'To having a lover. Now, rest.'

Louise wanted to say 'But I'm not tired', only it wasn't true. Her eyes were already closing, her body nestling against the warmth of his, relaxed as never before.

He whispered, 'Goodnight, my sweet.' And she felt his lips on her brow.

Yet, just before she drifted into sleep, it occurred to her with a strange, piercing clarity that he had never once said 'I love you'.

And on the heels of that came the stark and sobering realisation that he probably never would.

CHAPTER ELEVEN

THE thought stayed with her in her dreams like a dark thread in a golden tapestry, and waited for her when she awoke early the next morning.

She lay for a while, thinking. Her heart and mind might be counselling caution, but physically she was basking in a sense of well-being that she had never experienced before, while the events of the previous night unrolled in her memory in glorious, nerve-tingling detail.

She turned and looked at Alex sleeping beside her, watching the curl of his lashes on his cheek, the steady rise and fall of his chest. Then, slowly and delicately, she drew back the covers and allowed herself the indulgence of studying him in every detail.

With or without his clothes, he was heaven to the eyes, she thought, stifling a sigh, feeling the first helpless pang of desire stir anew within her. Lean, tanned all over and amazingly strong, as she'd learned last night.

She reached out a hand and touched his chest, letting her fingers stray over the flat male nipples. She bent her head and kissed them, then ran her fingers down, over his rib cage, to the firm stomach. She smoothed the clean line of his hip bone, and moved down to the long muscular thigh, where she paused, suddenly hesitant, realising that her tentative caresses were already having their powerful effect on him.

He said softly, 'Don't stop there—please.'

She withdrew her hand swiftly, helpless colour flooding her face as she wondered how long he had been lying there, observing her from under half-closed lids, that glinting smile playing round the corners of his mouth.

'So,' he went on, 'what happened to the shy lady who couldn't bear to look at me last night?'

She said, stammering a little, 'I think she died, and went to heaven.'

She paused. 'I—I didn't mean to wake you.'

'Whereas I,' he told her, 'had every intention of awakening you.' He turned onto his side, drawing her gently towards him. 'Like this,' he whispered, and began to kiss her, his lips gentle as they caressed and nibbled hers, his tongue warm and teasing as it found her own.

She yielded her mouth blindly, completely, the breath sighing in her throat as his kiss deepened, beckoned. As his fingers cupped her breast, stroking its rosy peak to renewed and almost startled awareness. Making her melt and burn with longing.

She said his name, softly, yearningly against his mouth.

He repositioned himself slightly, and without haste, raising her so that she was lying half across him, before entering her subtly and sweetly. Her breath caught, and her eyes dilated as they stared into his.

He moved gently inside her, controlling the power of his body to create a series of small, intense sensations, each one more concentrated and engrossing than the last, drawing her inexorably on.

At the same time he slid a hand down to the joining of their bodies, seeking her tiny hidden bud, brushing its tumescent heat with the tips of his fingers. Coaxing, enticing her to pleasure. Making her moan faintly, pleadingly.

Within a heartbeat, the rhythm of his body changed, became more forceful—more urgent. Taking her to some edge, holding her there for an endless moment, then releasing her into the dazzle and shimmer of a new, unguessed-at sphere of trembling, sobbing delight.

Afterwards, she lay, her face pressed into the damp wall of his chest, as she tried to recover her fragmented breathing.

When she could think, she said in a small, drowned voice, 'But you—you didn't...'

His lips touched her hair. 'I can wait.' There was a smile in his voice. 'For you.'

She raised her head, staring at him with eyes made drowsy from pleasure. 'You mean—again?'

'I hope so,' he said. 'Unless you have some objection.'

'Oh, no,' she said with a slight catch of the breath. 'None at all.'

He drew her close again, with a sigh. 'All the time we've wasted,' he said. 'All those endless days and nights when I didn't dare come near you in case you fought me off. I used to pray that you'd give some sign that you wanted me, too. Only you never did.' He shook his head. 'Even last night I was scared you might turn away from me. That you might still be hung up on that idiot you were engaged to, after all.'

She pressed her lips to his shoulder. 'You don't have to be unkind about him,' she murmured. 'I told you that David and I were never lovers.'

'I know.' His arm tightened around her. 'But I couldn't believe that he'd let you get away from him when I wanted you so badly. And when I saw him leaving the flat that day, I just lost it completely,' he added ruefully. 'Enforced celibacy clearly doesn't suit me.'

She was quiet for a moment. Then she said haltingly, 'But you haven't been—celibate, Alex. There's always been—Lucinda Crosby. I—I saw you together at that hotel. I told you so. And you didn't deny it,' she added with difficulty.

'I wasn't in the mood to confirm or deny anything,' he said with sudden harshness. 'Although I admit I should have dealt with it there and then. But I'd seen that bastard leaving, and you were there half-naked, just out of the shower. All I could think was that you'd been washing him off you, and it was driving me crazy.'

He paused. 'But if you want to talk about Cindy Crosby, we can do so now. Yes, I was seeing her at one time, and I'm not particularly proud of that. But it was over long before I met you, and I've never been even marginally tempted to resume the relationship. We're history.'

'But you were with her…'

'Briefly, yes,' he agreed. 'Because I was set up.'

'Set up?'

'Listen,' Alex said. 'I'd been approached by a guy I knew slightly who was looking for venture capital, but didn't want it generally known. He suggested lunch at the Belmayne because it was quiet and out of the way. I wasn't thrilled at the idea, because this weekend was coming up and I wanted to clear my desk, but I agreed to meet him for a drink.

'From the moment I got there, it was clear something was wrong. He was on edge, and unwilling to come to terms about his requirements, even though I'd made it plain I had no time to waste. I was just about to finish my drink and leave, when he said he had to make a phone call, and asked me to wait for him.'

He sighed harshly. 'Needless to say, he didn't come back. Instead, I was joined by Cindy, all smiles, with a table reserved in the restaurant, and a room booked on the first floor.

'I told her flatly that I wasn't interested, and that I was leaving. But she became insistent. Followed me outside. She said we'd been discreet long enough, and she wanted me back. That as long as we continued to be careful, Peter would never find out.

'I pointed out that Peter was only part of the equation. That she'd apparently overlooked the fact that I was also married now.' His voice hardened. 'She seemed to find that amusing. Told me that no one, least of all myself, could take my "ridiculous marriage" seriously.

'And that was when I walked away. In all, I was out of the bank for less than an hour, which my staff can confirm because I called back there briefly before I came home. I wanted to instruct them to take no more calls from Cindy's catspaw.'

She said with difficulty, 'Were you—in love with her?'

His mouth twisted. 'No, I haven't even that excuse. Our relationship was sexual—nothing more. A passing thing.'

He smoothed her hair back from her face with a gentle hand. 'Louise, I wasn't expecting to see her at the Belmayne. I didn't want to see her, and if you check with the barman and commissionaire at the hotel they'll tell you that our reunion was brief and unfriendly.

'But I know—none better—how easy it is to be deceived by circumstantial evidence.' He paused. 'Although I should warn you if Sanders ever comes prowling round you again, I plan to break his neck.'

She said, 'I think David came looking for comfort—needing to be told that everything would be all right. But he was disappointed. And he certainly won't be back.'

Alex bent his head and kissed her, slowly and deeply. Her response was instant and hungry, her body shivering against his. She began to touch him, her fingers exploring his bone structure and caressing his skin, trailing downwards without haste. And where her hands touched, fondled, her mouth followed, delicate at first, then moving voluptuously, all inhibitions flown.

Enjoying him in ways she had never dreamed she could. Finding, to her astonishment, that she could make him groan with need—with pleasure—in turn.

He moved suddenly, turning onto his back, his hands clasping her waist, lifting her over him, then lowering her gently onto the hard, sleek power of him.

Louise took him into her, gasping a little as he filled her, making her complete. Then she began to move on him strongly and fiercely, creating her own rhythms, her own suddenly fevered demands. He was the instrument of her pleasure, and she was his. Nothing else existed. All laughter had fled. There was no place even for words in this mutual agony of need they had created.

Louise flung her head back, arching her spine as Alex caressed her breasts, her nipples becoming pinnacles of pure sensation under the play of his fingers.

She reached culmination almost before she was aware, her voice moaning thickly at the sheer intensity of the spasms tearing through her, and heard him cry out in turn, his voice driven and anguished.

She felt herself falling, tumbling into some void, and found his arms closing round her, to hold her and keep her safe. And lying entwined with him, exhausted, she found peace, and even a kind of oblivion.

When at last Louise opened her eyes it was full daylight, and the bed beside her was empty.

She sat up slowly, fighting a ridiculous sense of disappointment, and pushed back her dishevelled hair, realising, as she did so, that she was still wearing the ruby choker from the night before. Blushing a little at the memories it evoked, she undid the clasp and put the necklace back in its velvet case on the night table.

She lay back against her pillows, stretching luxuriously, her body glowing, then tensed suddenly as there was a light tap on the door, which opened to admit Mrs Gillow, carrying a tray, which she set down on a table in front of the chaise longue.

'Good morning, madam,' she said comfortably, ignoring Louise's hasty dive under the covers. She drew back the curtains, flooding the room with sunlight. 'It's another beautiful day. Mr Alex is having breakfast with her ladyship, and asked me to bring this up for you.'

'This', Louise saw, was orange juice, a soft boiled egg, toast and tea, plus a single red rose in a small crystal vase.

'Oh,' she said, burrowing further into the bed. 'Well—thank you.' Mrs Gillow took pity on her, and fetched her robe, laying it tenderly across the foot of the bed. 'Will there be anything else, madam?'

'No.' Louise pinkened under the housekeeper's indulgent gaze. 'That's—fine.'

When she was alone, she put on the robe and trod across to the table. There was a note, she saw, propped against the vase.

'You were sleeping so peacefully, I didn't have the heart to wake you,' she read. 'But I thought your energy levels might need restoring.' And it was signed with the single initial 'A.'

The orange juice was freshly squeezed, the egg perfect, and the toast cut into neat soldiers. And she was hungry, she discovered. In fact, she was ravenous.

All the same, she wished they could have had breakfast together—on the first day of the rest of their lives. If, indeed, that was what it was. Or was she taking altogether too much for granted on the strength of one night in Alex's bed?

He'd spoken frankly about wanting her, and there was no doubt that her resolve to keep him at arm's length had simply increased his determination to possess her. And her own passionate, hidden desire for him had inevitably caused her resolution to crumble, just when she needed it most.

Well, now he'd had her, and there was no turning back. She belonged to him, helplessly and eternally, and the storm of her eventual capitulation had undoubtedly intrigued him. For a while, she could even prove a novelty for him—this token wife who'd given herself to him with such ardent lack of reserve.

But would it ever be more than that? Because she still had no idea how he viewed the future. Or what part she was expected to play in it. If any...

After all, he'd achieved his ambition, she reminded herself bleakly. Rosshampton was going to be his. She'd fulfilled the role he'd demanded, and, technically, her services were no longer required, and there was no need for the marriage to continue any longer.

Maybe the incredible pleasure he'd given her was simply a bonus, in addition to the money she'd been promised.

She winced and rose to her feet. Whatever the outcome, she told herself, it was clear they needed to talk—and soon.

She bathed and dressed in a cream linen skirt, and a sleeveless blue silky top, brushing her hair loose on her shoulders, and disguising the faintly swollen contours of her mouth with a neutral-coloured lustre.

She looked different, she thought, studying herself critically. Apart from the tell-tale shadows of fatigue, there was a new knowledge in her eyes. And a new vulnerability too.

As she walked along the gallery towards the top of the stairs, she saw Della Maidstone coming towards her, carrying a suitcase.

She checked in surprise. 'Leaving already?'

The other girl shrugged. 'Well, there's nothing to stay for. Cliff's taken yet another gamble that hasn't paid off. I did warn him that the old girl wasn't a soft touch, and that she wouldn't fall for his big talk, even if she was once sweet on his grand-father. But he wouldn't listen. He cleared out earlier in a hell of a temper.'

'I see.' Louise bit her lip. 'I suppose you'll both be returning to South Africa?'

'I certainly am, though I can't speak for Cliff. He owes too much money to the wrong people.' She looked Louise over, brows raised. 'You look as if you haven't slept all night,' she commented, a jeering note in her voice. 'Something tells me your husband's been celebrating his victory. If he's in a good mood, maybe Cliffy should try touching him for a loan—to make up for losing the house.'

'Are you very disappointed?' Louise asked awkwardly, aware that she was blushing. 'It is incredibly beautiful.'

'Sure, if you like this kind of thing,' Della said with total indifference. 'Not that we'd ever have lived here ourselves,' she added. 'Cliff knows a guy who's looking for somewhere to turn into a high-class health spa, and he'd have paid us top dollar for the place. Another little scheme that hasn't worked.'

She paused. 'And talking of schemes, I wish you luck with the baby. Cliff was mad as hell when I wouldn't oblige, but maybe you don't mind ruining your figure.'

Louise stared at her. 'The baby?' she repeated slowly. 'I don't know what you're talking about.'

'Oh, didn't your husband tell you?' Brief malice flared in the other girl's face. 'I can't say I'm surprised. That was one of the conditions that the old lady imposed. Apparently she wants to hear the patter of tiny feet before she dies.'

She gave a strident giggle. 'She told Cliff straight, and he tried to talk me into it. But I wasn't having any. No house is worth all that.' She shook her head. 'My God, but men can be ruthless when they want something, particularly the men in this family. I'm well out of it.'

She patted a stunned and silent Louise on the shoulder. 'So

now you have to come up with the goods instead. I don't envy you the brat,' she added, winking. 'But I guess you'll have fun trying. And at least it'll be brought up in the lap of luxury. So things could be worse.'

She went down the stairs, tugging the case after her.

Louise stood rigidly at the top of the stairs, her hand clasping the banister rail so tightly that her knuckles turned white. She felt numb, paralysed with shock and hurt.

Ruthless, she thought painfully, was not the word. How long would it have been before Alex told her the real motive behind his practised seduction—if ever?

She'd wondered why he hadn't told her he loved her. Well, now she knew, and it hurt so much that she was falling apart, breaking in pieces.

She supposed he deserved credit for not having pretended to care. He'd practised a kind of honesty in that. But the fact remained that in one night she'd gone, without warning, from being a token wife to a convenient womb.

Was he really so obsessed with the place that there was no room in his life, his heart for anything else? she asked herself in anguish. It seemed so.

And that was the worst thing of all. That he was prepared for her to be just another sacrifice on the Rosshampton altar. And one that meant no more to him than Cindy Crosby had done.

For a moment she knew a flash of sympathy for the other woman, who'd found herself discarded in the cause of expediency.

She must have been desperate to pursue Alex like that, she thought. To want him back at any price. But I can't do that. I can't...

I won't plead for what he can't give. And I won't let him use me—not any more. Because I couldn't bear it.

I have to be the one who walks away. I have to...

She turned and went swiftly back to the bedroom. She fetched her case, and began filling it, throwing things in at random.

But not the red dress she'd worn last night. Or the necklace. Because she couldn't stand to see either of them again—and remember what a fool she'd been.

When the door opened behind her she tensed, instinct telling her instantly who it was, even before his hands descended on her shoulders, and his mouth grazed the side of her neck.

She stood like a statue, fighting the involuntary quiver of her senses at his touch.

'Hi,' he whispered, turning her to face him. 'I've missed you.' He dropped a light kiss on her unresponsive lips, then looked at the half-filled case.

'Packing already?' He sounded surprised. 'Gran wants us to stay for lunch, if not for another night. I think she needs to talk about the house.' He gave a faint smile. 'Convince herself that she's made the right decision.'

'Well, I'm sure you can reassure her about that,' Louise said tightly. 'If not on all points. You'd have to wait a month or two for that.'

His brows lifted. 'Is this a coded message?'

'Oh, please don't pretend.' She stepped back from him, freeing herself quite deliberately. 'Not any more. You see, it just occurred to me that we had unprotected sex last night.'

'Did we?' He was frowning suddenly. 'I thought we made love.'

'And don't play word games either,' she said raggedly. 'It amounts to the same thing.'

'No,' Alex said, 'it doesn't, but let it pass. Is there some problem?'

'Only that I could be—pregnant.'

He was very still, watching her with narrowed eyes. 'Yes,' he said, after a pause. 'I suppose it's a possibility. But would that really be so terrible?' His mouth twisted. 'After all, we're married, or had you forgotten?'

'All the same,' Louise said, trying to keep her voice steady. 'I'm wondering why you didn't take—precautions.'

'Because I had none to take.' He sounded impatient. 'I don't keep a permanent supply of condoms in my wallet in case I meet a willing lady.' He gave her a level look. 'And you've never been that, anyway, Louise. You've gone out of your way to keep me at arm's length. I had no reason to think last night would be any different.'

He paused. 'But what I need to know is—why this is suddenly such an issue. It didn't trouble you when you were weeping with pleasure in my arms. So why now?'

She shrugged defensively. 'Because last night I wasn't thinking clearly. You're very good at what you do, Alex, as you've just obliquely pointed out. Only now it's the cold light of day. And I've just realised I've taken an appalling risk.'

He was silent for a long moment. Then he said carefully, 'Are you saying you find the idea of having my child abhorrent?'

She was assailed by a sudden unwanted vision of Alex cradling a tiny, shawl-wrapped bundle in his arms, his face rapt and tender.

No, she thought, her heart contracting. *Oh, no…*

She made herself meet his gaze. Heard her voice say coolly and clearly, 'We had a deal. A baby was not part of it. You wanted the house. You have it, and if your grandmother has imposed additional conditions then that is your problem, not mine.'

He said, 'What the hell are you talking about?'

'Children.' She swallowed. 'Apparently, Selina wants them here. An extra clause in the inheritance agreement. Della warned me before she left. Or are you going to deny it?'

'I deny nothing,' Alex drawled scornfully. 'Rosshampton is a wonderful place for children, and always has been. Selina believes that, and so do I.' He paused. 'What else did Della say?'

'Just that she'd refused point-blank to become the Rosshampton brood mare.' Louise lifted her chin. 'However, I wasn't offered the same choice.'

He was very white. He said, 'Is that—truly how you see yourself? With me as visiting stud, presumably?'

She was weeping inside, but she managed a shrug. 'You said it. I didn't.'

'Yes.' He was silent again, his mouth hard and taut, his eyes studying her as if she was a stranger. 'I can't believe we're having this conversation. What happened to the warm, adorable girl I left sleeping?'

Louise shrugged defensively. 'She—woke up. Discovered reality.'

'Reality?' he repeated incredulously. 'Is that what you want? Fine.' He drew a breath. 'You feel you should have been offered a choice? Then choose now, Louise. The deal—or the marriage I thought we began last night.'

She folded her arms across her body, creating a deliberate barrier. A gesture that, she saw, was not lost on him.

He said too quietly, 'I see.' He paused. 'So, a few hours ago, you were merely on loan—is that it?'

She said stonily, 'A few hours ago I was a little crazy, but now I'm sane again, and I want my life back. All of it. As we agreed.'

He nodded, his face too expressionless, too controlled. 'What happens now, if I'm allowed to ask?'

She swallowed. 'I—I'd like to go back to London, if you'll let me have the car. I'll move out of the flat—find a hotel.'

'Try the Belmayne,' he said, his voice icily cynical. 'I hear the beds are incredible.' He paused. 'I'll have the money transferred to your account, plus a suitable bonus to compensate for my unwarranted use of your charming body.'

She bit the inside of her bottom lip so hard she tasted blood. She had the feeling that she'd thrown a stone, and started an avalanche. That events were out of control, careering away from her to ruin and despair. That if she could only turn back the clock, she would handle things very differently.

Aloud, she said, 'And if there are—consequences?'

His smile touched her shrinking flesh like the lash of a whip. 'Then deal with them in whatever way you wish, darling. And send me the bill.'

She wanted to cry out—scream in pain and negation. Instead,

she lifted her chin defiantly. 'Naturally. And now, perhaps, you'll go. Let me finish packing.'

She turned to walk past him to the wardrobe, but he halted her, his hand hard on her arm. He lifted her as if she was a featherweight, tossing her onto the bed.

'Presently,' he said. 'But first, maybe, I should give you something to remember me by.'

'Alex.' She sobbed his name as he knelt over her, his hands going to the waistband of his jeans. 'No—*please*. You couldn't...'

He paused, looking down at her, the anger draining from his face, leaving a terrible weariness in its place.

'No,' he said at last. 'Fortunately for you, I couldn't. Because I have to live with myself after this.'

His icy glance glittered with contempt. 'I wonder if you can say the same, my sweet wife.'

He went from her, leaving her lying there, staring after him, her hand pressed to her mouth.

She thought, So that's that. It's over, finished.

And then, as the pain tore through her, I've lost him. What have I done? Oh, dear God, what have I done?

It was a long time before Louise could pull herself together sufficiently to finish packing, and when there was a knock at the door she tensed, hoping—praying—that Alex had come back. But even if he had, what was there to say?

I can't stay with him as things are, she told herself wretchedly. But how am I going to live without him?

But it was only Mrs Gillow at the door to tell her that Alex's driver was waiting, and that Gillow was ready to carry her bag down to the car. She murmured a word of thanks, and fastened the bag, her hands shaking so much she could scarcely close the zip.

The hallway was deserted and the main door stood open, offering instant escape, she realised, trying to feel relieved. But as she reached the foot of the stairs Lady Perrin appeared in the doorway of the drawing room.

'Louise, my dear.' Her tone was crisp. 'I hope you were not planning to go without saying goodbye to me.'

'No, of course not,' Louise said, guiltily aware that had been her exact plan.

'Come in, then, and sit down,' Lady Perrin directed.

Louise complied with reluctance, noting that Lady Perrin had closed the drawing-room door, indicating that she had more to say than the conventional words that normally sped the departing guest.

The older woman seated herself opposite, fixing Louise with an eagle eye.

'So,' she said, 'my grandson tells me you are leaving him. That you've decided to "take the money and run", as I believe the saying is.'

Louise's lips parted in shock. She said, 'You mean—you know?'

'About that nonsensical bargain? Yes, of course.' Lady Perrin nodded. 'Alex told me all about it when he came to inform me of your marriage. He has always confided in me since he was a small child, especially when he was in trouble. And on this occasion, I had to share the blame.'

She shook her head. 'However unhappy I may have been about his way of life, his choice of companion, I had no right to interfere. And I should have realised that if I threw down the gauntlet Alex would pick it up, for good or ill.'

Louise sat up very straight. 'Was that why you decided to give him the house? Because you felt guilty that you'd pushed him into marriage?'

'Oh, no. Rosshampton was always his—if he wanted it. He knew that.'

Louise was confused. 'But what about Cliff Maidstone? He thought he was in with a chance too. Something must have given him that impression.'

Lady Perrin snorted. 'I am not responsible for that young man's delusions. He also believed that I would be fool enough to invest in some non-existent company he was touting,' she added tartly. 'I'm afraid that bad blood tells.'

She paused. 'As it did with his grandfather, of course, who was twice as good-looking, and far more charming, and with whom I briefly fancied I was in love.' She smiled reminiscently. 'You see, I was engaged to my other cousin, Alexander, whom I'd known all my life, and it all seemed very staid and settled and not particularly romantic. So Archie was a very real temptation, and it was fortunate for me that he proved far more interested in getting away with the bank's money than he was in me.'

She sighed. 'All the same, when he was sent away I was convinced my heart was broken, so my parents very wisely brought forward the date of the wedding, and I married Alexander and went on honeymoon with him.' Her face softened magically. 'And discovered with him, my dear, more passion and excitement than I had ever dreamed of. Found, in fact, that I was not merely loved, but adored, and that I could love with my whole heart in return.

'When we were together in a crowd, he used to watch me across the room in the same way that I saw Alex looking at you last night. As if I was the centre of his world—of his universe.'

She nodded. 'I knew that when my grandson found a woman to love, there would be no half-measures, and I was right. I hoped that by this time his patience might have been rewarded. And as he sat through breakfast this morning in a dream, barely hearing a word I said,' she added drily, 'I thought it had.'

Louise blushed to the roots of her hair. 'Lady Perrin,' she began.

'My dear, couldn't you call me Gran, as Alex does?'

Louise stared down at her hands, welded together in her lap. She said in a low voice, 'He doesn't love me. He married me just to get the house. That's all it's ever been. And I can't bear it.'

'But he doesn't have the house,' Lady Perrin told her gently. 'He gave up all claim to it when he came to see me that day.'

Louise shook her head. 'But he can't have done,' she said in bewilderment. 'He—he wanted it so badly. He always has.'

'Once, perhaps,' the older woman agreed. 'Until he found something he wanted far more. Until, my dear, he found you. And, believe me, he made the sacrifice most willingly.'

'But what's going to happen to it?' Louise stared at her. 'Surely not Cliff Maidstone…'

'Certainly not,' Lady Perrin said briskly. 'At your husband's suggestion I'm making a gift of it to a charity that helps disadvantaged children. He's helping me set up a trust fund to cover the running costs.'

Louise said numbly, 'Then—*those* were the children you meant? But Della said—Cliff Maidstone thought…'

'Yes.' Lady Perrin looked rueful. 'I'm afraid that was pure wickedness on my part. A strong desire to see how unprincipled he was—and how far he was prepared to go to achieve his ambitions. Well, a few unguarded remarks from his wife gave me the answer to that.' She sighed. 'But I never intended to make mischief between you and Alex.'

'Oh, God.' Louise buried her face in her hands. 'Lady Perrin—Gran—I said the most dreadful things to him.'

'So I gathered,' Lady Perrin said drily. 'He looked shattered when he came to see me. And lonely, as he used to sometimes when he was a child. I'd hoped I would never see that look in his eyes again.'

Louise stood up. 'Where is he—please?'

'Down by the lake. I suggest you go through the French windows and across the terrace.'

Alex was standing by the water's edge, his tall figure dark and isolated against its glitter.

She said his name, and he turned slowly and looked at her, his face pale and deathly tired.

She said breathlessly, 'There's something I need to ask you.'

'Then will you please ask it, and go?' he said. 'As you can see, I don't take rejection well.'

She swallowed. 'Why didn't you tell me?'

He said slowly, 'There are so many things I should have told you—and didn't. Which particular one did you have in mind?'

'This house,' she said. 'Your grandmother told me you gave it up. Why, please?'

He said quietly, 'Don't you know?'

'I think so,' she said. 'I hope so. But, Alex, I need to hear you say it.'

'I gave it up,' he said, 'because I realised it would always have been a barrier between us. I wanted to be able to say to you—I want you, and only you. But if I'd accepted Rosshampton from Gran, you might always have wondered, in some corner of your mind, if I had used you. I couldn't risk that.'

'But you love it so,' Louise said urgently. 'It can't be too late. I'm sure she'd change her mind, if we went to her.'

'I don't want her to change her mind,' he said gently. 'I want us to find another house together, you and I, and make a home in it.'

'Why did you let me accuse you like that? Say those stupid, awful things to you? You could have told me the truth.'

His mouth twisted. 'Pride,' he said. 'I hated being categorised with Cliff Maidstone. And my rotten temper, which I promise I'll try to control.' He paused. 'Also, you have the power to hurt me, and make me look at myself, and ask questions as no other woman ever has. And that doesn't make me altogether rational, sometimes. I didn't know love could do that.'

'Why didn't you tell me you loved me?'

'I planned to—after breakfast,' he said. 'I was going to take you walking in the garden, your hand in mine, husband and wife stuff, and tell you that I fell in love with you when you dropped a pile of old clothes on my head, but that I didn't realise it until you came out of the house that day to drive off to Somerset.'

He shook his head. 'You were so hurt and bewildered, yet trying so hard to be brave. And I suddenly knew I wanted to pick you up in my arms and comfort you, and keep you safe forever.'

'You felt like that?' Her voice trembled.

'Oh, I had other less chivalrous impulses too.' He smiled a little. 'Like taking off your clothes and making love to you until we both fainted.'

'Suppose I'd refused to go with you that day?'

'Then I'd have become very well-acquainted with the motorway to Somerset,' he said. 'I wasn't going to let you walk out of my life. Just as if you'd left me today, I'd have come after you. You're my wife, Louise, and the only woman I'll ever want. And I shall love you until I die.'

He paused. 'Now, there's something I need to hear from you.'

She went to him then, walking into his waiting arms, feeling them fold around her. Sliding her arms round his neck to draw him down to her.

'You mean—that I love you too? Oh, darling, if you only knew how many times I've wanted to tell you.'

'I do know,' he said softly. 'None better.'

He kissed her, his mouth a tender affirmation on hers, and Louise responded, her heart on her lips.

'There is still one matter we haven't mentioned,' Alex murmured after a while. He gave her a wry look. 'You could still be pregnant.'

'Perhaps.' She smiled at him. 'But I doubt it. I think we need far more practice than that.'

'Then I suggest a swift return to London after lunch,' he said promptly. 'And an incredibly early night.'

As they turned to walk back to the house, Louise saw a movement on the water, and halted. 'Alex—look. The swans. Aren't they lovely? They've come to say goodbye.'

'Yes.' He put his arms round her as they watched the graceful birds swim majestically past them.

He said softly, 'Did you know that they mate for life?'

'How very wise of them,' Louise said, 'my dearest love.' And lifted her mouth for his kiss.

Queens of Romance

WIN

a romantic break for two
worth over £500!

To celebrate the special Mills & Boon® centenary
Queens of Romance collection, we are offering
you the chance to win a very special break for two
to Paris – worth over £500!

To enter, visit
www.millsandboon.co.uk
and answer this simple question:

What are the names of the two founders
of Mills & Boon?

Note: The answer to the above question can be found on
www.millsandboon.co.uk

Entries must be received by 31st January 2009

Good luck!

Terms & Conditions

For full terms and conditions see www.millsandboon.co.uk. There is no obligation
to purchase. To be eligible for any draw, simply enter via www.millsandboon.co.uk.
You must complete all details with your name and address for it to be a valid entry.
Those which have not been completed will not be entered into the draw. You may
also enter any draw by hand printing the words "Queens of Romance Prize Draw",
plus your name and address on a postcard. Send your postcard entries to: Queens of
Romance Prize Draw, PO Box 676, Richmond, Surrey, TW9 1WU. Entries must be
received by 31/01/2009. No responsibility can be accepted for entries that are lost,
delayed or damaged in the post. Proof of postage cannot be accepted as proof of
delivery. No correspondence can be entered into and no entry returned. Winners will
be determined in a random draw from all eligible entries received. Judges' decision
is final.

0208/25/MB129

Queens of Romance

An outstanding collection by international bestselling authors

HELEN
BIANCHIN
Their Wedding Deal

1st February 2008

JESSICA
STEELE
Engaged to be Married?

7th March 2008

MICHELLE
REID
A Passionate Bargain

4th April 2008

SARA
CRAVEN
Marriage Vows

2nd May 2008

PAULA
MARSHALL
Rogues and Rakes

6th June 2008

One book published every month from February to November

Collect all 10 superb books!

Queens of Romance

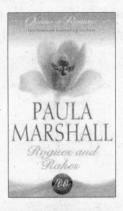

The Beckoning Dream

When her brother Rob was arrested, Mistress Catherine
Wood accompanied a stranger – pretending to be his wife!
– to Holland on a spying mission. With roguish charm her
'husband' made no bones about wanting Catherine in his bed,
while she was surprised how hard it was to hold him at bay as
they travelled into danger together…

The Lost Princess

Having never met her future husband, Marina Bordoni,
Lady of Novera, reluctantly set off to her wedding – only to
be kidnapped and held to ransom! Rescued by an arrogant
stranger, Marina began a mad trail across Italy. Flung closer
to a man than ever before, Marina shocked herself by
relishing every danger…and her rescuer!

Available 6th June 2008

Collect all 10 superb books in the collection!

100 Reasons to Celebrate

2008 is a very special year as we celebrate Mills and Boon's Centenary.

Each month throughout the year there will be something new and exciting to mark the centenary, so watch for your favourite authors, captivating new stories, special limited edition collections…and more!

www.millsandboon.co.uk

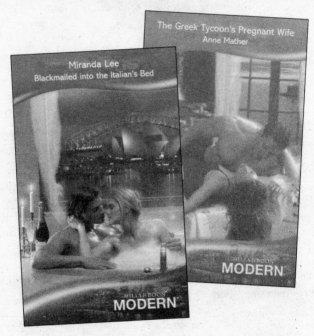